A SCI-FI GAMER FRIENDS-TO-LOVERS ROMANCE

PROTECTING HIS PRIESTESS

BOOK TWO
LOOKING FOR GROUP

SHANNON PEMRICK

Protecting His Priestess
Looking For Group | Book Two

Copyright © 2018 Shannon Pemrick
www.shannonpemrick.com

Cover Design by Covers by Combs

ISBN 978-1-950128-01-3 (paperback)
ISBN 978-1-950128-14-3 (hardcover)
ISBN 978-1-950128-02-0 (ebook)

For my player number two.

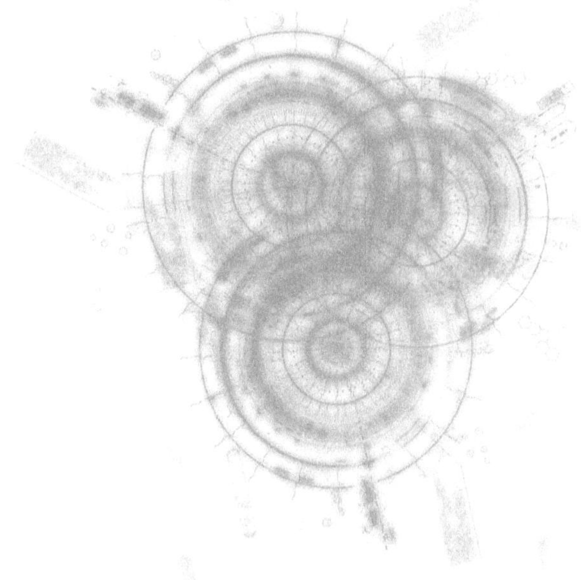

BOOKS BY SHANNON PEMRICK

LOOKING FOR GROUP

Spellbinding His Ranger
Protecting His Priestess
Summoning Their Elementalist
Binding Their Elementalist

VALKYRIES RISING

Valkyrie Destiny
Valkyrie Lost
Valkyrie Renewed
Valkyrie Restored
Valkyrie Confused
Valkyrie Condemned

EXPERIMENTAL HEART

Destiny
Pieces
Secrets
Exposed
Surrendered
Reborn

ORACLE'S PATH

Prophecy of Convergence
Prophecy of Unbroken Oaths

Prophecy Tested
Prophecy Chosen

See all books and learn more at
https://www.shannonpemrick.com

CHAPTER 1

Narissa sipped her coffee as she sat in the Monday morning Los Angeles traffic. She didn't understand how, in 2107, they couldn't come up with better travel ways to keep this from happening. Especially with self-driving cars being the only legal way to drive now.

Standard news played through the car speakers. Trouble at the UN summit meeting. The upcoming tech meeting Cybro Industries would be hosting, thanks to Narissa's new cybernetic design. The Peace Corps building wells in Africa. Fires breaking out in Oklahoma… again. Narissa was surprised there wasn't any mention of sharknados in that area at this rate. She didn't understand why people lived out there. They had earthquakes in Los Angeles, sure, but that area always seemed to be under some sort of threat by Mother Nature.

The newscaster mentioned Jason Atilon, and Narissa's fingers curled. That awful man had gotten the

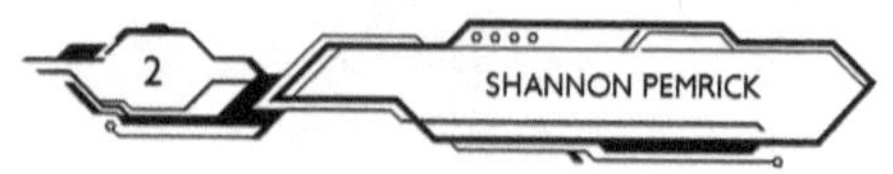

perfect sentencing for what he'd done to her friends, and she wished he'd stop getting so much attention. She especially hated that some people truly believed he didn't deserve his fate and came up with so many excuses why he was framed or misunderstood. *Reminds me of Nolan's trial.*

"Doctor Narissa," a smooth voice said from her car dash. "I've found an alternate route. It'll save us seventeen minutes."

She lounged in her seat. "That would be fantastic. Thank you, Picard. I like how well your new voice pack works in the car."

"I'm glad you're pleased. I will write up a report for the developer."

Narissa pulled out her phone. "While you're at it, can you check for scheduling changes today?"

"One moment." The car grew quiet, except for the news report and occasional honking of impatient drivers. "I do not have any changes."

That was peculiar. Mondays always had an influx of appointment change requests. "Are you sure?"

"I double checked."

"Is your system not updating again?"

"Today is August 29, correct?"

"Yes."

"Let me be sure that wasn't the only part of my system to update."

The car went quiet again. As he did his check, her car pulled out of the traffic and headed down the off ramp. Now free from the morning commuter traffic, her pace to work quickened.

"My programming appears to be fine, Doctor."

"All right, I'll just assume something else is up."

Fifteen minutes passed and Cybro Industries came into view, the large building towering over the others around it. Her car pulled up front and Narissa climbed out, making sure she had everything. *Phone, yep. Purse, yep. Tablet…* she sifted through her purse and then checked under the seat, but no tablet. *Shit.* That had all her notes she'd need today.

"Doctor, it's on the rear seat." Picard said.

Narissa glanced to the back and sure enough, there it sat, on the rear seat. "Thanks, Picard. No idea why I put it there."

The intense Los Angeles sun beat down on Narissa's dark skin as she made her way up the steps to Cybro Industries, her dark curls bouncing around her shoulders. Her shoes clicked on the stone and echoed through the lobby after she pushed through the rotating entrance doors.

A mousey young woman with thick-rimmed glasses sat at the reception desk. Her name plate read *Amy Smith*. Amy looked up from her computer and smiled. "Good morning, Narissa."

Narissa smiled back. "Good morning to you as well, Amy. Do I have any appointment change requests? Picard couldn't find any during the commute this morning."

She shook her head. "No, ma'am. It's been unusually quiet today. But your mother is already looking for you."

A deep sigh escaped Narissa's lips. "Joy. I was hoping I'd be able to start my Monday off right."

Amy gave a closed mouth chuckle. Narissa loved her mother, but she was difficult to deal with. And if she

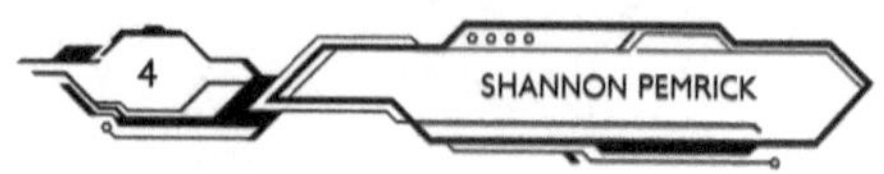

came searching this early in the morning, it was a near guarantee it wasn't work-related.

Narissa hopped into the elevator, checking her phone and sipping her coffee.

"Doctor, your car is now parked," Picard said.

"Thank you. You were right about the appointment changes. Amy confirmed there weren't any."

"That is peculiar. But I'm glad she was able to confirm it wasn't my system malfunctioning again."

Narissa agreed. She didn't want to have to go through that problem again.

The elevator came to a stop and the door opened. Narissa exited, making her way down the long hall of glass-enclosed offices and laboratories until she came to an office with a plaque reading *Dr. Narissa Okafor, EVP*. She pushed open the door and entered her office. Her mother wasn't there, but it'd only be a matter of time before she showed up. *Better prepare some work for myself as an excuse to keep the visit short.*

Narissa went about turning on her computer and sorting client files on her desk as she finished off her cup of coffee.

"Narissa," Picard said through the office's infrastructure. "I have successfully installed the new voice pack into the building database, and your analysis on the most recent prototype is ongoing."

"Excellent, thank you." Although he said the testing hadn't completed, she still ventured over to the far end of her office.

On a stand, surrounded by various scanning equipment, sat an artificial arm on a stress test machine. Bright lights flickered behind the clear fiberglass structure, and

pistons and other moving components moved about within.

Before she could check what data had finalized, her door swung open and a buxom older woman of dark completion strolled in.

"Mornin', Narissa, darlin'." Her words dripped with a heavy southern accent.

"Good morning, Mother." Narissa left the experiment alone and made it back to her desk, noticing a magazine in her mother's hand. "I hope traffic wasn't too horrible for you this morning."

"No more'n any other day," her mother said. "Found somethin' in'restin' this mornin'."

Here we go. She put on a smile and opened a few programs on her computer. "And what is that?"

Her mother sashayed over and placed the magazine on the desk, open to a specific page. "Look who jumped up th' list."

Yep. Narissa already knew what list her mother meant, but she humored them both all the same by looking at the page. *America's Top Bachelorettes* read the title. She found her name listed in third place.

"You've gone from ninth spot ta third in unda a year." Her mother wore a wide grin as she flipped to the page listing all the top eligible bachelors. "And your friend, Ajax, went up several spots s'well. He's in top five now."

Narissa sighed, though did allow her eyes to wander to the listing for a moment—and only for a moment. "Mother, just come out with it. I've got appointments to prepare for."

Her mother frowned. "Why must you be like this, Narissa? You won't go ta church n' meet the nice men

I've approved of there. You turn down e'ry date offer I find at conferences n' business parties. You even turn away from a very handsome, wealthy, and attentive man—a man who is now ranked fifth on the eligible list, mind you. Lawd knows I've tried ta help you get over Nolan for the last seven years. You haven't been receptive t'all, bless your heart. What more can I do ta ensure your happiness, pumpkin?"

She stared at her mother. "You are unbelievable. Have you forgotten what Nolan did to me? Or do you just not care because it doesn't fit this obscure idea on what you deem will make me happy?"

Her mother took a step back, offended by Narissa's words. "Bless your heart! I do care. That's why I want you ta find someone who makes you happy. Who'll give you th' family you once wanted. You're nigh thirty years old, Narissa. You won't be in your child bearing years f'eva, you know. Forgive me for puttin' that into perspective for you."

"Have you considered maybe I've changed what I wanted out of life?"

Before her mother could take in the response, Narissa's office door swung open. The two turned and spied a familiar tan-skinned man with strong features and large muscular build wearing a t-shirt and jeans entering. In his hands, he carried two cups with steam rising from them.

"Ajax?" Narissa looked at the time and then the artificial arm on his right side. "What are you doing here? Your cybernetic isn't busted again from the looks of it."

Ajax approached, his striking eyes warm as he locked gazes with her. Her heart fluttered for a brief moment.

His presence could command a room, if his looks didn't turn heads first. There was good reason Ajax hit the top five eligible bachelors in the US, and it wasn't because of how successful a businessman he was, though she believed he should be higher on that list. Per Shira's words, one of her best friends, he was every shade of sex on a stick. She agreed. Of course, she'd never tell anyone that. They'd think too much into it.

"I saw the news and thought I'd check on you both. I also brought coffee." He scrutinized them with his keen, dark eyes when she and her mother passed each other confused glances. "You two have no idea what I'm talking about, do you?"

Narissa and her mother exchanged glances again. "Uh, Picard?"

"My apologies, Doctor Narissa," Picard said. "The conversation between Missus Ayana and you was important. I thought it best to wait until it ended. There's been a situation in Uganda."

Her heart halted and her mother gasped. "Turn the TV on, now."

Her assistant did as she asked and flipped to a news station. A reporter spoke about the destruction of a small Ugandan village, clips of the devastation rolling across the screen.

"T—that's not where my baby is, right?" Narissa's mother managed out as she held her hands close to her chest.

"I'm afraid I do not know, Missus Ayana," Picard said. "Elijah and the Peace Corps have been on the move so often, we haven't received any location updates."

Ajax put the coffee on the desk and placed a hand

round her mother's shoulder to console her. Narissa appreciated the sentiment.

Civil war had broken out a week ago, after years of tension between the people and the Ugandan government. It was a hot topic during the UN summit meeting, and a main reason the summit hadn't gone so well.

Narissa's phone rang once and Picard answered it before she could ask for a name.

"Narissa?" came a familiar masculine voice over the speaker phone.

Her heart fluttered as relief flooded through her. "Elijah?"

"Elijah!" her mother screeched. She ran over to where the phone lay and scooped it up. "Elijah, babydoll, tell me you're somewhere safe."

He gave a nervous chuckle. "Safe is a relative term right now, Mom."

Panic flooded over their mother's face. Narissa would have smacked him if she could.

"Hey, Elijah, buddy," Ajax said. "Don't be giving your mother a heart attack, okay? She's worried sick as it is."

"Hey, Ajax. Did you bust up your arm again?"

"No, just checking in after I saw the news."

"Thanks, I appreciate you doing that. With Father away at the conference, someone has to look out for them."

"I may be a little brother, like you, but that doesn't mean we don't look out for our favorite ladies, yeah?" Ajax's eyes darted over to Narissa. Warmth rose up in her body and she had to look away.

"Stop gettin' off track," her mother scolded. "What do you mean you're relatively safe, Elijah?"

Narissa held up her hands. "Mother, please stay calm. I

haven't heard anything dangerous in the background, so he probably means he's still on the move. Right, Elijah?"

"You got it, Sis. We're evacuating a small village south of all the action. We're safe right now, but we're not taking any chances." The line grew quieter as Elijah muffled the phone to speak with someone. "Hey, I have to get going. We're about to move out. I love you both."

"Elijah, this is all extremely stressful," Narissa said. "Especially for you. If that heart of yours acts up even a little, you tell me immediately."

"You know I will."

"No, you come home," their mother said. "I'm plum frazzled to gray, Elijah. You come home where it's safe."

"Mom, I can't. I need to help these people. It's what we do, right, Sis?"

Narissa smiled even though he couldn't see. "You got it."

"I'll contact you both again when I'm able." The line then went dead.

"Elijah?" their mother said. "Elijah!"

"I'm sorry, Missus Ayana," Picard said. "He hung up."

Defeat crossed her mother's face, tugging at Narissa's heart strings. She understood how much this affected her. They thought they were going to lose him ten years ago to a bad heart. Had Narissa not created a replacement heart in time, they would have. And then, two years ago, Elijah broke to the family he would be taking the family work overseas to those who needed it. He'd work alongside the Peace Corps and planned to be gone for several years. Helping others was in their blood, everyone knew that. But that didn't make it any easier on their mother.

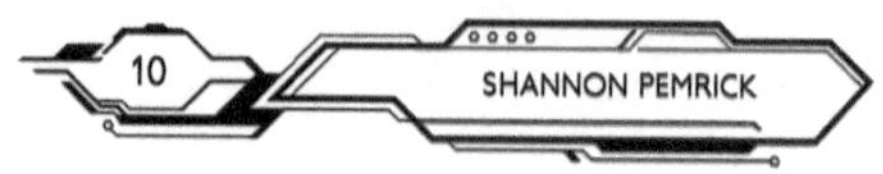

Ajax pulled out a chair and coaxed her mother to sit down. He then handed her a cup of coffee. "Drink this—decaf with skim, no sugar, just how you like."

Ayana took a deep breath, and she calmed. "Bless your heart, but there ain't no need. Ah'm fine now."

Her mother's ability to bounce back amazed Narissa. It didn't seem humanly possible sometimes.

"I shud go call y'all's father. I'm sure he's seen the news by now n' is worried sick." Her mother rose, ever graceful as any proper southern socialite, and headed for the door. "Number five shud be number one."

She winked at Narissa and left. Narissa shook her head.

Ajax cocked an eyebrow. "What was that about?"

She sighed and pushed the magazine to the edge of her desk. "My mother trying to remind me she thinks I'll only ever be truly happy once I remarry."

Ajax picked up the magazine. "What's this have to do with it?"

"Apparently I've been ranked America's third top bachelorette."

Ajax flipped through the magazine, though his eyes went to her more than the pages. "What idiots did they poll to make you only third on that list?"

Narissa snorted and opened a client's file. "People with a brain. I was beat out by an actress and our president's daughter. She's number one."

Ajax stopped flipping the page when he came to the rankings. "You mean barely legal party girl."

"Her actions aside, she deserves that spot with that pretty face."

Ajax's dark eyes snapped up to her. "I beg to differ."

Narissa had to look away, heat threatening to rush to

her face again. The way he looked at her sometimes got her out of sorts. She almost laughed. Acted was more correct. Most days he kept things friendly outside of work, and professional during work hours, but there had been a growing number of days he'd act out of the ordinary.

"My mother's comment, though, was directed to you." She knew she should change the topic, but the words came out of her mouth before she could think. "You made it into the top five eligible bachelor list."

"Yeah?" He didn't look at the magazine. On the contrary, he closed it and sat down on the edge of her desk.

Narissa tilted her head. "You don't sound excited. Most men would be beaming with pride."

Ajax's eyes darted down to his artificial arm. "We both know it's my money that got me there."

She tried not to frown. Her family prided themselves on the state-of-the-art cybernetic technology they put out on the market. Narissa was even dubbed a pioneer, due to her contributions that had radically changed how they were used in the last ten years. But the one thing they couldn't combat was the social stigma around them. Android. Half human. Freak. The terms went on. All her clients and friends with artificial parts dealt with them in one way or another.

Narissa placed a hand on his cybernetic arm and held his gaze, unflinching. "That's not true. You've got looks that turn heads everywhere you go." She chuckled. "Or have you forgotten those two ladies whispering about your tight butt when we went out for that run the other day?"

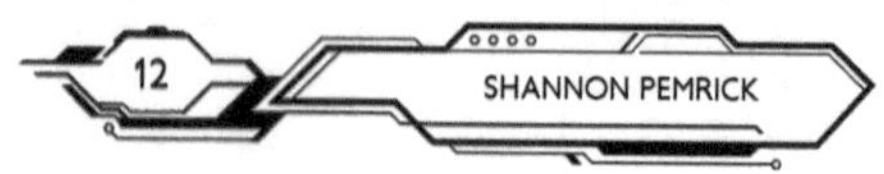

Ajax's brow cocked. "Tight? I don't remember that adjective coming out of their mouths."

A wide grin spread across his face and he pulled her close to him. The action pulled her partially into his lap. Her hands rested against his muscular chest as his hand held her firm by her lower back. "Are you sure that's not you projecting?"

Her pulse skipped and heat burned her cheeks. Here he went, acting weird on her again. "Of course not."

His grin deepened in a way that screamed dangerous and alluring at the same time. "You sure about that?"

"Yes—I have no opinion on your posterior, thank you."

"Oh, bringing out the fancy words now?" He chuckled. "I know I look like a dumb jock, but we both know I am bright enough to understand your sesquipedalian ways."

"Is that what they call it now?" a new voice said.

Narissa's blood ran cold. Her attention turned to the door where two women of similar age to Narissa stood. The light-skinned redhead with untamed curly mane and cybernetics all up her right side grinned wickedly at her. The tan-skinned blonde with a cybernetic right arm also smiled, but didn't project as much joy. Behind them, a lean, tan-skinned man of mixed racial heritage around their age leaned against the hallway wall. His dark eyes showed his amusement at the situation. *Shit.*

Without fail, her friends always caught her in some compromising position with Ajax that wasn't even her fault—or her intention.

Narissa pulled away from Ajax. She smoothed out her clothes. "Mercedes, Shira, Takashi, what are you doing here?"

Shira's green eyes sparkled. "I know we're a bit early for our appointment, but we didn't realize you two were mid-morning rompers. We would have been more courteous."

Narissa's face burned hotter. "That's not what's going on."

Mercedes' eyes twinkled. "You sure?"

Between the two of them, Mercedes had caught these interactions first hand more often. Narissa wasn't sure if it was due to bad luck, or excellent planning.

"I don't know if Narissa is into dumb jocks," Takashi said. The smirk he wore screamed "payback." Narissa suspected Ajax had pulled something recently.

Ajax ran his hand through his short, dark hair. "Wow, and here I thought it made me adorably irresistible."

The room echoed with laughter, the tension quickly releasing from Narissa. Ajax walked past the two women and draped his arm over Takashi's shoulders. "I shouldn't keep you from your appointments. Mercedes, I'm going to steal your boyfriend for a few hours."

"All right, just don't get so crazy you both end up in jail," she said. "I'm not bailing you out."

Takashi chuckled. "Don't worry. I'd be smart enough to run long before that became an issue."

Ajax's arm squeezed on Takashi's neck, trapping him in a headlock. "Yeah, we'll see about that. You ladies enjoy yourselves."

He dragged Takashi away, Takashi fighting the entire way to get out of the hold. He eventually managed to break free, and ran back to plant a kiss on Mercedes' forehead. He then rejoined Ajax.

A smile spread a crossed Narissa's face. "How sweet."

Mercedes stared after Takashi for a moment longer before looking at the other two in the room. A big smile spread on her face. "Yeah, he's a keeper."

Hearing those words elated Narissa. She and Shira had such a difficult time getting her to give their mutual friend and guildmate a chance that it almost felt like an impossible task.

Shira nudged Mercedes. "So, when are you two getting married?"

Mercedes' face reddened, making Narissa laugh. "We've only been dating three months."

"You've been friends for even longer." Narissa winked and went to pull their files. "And he gave you that special necklace."

"Yeah. Means you're basically engaged, right?" Shira said, sitting down in a chair. Her black German shepherd, Snake, trotted along with her. Narissa hadn't even noticed him. He was Shira's service dog, so it was expected for him to be quiet while working unless she was in trouble, but he was exceptionally quiet. *Maybe that's why he's named Snake.* She knew there was some sort of geek reference along with it, but there had to be more. *Why did I never ask her in the past?* She supposed it didn't matter all that much.

Mercedes touched the beaded necklace hanging from her neck. "I guess? It's like a promise ring, but gains more meaning as our relationship grows."

Mercedes then shook her head and pointed at Narissa. "Wait. Stop making this about me, when we should be making this about you."

Damn. She'd almost made it. "There is nothing going on between Ajax and me."

"Maybe you're not seeing something right now, but he certainly is," Shira said. "I mean, you can't honestly think the way he acts around you is him just being an over friendly guy. Not even you are that naïve."

She wasn't wrong. As much as she told herself Ajax was just acting peculiar every now and then, his actions had been going on long enough that she couldn't convince herself of her own ignorant bliss lie. *But Nolan…*

Narissa's shoulders sagged. "Look, I'm not going to discuss this. I already had my mother dogging me this morning, I don't need you two doing it as well."

Her two friends looked at each other, regretful for all the teasing. They both knew how difficult her mother could be on the topic.

Mercedes spoke. "How bad?"

"She felt the need to remind me of my ticking biological clock." She didn't need to mention the list. That one came up enough it was a given at this rate.

Shira grimaced. "That's going a bit too far in my book. Sure, you two are lucky to even have to worry about that, but you don't see me being spiteful enough to remind you of that."

Narissa gave her friend a sympathetic glance. The accident Shira had five years prior ravaged her body. Even though she'd survived, thanks to the tech her family provided, as well as all the hard-working medical staff assigned to her care, not everything could be saved. But what her friends didn't know, was Narissa had a secret she carried around the same topic. It was too painful to ever bring up in any conversation, so not even her two closest friends knew this hardship.

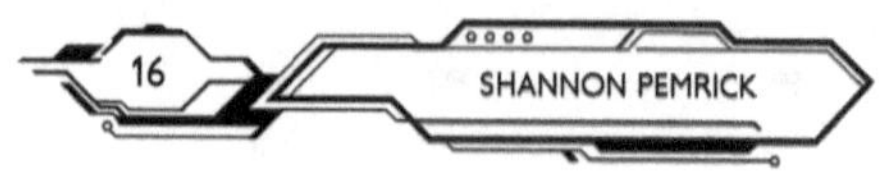

Mercedes wandered over to the cybernetic in the stress test machine. "What do you have going on here?"

Narissa appreciated her friend's choice to switch the topic. It wasn't good to let Shira, or herself, dwell in the past. "I thought of a way to improve the simulated nerves. That stress test is part of a computer analysis to make sure it'll work before I roll it out for volunteer human testing."

The past few months, she'd been working away on improving cybernetic technology. One of the many dreams of her clients was to see medical tech improve enough to establish full limb regeneration. Even though small body parts like ears and livers were possible these days to some extent, limbs and large organs weren't there yet. This gave her the idea to create simulated nerve technology in the cybernetics.

Since cybernetics connected to the individual's brain through advanced neuro-mods, and she understood the phenomenon around phantom limb syndrome, she knew it was possible to trick the brain into believing there were active nerves.

Mercedes, Shira, and several other volunteers had been working with her on testing this new tech, pushing it farther than she could have ever hoped. While it wouldn't be out on the market for some time, it gave her hope for the future of cybernetics and people.

Shira leaned back. "Will you be asking Ajax to test yet, or are you holding off a bit longer because of his accidents?"

Narissa shook her head and loaded Mercedes' file onto her tablet. "He hasn't had an incident in two weeks, but I don't trust it. These new cybernetics are far more

powerful than the current market. If he stresses these too much, it *will* kill him."

"I'm honestly surprised he's not in the hospital," Mercedes said. "And I'm more surprised you haven't gotten out of him what he's doing to end up in these predicaments."

Narissa frowned, her thumb tapping the side of her device. "He's stubborn. No matter how many times I ask him to stop doing whatever it is he's doing to blow up his cybernetic, or even tell me so maybe I can help him avoid the problem, he clams up or changes the subject. For what reason, I don't know at this point. But I can't keep allowing it to continue."

"You wrote up a termination contract, didn't you?" Shira guessed.

Narissa nodded and moved from behind her desk. "I finalized it last night with the lawyers. His visit today was unexpected, so I didn't get the chance to broach the subject with him. So I plan to get him in again and give him the choice—tell me what's going on, or sign the contract. It's not just the company's integrity at stake. He's a friend and I can't sit by and watch him kill himself."

Shira smirked. "You could also refuse to heal him in raids anymore."

Narissa laughed. Shira was referring to Lusara Fates, the most popular MMORPG, massively multiplayer online role-playing game—a fantasy world filled with made-up playable species, adventure, and social interaction. The game's popularity was all due to its ability to craft brilliant storytelling, compelling encounters for PvE, player vs. environment; balanced PvP, player vs.

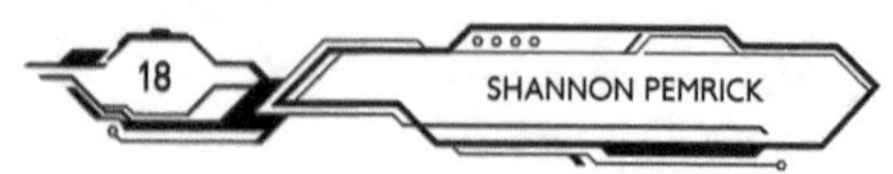

player; and unique economics that meshed with the real world, making it possible for people to make a legitimate living inside the game if they so pleased.

Its major selling point, though, was its unparalleled integration in the advanced gaming chairs Ajax had created. Full neuro-simulation, allowing someone to experience the game as if they were actively living in the world. The coding Lion Rage Games used allowed for some *interesting* experiences. That included quite real personal relationship capabilities.

The three of them, along with Ajax and Takashi, all played this game and were members of the same guild, a group that came together and forged strong bonds akin to a second family.

"I suppose I could do that, but it would affect everyone else in the raid group, too," Narissa said.

A raid was an end-game aspect of PvE that required group cooperation. Narissa mained a priest for this, a healing class. Ajax, the main focus of her healing during a raid, played a berserker, a tanking-class type that put out minimal damage, but could take heavy hits and had abilities to keep enemies off other players. He'd made it clear on a number of occasions he didn't like it when someone else healed in her place.

Shira shrugged. "Wouldn't affect me any."

Shira and the two men she had following her around like little puppies, Jasper and Zach, focused on the PvP aspect and never jumped into the raids.

Mercedes chuckled. "I wouldn't mind. It'd be funny watching him beg you to heal him."

Narissa couldn't stop herself from smiling at the image. "True. But it certainly wouldn't be tonight that it'd happen. Don't want to freak out the newbies and all."

"Oh, that's right." Shira looked to Mercedes. "That's Emi and Rei, right?"

Mercedes nodded. "Yep. We finally convinced Emi to give it a shot."

Hearing the woman's name sent a pang of sympathy through Narissa. Emi had been the center of all of Jason Atilon's crimes. A close friend of Takashi and his sister Rei, and eventually Mercedes and Shira over these past few months. The guild got to know her little by little as they tried to help her get through the ordeal, after Jason had been exposed after messing with Takashi and Mercedes one too many times.

They'd inducted her as a full member, and their guild master, Darius, also managed to snag her a special class code for the upcoming expansion next month to try out, thanks to how long he'd worked at Lion Rage Games. Of course, only a handful of people knew what he'd done. Everyone else thought she'd been one of the randomly selected players to help hype up the new expansion release, *The Old Kingdom*.

"Of course, if we keep stalling, it's going to make me late for my other appointments today, and keep me from playing tonight," Narissa said. She pointed for Mercedes to sit in the patient chair. "We'll start with you, Mercedes."

Her eyes narrowed as she complied. "You just don't want to go back to talking about your little secret love affair with Ajax."

Heat rushed to Narissa's face. "Would you drop it?"

Shira laughed. "Never."

Narissa opened the required files, swiping some to a nearby computer. Today was going to be a long one with these two.

CHAPTER 2

jax swiped his key to unlock his door. His red merle Australian sheepdog, Helios, sat at his feet, his tongue lolling out. His fleabitten and lovable mutt, Crash, on the other hand, bounced about as if Ajax hadn't taken them out for their run at all.

He opened the door to his spacious penthouse and unhitched them from their leashes. Helios trotted to his water dish, while Crash bolted through the living room at top speed, missing a turn and crashing into an ottoman. Ajax shook his head and as he laughed. He never tired of her antics.

"Ajax," a computer voice said from his suite's infrastructure. "You have a meeting request for tomorrow morning that came in."

"Thanks, Kirk." Ajax tossed his keys into a bowl and went to change out of his running clothes. "What's the importance? I'd like to get some work done."

He'd spent half the day hanging out with Takashi. It

wasn't every day they were able to get together, so he was fine with putting off work for a bit.

"Your mother set something up with investors."

He frowned and pulled his shirt over his head. "Great. Accept it."

Investor meetings took far too long for his liking. But GameTech needed them, and as CEO, it wasn't like he could just skip out.

Once he finished throwing on some clean clothes, he opened his phone and scrolled through social media while prepping a light dinner. Narissa and the girls had posted a few times. No pictures, but a few status updates. It looked like Mercedes and Shira had managed to get Narissa to have some fun between appointments. That made him happy.

Sure, it was a Monday, and most people worked hard during the week, but Narissa overdid it. If he didn't check in on her every now and then, she'd work long into the night and never make herself a priority.

Ajax looked at the time. They had an hour before the raid. *I should make sure she's going to make it.* It wouldn't be the end of the world if she didn't, but Ajax would rather she be there. Narissa was the best healer in the guild, and with them showing some of the newbies the ropes of raiding, a confident and capable tank healer helped.

He pulled up her contact. Plus, he just wanted to spend more time with her.

Don't forget, we raid tonight.

He sent the text and a moment later she responded.

I'm on my way home now.

He drummed his fingers on the counter. He could leave it at that, but she'd lied to him before about not being at the office. It also allowed him to keep the conversation going a bit longer.

Prove it.

Ajax had a fifty-fifty shot if she'd take the bait. Sometimes she did, others, he got a view of her car dash and a metaphorical rejection.

A photo came through and a grin slid up the side of his face. Her perfect face looked back at him, Mercedes sitting in the back seat behind her, making a goofy face. Ajax slid his thumb over his screen, focusing only on Narissa. Those beautiful brown eyes and dark curly hair—full lips pulled into a brilliant smile. It should be illegal for a woman to look this gorgeous.

"Ajax," Kirk said. "Do I need to inform your guild-mates you're going to be late, so you can have some time with your phone?"

Ajax snorted. "What do I look like, some creep?"

"You have saved a far greater number of her photos to your computers than any other friend you have."

Ajax put the phone down. "I haven't saved *that* many."

"You have sixty-three on your phone alone."

Did he really? *Shit.* Made him look a bit pathetic. He was going to have to delete some.

"When are you going to outright ask her?" Kirk asked. "There's only so long you can keep up your current antics."

Crash came up and pawed his leg with a cybernetic limb. Ajax bent over, scratching behind her torn ear. "I heard her ex's name today. From the sounds of the conversation, she's still hung up on him."

"Is she, though?"

This challenge confused him. "What do you mean?"

"Didn't Mercedes say once that Narissa's divorce was a messy one? It was the sole reason she never spoke of her prior marriage."

Ajax's lips twisted. "Doesn't mean she was the one who wanted it."

These past few months, he'd tested how available she may be. Close contact got her flustered, something he quite enjoyed seeing. Even today, it had been just as satisfying to pull her close and watch her fumble about. But her reaction was mostly out of resistance. He wasn't stupid. He knew women well enough to see that sign. So she either wasn't interested, or wasn't over this... Nolan.

"If you would like, I can do some research on the matter."

Ajax retrieved his phone and headed for his gaming room. "I told you, I'm not a creep. I'll just ask her about it."

"Will you, though?"

Ajax stopped. "What do you mean?"

"I'm beginning to wonder if you're projecting your own uncertainty onto her."

He looked down at his artificial arm. Maybe he was. He'd known Narissa for several years now. They made great friends, and she didn't have any issues with cybernetics. He'd had his fair share of breakups and date fallouts because of his. In the end, it was his money that drew all those women in. Narissa was different, though.

She was a successful woman who didn't care for the size of one's wallet. She only cared about the person's integrity. It was one of the many things that drew him toward her.

Narissa was one of the most beautiful women he'd ever met, yes, but that wasn't her only flawless feature. She had wit and intelligence that brought him to his knees. A sense of humor that matched his, and her interests, though not entire the same as his, did overlap. She was the perfect woman wrapped in one hell of a delectable package he ached to indulge in.

Ajax clenched his artificial hand. But was he good enough for her?

Two cold, wet noses touched his skin and he jumped. Both Helios and Crash stood at his feet, wagging their tails. Ajax smiled and petted them both. "You two are always coming to my rescue."

His phone beeped, and he checked it to find a raid reminder flashing on the screen. "It's almost showtime. Better log in and group up with the others."

He looked down at the furry faces at his feet. "Be good, you two, while I'm getting beat on for the next three hours."

Ajax continued to his gaming room, only pausing when he made it to his "lab." A long cylindrical pod sat in pieces in the middle of the room. Gazing upon it, he had the urge to continue his secret project, but the desire to raid alongside his friends and Narissa tugged harder.

He entered the gaming room, briefly gazing around at his collection of tabletop, PC, and console games

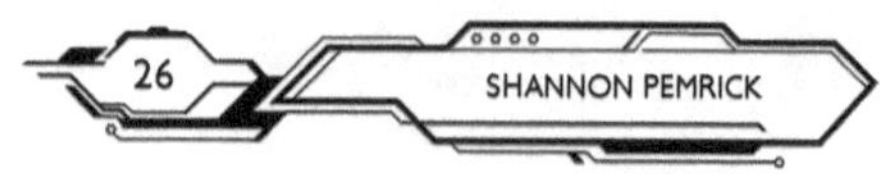

and devices. He had a few vintage systems, an Xbox 360, Nintendo Switch, and even a PS1, but after seeing the impressive selection Mercedes had a few months back, he'd been on the hunt to improve his own. What kind of gamer or game company CEO could he call himself if he didn't?

Directly in the center of the large room sat his VR gaming station—a specialized curved chair with all the necessary gear to suck him into the virtual world, and hanging screens to allow him any out-of-game prompts, from selecting a game to managing business tools.

Ajax powered up the chair and checked to make sure all signals were good. He didn't need to; he'd designed this with so many fail safes and warnings it wasn't needed, but habits died hard.

He sat down in the chair and used the touchscreen displays to set up Lusara Fates and check his friends list. Jasper and Zach were locked in a PvP match, the former using his rogue class, a stealthy melee DPS—damage per second—a class good for high damage but extremely low defense, and the latter using his warrior class, a heavy-armor melee class built for either tanking, high defense and lower offense, or DPS with average defense and high damage.

His best friend Darius was online, locked into his dragoon class, a long-reach melee DPS with some jumping and magic capabilities that emulated dragons. He resided in the guild hall—no surprise there. As the guild leader, he made it a point to be early to raids if he was going to make it. Their shared best friend and Darius' roommate, Kiara, also sat in the guild hall, having chosen her favored beast tamer class, a melee DPS class that fought alongside two animals.

Ajax enjoyed the differences in this class and the ranger class Mercedes favored. Both utilized pets, but the benefits and handling of the animals differed.

Other guildmates were on, but none slated to join the raid. It was still early, so they'd trickle in. Ajax preselected his berserker, a melee class with a raging mechanic, and his half-orc avatar, a human and orc hybrid race, keeping his login loading time down, and relaxed to allow the neuron equipment to do their job. His eyes grew heavy and then his consciousness shifted.

Ajax opened his eyes when familiar sounds of the Guildhall filled his ears. He sat up in the bed he'd last logged out on and peered around. He resided in a small room, sparsely decorated with the bed, dresser, washbasin, and a couple of trophies he'd collected over the years of playing, and chose to store in his room.

He slipped off the bed and exited the room, making his way into the main gathering hall. People ran about doing whatever it was they did, beyond causing a drunken ruckus, which many of the guildmates did well, some even holding a champion belt for their antics.

In a far corner, at a table, sat a man with long raven hair, clad in dark plate armor. With him was a short buxom elven woman with flaming red hair, and two creatures sitting at her feet—a drake, a wingless dragon-like creature, and an owlcat, a magical black tiger-like creature with wings. Ajax grinned and beelined toward the two. They greeted him with warm smiles as he approached.

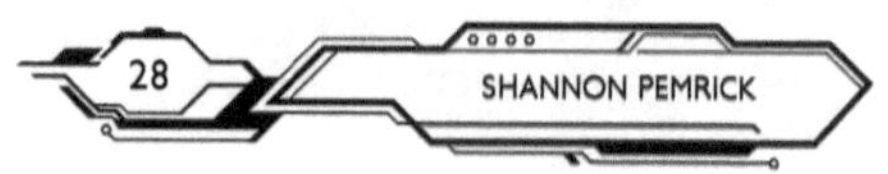

"Darius, Kiara, it's good to see some people are on time," he said.

Kiara snorted. "We're always on time because Mister Punctual can't stand to be late. We always expect you to be next." She grinned. "Unless, of course, a particular priestess is distracting you."

Ajax avoided eye contact. Only she got him to do that with this particular topic. Being like a younger sister to him and Darius, the way she brought the topic up made him feel weird. Pleased with the reaction, Kiara sat back and consumed her mug of ale. Drinking and eating were strange concepts in the game. While it had no physical effect on the body, the gaming chair's technology, mixed with the game's coding, tricked the brain to believe was under the effects of whatever you consumed. It made taking potions and other game-specific items quite the experience.

Ajax turned when two people approached. He smirked at the outrageously dressed half-orc man accompanying an elven man garbed in leather and other natural materials. "Donovan, Ronan—it's been a while since we last saw you. Glad you could make it."

Donovan played a bard, a magic-based class built on continual short-term DPS buffs for the raid, with the occasional attack spell for a pinch maneuver. His brother, Ronan, preferred the druid. A versatile class that could go magic range, or melee DPS. They also had the capability for healing, much like how Shira's elemental class could.

Donovan grinned. "Yeah, the vineyard is keeping us busy right now. Going to have a great harvest this year."

The two ran a winery up in Napa. Family business

they'd recently been handed full-time, or that's what Ajax knew, at least. It took away a lot of their free time depending on the time of year, so the guild saw them intermittently.

"We figured if some newbies wanted to learn the ropes, we could spare a few hours to ensure some more-experienced players were there to help out," Ronan said.

"Well, I know I'm grateful for another healer."

Everyone turned to see six individual approaching. The one leading them, a lovely umber-skinned elven woman with flowing black hair, garbed in a high-collar silver and blue robe. *Narissa.*

She appeared regal. It was sexy. *Narissa makes priests sexy.* His mind paused. *Is that a sin to think?* She may have to make him repent. He may enjoy that.

Next to her was Mercedes, having picked her elven ranger per usual. Her pet this time around was a magical cat she called Lo'quena. The dark-haired elven sorcerer with them, an arcane spellcaster DPS class, was Takashi.

The buxom human woman clad in half-plate was none other than Shira, as her elementalist, a natural magic-user class focusing on elemental abilities like fire and water to either heal or damage. He hadn't expected to see her, and instead figured she'd jump right into PvP matches. PvE wasn't really her thing.

The two women with them were the newbies. Rei, Takashi's sister, and Emi, a friend of all of theirs, and Takashi's ex. He found their friendship interesting, as he knew very few who stayed friends with their exes, but if it worked for them, he had no business saying anything about it.

Rei played a rogue Azázil, a half-demon species, and

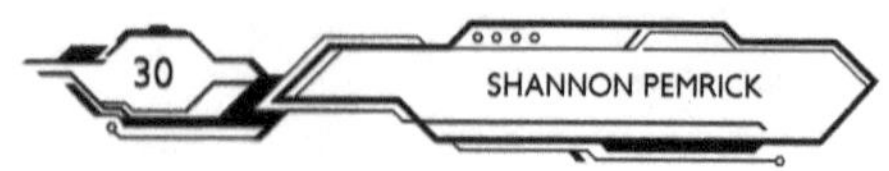

Emi played something completely different from everyone—the brand new siren class and merfolk race. He didn't know much about the class, but the avatar was interesting. A rather alluring figure and features, her ears and hands had webbing, and her eyes sparkled like light on water. From what he knew, if she ever jumped into a pool of water, her avatar would give her fins of some sort, much like how Ronan could use a spell to take an aquatic animal form.

Ajax crossed him arms. "Well, I'm glad to see we managed to keep the newbies instead of scaring them off. And we gained another unexpected player, too."

"Eli had to bail again," Shira said. "So I offered to sub in. I'm no raider, but"—she tossed a thumb at Rei and Emi—"that should help these guys get comfortable. Can't get worse than me."

Mercedes laughed. "You're all going to do fine. It's not that difficult."

Emi kicked her feet on the ground. "You guys sure about this? I still don't understand this class very well. I might just get you all killed."

Darius laughed. "Don't worry. We picked an early expansion raid to ease you in."

She still didn't look convinced. Ajax had learned a few things about Emi. She was as smart and talented as she was pretty. But after the Jason thing, her confidence had taken a hit. This environment the guild had, a surrogate family if you would, did help her, but there was only so much they could do before she needed to take charge.

Ronan strolled over to Emi and wrapped his arm over her shoulders. "You only have to focus on learning. The rest of us will have you covered."

Donovan joined her on the other side. "And if we die, we die. Not the end of the world. We'll discuss what may have gone wrong, and work together to learn and fix."

Rei fixed her eyes on the two brothers, not that it wasn't expected. She had a bit of a protective streak for her friend.

Emi gave a meek smile. "Okay. If you all say so."

Donovan patted her back. "We do." He then pointed to Rei. "We've got faith in you, too, newbie number two."

Rei crossed her arms. "I'm not a novice at this game, dimwit. I've been playing a long time."

Ronan whistled. "There's some venom in that tongue. No wonder she picked a rogue."

Rei smirked and tossed a dagger into the air.

"Boys, don't be picking a fight with my newest intern now," Narissa chastised. "She may be working on your cybernetics when you come in next."

Ajax held up a hand. "Hold up. New intern?"

This was the first time he'd heard of it. He didn't even know Takashi's sister was in the field—or trying to get into it, at least.

Half of Rei's lips slid up the side of her face. "Yeah. I just have to pass these next two semesters, and the big mid-degree test, and I'll have secured my spot as a summer intern at Cybro Tech."

Mercedes squealed and held onto the young woman. "I'm so glad you listened to me. You are going to do great there."

"I hope so," Narissa said. "Her portfolio is impressive for a second-year student. I'd like to see how much she'll improve in a real lab."

Rei ducked, her face reddening. It made Ajax smile.

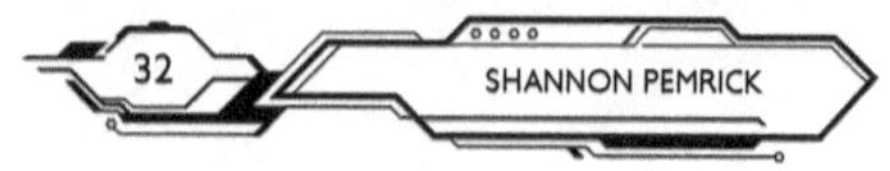

Rei had a bit of an attitude, so it was nice seeing her embarrassed.

"Let's get moving," Donovan said. "I'm interested to see how different this new class is to my bard."

Ajax took the cue and hauled Narissa onto his shoulders. "I have my priestess. I'm set."

Narissa looked down at him. "Excuse you. Put me down, you barbarian."

"Now, if I were that, I'd have thrown you right over my shoulder and ran off." He winked. "And that's quite tempting."

Her cheeks tinted as she rolled her eyes. He enjoyed getting that response. It wasn't outright denial that she hated the idea, either.

Darius stood up. "Well, while those two flirt, the rest of us can get to raiding. I'm excited to see Emi use this class. I've only caught small glimpses at work during the testing phases."

Emi's eyes lit up. "You work for Lion Rage?"

He grinned. "I'm part of the art department."

"That's really cool." She looked to Ronan and Donovan, who were still hanging off of her. "I don't think I've met either of you before."

"Donovan."

"Ronan."

Emi smiled. "Well, it's nice to meet you both. I'll try not to get you killed."

Kiara jumped to her feet. "Okay, let's get this party started. I want to rip my claws into a boss."

The group snickered and headed for the flight master, Ajax still carrying Narissa. She didn't complain this time. Instead, she looked quite pleased to be carried like a person of importance. *Like the queen she is.*

"Wait, hold up!"

They all turned to see two tall elven men of muscular builds, garbed in leather and plate armor respectively, running after them.

Shira's brow creased. "Shouldn't you two be in twos matches?"

"Yeah, but when we received your message you'd be grouping up for the raid, we thought we'd join yah," Jasper said, his thick Boston accent clear.

"We thought it be a wicked fun change of pace," Zach said, his accent far less pronounced. "Serenity even went down for bed easy today, so we're less likely to be interrupted."

Mercedes snickered. "More like you couldn't get her for three's matches, so you're following her like two little puppies."

Shira shot her an ugly look, but the two men didn't exactly deny it. The three had a unique relationship, one that seemed to be building into something stronger these past few months. The ladies insisted Shira would end up joining the little family unit, but Shira seemed adamant about keeping them at arm's length. *What is it with the women in our guild being so afraid of relationships?* Mercedes and Takashi had only recently gotten together, and they'd danced around each other for a few years.

Kiara looked to Darius. "What do you think? It'll up the difficulty a bit based on our numbers, but I think we can handle a half-noob group."

Darius nodded. "As long as the healers are okay with it. I know Ajax and I can tank it no problem."

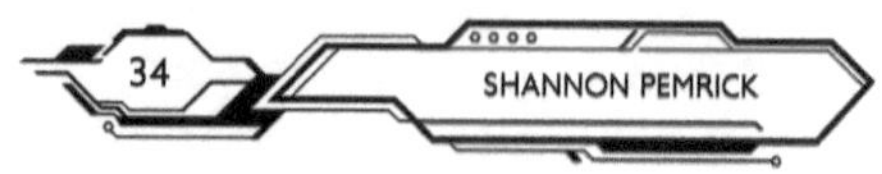

Ronan nodded. "I'm fine. If things get too hairy, I'm sure Shira wouldn't mind switching to a third healer."

Shira nodded. "I could do that."

All eyes fell on Narissa. She smiled. "Does Ajax have undying faith in my healing abilities?"

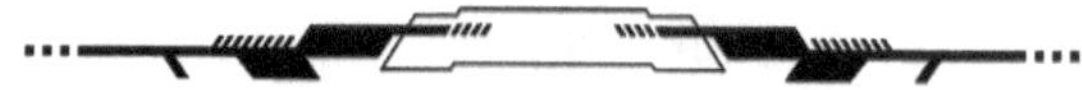

Me and my big mouth. Narissa threw out another heal on Shira, while Jasper and Zach cheered them all on in their ghostly forms. The two hadn't listened to Darius' mechanic instructions and took a nasty blow from the boss, killing them instantly. This freaked Rei out, and she fumbled with her rotation and subsequently, her footing, and found herself right under the boss's next attack. She watched on, amused at the group's uncoordinated attempt, rather than being upset with her misfortune.

Kiara rushed around, attacking at all angles she could, directing her pets to flank or aid as she saw fit. Mercedes' pet also added to the animal chaos. One of the pets tripped Darius up, a common issue with the AI creatures, and both Narissa and Ronan focused their healing on him to keep him up. Donovan pranced around playing up his bard persona, sometimes getting in the way of others as they repositioned to evade some of the bigger attacks. *It's like herding cats!* Though, it wasn't like she didn't expect such craziness.

Even with a group of skilled raiders, it was chaos as a healer. And her guild had the easier going runs of the ones she'd been in. There were some people she'd never offer to help again.

Narissa threw on a temporary shield for Ajax and

glanced over to Emi. She concentrated hard on her current long-term haste buff, the lovely sound of her class' song echoing through the chamber. Of all the people in this raid, she had far exceeded everyone's expectations. It helped that Darius took the time to ease her into the group setting by pulling small trash groups, minor hostile NPCs—non-player characters—for her to get a controlled feel for her class. They'd all learned the reason for her original unease. Solo play and group play changed how her class functioned. Solo, her buffs were instant and she had more attacking mechanics. Group, her buffs became channeled, and many of her attacks became new buffs.

Narissa had never seen anything like it before. It was quite the intuitive class. But that definitely meant it was geared for the more experienced players. Emi was in good hands, though. Donovan ended up being the greatest help, knowing how bards worked and all. Even with the clear differences in the way their skills worked, it eased a lot of fear from Emi.

Narissa screeched when a wayward attack came at her. She dove out the way, landing on her face, but at least she'd missed the attack.

"Sorry!" Darius called out.

"Deflect away from the healers, please." She knew it wasn't necessary to say, he wasn't new to this, but the fact he made such a noob mistake irritated her.

"Yeah, especially *my* healer," Ajax called out.

She shook her head as she used a small heal on him and got to her feet, though she was tempted to stay where she was. At that vantage point, she got a good view of him. And game avatar or not, he had a nice butt. *Focus, Narissa.*

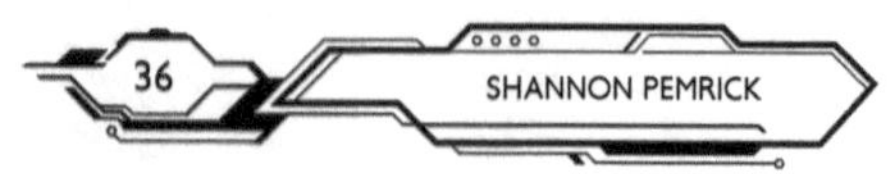

The behemoth of a boss lifted his spiked club into the air and swung it down. Everyone scrambled to scatter but Takashi. He'd chosen the wrong spell, locking him into the cast. His health *blipped* to zero. Narissa cringed. Such a rough attack. It could even one-shot a tank if they weren't paying attention. It didn't help that with the nerve simulation, pain was a thing. It was gated, keeping the physical body from going into shock so the players could continue enjoying themselves. Of course, many in the game culture believed that to enjoy certain classes, or even aspects of the game, like PvP, you had to be a bit of an adrenaline junkie, or maybe even a masochist.

"I think this one is a wipe," Darius shouted.

That meant they were all going to die and have to start the encounter over. Not such a big deal. Even with the problems, their group had gotten the boss down to twenty-five percent health.

"I ain't quittin' yet," Kiara said, the Scottish brogue she tried to keep at bay coming out in her excitement, as usual.

"If we're counting this one as a loss, can we try something crazy?" Emi asked.

Narissa cocked her head before spamming a couple heals on Ajax after not mitigating damage appropriately. What had she thought of to get them out of this pickle?

"Let's hear it," Darius said before launching himself up into the air and slicing down on the boss with his weapon.

"I have an ability steal," she said. "I've built up enough lure resource to use it."

That was one of two resources a Siren had, adding to the class' complexity. They used mana, like her own class did, but depending on the buffs a siren used, built up a second resource for an ultimate move.

Ajax dodged an attack and slammed the boss with his giant axe. "How does it work?"

"I can pick from a small list of abilities based on who is alive in the raid composition. Kiara has the most useful one from my search—some sort of bestial wrath ability."

Kiara slashed at the boss, her two pets following up with their own attacks commanded by her, and she peeked around the boss' leg. "Ye could do that?"

Emi nodded and channeled a shield around everyone when the boss came in for its devastating club attack. That didn't mean they could take the blow head-on, but if someone fumbled, that would give them a fighting chance. Mercedes found herself clipped by a spike. It took a chunk of her health, but nothing Ronan couldn't heal while Narissa focused on Ajax.

Darius taunted the boss, to allow Ajax to recover from the debuff stack mechanic. This forced her full healing effort—a shield and several more strong heals. He tossed her a heart-stopping "thank you" smile.

"I'm pretty sure it'll also give your pets an added buff," Emi said, once they were sure everyone had their bearings. "I'd like to stack it with Donovan's haste buff, too, since I can't channel two at one time."

A wide grin spread across Donovan's face. "I like this plan—let's try it."

"Bestial wrath will force healers tae attack," Kiara warned. "It's a type o' frenzy mechanic."

"The channel only last thirty seconds," Emi said.

Ajax and Darius nodded at each other before rolling from a kick. "We can handle that amount of time."

Narissa and Ronan exchanged glances. They could throw off a temporary shielding for each tank before everything went down. That would help with their survivability.

"I don't have enough mana to keep prolonging this fight, so if we're going to pull out a miracle, this would be the time," Ronan said.

She agreed.

"Then everyone get ready," Darius said.

He counted down, and on one, Donovan activated his haste, Narissa and Ronan placed a shield on their tanks, Kiara used her special ability, and then Emi pulled off her special move, the eerie song spilling out of her mouth.

Power and emotion welled up inside Narissa. An urge to maim and tear at this boss compelled her to no longer heal, and instead call forth a beam of holy light from the heavens. Her friends around her went full force on the boss, its health dropping quickly.

Ajax roared at the boss and slashed it with everything he had. If it weren't for this spell compelling her, Narissa would have found herself distracted by such a sight. There was something about the way Ajax went full berserker that excited her. Even with the spell controlling her attacks, an image of him tossing her face-down on a bed and making her writhe in pleasure shot through her mind. *No, brain, not that kind of excited.*

Emi's spell ended, the effect of drained mana hitting Narissa immediately. She didn't have much left, and both Ajax and Darius could benefit from it. Narissa threw the last two heals she could muster onto Ajax and collapsed to her knees.

The boss had five percent health. That boost had really pushed this for them. They could finish the rest. She knew it.

Darius fell dangerously low on health, and Ajax had to activate his last damage mitigation ability to make up for Narissa's failure. Emi got off one temporary shielding onto Darius while Ronan threw out three more heals. Emi fell to one knee but wasn't ready to throw in the towel.

This impressed Narissa. She'd never seen such determination in this woman's eyes before. It was if there was a whole other person locked inside her that was able to come out when pushed. Narissa knew that feeling all too well. Nolan had stolen a lot from her, and a large piece of who she once was. Every now and then she'd be reminded that person may still be there, Ajax the biggest enabler, but she wasn't sure how real that other person was anymore. *Or how real this current me is.*

The boss' health fell more, Shira catching a lucky break with several critical hits and procs, and before they knew it, the beast fell, its health reduced to zero. It took several moments for the group to register the win. When they did, cheers erupted through the chamber.

Donovan rushed Emi and picked her up, spinning her around. "You're amazing!"

"I just have a lot of time to think during channels, that's all." Emi laughed. "Put me down, you're going to make me sick!"

Donovan listened but didn't exactly let her go.

Ronan came over to her and tucked a flower in her hair. "Permanent raid spot for this amazing woman, for sure."

Emi ducked her head, her face reddening. "Stop. You're embarrassing me!"

The group laughed. Narissa went about channeling a mass revival spell, also keeping an eye on the two brothers. They were an odd pair, but they were acting a little extra peculiar with Emi.

Rei ran over to her best friend the moment she was revived, and gave her a bear hug. "You deserve the praise. That was awesome!"

Emi's face changed to a darker shade. Ajax wandered over to Narissa and then practically flopped on her. She let out an "oof."

"Get off me, you big lug," she complained.

"I'm exhausted. Carry me."

Narissa laughed and tried to push his heavy mass off her. "Not going to happen. You're going to crush me!"

Ajax sighed and stood up. Narissa squealed when he threw her over his shoulder. "All right, I have my priestess, I'm ready for the next fight."

Narissa shook her head. The rest of this run was going to be interesting.

CHAPTER 3

Narissa organized some digital files. She didn't have many clients or meetings today, so she thought she might actually get work done on some of the prototypes—though she wasn't sure her mind would allow for the right focus needed.

Last night's raid had been amazing. Both Emi and Rei had proven to be naturals, and also had more fun than they expected. Both as players and their class choices they added a dynamic to the raid group that they'd all benefitted from. Rei and Emi both hit it off real well with Donovan and Ronan, to boot. Narissa hoped this would encourage them to make stronger friendships within the guild.

Narissa glanced up from her computer when the door opened. She smiled at the sight of Ajax entering. "Hey, what are yo—"

Her eyes zoned in on the mangled cybernetic arm

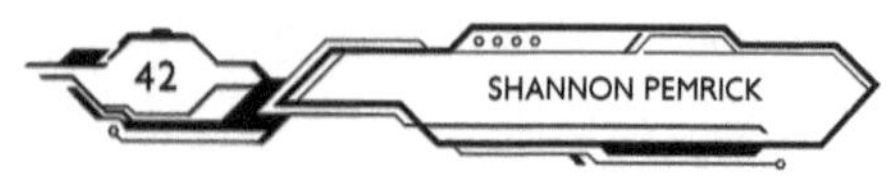

hanging limp on his side. Fear flashed through her. "What the hell did you do?"

He glanced down at the arm. "I had a small accident. Can you pencil me in for a fix?"

"Y—you had an accident?" She couldn't believe what she was hearing. That was his explanation? Her fear burned into rage. She rose from her seat. "You had an accident? That's how you're going to explain yet another mangled arm?"

He rubbed the back of his neck, his gaze falling elsewhere but her. "I know you hate me saying that, but—"

"But what?" Her volume rose. "But you can't tell me what the hell you're doing to cause this kind of damage to yourself? Is that what you're going to say, again? Because I'm not going to accept that, Andrew."

His eyes went to her for a moment then fell back on the floor. "Well, at least you're not mad enough to use my first name. I appreciate that."

She was the only one to call him that. It wasn't his real name; she swore to never speak it or tell anyone what it was, as he hated it so much, but it was his middle name, making it an acceptable alternative when she didn't want to call him Ajax, the name he'd adopted for some reason that he never told her.

Narissa's fury twisted and knotted inside her, making her unable to process. She sat down, and rubbed her face. "Andrew, do you honestly not understand how dangerous this is? Do you not listen to me every time I explain the strain this puts on your neuro-mod and your brain? Do you not care for some reason?"

She looked up at him with pleading eyes. "Please tell me what's going on."

Ajax hesitated and she didn't understand why. Why couldn't he just be honest with her?

"I'm sorry, Rissa, but I can't tell you right now."

On a regular day, she liked it when he used her nickname. She had to admit, to only herself, she liked how it rolled off his deviously tempting tongue. But today, it just made her angry.

"I promise you, this project will improve and these damages will stop, very soon."

She pressed her lips into a thin line. So that was how it was going to be. She had no choice. She reached into her desk drawer and plucked out a tablet, pulling up the contract she'd gone over with her legal team. "Come over here and sign this, then. I can create a paper version if you'd prefer that, as some people still do these days."

He approached. "Sign what?"

Narissa pushed the tablet forward. Ajax took a seat, pulling out some blue-light-blocking glasses to look the contract over. Narissa typed up gibberish on her computer, else she'd struggle to keep her composure. Mister Sex-on-a-Stick got way sexier when he put those glasses on. She couldn't explain it, and she hated it.

Ajax put the tablet down. "A termination contract? Are you serious?"

Narissa took a deep breath. "I am. There are two reasons for it. One, is because of our company's reputation. You are our only patient who ruins their cybernetic at the rate you do. Not even physically demanding and sometimes hazardous jobs cause this type of damage so regularly. By fixing your arm each time you ruin it, even if we're paid, we're condoning your actions. We cannot allow it to be seen that way."

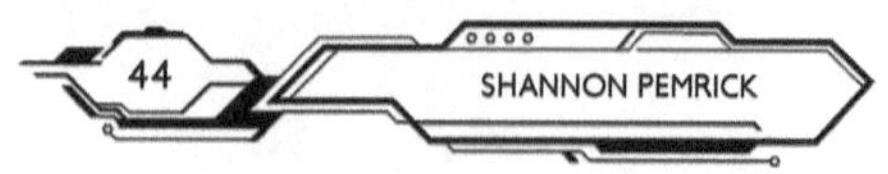

She took a moment before continuing. "The other reason is more personal. You're my friend, Ajax. And I can't continue to sit by and let you kill yourself over some project you think is so important you have to keep it a secret."

Her shoulders sagged. "Even with all the dangers, no matter what I say to you, it doesn't seem to matter, and there's only so much of that I can handle."

She wasn't looking at him anymore. Disclosing that truth hurt more than she wanted to admit. It brought her mind dangerously close to remembering what Nolan did to her. How he'd undermine her and refused to acknowledge anything important she'd put forth. She vowed to never allow anyone to do that to her again. This wasn't the same, but it was too close for comfort.

"Rissa, I—"

"My apologies for interrupting, Doctor Narissa, but you have an important phone call from Officer Dylan," Picard said. "He's on your cell line."

Narissa's brow furrowed as she sat back in her seat. *I haven't spoken to Dylan in quite a while.* "I wonder what he wants."

Dylan was her neighbor, and one of the main officers to have helped her with her messy divorce. She'd also helped him out, or one of his brothers in blue, on miscellaneous police matters in regards to cybernetics. But lately, both had been so busy, it'd been a while since they last spoke.

"I'm afraid I don't know, Doctor," Picard said. "He said he could only speak to you about the matter."

She chewed on her lower lip, a deep sense of dread settling heavy in her stomach. She looked Ajax's way.

"You think about this conversation and we'll discuss it when I'm done with this phone call."

She snatched her phone from her desk and went to the corner, answering the call. "Hey Dylan, how can I help you?"

"Narissa, are you alone right now?" His tone was unusually gruff.

This concerned her. She glanced back at Ajax, who was watching her, and not going over the contract. "I have a client on the other side of the room. Is that a problem?"

"Do you trust them?"

Her fingers tapped her phone. "Dylan, what's this about?"

"I need you to understand I'm just the messenger. When we're done, you need to go talk to your lawyer right away. Understood?"

Her blood ran cold. Before the words came out of his mouth, she already knew who this was about.

"Nolan is getting out on parole."

She almost dropped her phone. "No… he can't… Parole? He's getting out on parole?"

Ajax's chair squeaked as he stood up.

"Dylan, how is he out on parole?"

"I'm afraid it's all I can share on this line, Narissa. You're going to have to talk to your lawyer about the rest and what you can do."

Narissa found it hard to breath. *This can't be happening.*

"Narissa, are you still there?" Dylan asked.

"Yeah… I… thank you for telling me. I'll call my lawyer right away."

"I'm really sorry to have to be the one to tell you. I know how unfair this is."

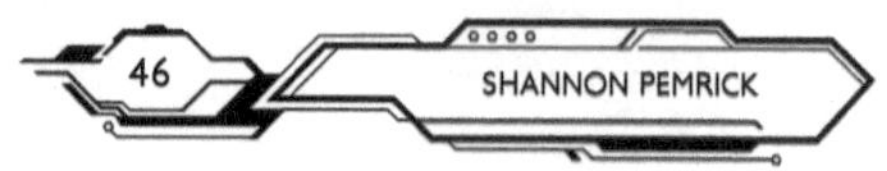

"It's not your fault. I'll talk to you later." She ended the call, numbness overtaking her. This couldn't be happening.

"Rissa?" Ajax said. "What's going on?"

Narissa took two shaky breaths. "Picard, I need you to call up Anastasia to fix Ajax's arm on my behalf." She headed for the door. "I also need all of my appointments canceled or moved to someone else to handle. Apologize on my behalf, but an emergency has come up."

Ajax stepped in her way and placed his good hand on her shoulder. "Narissa."

She looked up at him, finding his gaze intense.

"What is going on?"

She hesitated and then shook her head, moving around him. "I'm sorry, Ajax. I need to handle something. Anastasia is one of my best technicians. You'll be in great hands with her. She'll also only get your nickname in the client files."

He tried to stop her again. "I don't care about that. I've never seen you this freaked out before. Who is on parole that scares you so much?"

Narissa opened her mouth, the words lodging in her throat, and then she headed for the door. "I'm sorry, I have to go."

She rushed out for the elevator, speed-dialing her lawyer.

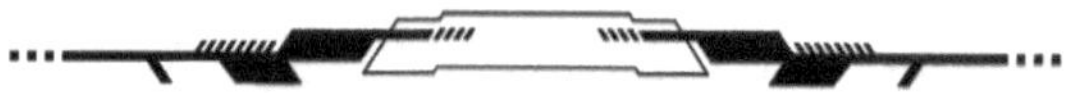

Ajax paced in his work room like a caged animal. Frustration gnawed at him and he checked his phone. Still no response.

After the incident in Narissa's lab this morning, he'd done nothing but worry. She hadn't responded to any of his texts or calls, and no one else had heard from her, either. It was now seven at night and still he hadn't heard a peep.

He ran his cybernetic hand through his hair, stopping mid-motion to look at it. True to her word as always, the woman Narissa had assigned to fix his arm in her stead, Anastasia, knew her stuff. She worked almost as efficiently as Narissa. She was also pleasant to talk to and didn't press him for any conversation that leaned too personal, though she did give him those looks he'd seen from many other women. The looks he wished Narissa would give him.

"No matter what I say to you, it doesn't seem to matter..."

Irritation flared up within him, and he tossed a wrench at the broken machine on the far end of the room. The problem was, what she said did matter. Every time she cautioned and pleaded with him to stop or to tell her what this project was, it hit him hard.

And the way she looked so defeated in the office today, after saying those words... He rubbed his face. *I'm such an ass.*

It was no wonder she didn't trust him, let alone see something in him. Why should she? All he had to do was get her to agree to not speak about the project until it was revealed, but no. He had to keep his mouth shut altogether to make his stupid reveal all that more amazing, as if one more person knowing would ruin it.

His phone went off, the new Star Trek ringtone he'd picked out just for Narissa working perfectly. He snatched the phone to read the text.

I'm fine. Don't worry.

Red signals the size of the USS Enterprise went off in his head. Not only was that response too short and vague for all the messages he'd sent, he very well knew not to trust that "I'm fine" line. Everything was not fine. But she'd never tell him what happened. And why should she, when he kept things from her too?

He plopped down in a chair. What was he going to do?

Ajax's footsteps echoed down the quiet hallway. He'd spent all night and most of today wrestling with this idea of confronting Narissa. She wasn't going to give information willingly if it was a big problem, so he needed to have leverage. *That still sounds so devious.* It wasn't his intention. He just wanted her to open up to him, and if he had to offer up information of equal value, then so be it. If he wanted something to potentially come of the two of them, then he'd have to be more forthright anyway. *Something Father never figured out.*

Ajax opened the door to Narissa's office, and found her working away on her computer. She peered up from her work and then sat upright.

"Ajax." She looked at his arm. "Oh thank god, your arm isn't busted again. You didn't sign the contract. I hope you have a good reason for it.

He pulled up a chair. "Hi to you, too."

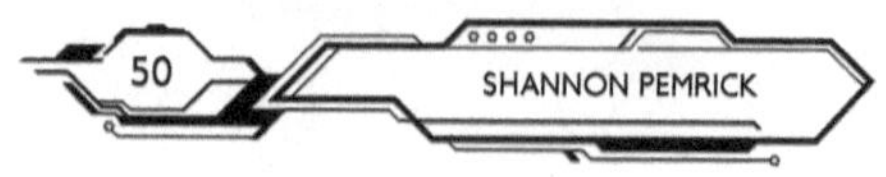

Narissa gave him a long, hard look. "You're not off the hook, mister."

He chuckled. "I wasn't expecting to be. It would just be nice to have a nice greeting exchanged before we talk."

Narissa sighed. "Sorry. You're right."

He waved her off. "Not a big deal."

She gave him an unamused look and he grinned. He enjoyed messing with her.

"So, can we talk about your issue?"

He nodded. "Yeah, but we also have to talk about yours."

She pursed her lips. "I don't have an issue."

"You know what I'm talking about, Narissa. You can't give me an 'I'm fine' line after running out of here in a panic and expect me to believe it."

Her gaze fell. "I'm not going to talk about this, Ajax. You don't need to involve yourself."

He put his feet up on her desk. Narissa narrowed her eyes. She hated feet on the desks. "Look. We either both tell our big secret, or we keep them and continue with our lives. No contracts."

She shook her head. "You know I can force that contract into effect, whether you agree to it or not. We can refuse to continue working with you. Contracts are just cleaner."

"But you won't do it, because it's you. I know you. You wouldn't resort to that." He reached out and grabbed her hand with his artificial one. "Tell me what's going on, Rissa."

She swallowed, conflict and fear flashing across her eyes. Whatever this issue was, it was bigger than she wanted him to see. *I knew it.*

"Okay." She finally said. "I'll tell you. But you have to tell me what's going on with you first."

He smirked and leaned back in his chair. "I'm working on a new gaming machine. One that is better suited for those who can't, or struggle to sit for long periods of time. It also adds for greater stability to the neurological link."

She stared dumbfounded. "That's it? That's your big secret for blowing up your arm?"

"Not even the least bit excited? Wow, tougher crowd than I expected." He kept his smirk where it was, so she wouldn't think he was serious.

Narissa ducked her head. "What did you expect from me? Yes, the idea sounds amazing. But you come in here, nearly killing yourself all the time, and I find out it's because you don't have safety protocols in place for cybernetics?"

He held up his hands. "Hold on. Back up here. This new design is a prototype. While it functions the same as the current chairs, it's a bed style that encases the user, thus causing its own host of issues. I didn't intentionally make it so I'd have to see you every other day in a mangled state."

He chuckled. "As you've told me before, I don't have to nearly kill myself as an excuse to stop by." His eyes ticked to her, making contact. "It'll never have to be an excuse to see you."

Narissa clasped her hands together and tucked her elbows in, her face tinting a shade. Unfortunately, that just accentuated her chest, making it hard for him not to stare, which was a chore in itself. She got her looks from her mother, he'd admit that. Those two hit a genetic

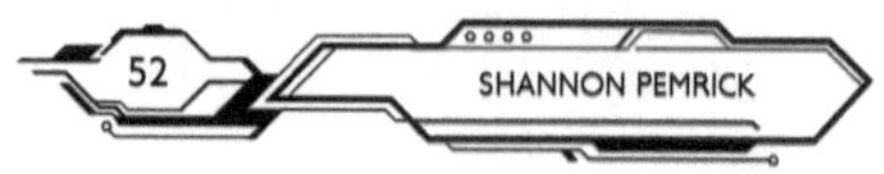

lottery with their perfect figures—curves in all the right places. If Narissa stood up now, he'd about die—or bend her over the desk. That last idea was tempting.

He made an open-handed gesture to her and tried to shift the topic, along with his internal focus. "Okay. Now that I've shared my super-duper secret, it's your turn."

Narissa caught her bottom lip with her teeth and her eyes tightened. She stood and took slow steps as she paced.

Fuck. She had to get up and show off that body. And she wore a skirt today. Bending her over the desk was even more tempting.

Ajax shifted in his seat, as subtly as possible so she wouldn't realize why. He needed to focus. This was serious.

Narissa came to a stop, standing in front of her desk again. "This is all about my ex-husband, Nolan. He's… getting out of jail."

Ajax straightened. Jail and Nolan were not two words he expected to hear in the same sentence.

Narissa sat down in her chair taking a deep breath. "You don't even know what I'm talking about. I've never told you about that."

"I know you're divorced," he admitted. "Mercedes mentioned once that it was a messy one."

"Messy…" Narissa half-laughed—one of those forced, defeated ones. "I wish it'd only been that. I met Nolan eight years ago at a conference, and we hit it off well. We decided to keep in contact, and before I knew it we were dating and then getting married. He was attentive, caring, supportive of my work, and wanted a family—everything I wanted in a partner."

She clasped her hands together. "We moved into a nice house that'd be perfect for the family we planned. I was so happy. And then… I wasn't. It was seven years ago I was divorced. I met, married, and divorced a man in a course of one year."

Her gaze fell to the desk. "He started acting strange six months into our marriage. It began with him canceling dates, or having to go out of town out of the blue. Then he'd get angry when any achievement I made came up, or he'd brush positive things off as if they were nothing. Or even dismissed my knowledge as if I didn't know anything at all."

Narissa's lips pressed into a thin line. "I tried to talk to him about it. At first, he'd push me away. Then, as I became insistent we work things out or go to counseling, he would apologize for his behavior and tell me he was just stressed with his job and things would get better. But they didn't. They'd always go back to before we'd talk, and I wasn't the only one who noticed anymore. So I had someone look into it. Around this time, I started to feel ill. I went to the doctor, and found out I was pregnant."

Concern grew within Ajax. Narissa didn't have any children.

Her face contorted with a type of pain that sent an ache into Ajax's chest. "I was so happy. I couldn't wait to tell Nolan. Young, twenty-two year-old me believed that maybe if I told him, he'd be happy again, and our marriage would be fixed. If twenty-two-year-old me had been smart, she wouldn't have done that. Or did what came next."

Ajax pulled his seat closer, compelled to keep listening, like someone watching a tense thriller movie.

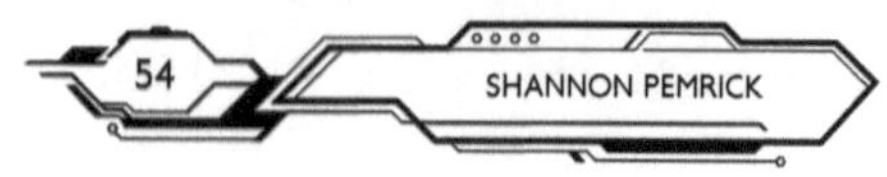

"I was at the office, organizing some files. I'd just revealed the news to my parents. They were so thrilled, but promised not to say anything until I told Nolan. That's when the individual I'd tasked with checking in on Nolan came to me. He accused Nolan of embezzling the company's money. I didn't believe him at first. Why would my husband do something like that? Then he showed me the proof. Millions of dollars, redirected elsewhere and 'lost.' All right under our noses."

Narissa's hands shook. "I went to confront Nolan. What I found was him in bed with my intern. Then it went downhill."

Narissa's hands fell to her stomach, concerning Ajax.

"He sent the intern out and we exchanged heated words, until he pulled a gun." Narissa squeezed her eyes shut. "Two shots. I lost my baby, and if it weren't for a neighbor who had called the police about a domestic disturbance before the gun being pulled, I would have been dead, too."

Narissa's entire body shook now, tears streaming down her cheeks. Ajax couldn't believe what he'd heard. He thought she'd been hung up on Nolan, but this, this wasn't that. This was... he traumatized her. Nothing could have prepared Ajax for this story, and she'd lived through it.

He jumped out of his seat and scooped her up in his arms, holding her close as he sat on her desk. He stroked her head, hushing her softly.

"And now... they're letting him out on parole for good behavior. A twenty-five year sentence, he's only serving seven."

Rage flared in side Ajax. Were they mad? What would compel them to do something so idiotic?

He grasped her face firmly in his hands and pressed his lips against her forehead. "He will never touch you again, Rissa. I swear it."

The office door opened, and the two looked at Ayana standing in the doorway.

"Oh, my." She blinked rapidly before turning away, but not before a wide grin spread across her face that meant only one thing. "I'll leave you two be."

"Mother, don't jump to conclusions," Narissa warned.

"I ain't a blind ole woman yet, darlin'. I know what I saw." She waved her fingers. "I'ma pick your father up from the airport."

Her eyes darted back to them. "Y'all behave now, y'hear? I don't want any lewd sinnin' on company prop'ty, especially not involvin' my daughter. Just look at'im! Bless his heart. Brin' him ta church, Narissa. And yourself while you're at it."

Ayana sashayed down the hall. Narissa pinched her nose while she sighed. "My mother is a piece of work."

Ajax laughed. "I'm more focused on this 'lewd sinnin' she mentioned. Is that what we're calling office romps now?"

Narissa shook her head. "Watch, tomorrow she'll call it devil nesting or something. I swear, she makes these phrases up sometimes."

Ajax reached out and wiped away a stray tear running down Narissa's face. Her eyes widened and then she frantically wiped her face, as if it were shameful for her to have expressed such emotions while retelling that awful story.

He grabbed her hands. "Stop. You don't need to be ashamed."

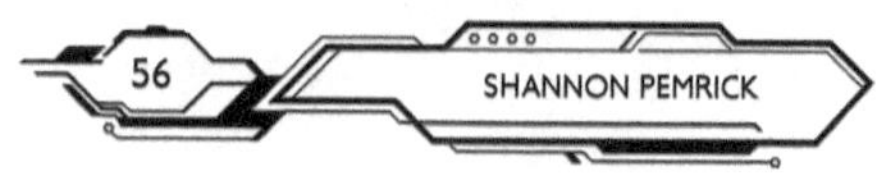

"I…" She pulled her hands free and dabbed her eyes again. "I think I ruined my makeup. Shit. I told myself he'd never do that to me again."

Ajax lifted her chin. "You look beautiful."

Narissa froze, and then after a minute composed herself and looked away. "You're just saying that to make me feel better."

He frowned and watched her rummage through her purse for a mirror. Everything made so much sense now. Nolan took everything from her. Her confidence. Her sense of worth. Her safety. It was no wonder his own advances didn't have an effect. Nolan scared away the idea she could be happy with someone. *He still has too much of a hold on her.*

"So, when is Nolan out?" He should drop this topic, for her sake, but he couldn't let it go. He needed to know what he could do to help her.

Narissa took a moment to respond. "Friday."

Two days from now? *Shit.* That didn't give anyone time to prepare. "What's going to be done to keep him away from you?"

She plopped down in her seat and let out a flat laugh. "Papers. I placed no trespassing orders immediately, and I'm going through the process of a restraining order, but that takes time." She reached under her desk and pulled out a hand gun. "And I have this."

He looked at the weapon and then her, and then the weapon again as she stored it away into a holder strapped to the underside of the desk. She had a gun in her own place of business because she didn't feel safe.

"I also have one at the house, and am getting the permits to have one on me at all times."

Correction, the system was failing her so much she needed three to feel a tiny bit safer.

"My lawyer also suggested I get a dog, which I'm considering. I'd definitely feel safer, trained for protection or not. I'm not going to feel safe at home with Nolan roaming about, even if he doesn't know my address."

This wasn't okay. His anger rose again. This was far from okay. *That son of a bitch. I'll tear him apart if I ever seen him!*

"Be my business partner," Ajax blurted out.

Narissa's brow furrowed. "What?"

Wow, way to go, genius. He'd been thinking about this proposition this morning, due to the nature of his project, but knowing Narissa wasn't safe alone, this would keep her with him more often. And he didn't trust anyone but himself to keep her safe. Nolan wasn't getting anywhere near her if he had anything to say about it.

But, he could have verbalized the idea better. "Yeah, it's exactly what I said. You are the cybernetic queen—"

She chuckled and looked away, her face reddening. "I'm no queen."

Ajax lifted her chin so she'd see the sincerity in his eyes. "Yes you are. And you're going to be treated like one while I'm around."

Her mouth opened, but nothing came out, her cheeks still a shade darker than the rest of her, just as he'd hoped. Nolan may have lied when he said he valued her, but Ajax wasn't that loser. She'd know what real attention was.

"I need your help," he said. "I thought I could do it alone, but there's only so much one person can accomplish. And I've come to that point. I can't bust through this brick wall like the Kool-aid man could."

That got her laughing so hard she almost fell over, which got him laughing. They eventually calmed and she smiled at him. "You sure you want someone like me to help you with this super-secret project?"

Ajax shook his head. "Not someone *like* you. Exactly you. You're the brains behind cybernetics. If anyone can figure out why my machine is prejudiced against them, it's you. And once we figure out where the problem lies, I can fix it, and make this new pod safe for everyone, like it should be. It'd be great for both our companies' reputations, too."

He held out his hand. "So, what do you say? Partners?"

Her eyes showed the idea excited her, and her mouth tried to move several times before words finally came out. "Yes. Yes, absolutely. Oh, wait. Picard, can you check to make sure I can do that without any conflicts?"

"Let me check, Doctor."

"I still can't believe you named your assistant Picard."

She pointed at him. "Hey, it's better than Kirk."

"Take that back. Captain James T. Kirk is the best captain."

"How dare you claim that! Captain Jean-Luc Picard out classes Kirk. There's never been any contest. And besides, no self-respecting Trekkie would ever trust an AI named after Captain Kirk."

"Ajax, would you prefer I change my data to be named Spock?" Kirk said from his phone. "Statistically, Trekkies have a greater fondness for this character. It may be better received."

Narissa pointed to the phone. "See, he gets it!"

"That's it, this friendship is over."

She crossed her arms and stuck up her nose. "Fine. Leave."

He did, right down the hall where he stopped just out of sight. He wasn't actually mad. This kind of "bickering" was normal for them. He was an OG Trekkie through and through, but Narissa had been raised in a ST:TNG Trekkie family. Of course the one thing they could agree on was that all other Star Trek variations were inferior.

His phone rang and Kirk spoke up. "It's your mother."

He sighed and answered. "Hi, Mom."

"Oh good, you answered this time."

His brow rose. "This time?"

"Yes. I've been trying to get a hold of you for the last fifteen or so minutes."

Kirk must have blocked his calls. "Sorry, Mom. I was dealing with something important that required my full attention."

"Oh really? Did it perhaps have anything to do with charming the pants off that friend of yours?"

He chuckled. "She's wearing a skirt today, actually."

"Even easier. Sounds like her mother didn't find out either, else I'd be planning your funeral."

His mother caught onto his interest in Narissa before even he noticed it himself. She approved, telling him he deserved the best and that was Narissa, making him happy. He had a great relationship with her. She was always there for him when he needed some wise woman counsel. Or a swift kick in the pants.

"No, nothing happened this time. We were talking about some other things."

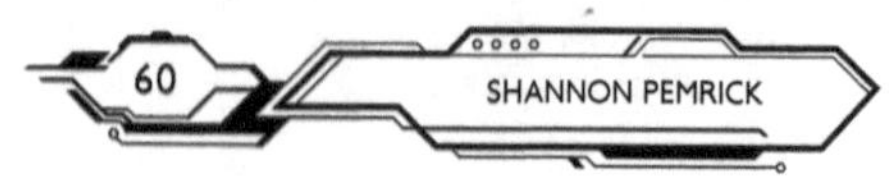

"Sure, sure. And when you want to be honest, tell me and I'll give you some tips that'll be sure to keep her happy and coming back for more."

Ajax shook his head. "Mom, what did you really call me about?"

"Dinner. The investors were so pleased with the meeting, they've invited us to dinner."

He let out a mental sigh of relief. That meeting had not gone as smoothly as he'd hoped. He'd been so distracted because of Narissa, and they noticed. It seemed, though, he had lady luck's favor, and his attempts to sweet-talk himself out of that fumble worked. "You think they want to discuss the new project?"

"I know they do. You did drop a hint about it when explaining the company's goals for the next five years, and they're going to want to know what their money is going toward."

Ajax rubbed the back of his neck. He'd hoped to keep it secret for a while longer, but they were investors. They funded these improvements. "All right. Usual time and place?"

"Always. And your sister won't be able to make it."

He didn't expect she could. She was in the middle of her own project, and her work ethic was almost as crazy as Narissa's. So he gave her lenience when it came to after-hour meetings.

"I expect you to bring a date, too. I don't care how short notice it is. I doubt you'll have an issue inviting Narissa."

She would jump from assuming that'd be the woman he'd ask, to making that decision. But she wasn't wrong this time. "I'm already ahead of you on that, Mom."

"Oh?" He caught the interest in her voice. "Do tell, as you wouldn't have been speaking to me so freely earlier if she'd been in the room. Unless—"

"I asked her about being my business partner on this new project."

His mother sighed. "Shoot. I was hoping you'd say you two were already planning on giving me grandchildren."

"Mother."

"What? Your sister said 'no way in hell,' so that leaves you. And Narissa seems like a nice family woman."

Ajax shook his head. "One thing at a time, Mom. Please?"

"Well, that sounds promising at least. But on topic, she said yes to the proposal?"

He'd let his mother know of the idea before heading over to confront Narissa. He wanted to be sure the move would be approved of. The words out of her mouth amused him. *It's about time! You should have brought her on sooner, like when you were designing the first model.*

It didn't matter he hadn't met Narissa until long after. It became a "Well, you should have met her sooner" type of talk.

"Yes. She was surprised, but eager to say yes." He knew she told her assistant to check the legalities, but he'd already run that. When he walked back into the room, things would be all set.

"Good. Now, get to work charming a ring on that finger." The line clicked, leaving him to stare at his phone. Ayana wasn't the only piece of work in these families.

Ajax made it back to Narissa's office. She smiled at him. "You took so long, I thought that may have been the fight to end all fights for us."

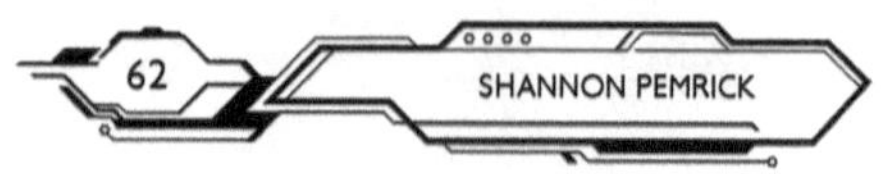

He snickered. "No, it'll take a lot more to get rid of me."

She continued to smile. "Good, because we're partners now, and I'm not chasing you all over Lusara to keep you from blowing up that arm of yours."

The reference to the MMO made him grin. Could she get any more perfect? "You free at seven?"

Narissa opened her mouth, her eyes saying she wasn't sure, and Picard answered. "You have no appointments or family events."

She nodded. "I guess that's my answer. Why?"

He wanted to offer to partner up and do something fun in game, but… obligations. "I have a dinner to attend with some investors. I'd like you to accompany me, as my new business partner and dinner date."

Narissa grinned. "Thanks to the order of your wording, my answer is yes."

CHAPTER 5

The makeup brush pressed against Narissa's cheek as she finished the final touches. She'd spent the last hour making sure she looked perfect—her eyeliner was on point, the blue dress hugging every curve of her frame, and every curl of her hair in its place. Investor meetings were important, and she needed to make a good first impression. That wasn't to say she wouldn't put this effort in if it had just been her and Ajax. *Not that he'd ask me out on a date for two.*

She still couldn't believe he'd asked to be business partners. And for such an amazing project. She wished she'd acted more appropriately when he revealed it to her, but she'd been honest. A game pod prototype wasn't worth blowing his arm up in secret for this long. Now that she was going to help, that'd hopefully stop.

Ajax had forwarded the contract over to seal their partnership, and he'd also forwarded a large packet of information for her to go over. Per his claim, it was just introductory information, and the rest would come to her once she got through it. It both made her nervous and excited.

She brushed the makeup brush over her forehead and found herself touching the spot where he'd kissed her with her fingers. She hadn't planned on telling him about Nolan, ever. She didn't think he needed to hear those problems. So she certainly hadn't expected to confess everything to him today in her office, but she was glad she had. A weight lifted off her chest the moment the words came out.

And the way he held her—his promise to keep her safe—she believed it. She felt safe with him—like nothing could ever touch her as long as he was around.

Her phone went off, the Star Trek Next Generation theme song rang away. Ajax's name came up on the screen.

I'm outside. Early, I know. If you buzz
me in, I can greet you at the door.

No need. I'll be out in a minute.

His response came back with a frown emoji. It made her laugh. When she calmed, she stared at her phone instead of finishing her task. *Maybe the girls and my mom are right.*

Maybe she did have a chance with him. His actions as of late really were borderline flirting. *Please, Narissa, they crossed that line a long time ago.* And the rage building in Ajax after finding out what Nolan did, she thought it might rival her father. She swore she'd be seeing Ajax in court for murdering the bastard.

Narissa hadn't dated since Nolan. She couldn't find it in her to trust someone like that again after all she'd gone through. Even in the last seven years, she maybe had three nights with different men that were never intended to go further. They didn't leave a lasting impression on her, that's how great they went. It all left a bad taste in her mouth. Jaded is what some would call it.

Ajax tempted her to be daring—hopeful for something she believed just didn't exist for her. But she wasn't sure now if she wanted to risk her amazing friendship on something that may not be as great as it seemed.

Her phone went off again.

> *Are you sure I can't come up there and meet you?*

She shook her head.

> *I said I'm almost done. You'd be halfway up the stairs by the time I leave.*

> *You underestimate my power walking skills.*

She threw her head back as she laughed. He was something else. Narissa put the phone down and dusted one final area on her face, checked herself over one last time in her full length mirror—*Nice and sexy. Good, good*—and snatched up her shawl and clutch from her bed.

Her heels clicked on the floor as she moved through the small, modest one bedroom apartment. She'd been raised not to flaunt her money, and since she spent most of her hours at the office or in the game, she saw no reason to invest in a lavish lifestyle.

Leaving her apartment, she descended the stairs. At the bottom, some of the local children played. One of the older girls watching them, she was maybe thirteen, stared at her. "Narissa, you look ready to walk the red carpet!"

She chuckled. "Thank you, Ellie. I feel very pretty."

One of the smaller children looked up at her. "Are you going out on a date?"

"I have a work dinner to attend."

One of the mothers poked her head out of an open door of an apartment. "I hope it's with the handsome man sitting outside. I've been watching him since he first arrived." Her eyebrows rose a few times. "He's quite the catch."

Narissa laughed. "As a matter of fact, he's my date."

"Well, don't let that one get away."

Narissa smiled, and left the building, wishing them all a good night. She found Ajax leaning on the hood of his red 2107 Corvette. He liked his cars fast, and he had good taste in them. And he looked good in a suit—real good. Ajax was a fine specimen of a man. He needed to wear suits more often.

Ajax looked her way and his mouth fell open. He also almost dropped his phone. *Test subject has passed the look test.* She was going to make Ajax a happy man at this dinner. It was the least she could do for what'd he'd done for her today.

An image of him unzipping the back of her dress after the party flashed through her head. She shook it out immediately. *Not okay.* Another one popped in,

this one of them sneaking away for a moment during the dinner. The two of them just out of view while he lifted up—*Stop it! I'm not even that type of woman!*

Fantasies, maybe. Sure. But real life wasn't a fantasy. *Real life is pain, not pleasure…*

Ajax struggled to say something for a moment. "You look amazing, Rissa."

God did she loved hearing that name from him. Her lips curved into a deep smile. "You look great, too, Andrew."

He looked down at himself. "It's a suit. Nothing special."

"It's the person inside the suit that makes it special." The moment the words left her lips, she'd wished she'd been smart enough to use other words. That compliment sounded cheesy as hell.

Ajax's shoulders moved as he looked away and struggled with a comeback. *Is he blushing?* Maybe cheesy worked for him. He was a bit of a cheese-ball anyway.

He opened the car door for her. "Shall we?"

Narissa slipped into the impressive car, finding it cleaner than it'd had ever been in her life of knowing Ajax. Why, she wasn't sure. It wasn't like the investors would see, and she'd already seen this car at its worst.

Ajax jumped in and the car pulled out of the parking spot, speeding off into the city. "Cute place you have. I expected you'd have a home, not a small apartment."

She'd forgotten he'd never been by her place before, or she his, until he texted her, asking for the address. "I like living in a small place. It's just me and I don't own a whole lot, so no need for a big home."

"A billion-dollar woman who doesn't have a need for

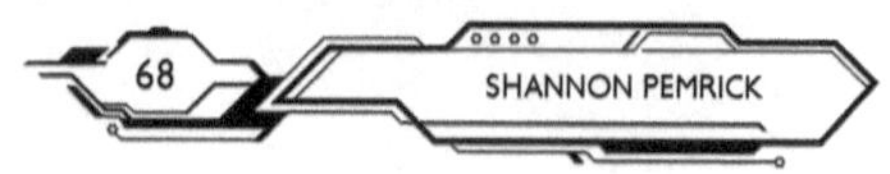

a personal shopping mall for her collection of over-priced clothes and year's supply worth of shoes." Ajax chuckled. "That's a first for me."

He turned to face her. "Who were those other people there? Seemed like there were a lot of kids."

Narissa nodded. "I rent the building out to low-income families. Most of the families in the apartments have kids."

"Wait, you own the building?"

"Yeah. I also own a few of the buildings nearby that I rent out for low income. They're some of the best maintained low-income buildings you'll find in L.A."

He smirked. "Doctor Narissa, helping people in any way she can."

She looked away. "Yeah, that's me."

The car pulled into the parking lot of Dion Taverna, one of the best restaurants in the area to get your hands on some Mediterranean cuisine.

Narissa removed her seatbelt, but Ajax stopped her from getting out. "Hold on, I have something for you."

She cocked her head. "What do you mean?"

He reached into the console and pulled out a small, wide box with a ribbon. Narissa's eyes grew wide. She really hoped this wasn't what she thought it was.

Then he offered it to her. "I saw this and thought of you. When you told me the color of your dress, I knew it'd be perfect."

"This had better not be jewelry."

He smirked. "I'm glad you're not wearing a necklace tonight."

She knew it. She refused to take the box. "I'm not accepting this."

Ajax grabbed her hand and made her take it. "Open it and see what it is. I know you'll like it."

She sighed, her shoulders sagging, and undid the ribbon. She opened the box and her breath caught. Glittering inside was a necklace made of white gold, tanzanite, and either diamonds or cubic zirconia, depending on your preference. She knew, because she'd been eyeing this one for weeks. Narissa even told Ajax about it when she couldn't decide if she should buy it or not. He'd advised her to wait. Now she wondered if this was his plan all along.

"Andrew…"

"Before you freak out, it's not diamonds. I know how much you don't like them."

Overpriced shiny rocks, she always called them. She would never buy them for herself, and told others to consider an alternative if they ever insisted on buying her jewelry.

She looked at the necklace and then him, and then the necklace again, trying to process this. "You didn't have to…"

"I know." His lips curled up half his devilishly handsome face. "That's why I did it. And no, you can't refuse or give it back. I won't allow you to."

He opened his door. "Give me a moment and I'll help you put it on.

Narissa continued to stare at the necklace, unable to process why he'd go out of his way to buy her this. It wasn't a money thing. They both had the money to buy it without breaking the bank. So what compelled him to remember she wanted this piece, and then buy it for her?

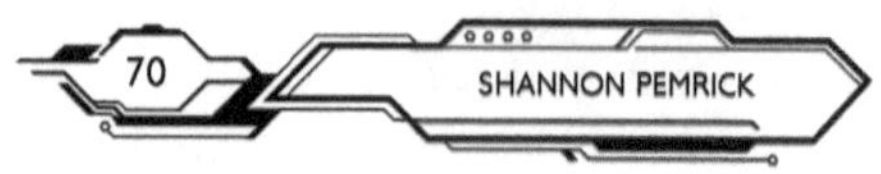

She loved tanzanite. It was such a beautiful stone to her, and also happened to be her birthstone, so win-win.

Are the girls right? Or is he just being nice because of what happened earlier? This would be a bit extreme in her book. Ice cream would have sufficed. Well, ice cream was a good go-to for just about every problem and non-problem.

Ajax opened the door and leaned in. "Let me have it."

"Careful. That sounds like permission to punch you for buying this."

He grinned right up next to her ear. "But you won't."

His hot breath sent goose bumps down her spine. Her breathing stopped momentarily.

Ajax reached around her and took the necklace from the box. He wasn't going to let her refuse, so she chose not to fight him. Narissa pulled her hair up, giving him easier access to clasp the jewelry. Ajax's hands brushed her skin as he got the clasp taken care of, sending a jolt through her and a question of what it'd be like for those strong hands to touch more of her.

"There," he whispered before pulling away and offering her his hand.

Narissa let her hair drop, fussing with it in the visor mirror so it'd be perfect again, and then allowed him to help her out of the low-sitting car. She wobbled on her heels, but he held her close so she wouldn't fall. The Los Angeles evening heat felt cool compared to the heat sizzling between them as she stared into those dark, captivating eyes of his.

"Thank you for catching me," she finally said.

He smiled. "I told you I'd keep you safe."

She pulled away, smoothing out her dress. "You said you'd keep me safe from Nolan."

"Was I that specific? I was pretty sure I meant in general."

Narissa shook her head. "Should we head inside? We don't want to be late."

Ajax checked the time. "We're right on time, actually."

He offered his bent elbow. She linked her arm into his and the pair headed for the restaurant. "Andrew, just so I know, what name should I call you by around these people?"

"Go with Ajax for tonight, if you would." He smirked. "I don't let just anyone call me Andrew."

"I feel honored."

His grin deepened. "I know."

She chuckled. The references the two made with old geek culture, at the rate they could, was refreshing. It made it hard to not want to find more things in common with this man.

The two entered the building and the hostess showed them to the area reserved for their party. An older woman with wavy, dyed black hair and bright blue eyes sat at a table in a private room, alone. She looked up when the two entered with the hostess and smiled widely, immediately standing.

"You finally arrived, Eu—"

Ajax's eyes narrowed. "Mother, what have we discussed with using that name in public, especially on days we're speaking with important parties?"

His mother huffed. "I don't know why you hate your name so much. Narissa, you think it's a good name, don't you?"

She understood his mother's attachment to the name,

but she had her own opinions of it. "Sorry, but I'm not a fan, either."

"It's a good name you give to smart boys." She sighed. "I should have called you Einstein. Or Theodore. Maybe then you would have used it."

Ajax grimaced and Narissa giggled. His mother had some strange tastes in names. His sister, Allyson, was lucky she came out with a good one.

His mother waved Narissa over. "Come here, Narissa. It's been so long since I've seen you."

Narissa smiled and the two exchanged a nice hug and kiss on both cheeks. "It's good to see you again too, Ms. Williams."

She wagged her finger at Narissa. "Sophia, remember, dear? Or Mom."

Ajax gave his mother a stern look. "Mother…"

She waved him off. "I'm just teasing. Lighten up."

Unlike him, Narissa found it funny. Her mother would do the same, given the chance.

"Oh, looks like they've all finally arrived," Sophia said, looking past the two.

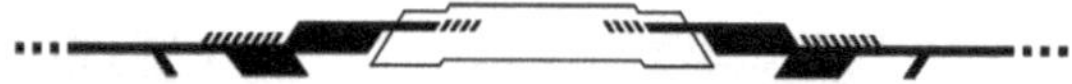

Ajax turned to see four men and one woman being led into the room by the hostess. All of the men were middle-aged or older, and wearing their best attire. Only one stuck out from the bunch—the oldest-looking of them, who wore a cowboy hat and boots. *Texans.* He thought the stereotype was just that, but Adrian said otherwise.

The woman, Lisa, was far younger, closer to his and

Narissa's age. She was his biggest investor, always championing for inclusive tech. It's why she had such a big interest in his company. Ajax prided himself on that prospect. And with Narissa here, it'd only improve his relationship with Lisa.

"Only five of the seven?" he muttered to his mother.

"It appears so." She sounded just as unnerved.

Missing investors at a dinner like this was not a good sign. Hopefully there was an explanation. From the looks of it, Daniel and Serge were the missing heads, and they came from the same company. If they were uninterested in funding, it wouldn't be as large a loss.

"Do I need to teach you how to stay calm?" Narissa said in a hushed tone.

A grin spread across his lips as he bent closer to her ear. "Careful, I might like that."

His mother cleared her throat. "And you, young man, will behave yourself in public. Or I will use your name against your wishes."

Narissa giggled while he straightened up. She'd make good on that promise if he wasn't careful.

"Mister Jackson," one of the men said as they approached.

Ajax turned and shook hands with the older gentleman. "No need to be so formal, Dale. Ajax is fine."

"As you wish."

Ajax shook hands with the others, and Liam took notice of Narissa as they all went to greet the two women. "And who do we have here for a new face?"

Adrian let out a boisterous laugh and pushed his way forward. "How do ya not know of *the* Doctor Narissa Okafor?"

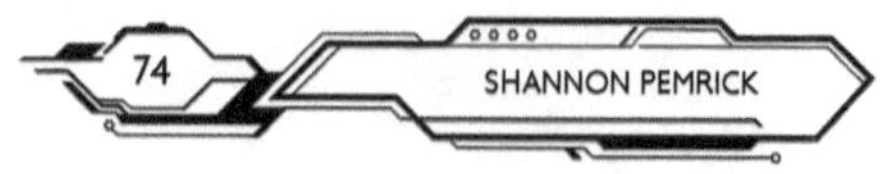

Liam took a step back, startled. Ajax was surprised as well, but more with how friendly Adrian and Narissa greeted each other.

Narissa kissed him on the cheek. "It's good to see you again, Adrian."

"You too, Narissa. Been too long," he drawled.

Ajax pointed to the two of them. "You know each other."

Adrian lifted his hand, an artificial one. "Narissa is one of the best in these parts. How could I not go to her?"

Narissa poked him in the shoulder. "He just needs to learn to stop by for more regular checkups."

He waved her off. "Still young blood runnin' wild in these veins, little missy. I don't need some doctor tellin' me what's best for me."

Her brow rose up and then down once. "Yeah, that's why you still have both your hands."

The room filled with laughter. Lisa shook her finger at Narissa. "I like her already. Name's Lisa."

Narissa shook Lisa's hand. "Pleasure."

"But, before we continue with these introductions"—Adrian gestured to the waitress standing patiently behind them all—"I think we all should order a drink. Budweiser, ma'am, if you don't mind."

The waitress nodded and took the order of the other men, all ordering a beer or spirit of some kind.

Narissa ordered next. "Would you have any brands of Barolo wine?"

The hostess nodded. "We have one, it's aged twenty-five years."

Narissa smiled at her. "That'd be perfect."

"Add another glass with that," Lisa said, as she found herself a seat at the table.

"And a third," his mother added. She lowered her voice to Ajax. "She's got good taste."

Ajax ordered a water, gaining a few looks from the men.

The waitress left, and Adrian took over Ajax's attempt to introduce Narissa to Dale, Liam, and Mason. He did so all the while touching her upper back, sending a rush of irritation and envy through him. Ajax was just glad the old gentleman didn't place his hand any lower.

"This project of yours must be mighty big, Ajax, if you've got Narissa here as an investor, too," Adrian said.

Before he could answer, Narissa spoke up. "Oh, I'm not here as an investor. I'm his business partner."

All of them took interest in her and then Ajax. He gestured to the table. "Why don't we sit down so a proper explanation can be given? It has to do with the new project."

Ajax pulled out a chair for Narissa and then sat next to her. Adrian sidled up on the other side of her, and Lisa took the seat across from her. She looked eager as always. Ajax suspected she would be upon hearing Narissa's involvement.

Mason spoke up once everyone was all seated. "Before we start, I must ask, are you really a doctor?"

Ajax didn't understand the reason for the question, but Narissa took it in stride. "Yes. I have a doctorate in biomedical engineering, and I'm a licensed surgeon. It allows me to perform neuro-modification surgeries without the need to bring in another party beyond a few nurses."

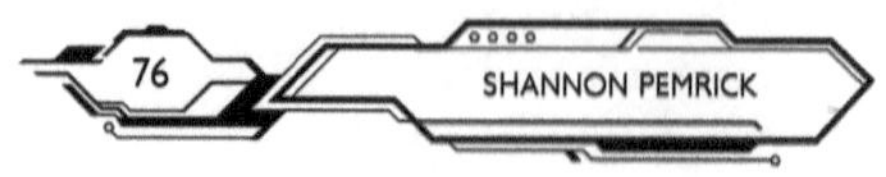

Lisa gave Mason a sidelong glance. "Have a problem with a woman being so successful?"

Mason shook his head. "Not at all. She just seemed rather young, is all."

Narissa's lips spread into a deep smile. "I graduated high school at fifteen. Those extra two years made it easier to excel in my double major. All the while saving my brother's life with my revolutionary tech."

"You did that when you were around twenty, yes?" Dale asked.

Narissa nodded. "Yes. And I used that work to complete my degree in record time, and jump right into creating the cybernetics our company uses today."

Liam leaned back in his seat. "Fascinating. Now, Ajax, can you tell us more about this secret project of yours, and how our lovely doctor fits into it all?"

Ajax looked to his mother, who pulled out her phone to work up the file transfer. The waitress returned just then to deliver their drinks and take their orders. It was common for these to be more business-focused right off the bat, so everyone had picked out their meals ahead of time. Even Narissa knew the drill.

Once the waitress left, he addressed the investors. "My mother is transmitting a file to each of you. I have a condensed and easy-to-follow information packet for you all, on the latest virtual-reality gaming chair we're developing." He chuckled. "Well, *chair* wouldn't be the correct term for this one."

He went on to detail the new design for them all, including the benefits of stability, user health, and wider inclusion, which the current construction lacked. This grabbed Lisa's attention. He knew this design would reel her right in.

"How customizable is this design?" Lisa asked. "I wonder how well it'll accommodate the disabled and little people at the same time."

"We're still working out the technical aspect of accommodation, but it'll occur for most in the gel padding. For more advanced needs, we may need to construct a customized machine, which, as you may imagine, would be pricey. There's also no way I can currently guarantee the extent of the customizable capabilities at the moment. I still need the prototype to function correctly."

"Will there still be a weight restriction with this design?"

He nodded. "There's only so much we can allow these devices to hold before they collapse."

Lisa didn't like that answer, he could tell. Luckily, Narissa came to his rescue. "Weight restrictions also encourage healthier living styles. Not even I can give a prosthetic to just anyone. They have to be within a particular level of overall health, else they're more likely to fail. Even my life-saving designs can't be used on everyone."

Lisa nodded. "I suppose you're right."

Liam flipped through the leaflets. "This is quite the fascinating design you've come up with. This begs the question, why do you need Narissa's assistance?"

The pair glanced at each other, and he nodded to let her take that; he trusted her to handle it correctly. She'd handled Lisa better than he could have.

"The current prototype has a major flaw," she said. "It

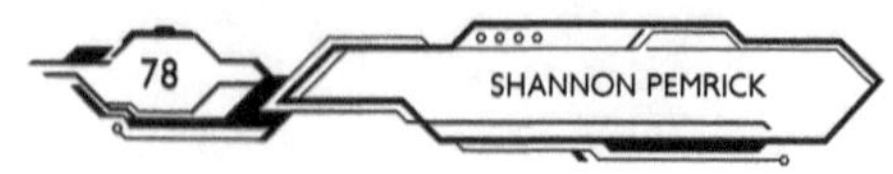

doesn't interact well with low-grade or even high-grade cybernetics, like the ones Ajax and Adrian have. This obviously could present a problem for a great deal of the population if they can't get into the pods without potentially risking their life."

"That is a mighty big problem, indeed," Adrian said.

"This is why Ajax has come to me."

"And so he stops hurting himself," his mother muttered.

This grabbed a few people's attention. *Great, thanks, Mother.* Liam spoke. "Those are troubling words."

She waved him off. "Don't worry. Narissa would have killed him and disposed of the body before this thing could ever do him in."

Everyone laughed. Ajax even found it funny, because she wasn't wrong. When he'd come in for his fix, the fury in Narissa's eyes screamed he was a goner for sure.

Narissa went about getting them back on track. "When Ajax decided to finally include me in on his little secret, it was just a consultation—something I do regularly for many companies who run into issues such as this. But, we soon realized that a consultation wouldn't be enough."

A lie, but sometimes that's what was needed, and it wasn't going to hurt them. Narissa peered around at the investors. "This design has a great deal of potential. As we all know, virtual reality programs of all types, not just games, have sprung up because of Ajax's work, and it has changed many lives. It's imperative the design continues to improve, and this new style will be the next big step."

The meeting continued for another hour and a half,

each investor having questions and testing the waters with Narissa's involvement. When it finally ended, Ajax led Narissa to the car after seeing everyone off.

He shut the door and sighed, leaning on his steering wheel. While a good outcome in the end, that had not been fun. He was glad the investors took to Narissa's and his new partnership well. It was stupid to him, how he could potentially lose investors for something like that. *I think she's really what sealed this deal, if I'm honest.*

Lisa loved her, no question. It was the men that grated him. But Narissa knew her way around them, he'd give her that. It was no wonder she could command a boardroom and got what she wanted ninety percent of the time. *And really, who wouldn't want to please this woman? Besides that loser of an ex of hers.*

Her good standing with Adrian didn't hurt, either. For such an easygoing man, he was one of the more fickle investors. *Thank whatever god is out there for that miracle.*

Narissa giggled next to him. "Are you okay, Eugene?"

He threw his head back and groaned. "Dammit! I thought I'd actually make it through tonight without hearing that name."

Narissa rolled on the console in a fit of laughter. "I'm sorry. I'm sorry, but I couldn't contain myself. Your mother had to try so hard not to use it."

He scowled. "At least you think it's funny."

She calmed herself and looked up through those gorgeous curls of hers. "Oh, don't be mad."

He leaned over and brushed some of her curly silken stands away from her captivating dark eyes. "I won't be mad if you agree to go away with me for a bit. Say, a week?"

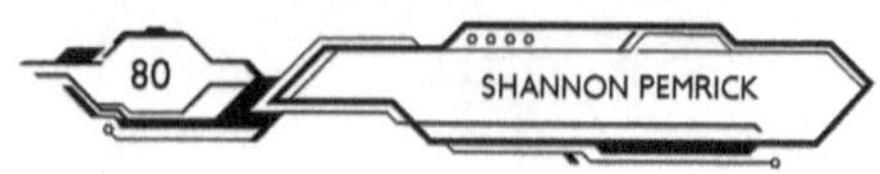

Her brow knitted and her lips pursed as she sat up. "Huh?"

Ajax had been thinking it about this all night after inviting her to dinner. He needed to ensure she was not only physically safe from Nolan, but mentally as well. This idea also allowed him to have her to himself for a while.

No more games and dancing around. He was going to have Narissa. And spending this time with her would expedite that. "Let's get away from L.A. for at least a couple of days. It'll be fun, and one-hundred percent stress-free, I promise."

As long as she cooperates, that is. It would be hard to show her the perks of being with him if she resisted his advances. "Bonus, you won't have to worry about Nolan at all."

She chewed her lip, sending a wave of arousal through him. He wouldn't mind helping her with that. "I don't know if I can take more than the weekend off. I have appointments to worry about."

"Doctor," Picard said from wherever she hid her phone on her person, "You are free of appointments until Wednesday, and those could be handled by another employee."

Her brow ticked up. "None on Monday, really?"

"So far, yes."

"Odd."

On a normal day, Ajax would be concerned, but today, it excited him. One less thing to get in the way of her saying yes. "I'll plan everything. I'll even give you a list of items you will definitely need on the trip. It'll also be treated like an *off the grid* situation, so no one follows us. Means we'll drive to this destination."

She peered up at him. "But I can't know where we're going?"

"It'll be a surprise. I promise, you'll love it."

Narissa took a few more moments to think and then shrugged. "Why the hell not?"

He grinned and started the car. "Great. We leave tomorrow."

CHAPTER 6

arissa went over the list Ajax had forwarded to her late last night. Most of it was standard: good walking shoes, specifically ones that could get wet; enough clothes to last a week, maybe more in case of accidents; toiletries, and the like. But two items on the list were odd. He'd told her to pack at least one set of warm clothes. The other one, she had to go out and buy this morning, and not willingly. Ajax listed a two-piece bathing suit. A complete contradiction to the first item.

There was no explanation, of course, for either item, and when she asked about it, he refused to give away the surprise. Though, he did assure her the specific type of bathing suit was important, even after she'd told him she wasn't comfortable with the request. He'd seen her in a bathing suit before; that wasn't the issue. She just didn't wear that type of bathing suit anymore. Not after the incident with Nolan.

She touched her stomach. She had some visual reminders she didn't want anyone ever seeing. Instead, monokinis were her choice, and she always picked ones that covered her in just the right places. She could look sexy and feel comfortable in those. She had packed that one just in case she could get away with it when the time came.

Her office door opened and her mother sashayed her way in. "Narissa, honey, are you sure about this trip o' y'alls?"

Narissa put her list away. "Of course, mother. Why?"

Her mother touched her face far too dramatically. "Oh, babydoll, I just don't like the idea of y'all going somewhere unknown, just you and a handsomely temptin' young man. So many temptations."

Narissa shook her head and took a sip of her coffee. "Mother, it's going to be fine. I can take care of myself."

She sighed. "All right, but don't be lettin' him ring the devil's doorbell, y'hear?"

Narissa choked on her coffee. "Did you really just call it that?"

Her mother waved her hand and rolled her eyes. "Would you prefer a different term? A hoo-hah? Hooded lady, perhaps?"

Narissa's face burned hot as she held up her hands and found herself unable to look at her mother. She wasn't sure if she should laugh or not. "Mother, stop, please."

Her mother crossed her arms. "Okay, but keep in mind the devil'll tempt you with that man. As much as I approve o' him, you keep them sinna thoughts away 'til you's married him."

"Who is marrying who now?" a familiar male voice said.

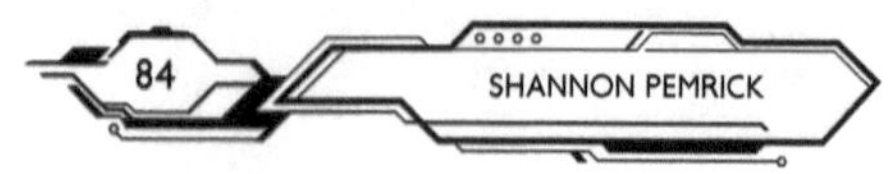

The pair looked back to see Ajax standing in the doorway. He leaned against it, his t-shirt and jeans clinging to every delicious muscle of his. Had she not been so worked up because of her mother, Narissa would take a moment to appreciate temptation before her. Instead, she mouthed "save me" to him. She'd had enough of her mother's antics.

Her mother sighed. "From what ah'm told, not y'all, unfortunately." She strolled over to Ajax and patted him on the cheek. "You behave around my baby, y'hear, Sugar?"

He smiled. "Don't worry, Ayana, Narissa is going to be safe with me."

She looked him up and down and then glanced back at Narissa. "S'pose if y'all give me a grandbaby, I cans forgive you for sinnin' while y'alls away."

Narissa groaned and slapped her hand into her face. "Goodbye, Mother."

Her mother hummed to herself as she waved goodbye and left. Narissa shook her head.

Ajax wore a bemused smile. "Ready to go?"

"Yes, before she decides to come back with more crazy 'advice.'"

He chuckled.

Narissa followed Ajax out; he insisted on carrying her suitcase for her. *Men.* She pulled her dark sunglasses over her eyes when they came down into the bright lobby, and said goodbye to Amy as she passed. When they stepped outside into the unrelenting Los Angeles heat, she found a Jeep Rubicon sitting out front. *When did he get a Jeep?* And where were they going where he'd need to swap out his favorite sports car?

They approached the Jeep, and she jumped back when two excited furry faces popped up in the back window. One was a red merle Australian sheepdog, and the other was some sort of scrappy, flea-bitten mixed breed of the same size with a torn ear. Both had lolling, excited tongues as they stared at her.

Ajax laughed at her. "It's all right, they're friendly. They'll also be our copilots on this trip."

Narissa opened the front door, the air-conditioned air hitting her warm skin, and the Aussie greeted her first, with bright blue eyes and happy licks.

She knew these two, Helios and Crash. While she'd never met them, Ajax posted about them all the time on his social media. They went everywhere with him. Narissa gave Helios a good scratch along the neck and behind the ears before Crash pushed his way into her hands. She immediately noticed the dog's cybernetic front right limb. She'd seen it before in the photographs, but never saw an explanation anywhere.

"They're adorable," she said to Ajax. "I'm glad I get to finally meet them, rather than vicariously through social media."

Ajax's brow rose. "I thought I brought them with us a few times on days we chose to go to outdoor eating places for lunch."

Narissa shook her head. "Nope. Though I wish you had. They're good boys."

Ajax finished storing her suitcase in the back and went to the driver's side. "*She*. Crash is my baby girl."

Narissa situated herself in her seat and then scratched Crash again. "Sorry. I assumed, since Crash isn't all that lady-like."

Ajax chuckled. "Oh, she's no lady."

Narissa laughed. She'd probably find out exactly what that meant during this trip.

The Jeep roared to life and they set a pace through the city. The two rode in relative silence, Narissa lost in her own thoughts of where they may be going, and the danger that was her ex-husband. She shouldn't think about him—shouldn't give him a moment's thought and let him win—but fear gripped her, paralyzing every other thought that she wished would come and overpower these ones.

A cold, wet nose touched the back of her arm and she jumped. She found Crash staring up at her with big brown eyes.

"Well, at least one of us got your attention," Ajax said.

She found him shuffling a deck of cards. Not many people had physicals cards anymore. Most used card machines. They displayed cards on a screen or hologram, and you could set up any game with any rules you wanted. They were perfect for road trips like this, but she knew Ajax well enough to know he liked the feel of the cards in his hands. Using physical cards had a different feel in a game as well.

Narissa rubbed her arm. "Sorry, lost in thought."

"That's what I was worried about. I don't want you going anyplace dark on me, you hear?"

It was hard for her not to smile. His caring nature was a refreshing twist to her own dark thoughts. She needed to think of something that'd keep her from going back to that place. Crash pawed her, begging for attention. Narissa pat the adorable pup, giving her just the impetus to keep her grounded.

"So, why Crash?"

"Not, why Helios?"

She found that counter interesting. "Well, that one is fairly easy. Helios is the Greek titan of the sun. As a red merle Aussie, it seems like a fitting name."

"You know the term for his coat color."

She gave a sheepish smile. "We had a red merle corgi for a family pet when I was a kid. His name was Bruno."

Ajax chuckled. "Cheeky. Well, your reasoning is mostly correct, but it's missing one thing. He's my sun. Rises when the sun does and goes down just the same. He's eager to get me outdoors, and always reminding me to live a full life."

As he spoke, she watched his features soften, and the love he had for his four-legged friend projected outward in an uncontained way. The adoration was heartwarming. "I love how you put that. It was poetic in a way. And now I wonder if Crash is anything close to as poetic as her 'brother.'"

Ajax laughed. "No, not really. That is quite the long story, though."

"Well, depending on where you have plans to take us, we may have time to hear it all."

Ajax hesitated, piquing her curiosity. "Okay, I guess I can't keep this surprise for long. You *are* in the car with me now. We're going to my family's vacation home in Oregon."

Her eyes widened. "Oregon? We're driving all the way to Oregon?"

Ajax chuckled. "I had a feeling you'd react that way. I do have plans to stop halfway through the trip, for us to rest at a motel."

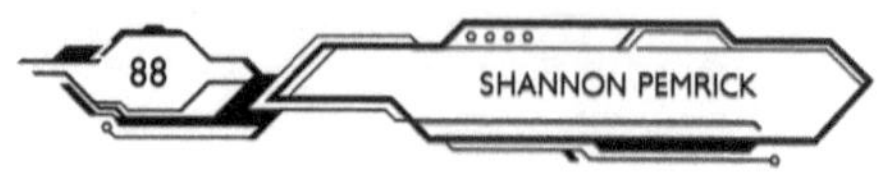

Her heart stopped. "A—a motel?"

Ajax's head flew back as he let out a boisterous laugh. "Oh boy. I knew this could get interesting with a city girl like yourself, but now I know how much of a luxurious spoiled life you've had if you're reacting that way to the word 'motel.'"

Dread sat deep in the pit of her stomach. Modest living was one thing. But this—What kind of dirty, cockroach-infested place was he bringing her to? *Oh great, my mother just came out.*

Ajax held up a hand. "I promise it won't be a thing of nightmares. It's dog-friendly; that's why I planned it."

"I can confirm it's not a shady business," Kirk said through the dash of the Jeep. "You have nothing to worry about."

He was telling the truth. She knew it, because motels weren't sleazy places—most of the time. They just had a different layout. But now she needed a distraction for the creepy thoughts running through her head. "So tell me Crash's story."

"Well, her story is deeply tied with mine." Ajax sat back in his seat, still shuffling his cards. "It was about two months after my accident. I wasn't doing well adapting to the loss of my arm. I refused a prosthetic of any kind; I quit medical school, even though neurology didn't require me to have two functioning arms—"

Narissa tilted her head. "I didn't know you were planning to be a neurologist."

He smirked. "I'll get to that in my story. I think. If not, we'll discuss it after."

Narissa chuckled and let him continue.

"As I was saying, I hit a low point. I lost interest in

almost everything I loved, and I couldn't do a lot of the basic things in life without a great deal of extra effort. I was miserable." He reached for the dash, under the stereo, and slid out a tray. "I self-medicated by drinking the day away. There wasn't a moment I didn't put my liver under stress."

He hooked the tray to the console between them, creating a makeshift table, and placed his shuffled cards down. "Until my sister returned a video game she borrowed, along with a strange new controller. A gift from our father. He'd designed it for the benefit of those who had only one functioning arm, and wanted me try it out."

Narissa's brow knitted. "Why didn't he give it to you personally?"

Ajax's mouth spread into a thin line. "I don't have the best relationship with him. My parents didn't have a happy marriage, and after they divorced, he didn't waste time remarrying. Not only did the quick switch put me off, I didn't like his new wife. I still don't. She's not a nice woman."

"And you still tried out the controller?"

Ajax nodded. "I don't get along with him, but he's a brilliant man. His company focused on unique game controllers and accessories, and he made a killing from it. If anyone could create a universal one-handed controller, it'd be him."

A small smile spread across his face. "And seeing the controller gave me a sense of longing. I hadn't done anything except drink for two months. I needed to find something to give me a reason to put the bottle down."

Ajax split the deck into two, sliding them evenly apart

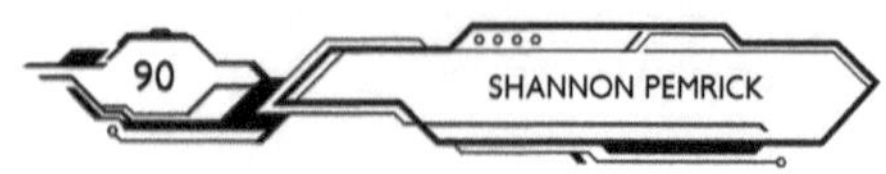

for a game of war. Narissa smiled. It was her favorite card game growing up. *I don't think I ever told him that, either.*

"The controller ended up being garbage, but as a first attempt, I didn't expected perfection. One good thing that came from it—I slowed my drinking, and went about teaching myself how to play games with one hand. Even VR wasn't easy, since you needed a controller along with the headgear."

The two of them started the game, Narissa winning the first round. "Relearning was tough, but it worked. My self-medicating became a little less hazardous to my health as I quit drinking and played games all day. It didn't bring me out of my slump, but it was a start."

Ajax won the next round with a ten over her three. "Then one day I found a pawnshop ad selling an old original PlayStation One console. It came with two controllers and three games: Spyro, Croc, and Crash Bandicoot. All for the low, low price of four hundred dollars."

Narissa choked and it stalled her next card play. "Four hundred dollars?"

He won again. "For such an old system, that was a steal. I called them up right away to see if they would hold it for me. The clerk could only hold it for thirty minutes because of the rarity. I got down there with three minutes to spare. After making sure it was in as good of a condition as they claimed, I walked out four hundred dollars poorer."

Narissa shook her head and revealed her next card in the deck. He did as well, and they were the same. The two grinned and flipped another card—the same number. They flipped again—Narissa's was higher. Ajax hung his head and Narissa gleefully collected her cards.

The game continued, as did his story. She was starting to wonder when Crash came into all this, but also liked listening to him. She knew about the depression he'd gone through after the accident, but this was the first time he'd gone into such personal detail. *Doesn't help that I've tried harder than I should have been to keep him at a distance.*

"As I walked back to the car, I heard a crash in an alley, and then a pitiful whimpering. My curiosity got the better of me and I took a look. Crawling out from under a tipped-over box, covered in filth, was a small puppy. Tiny, flea-bitten, torn ear, and malnourished, there was no way he had ever seen a loving home. He whimpered and crawled for me, or at least, tried to. The pitiful thing's front right leg dragged on the ground, as if it couldn't use it at all."

He won the next round. "I pitied him. I wasn't in any shape to be caring for a puppy, let alone one that needed intense care like this one would, but I wasn't going to leave him. So, not only did I get a new system, but I picked up a puppy *temporarily.*"

Narissa chuckled, and the two of them ended up in another war when they pulled the same card. This time Ajax won after four card flips.

"Brought the tiny thing to the vet, found out he was a *she*, was barely six weeks old, and spent an insanc amount of money to make sure she was going to make it." He looked back at Crash, who sat in the back wagging her tail. "She'd cry every time the vet took her from me. It hurt. So, of course that temporary became permanent, and it became the best decision of my life."

He smiled and drew a card. "I no longer had just me

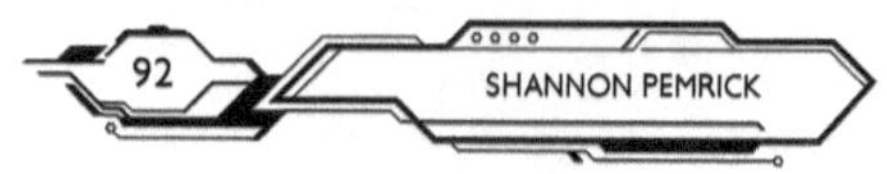

to worry about. I had to focus on her and make sure her needs were met. I had to get back out in the world. She got me to run and hit the gym again. I socialized. I ate right. I found a love in my old hobbies again."

Ajax looked at her with those dark eyes of his, gripping Narissa tight. Her breath hitched. "She saved me from myself. Some scraggly, flea-bitten mutt that had no chance of surviving on her own."

Narissa held his gaze for a moment, her body growing warm, before tearing way and flipping a card. "So, when did the name come about?"

Ajax laughed. "It was after she'd gone through surgery to remove her bad leg. She'd been born with a deformed leg. With more life in her with my nursing, she became one hell of a rambunctious terror. Flying around the house at top speeds. But she couldn't turn or stop, and collided with anything in her path."

He shook his head and flipped a card, losing to her. "I was playing Crash Bandicoot when she crashed into the couch one day. And that's when it hit me." He pet Crash when she stuck her nose up front. "Name stuck, and here we are."

Narissa leaned back in the seat and pulled a leg up to her chest. "Thank you for sharing that with me. It was far more touching than I would have expected. While I've seen your file, including your psychiatric information, I didn't know she was the reason you turned back around. Though, none of that really explained your career path attempt as a neurologist."

He chuckled as he rubbed the back of his neck. "Yeah, that's true. Well, my family is fairly diverse in their career choices, though a lot of them fall into the tech industry.

Because of my father's company, and my mother's career working as a game designer, a lot of people assumed Allyson and I would follow. Allyson did, she loved art and modeling, so got into game art and paved a path for herself that way. Me, I was fascinated by how we as humans work and how complex we are on a neurological level. So, I chose to pursue it. Until my accident."

Narissa's head cocked. "Why didn't you go back after you started getting back to your old self? What pulled you into the gaming industry?"

He nodded his head toward Crash. "Her. After she got me back on my feet, I went out and obtained a low-grade cybernetic, the one you replaced. I found I was able to do all the things I used to again, especially when it came to gaming. But the realization that I shouldn't have to, hit me. I started to think about all those people out there who couldn't afford a cybernetic, and how much easier it could be for them if there were simpler ways of doing things. Even if it was just a hobby they'd lost the ability to enjoy."

Ajax flipped over the last card in his deck. "So, I set out to make gaming easier for people like me. I planned for something simple, a chair that made it easy for people to customize their setup to adapt to their needs. But as I sketched it out, I realized that wasn't going to be enough. And that's where my neurology background came into play. If I could hook players up through their mind, they wouldn't need to worry about some controller."

Narissa watched as his eyes lit up as he told this part of his story. The excitement it brought him reminded her so much of herself. She'd assumed he'd made the gaming chairs for the sake of revolution. She never expected such a pure, selfless answer such as to just help people enjoy a small aspect of their life again. *It's a lot like me.*

"It took me two years to get it all right, and the end product was so much more robust than I was expecting. I teamed up with my mother and sister to get games ready for its big release, and the wave of popularity and fame that came after it"—he chuckled—"Let's just say I never dreamed it'd get as crazy as this."

"From a relative nobody trying to find purpose in life, to L.A.'s fifth top bachelor and gaming revolutionary." Narissa shook her head. "I'd say that's definitely not something you ever expected when you decided to go down to a pawn shop one day because of an ad."

Ajax threw his head back as he laughed. "When it's put in such simple terms, it's just amusing to think about, and sounds like the premise of some chick-flick."

Narissa collected her cards to count. "Ah, but then the main lead would have to be female, and need a heavy helping of romance piled on top."

A half-smile curled up the side of Ajax's face, sending a jolt down Narissa's spine. "Who said there wouldn't be?"

Was that directed to her? *Don't be silly.* She looked down at her cards and counted them. "I've got twenty-eight cards. Think you can beat my ass this next round?"

Ajax smirked, his eyes glinting a dangerous shade, and shuffled his deck. "I'd rather slap it instead."

Heat rushed to Narissa's cheeks, an image of him bending her over and slapping her bare rear popping into her mind. *Get out! Get out! Get out!* She needed to change the subject and fast.

Narissa took a deep breath and shuffled her cards. "Thanks for picking this game. It's been a long time since I've gotten to play."

He regarded her for a minute. "Did you used to play a lot in the past?"

She nodded. "My brother and I would play all the time. That and spit."

He snickered. "That was my sister's favorite game. It drove up her competitive nature."

They each pulled a card from their decks and started their second round.

Narissa pet Helios when he begged for attention. "So, what's his story? Simple, or epic like Crash?"

Ajax glanced at Helios. "Nowhere near as epic. A family friend was an Australian sheepdog breeder for agility."

Narissa sort of knew what that meant. It was some sort of dog obstacle-course sport that was all time- and precision-based, if she wasn't mistaken.

"She gave us a call when she couldn't find a good home for two puppies from her most recent breeding, as they had naturally stumpy tails, which wasn't desired in the agility scene. She asked if we were looking for new family members, and we figured we'd go down to check them out. The two left were a red merle male and blue merle female."

Ajax grinned. "We fell in love with them instantly. I picked up the boy, and Helios came right out of my mouth. Of course, my sister being competitive, couldn't allow me to outdo her, and picked an equally fitting name for the girl, Selene."

He pet Helios when he poked his head up front. "We

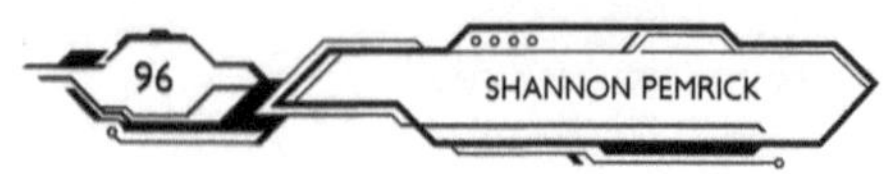

took them back to my place, and Crash connected even quicker to them. And even though my sister and I lived separately, forcing the two siblings to live apart, we were sure to let them see each other all the time."

He chuckled. "And in the end, we picked the perfect ones for ourselves. Helios is an early riser, like myself. And Selene is a late riser and even later one to count sheep, so to speak, like my sister."

Narissa laughed. "Makes their names all that more fitting, too." She grinned. "Almost as if the Greeks had planned it themselves."

Ajax grunted. "I hope not. This story will end in disaster if that's the case."

The two laughed.

"So," Narissa said when they calmed. "Why a vacation home in Oregon?"

Ajax threw down his next card. "You'd be surprised how stifling it can be living in a city. So my father built a house in a dense part of the forest just outside Mt. Hood Village for us to go there to relax and generate ideas as needed. Even after the divorce, that didn't change."

A smile came to Narissa's face and she flicked her lost card to him. "That sounds amazing. I can't wait to see it with my own two eyes."

His dangerous half-smile returned to his face as he drew from his deck. "Me too."

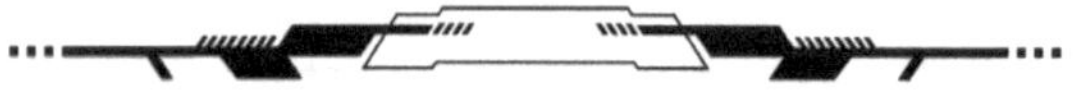

About eleven hours into their trip, including a couple of pit stops, they'd finally reached Medford, where they'd hunker down for the night. Ajax cast a few glances out the window as they rolled through town, seeing what possible new buildings or attractions had come in since he'd last stopped here few months ago. Or was it a few years? He traveled so much he had a tendency to forget.

The car pulled into the motel parking lot and Ajax kept it running for the dogs while he got the room key. Narissa accompanied him to the desk. The gentleman at the counter greeted them with a warm smile.

"I booked a room this morning under Jackson," Ajax said.

The man looked it up on the computer. "Ajax Jackson? One room, double queen, pet-friendly, for one night only?"

He nodded and held up his phone with all the dogs' required documentation. "That's the one."

Ajax noticed Narissa shift uncomfortably. He made a mental note to keep a closer eye on her. She'd done well in the car. He'd kept her occupied and even went over some business details with her when she insisted she get some work done. He honestly could care less if they made progress in the next week. Work was the farthest thing from his mind.

The desk clerk punched the dogs' information in and then handed him the phone back along with a key card. "Checkout is at eleven. Enjoy your stay."

"Thank you. Have a nice evening."

He held the door open for Narissa, and the two hopped back into the Jeep to park in front of their room. It was on the bottom floor and not too far from the office.

"If you get the dogs, I'll grab the suitcases," he said to her once they'd parked.

Narissa nodded reaching into the back for the leashes. "I can do that."

The dogs eagerly jumped out and sniffed around as he pulled their bags from the back. Narissa's laughter caught his attention as he slammed the hatch shut. Peering around the vehicle, he found Crash bouncing around like the lunatic she was. He was going to need to go for a run with her before the night was over.

Ajax opened the room and entered, Narissa and the dogs close behind. She let them loose the moment the door shut, and they bounded around, sniffed, and then claimed the closest bed to the door. "I guess that's my bed."

Narissa gave a closed-mouth chuckle as she looked around.

His brow furrowed. "You okay?"

"Yeah." She grinned at him. "Just checking for cock-roaches."

"Well if you find one, it won't last long with Crash here. No need for a cat when I have her."

Narissa's face scrunched. "Eww."

Ajax put the bags down in front of each bed and noticed she still didn't look okay. "Rissa, something wrong?"

She shook her head. "I'm just overthinking. I'll be fine."

He frowned. *Knew it.* "If you'd feel better about an upstairs room, I can look into—"

"No, it's okay. Really." She touched her stomach. "I think I just need some good food in me."

A grin spread across his face. "Well, let me feed these two crazies, and I'll treat you to one of the best steak-houses in the area."

She placed her hands on her hips. "You don't have to pay for everything, you know."

He chuckled. "But I'm going to."

She huffed. Ajax pulled out the bowls and food for the dogs, Crash impatient as always. Her wiggling butt as she tried to listen to his "sit" command got Narissa chuckling.

Once they were fed, the two jumped back into the Jeep.

"So, where are you taking me, so I know how overboard you're going?" she asked.

He snickered. "It's called Over Yonder Bar and Grill. It's not pricey, and the food is great."

"Over Yonder…" She shook her head. "Well, as long as they can grill up a good steak, I won't make fun of their name."

"You're in for a treat."

He and Narissa sat down at a table with an umbrella, cups of ice cream in hand. Helios and Crash wagged their tails, eager for the "doggy ice cream" he'd gotten for them. After their nice dinner, Narissa developed a craving for ice cream, but wasn't interested in the choices at the restaurant. He decided to grab the dogs and bring them along.

Narissa dipped her spoon in her overly-loaded peanut butter ice cream with chocolate and peanut butter sauce, and all things peanut butter candy. He pegged her more of a mint or bubble gum fan, but apparently not. What else didn't he know about her that he should?

Oh, that's one. Ajax set down the bowls for the dogs,

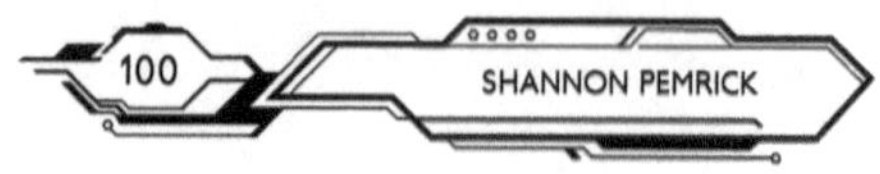

who eagerly gobbled up their treat. "Hey, I wanna know something."

She stuffed a giant spoonful of ice cream into her mouth and looked at him with wide eyes. "Hmm?"

He chuckled. "What got you into gaming? I just always accepted it, because why not. But now I'm curious. I doubt it was because of your mother. She doesn't seem the type."

Narissa nodded. "You'd be right on that. She got me into the sci-fi stuff, though. She's a huge trekkie. She's also a bit of a Pokemon fan."

This surprised him. He didn't peg her as the type, either.

"My dad is the gamer in the family. Not as crazy as some of our friends, or you, with the old consoles, but he started Elijah and me off on handhelds and PC games. We'd go to conventions every now and then, and Elijah at one point was going to be a professional gamer, which both our parents supported." She ate more of her treat. "Then I met you and was opened to a completely new world of gaming."

He'd forgotten he was the reason she got into Lusara Fates as much as she had. "Well, Darius did want me to help recruit for the big game he finally got to work on."

Narissa laughed. "Sorry. I got this image of you two being all sketchy on a street corner, trying to peddle the game like two drug dealers."

Ajax's head flew back as he laughed. "It's funny you say that, because Kiara told us to do that."

Narissa's face scrunched as she smiled. It was cute. "Sounds just like her."

Crash, now done with her treat, sat in front of Narissa,

staring up at her. She did well ignoring her canine friend until she sat up on her back legs and pawed the air. Narissa's face twisted as she was overcome with the adorableness of his sneaky mutt. Allyson was teaching her tricks behind his back, it seemed.

"Yes, you can give her some of yours for that," he said. "Just be careful of the chocolate, of course."

Narissa scooped some peanut butter ice cream and fed Crash right from the utensil. Helios padded over, expecting some, too, which she also gave. Ajax pulled out his phone and snapped a few quick pictures. It was too cute a moment to let go.

Narissa's eyes narrowed at him. "Hey. No unauthorized pictures."

He snapped another one with her displeased expression. Her eyes narrowed, and she swiped for the phone. "Give me that."

Ajax grinned as he held it out of reach. "Oh, no."

She launched out of her chair and tried to take it. He continued to hold it out of reach as he fought to keep her away. Well, away from the phone. She practically sat in his lap trying to get the device. He didn't mind her close proximity one bit.

Her chest brushed against his, and he couldn't resist the urge to glance down, only to be blocked by the t-shirt she wore instead of something low-cut.

Narissa continued to grab for the phone, each feather-light brush of her fingers against his skin or bump from her chest getting to him. "Rissa, you're causing a scene in public, you know?"

"Well if you'd just let me see how stupid I look, then I wouldn't have to."

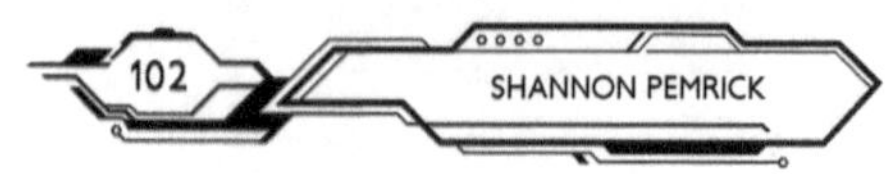

"You don't look stupid in any of these."

"Then let me see for myself."

Her chest bumped him again, this time a little higher, and he couldn't take it. Something needed to change here or he might just do something he may regret. Ajax flipped her so she sat crosswise on his lap. She let out a startled "eep" and looked up at him.

Those dark pools and tempting lips. Her curves forming to him just right. Her ass sitting right on—*Fuck.* This wasn't helping at all.

Ajax held up his phone. "You can look, but I hold it."

Narissa pursed her lips and then just up and snatched the phone. He shook his head. She looked over each photo of her. "These aren't bad."

"See?" He reached for the phone. "And I'm posting the ones of you feeding the dogs to social media."

Her eyes narrowed at him and she held the phone out of reach. "I didn't give permission."

His brow ticked up. "Is there a reason not to?"

Narissa's lips pressed into a thin line. "Isn't this supposed to be an *off-the-grid* trip?"

"No one will know where we are." He shrugged. "But if you'd really rather I not, then I'll just save it as my phone background."

"Already done, sir," Kirk said from the phone.

The two laughed. She then spoke once she'd calmed. "Okay. But I get to sign off on the crazy caption you plan on concocting."

She made it sound so devious. On the contrary, he was just planning to show her off to his social media world and subtly claim her. *It'll be far less subtle once I figure out how to get around this Nolan issue.* "That's fine."

Still in his lap, she pulled up the image he directed and helped him post. While he one-finger typed, because she wouldn't relinquish the phone, his free hand found purchase on her hip. She either didn't mind or didn't notice. He was happy for the lack of fight. Having her here like this felt right.

Narissa's brow ticked up at him when he finished his wording. "Most beautiful woman in the world? Really?"

He didn't see a problem with the wording. He grinned. "Well, it's true."

She scoffed. "Pick something else, you cheeseball. Something that makes way more sense."

Ajax snickered and posted the image. "It makes the most sense."

"Andrew!" Face scrunched with irritation, she moved the phone out of his reach and went through it.

Alarm flared up in him. "Hey, don't go through my photos just out of spite."

"I can, and I will." She laughed when she came to an image of his sister making a goofy face. "That is Christmas-card worthy."

He'd agree if he weren't so focused on getting his phone back. "Narissa, give me my phone back."

She grinned at him. A type of grin that excited and scared him. "Afraid I'll find some nudie images you downloaded from some porn site?"

He hadn't thought of that. He'd been far more concerned with her finding out about the photos of her he had. He'd done a poor job of removing ones he didn't need.

"Ajax is trying to make sure you don't see all the photos he has of you saved to his device," Kirk said.

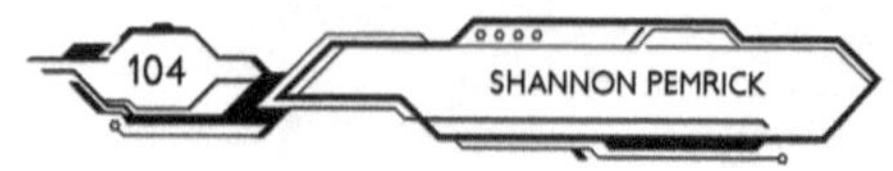

Narissa's brow knitted and she glanced at him. He swallowed hard and reached for the phone again. "No, he's lying. It's definitely the excessive porn pictures I've got."

He'd rather be caught with that than labeled a creep—he wasn't—and watch her run for the hills. Narissa pursed her lips and then swiped for another photo. *Balls.* One of her popped up. He'd snagged it while she'd worked on his arm.

Narissa's eyes cut to him and he swallowed, his shoulders tensing. This wasn't good. He grabbed the phone, but her grip was nothing to sneeze at. She swiped to the next photo.

This was far less incriminating, though no less awkward. Dark skin, curly hair, and sensually posed. Bella Stazra, a popular actress. Though, his reasoning was a bit more in depth than just because she was hot and had quality images to use.

Narissa cocked her head. "That's far tamer than I was expecting for you."

He pulled the phone away, this time successfully. "What do you mean?"

She shrugged. "I pegged you as kinkier."

Ajax leaned back in his chair, his mouth sliding up the side of his face. "Who said I'm not?"

Was she? He struggled to figure out what she may be into. He wouldn't mind exploring those options with her.

Narissa chuckled and slid off his lap to go eat her now-melting ice cream. Was that reaction good or bad? More importantly, did she really have to leave? The distance between them felt wrong—empty. He wanted to pull her back, just to have her there against him.

Narissa ate her treat, the air between them not awkward in the least, as much as he expected it to be after what she'd seen. Ajax studied her. "You don't seem to mind I have porn on my phone."

She shrugged. "I'm indifferent to it as long as you're single." *Good to know.* "If you're in a relationship, set ground rules that everyone is happy with. And if your partner is okay, then so be it. Some use porn, some, like me, use romance novels."

His brow ticked up. "Oh, really? So you must be into that *50 Nights of Heaven*, or whatever that ridiculously popular book is that's being turned into a movie."

Narissa snorted. "No. That book was garbage in my humble opinion."

Humble? With that type of response? "Why don't you like it? The writing not to your tastes?"

"The writing was fine, it was the author's poor research on how poly works. It was more like a fantasy built by some repressed thirty-five year old soccer mom who's been lucky to know what an orgasm is. If she'd just done some research, like talk to a few people in poly relationships, she'd have known how to write that all better. Plus, one of those guys was such an abusive asshole, I couldn't stomach it anymore."

Ajax ate some of his ice cream. "You sound like you have experience in that area."

"Abusive assholes? Of course I do." Ajax gave her a long look and she laughed. "I know. I know. The answer is, not firsthand experience. I just know a couple people who are poly. Each are quite different, which shows there's no one real way to make it work, but they'll even tell you that book is a train wreck.

No poly relationship would last if it were handled that way."

Ajax bit down on his spoon, only to realize he never scooped out any ice cream. "Shira, Jasper, and Zach one of them?"

Narissa laughed. "No. That relationship, or whatever it is, is complicated. Donovan and Ronan's parents are in one; I've known them for a while. And based on some conversations involving Donovan and Ronan, they might have similar tastes in relationships, since they share a partner."

Ajax already knew that. But he also had spent more time with them than she had, even though she'd known them longer. That didn't interest him, though. "What is Shira's issue with taking her PvP partners up on their less-than-subtle advances?"

Narissa chuckled and finished the last of her ice cream. "Shira is a mess of issues. That's what it really comes down to. She's got her reasons, and it's hard to convince her to step around them."

"Is there anything that isn't too personal to share?"

Narissa pursed her lips. "She has a 'no hooking up with guildmates' clause. She'd been on the fence about the idea for a long time, but after a really disastrous hookup with that former guildmate, she put a hard stop to it for the future."

Ajax remembered that. Man, was that a messy issue, and it wasn't even her fault. The guy was a lunatic.

Narissa's phone went off and she checked it. She texted something, and then set her phone back down.

His curiosity piqued. "Anything important?"

She shook her head. "Just my dad telling me he was

flying one of our surgeons out to his location for a new client. They couldn't meet us, so he made a house call. I guess he's getting right on that treatment."

Ajax smiled. "It's great you do that for people."

She smiled back. "It's what we do."

Crash barked and whined, pawing Ajax's leg. He sighed. "No more treats. We should really get you exercised, though." He glanced at Narissa. "You could join us, if you want."

She nodded. "Sure."

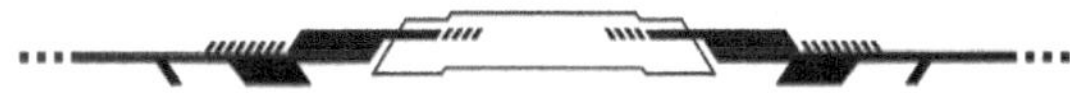

Ajax opened the door, Helios and Crash bolting in. He wiped the beads of sweat from his brow. That'd been a good run, though the dogs being cooped up in the car meant he still hadn't gotten all their energy out. Tomorrow would be good for them, with the plans he had.

Narissa sat on her bed, tablet in hand. Her hair was wet from a shower, but her day clothes were on. She'd bailed on him halfway through the run, complaining about feeling sweaty and gross. That was half the point of exercise. But she didn't care.

That had to be one of the first things he'd found different between them. He didn't think it was a problem, but it'd be good for her to work out. Her health should be important to her.

But regardless of that, he wouldn't let it get between him and this crazy-smart, sexy geek of a woman who drove him wild.

"You know, you can make yourself comfortable," he said, hanging up the dog's leashes.

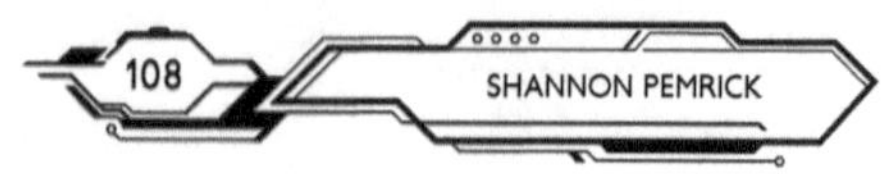

She looked up. "I am comfortable."

This answer perplexed him. It was late enough that they'd be getting to bed soon for their early rise in the morning. And yet she wasn't ready for bed. Was she feeling anxious? Nolan wasn't out of prison yet, so she should be fine. She could just be one of those people who didn't walk around in their night clothes. He decided to keep an eye on her to be sure, and not press the matter. Yet.

"I'm going to jump in the shower." Nothing crazy, as he'd take a longer one in the morning. Just a quick scrub for the sweat.

Narissa went back to her tablet. "Okay. I'm just working."

Working—of course she was. He needed to fix this workaholic lifestyle she had. "You could also join me. Would be more fun."

She chuckled and focused on her work. "I'll pass."

Wow, boner killer. Ajax grabbed some shorts and hopped into the shower. After a quick scrub down, he was out. He slipped on his shorts and towel dried his hair as he left the room. Narissa hadn't moved, nor had she changed clothes. He wasn't gone long, but still.

Narissa looked at her phone when it went off. She smiled and texted the person back. The smile put him on edge. It wasn't a casual one you'd get from a friend or family. It fell in line with what he'd expect to give if she ever received a good morning text from someone special. *I should do that. Why haven't I done that?*

"Your dad again?" He shouldn't pry, but the idea someone else was vying for her attention didn't sit well with him.

She glanced at him, and then put the phone down to go back to working. "No, that was Dylan."

Dylan? Who was Dylan? She'd talked to someone the other day by that name. That was the night she found out about Nolan getting out. Was it the same Dylan? "Dylan?"

She nodded and scrolled down on her tablet. "He's a friend of mine."

Great. He did have competition.

"He's also the police officer who's been by my side through this whole Nolan mess."

Ajax sat down on his bed, scratching Crash when she pawed him. Even with that information, he wasn't getting a good feeling from this. "What did he want?"

She giggled. "Someone is nosey."

His gaze fell onto his dogs. "Sorry, just curious."

"Uh huh." Even she could see that was a horrible lie. "He was just checking on me, since Nolan will be out tomorrow."

"That was nice of him." His words came out a little emptier than he wanted. It was nice he was looking out for her, but she was here with him. She was safe—he almost sighed. *Dylan doesn't know that, shithead.*

He really needed to get himself under control. "Did you tell him I've got your back?"

She rocked her head. "More or less."

His ego took a little bit of a hit from that for some reason. He wanted to change the subject. She was safe with him, and that's all that mattered. "I'm going to get some rest. You should, too. We have an early morning tomorrow."

Narissa nodded and stored her tablet. Ajax cocked his

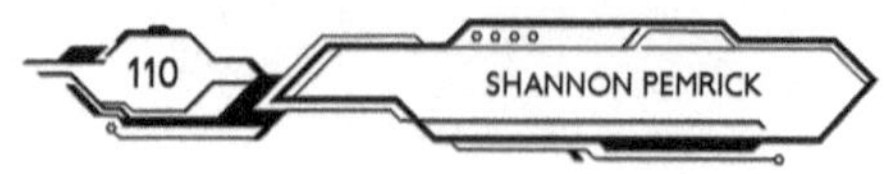

head when she still didn't change out of her day clothes. Something was up. "Don't tell me you're sleeping in your day clothes."

She avoided looking at him. "When you told me to pack sleep wear, I didn't think about the prospect of us sleeping in the same room…"

His brow ticked up. "Is my little priestess a nude sleeper?"

He liked the idea, the tantalizing image peeking up through the back of his mind.

Narissa's cheeks darkened. "No. And stop calling me your priestess. It's weird out of game."

He relaxed on the bed. "That's too bad. I thought I'd finally found someone else who understood the benefits of sleeping in the nude."

"What?" she shrieked, her eyes wide as she stared at him.

He rolled on his back as he laughed. "I'm teasing. Mostly. I do normally sleep that way, but for your benefit I planned to wear shorts to bed."

She calmed down and placed a hand on her chest. "Bless your heart."

Ajax found interest in the wording. He'd only heard Ayana say that phrase. He didn't know what it meant, but he got the feeling it wasn't as complimentary as it may sound. "So, what do you sleep in? A night gown?"

Her gaze fell away to her lap, though ticked back up to him for a moment before falling again, her cheeks reddening a bit. *Oh really?* That got his blood simmering. Ajax pegged her as more a tank top and shorts type of woman, but he could get behind this.

He knew it wouldn't be something frumpy. Sexy was

something she enjoyed in her wardrobe choice. Even her bathing suit choices proved that.

"Well, if you would prefer to wear one of my shirts, I'll be more than happy to loan you one." He found himself grinning at the prospect. He wouldn't mind if she slept in his shirt.

She still didn't look at him. "No, that's all right. Thank you though."

He didn't understand. She could wear sexy clothes and not blink an eye, but sleep wear was an issue? He wasn't going to press, though. Her reasons were hers, and if she didn't want to be open about it just yet, he couldn't pry. That'd only push her away from him.

Ajax shrugged and lay back. "All right, that's fine. Do what makes you feel most comfortable."

Narissa sat on the edge of the bed, facing away from him. He watched, curious what she'd do. When she reached for her suitcase, he was intrigued. She pulled out something purple and black and then went into the bathroom, closing the door behind her. He rolled onto his side, waiting.

A few minutes passed before she returned, this time with a fitted violet silk nightgown with black accents, her day clothes tucked in her arms. The nightgown cut low around her breasts, and thin straps were all that kept it on her tempting body. His own body heated again.

"No comments," she warned as she went to store her clothes.

Ajax held up a hand. "Hey, I wasn't going to say anything."

No, he'd rather snap those flimsy straps and let the gown fall the floor, exposing every inch of her. Or pin her against the wall and slowly slide his hand up and under to explore what lay hidden underneath. He'd leave no part of her untouched, finding out what excited her when, and hearing her little gasps and moans of pleasure.

Ajax rolled onto his back to stare at the ceiling. At this rate, he'd require a cold shower to get him through the night, and he didn't need any more temptation that could ruin his carefully laid-out plan.

Narissa settled into her bed and Crash jumped over, curling up beside her. Narissa smiled and pet the scraggly mutt. "I guess I get my own dog tonight, too."

The affection she showed his dogs elated him. He'd thought she was more of a cat person throughout all of these years knowing her. But she may just be as big a dog person as him. Even if she just liked his dogs, it was one less thing he had to worry would get between them. "She'll keep you safe. But if you feel you need added safety, let me know."

She snuggled into Crash. "Bed's full."

Ajax chuckled and reached up for the light. He'd get his chance. And when he did, she'd find out just how much space he'd fill on the bed. And in her.

CHAPTER 7

arissa stirred, her mind foggy. Odd grunting pulled her from her sleep. She sucked in a deep breath and stretched, finding her sleeping partner had remained curled up with her all night. Crash's tail thumped on the bed as she gazed at Narissa. But that wasn't the source of the sound that woke her.

She glimpsed over at Ajax's bed to find it empty. Then she saw him, his back rising up from the floor and then lowering again. She sat up. Ajax was doing pushups on the far side of the room, Helios apparently imitating him, bowing down on his front paws and then standing back up, in step with Ajax. The sight made her giggle.

"Sorry," Ajax said between grunts. "I didn't mean to wake you. The manager of this place wasn't thrilled I was doing my morning workout outside, especially so early. Thought it'd disturb the other guests."

Narissa's eyes followed his movements some more, watching every muscle flex and respond to the workout.

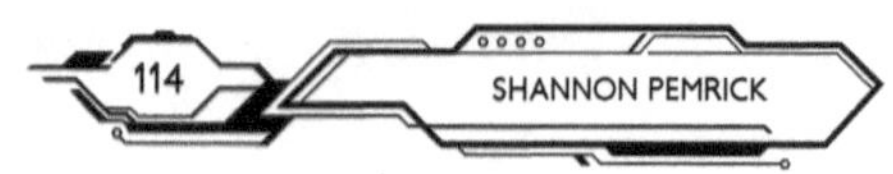

She licked her lips, a prick of desire bubbling deep inside her, before shaking her head. "You really can't go a single day without torturing your body, can you? Not even on vacation."

He locked his artificial arm in a straightened position, and with surprising balance he lifted his real arm up and flexed, showing of those impressive muscles of his. "You don't get these by sitting on the couch all day eating fried chicken."

She grunted. "Tell that to my family. Fried chicken, jambalaya, and corn bread was a staple in my home. And regular workout routines were only something health nuts had."

Ajax pushed himself to his knees, his brow cocked. "I know you bailed fairly early on in the run last night, but you can't tell me with a figure like yours"—he gestured to her—"that you don't work out, even in the slightest."

Narissa tapped her lips with a finger. "Nearly killing yourself working is considered a workout, right?"

Ajax hung his head and shook it while he chuckled. "We need to get you a healthier lifestyle."

She cocked her head, her curls falling to the side. "Are you going to be my personal trainer?"

A wicked grin spread across his face. It made her glad she was sitting and not standing. That sinful grin had a habit of making her knees weak. "If you want me to be."

Might not be a good idea. Between that devilish smile and tempting body of his, she may not be able to focus on a workout.

"My first instruction would be to get you out of bed. Because"—he gestured to Crash—"she refused to leave your side, even for the prospect of a walk."

Both dogs' ears perked at the sound of the "w" word. Narissa laid over Crash and scratched her belly when she presented it. "That's because she's the best protector ever."

Crash's tongue lolled out as she enjoyed her pampering.

"Stealing my thunder, Crash," Ajax muttered. "Should have left you home."

Narissa laughed into the pup's chest, which had Crash thinking it was okay to start giving her kisses. Narissa squealed and pulled away from the dog, but she followed. Helios, not wanting to be left out on the love fest, hopped onto the bed and joined the fun. Narissa wiggled and writhed as she laughed and tried to command the dogs to stop despite her laughter.

Ajax watched on, amused, for a few moments before finally helping her. "All right you two, enough."

Narissa took a deep breath as the dogs jumped off the bed and then wrestled with each other. "Thank you. That's a bit more love than I was prepared for this morning."

"I'd say I was doing it to save you, but I'd be lying." He bent over and kissed her on the cheek, sending heat all throughout her body. He smirked as he pulled away and then called the dogs. "Let's get you both walked before the next leg of our trip."

Narissa touched her cheek as he walked to the door and hitched the dogs to their leashes.

"Oh, and Rissa?" He glanced back. "Nice panties."

She gasped and looked down at herself, finding that in the commotion her nightgown had pulled up, revealing the lacy garment underneath. *Oh... my... God...*

Ajax chuckled and left. She wanted to scream into

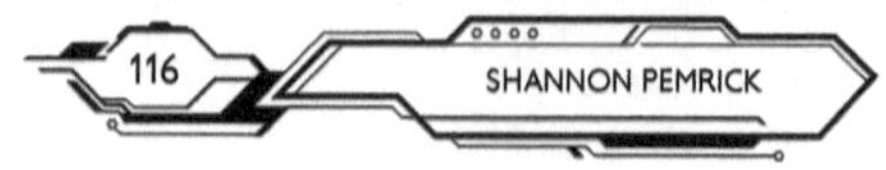

a pillow. She knew wearing this was a bad idea. Why hadn't she come prepared with something else just in case? *Though, it could be worse.* She could have been stupid and worn a thong instead. Her face warmed even more at the thought.

Narissa bolted out of bed and went about collecting her clothes and items for a shower. She couldn't let this get to her. It was just a peek at her underwear. Nothing to freak out about like some high school girl. It wasn't like the top of her gown had been pulled down.

She froze and looked down. The nightgown was a little low for where it normally sat, but nothing worrisome. She let out a breath of relief and went to take her shower. The sooner she let this roll off her, the less awkward it would be to sit in the car with him for the next several hours.

But as she set out her items in the bathroom, him kissing her cheek came back to her mind. She touched the spot on her face again. What had gotten into him enough to do that?

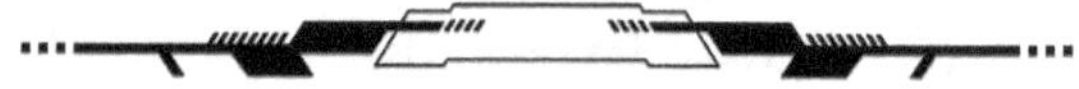

Ajax chowed down on a burger, his second that he'd grabbed during their lunch stop. He knew he should have only gotten one with the pick-me-up coffee, but he also knew that once they got to their next destination in a few minutes, he'd burn off the calories.

Narissa sat in the passenger seat, going over… something. She'd insisted on working. He wasn't sure if it was because of what he'd pulled this morning or not. He hoped not. It was meant to be harmless.

He looked down at the information on his phone. Not only did she expect to work, but she expected him to as well. Narissa insisted that if she was going to learn how his machines worked, he needed to know the basics of cybernetic functions. She wasn't wrong. This was the whole reason the new design wasn't ready for reveal. But he'd prefer to do something fun with her. Card or car games, twenty-twenty questions to find out what else he didn't know about her, or whatever they could come up with that was more stimulating than reading.

Of course, Narissa seemed to be enjoying herself. She hadn't quit smiling. Until now. Her phone *tinged* and whatever it alerted her to had changed her mood dramatically. "Everything okay?"

She pressed her lips together and then nodded, swiping something off her screen. "Before you asked me to come on this trip, I set a reminder for myself for the time Nolan would be getting out. I forgot to remove the reminder so it wouldn't distract me from the trip."

Ajax frowned. He'd really hoped he could have gotten her through the day without Nolan getting in the way. She also didn't express how the reminder affected her; just explained the situation.

He reached out and touched her shoulder. "How are you feeling?"

Narissa gave him a smile that screamed forced. "I'm fine."

He gave her a stern look. "Rissa."

Her shoulders sagged and she frowned. "Okay. I'm nervous. I don't know what's going to happen now. He could just leave me alone, or more realistically, he's

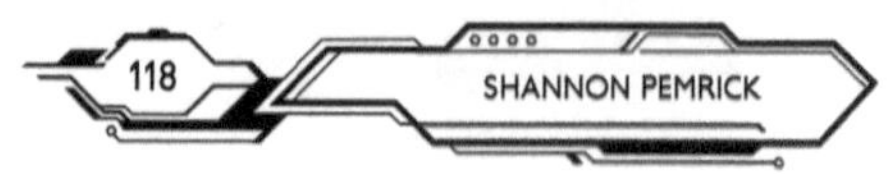

going to try to get back at me for what happened. I just know this good behavior bullshit is a ruse."

"You're safe here with me, Rissa," Ajax said. "There's no way he'll know where you are."

She wouldn't look at him. "Yeah, but what about when I return home? It's not like I can stay away forever."

He ground his teeth together. He hated this. Even if this asshole never showed up, the damage he'd done to her would make it so she'd never live in peace again, as long as he roamed about. "Don't think about that right now. Live in the moment without him, and leave the planning for dealing with what comes after to me."

Her eyes cut to him. "But it's not your job to do so."

Ouch. That hurt his ego. Twice in the last twenty-four hours that had taken a hit. "I know, but I'm making it my job."

Her beautiful eyes didn't hold back her confusion. "But why? Why go through all this for me?"

There were those insecurities Nolan caused. Ajax lifted her chin so he could look directly into her eyes. "Because I can, and you're worth it."

A deep flush spread across her face, reaching her ears. She stared back at him a moment before tearing her eyes away. He couldn't say he wasn't disappointed by the rejection. She needed more time.

Narissa scrolled through her phone again, stopping at something new. Her nose scrunched. "Dammit."

A slight bit of panic rushed down his spine. "What?"

She sat back in her seat, her phone hitting her lap. "Shira rejected my proposal again."

He relaxed. That was better than a Nolan topic. "What proposal?"

She tilted her head to look at him. "You know how she lost her modeling career because of her accident?"

He nodded.

"Well, we're trying something new with the company. We want to shift the human aspect into our advertising. I believe this will help with reducing the stupid stigma people have to put up with. And because Shira had a great modeling career in her pocket, even if it's been almost six years since she lost it, I thought she'd be the best candidate to help us jump-start the campaign."

She chewed her lower lip. "I thought it'd also help her with her self-esteem issue, since she can't stand cameras at all right now. And Jasper and Zach can't seem to convince her to meet them."

Ajax leaned back. "Is that why she always says no?"

"Some of it. There are some other underlying issues I'm not at liberty to discuss."

He understood. There'd be a lot of things she'd have to keep from him due to confidentiality.

Narissa sighed again. "I don't know how to convince her this is a good move for her. It's not even about having her help me lead this campaign. I want her to have the life she had back. Even if it's a little different. I want her to use that attitude of hers and give the world the middle finger when it comes to their option of her cybernetics. To be a bit spiteful and prove them wrong, instead of hiding in a game."

Ajax watched the different expressions play off her face. This idea was fantastic, both the new advertising and trying to help Shira. Her passion knew no bounds. He reached out and grabbed her hand with his artificial

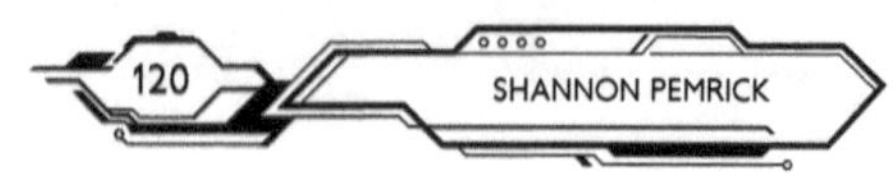

one. She didn't flinch—she never did. Not like the other women he'd pursued in the past.

She meant it when she claimed to not care about the limb. She was sincere in her claim it didn't make him or anyone else less of a human. Narissa was what everyone should be. Accepting and understanding that sometimes shit happens and you do the best you can to make everything work. Even if that meant relying on a robotic component to let you live a normal life.

"You'll figure this out." He smiled. "You're smart like that."

"My apologies for interrupting," Kirk said from the dash. "But we have arrived."

The pair gazed around at their surroundings. The car had pulled off the main road during their discussion, and now tall cliff faces and dense forest covered the landscape. Ajax rolled his window down, the sounds of active forest and running water echoing into the quiet car.

"Where are we?" Narissa asked, her eyes wide. "Narnia?"

She sputtered a laugh, making him smile.

"Somewhere in the Columbia River Gorge area."

Her brow ticked up. "Somewhere?"

"I missed the sign, but I think we'll be coming up to the Oneonta Gorge soon."

"The gorge is after our turn-off," Kirk informed. "Unless you'd like to change which service road we take."

Narissa look at him, confused. "Service road?"

"Yeah, I know a ranger up here. He lets me use the service roads as long as I call ahead first. Lets me see areas that others can't." He smirked. "And some parts only vehicles like my Jeep can get through."

"I don't think I understand. Why are we out here?"

Ajax shook his head. "For a smart woman, you surprise me. This is one of the stops we'll make. We're staying here the night before making it the last few hours to the house."

"We're camping?" she shrieked. "Like sleeping-on-the-ground-and-no-modern-amenities camping?"

He threw his head back as he laughed. If she'd done any sort of camping, it was probably at a campground in some sort of RV. "This going to be fun."

"Um, no, I disagree."

"Ajax, we're coming to the turn-off soon," Kirk said. "I'd recommend you make safety preparations."

Narissa's eyes widened and she started going into a panic. He tried to calm her. "Kirk, better wording next time, please. You make it sound worse than it is."

"My apologies, but your driving is something to be desired."

Narissa stared at him. "You're turning off the self-driving?"

"It can't function on these roads, so I did all the testing to be able to drive off-road."

She looked around the car. "Are there any other seatbelts?"

He smirked and pulled the crossover chest straps hidden behind her seat. She swallowed hard as he helped her strap in. This did make it look bad, but it was just to keep her from bouncing around too much.

The Jeep pulled off the main road and came to a stop. He hopped out and opened the back door to strap the dogs in. They didn't cause a fuss, as they were used to trips like this with him. He couldn't help but make a jab at Narissa. "See, they don't fuss."

She crossed her arms and looked out the window. She'd change her tune soon enough. He grinned as he hopped back into the driver's seat. *This trip isn't the only thing that'll get wild by the end.*

Ajax strapped in and then threw the Jeep into gear, taking off down the service road. The road was easy going for a bit, earning him unamused looks from Narissa. He just knew she was figuring he'd psyched her up for no reason. But not too long into the path, it got a bit bumpier, and then wild.

The Jeep jostled them around as they rode on the uneven ground, took sharp corners, and drove over large rocks and logs. Narissa grabbed the support handle above her head, but he caught the smile on her lips. It was working.

The ground smoothed out for a moment as they reached a dip down into a river with several inches of water running through their path.

Narissa's eyes ticked over to him. "You're not."

Ajax grinned and rolled up his window. "Hold onto your halo."

His foot on the gas, the Jeep shot down into the water. It splashed up onto the hood and windshield, rolling off quick, as he plowed through until they reached the embankment on the other side. Like a champ, the vehicle soared up and over, and hit the bumpy terrain on the other side. Narissa's laughter brought excitement to him as he maneuvered the tough, beaten-up road, until he laughed along with her.

Soon after, he pulled off the service road onto, another branching road. This led to a small clearing where he pulled up to park.

He looked to Narissa. Her eyes sparkled as she smiled. "Okay, I admit it, that was fun."

He patted her leg. "Told you. Have some faith in me."

Narissa snorted.

"Next time, I'll have Darius and Kiara come out with us. With a partner, we can go on crazier drives."

Her lips curled into a deep smile. "That sounds interesting. I might have to take you up on that offer."

Ten points for Ajax. He'd have to keep his game in top shape if he was going to keep this up. The more he impressed her like this, the better chance he'd have with her.

He unhooked his harness and she touched hers. "Are we getting out?"

"Yep, this is where we'll stay tonight."

She looked around as she fumbled with the clips. She sighed and pouted as she looked to him for help. Ajax smirked and gave her a hand. Once she was free, they jumped out and he released the dogs. They ran about, checking out the new smells.

Narissa took in their surroundings. "It really is like we've jumped through a portal into a fantasy world, isn't it?"

With a smirked, Ajax came up behind her and placed his hands over her eyes. She squeaked but didn't fight him. "Listen."

She did, and a big smile spread across her face. "It's so beautiful."

"This is what you'll hear for the next few days. The

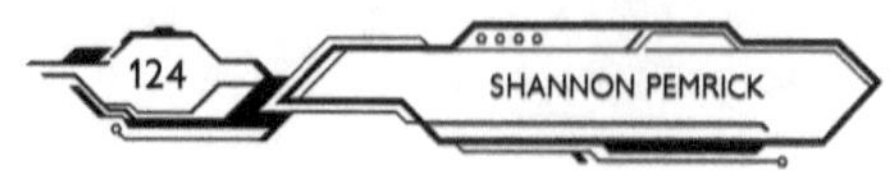

forest around the vacation home isn't this dense, but it has all the same sounds to greet you in the morning, through the day, and then to lull you to sleep."

She pulled his hands down and looked up at him with those hard-to-resist eyes. "Thank you. I think this is just the environment I needed."

He smirked. "You still don't get running water until tomorrow."

She let out an aggravated sigh. "I guess I'm going to have to deal."

"And no outhouses."

Her eyes widened. "Then where do we go?"

He snickered and called the dogs back. "Dig a hole."

Crash bolted through the clearing, disappearing into the underbrush. Helios followed after her, but when Ajax called for them again, he came right back. Crash took a moment longer to return.

"All right, now with these two accounted for, we can set up camp."

"You're going to have to teach me how to set up a tent," Narissa said.

"No, I'll be fine setting up."

She placed her hands on her hips. "I'm able to do manual labor."

He grinned and flipped a latch on the roof of his car. She cocked her head and watched him do three more latches. He then lifted the back end up and secured the support arms into the locked position. He looked down at Narissa, to find her eyes wide. "It had nothing to do with your ability to help. Two people would just be unnecessary."

"That's a tent? I don't have to sleep on the ground?"

Her excitement made him laugh. "I wouldn't be that cruel to you. It's also a lot safer. Just in case a bear walks through here."

Her face lit up. "I might see a bear?"

This threw him. She'd freaked out over a motel, no running water or modern amenities, and even sleeping on the ground. But a bear was exciting? "Uh, yeah. I can't guarantee it, but it's possible."

"Well, if I get to see more than a fox, opossum, and squirrel, I'd be stoked."

He tilted his head. "You've seen foxes?"

She nodded. "We have a few that like my apartment building."

Ajax knew foxes in urban areas weren't uncommon, but he'd never gotten the chance to see one himself. They were fairly elusive creatures. "Well, once we're set up, we can go for a hike. Maybe we'll see something."

Her smile widened. "I'll go collect firewood, how does that sound?"

"That sounds like a perfect idea. I'll build the fire pit after setting up the site. One of the dogs will follow you, most likely, so just keep your eye out every now and then."

She nodded and slipped on some better shoes before running off, both dogs choosing to follow her. Even if she wasn't wandering off too far, he was comfortable she'd be safe. That allowed him to focus on getting this place set up quick. He had a lot to show her today.

CHAPTER 8

arissa gazed around as they hiked through the forest, just as enchanted with the scenery as when they'd arrived. A woodpecker hammered away in the distance, and Narissa tried to find the little avian creature. She squealed when a Cascades frog jumped out into their path, and freaked out when Crash went to investigate it, thinking she was going to eat it. She wasn't wrong. Ajax always had to keep an extra eye on Crash.

Small birds flittered about above them, snagging Narissa's attention once she knew the little frog was safe. Ajax couldn't put words to why her reaction to this place enthralled him so much. Maybe it was the genuine reaction that got him. She didn't shy away from asking him questions about the local flora and fauna. Or even survival tips if something were to happen while out in a place like this. If this kept up, he may just be able to convince her to make this a regular thing for the two of them. And if not regular, an annual trip at least.

Narissa's gazing made her oblivious to the terrain and she lost her footing. Panic overtook him as she fell and rolled down the sloping path a little way.

"Ow…" she complained.

He rushed over to her and fussed as she lifted herself into a sitting position. "Are you okay?"

She winced as she stretched each of her limbs. "Yeah. That's going to bruise."

He tried to check her himself, but she pushed him away. "Really, I'm fine."

"I just want to check. That was a bad fall." He brushed away the soft curls from her face. "You could have hit your head."

She pushed him away again. "I said I'm fine. I'm able to take care of myself."

Ajax frowned. That wasn't why he was fussing. He sighed and let it be. Narissa got to her feet and dusted herself off. Ajax caught the sight of a scratch on her arm.

He touched it. "We'll need to make sure we clean that."

Narissa took a look. "Is it so bad we'd have to go back?"

Ajax shook his head. "No."

He was actually happy she wasn't going to let this little problem get in the way.

The two of them continued on, Ajax keeping a close eye on her in case anything from that fall reared up.

The sound of rushing water echoed through the dense trees. He stopped when something brown caught his eye and then motioned for Narissa to do the same. The dogs became alert, but listed to his hand signals.

Narissa looked at him, confused. "What?"

He pointed to the creature in the woods, keeping his voice low. "There's a doe over there."

Her gaze followed his hands and her eyes lit up. The doe stopped foraging and stared right at them. Her nose flared and her foot stomped before she turned and bounded farther into the forest, her black tail flagging them. Helios took a few steps forward, his eyes intent, and Ajax was quick to correct the behavior.

Narissa latched onto his arm and squealed. "That was amazing!"

He chuckled. "Even if it wasn't a bear?"

She nodded.

Ajax pressed on. "Good. I was worried the dogs would scare away anything skittish like that, so I'm happy I was wrong."

"Do you think we'll see anything else?"

"Hard to say. Sometimes you only hear the sounds of the forest, while other times critters cross your path all the time."

Narissa gazed around some more. "Well, I hope I can see just one more critter like that. That'd be amazing."

Ajax smiled. "Don't forget, we still have the house. We're bound to see wildlife there, too."

"True."

The terrain became difficult then, forcing the pair to focus on their footing. The dogs, however, bounded around without a care. The ground evened out when they came to a rocky riverbed, the water a few inches high.

Narissa squeaked when her feet plunged into the water. "So cold!"

Ajax dipped his hand in and splashed it onto his neck. "Yeah, but it helps cool you off in this heat."

"Yeah, I suppose."

"You'll get used to it soon enough." He changed course to walk upstream.

Narissa didn't follow. "Where are you going?"

"Follow and you'll see." He smiled. "I promise it'll be worth it."

She complied, her curiosity clear. The four of them trekked upstream, the water's depths rising and falling. Helios and Crash barreled through, having the time of their lives. The pair laughed at their excitement. *It must be nice being so carefree all the time.*

As they hiked, the ground beyond them rose high above until they were moss-covered cliffs. This sight continued before them, until the river turned a bend.

Narissa looked around. "I feel like I'm on some hunt for lost treasure."

"Mercedes and Takashi should come here, then," he said. "They'd have a blast."

She laughed. Those two had way too much fun with those game hunts, in his opinion, full of puzzles and traps and stuff. It was like Indiana Jones, but with magic rather than voodoo curses. He'd take beating up monsters for loot over that craziness.

Narissa stopped to touch the gorge's vertical surface, her fingers digging into every pocked, cracked, or mossy surface. Her exploring had him thinking about these walls, and he caught himself absently touching them as well with his artificial limb.

He peered up higher, looking for spots one could rappel down from. *I wonder what it'd be like...*

A soft hand touched his real arm, bring him back to reality. Narissa stared up at him. *Those eyes again.* "Are you okay, Andrew?"

He shook his head to clear it. "Yeah. Just got lost in thought about the possibilities of rock climbing this gorge. Seems like it could be fun to rappel down in."

"You rock climb?"

"I used to." He found himself touching his artificial arm. "Until my accident."

Narissa tilted her head, her hand still touching him. "Is that how you lost it? You didn't want to talk about it when you became a client of ours."

He nodded. "Yeah, it stung too badly still to retell the story again. But don't worry, it wasn't one of those *127 Hours* movie kind of situations. I've always been an adventure seeker. Darius, too. It's why we did everything together. Worried Kiara sick as we got older."

Ajax shook his head. "One day, we'd planned to go out rock climbing, but something came up and Darius asked if we could go another day. I agreed, but still wanted to go out that day. I knew it was stupid to go alone, that there was a reason we had a buddy system in place, but I'm the stupid jock."

Narissa's eyes softened. "If that term upsets you, Andrew, we can stop teasing you. We figured it was okay in jest be—"

He smiled at her. "It *is* okay. And really, it's true. I can use this brain, but that day, twenty-three-year-old me didn't. Like an idiot, I went out. And one miscalculation and loose boulder later, I found myself pinned. I was lucky enough to be found by another climber, but my arm was done for."

Ajax clenched his cybernetic hand. "Darius and Kiara had tried to help me through that time before Crash came along. They stuck by me through that hell I put myself through, even when I tried to push them away. And after I started bouncing back, they thought I'd be my old self again. Darius thought he'd get his adventure buddy back."

He shook his head. "After I came out of my depression, I told myself I wouldn't do anything stupid like that again. I'd always have someone with me, and I wouldn't do something so life-threatening again. Darius was disappointed. Kiara, on the other hand, was ecstatic I'd had some sense knocked into me and wished Darius would do the same."

Narissa pursed her lips. "This difference in opinions, does that have an effect on why the two of them aren't together?"

Ajax chuckled. It was no secret to anyone who knew those two, there was something there they both denied. "Pretty much. They've been tossing glances at each other since we were teens. But Kiara wants someone stable, and Darius wants someone who is adventurous and daring. One of these days they're going to have to budge on something, because I'm not sure if I can handle their dancing around much longer before I get involved."

"Just don't lock them in a closest. That's too cliché."

He scratched his head. "Okay, Plan B."

Narissa snickered and then rubbed his arm. "Thank you for sharing that with me. It actually made me think of Elijah. He was always into the outdoors. Never wanted to be inside." She laughed. "He even had his very own tent outside because we didn't have a tree for him to have a tree house."

Ajax lifted her chin. "I'm glad I can remind you of him. I know you miss him."

She nodded. "I'll be happy when he returns home finally."

His beautiful doctor took a deep breath and then pushed on. "Shall we?"

Ajax frowned. He didn't like that she pushed away. He wanted her to feel comfortable talking to him, even about heavy things. It's why he shared his story. He'd come to accept it, sure, but now and then the reality bothered him. Telling her just now lifted a weight he didn't realize he had on his chest. And in the end, he wanted her to know everything about him.

The pair trudged through knee-deep water, Narissa struggling at times. She insisted she was fine, but he could tell her leg was bothering her. He couldn't get through her stubbornness, so he'd have to keep watching her. This continued for at least a mile until they came to a dead end with a gorgeous waterfall. Narissa gasped, stepping closer to the wondrous sight. Crash and Helios drew up beside her. Ajax took out his phone and snapped a picture. Everything he wanted was right there in front of him.

Narissa looked back at him, the brightest smile he'd seen from her on her face. He snapped another picture. She pointed at him. "Hey!"

"What? I'm just saving the moment."

She waggled her finger at him. "No butt pictures."

He moved toward her, a grin curling up half his face. "If I was going to do that, I'd tell you to climb up on the Jeep while I watched."

She scoffed.

Ajax drew up right behind her. "Here, let's get one of us both. That should make you feel better, right?"

She leaned into him, smiling. "I like that idea."

He wrapped his arm around her waist, her perfect form fitting just right into him, and they snapped two, one with the waterfall behind them, and one without. He would have tried for a few more, to keep her close, but the dogs' splashing about became too much to deal with.

"The water closer to the falls is deep enough to swim in. Let's take a dip to cool off, and then head back."

She nodded. "I like that idea. Though this water is so cold, it won't take too long to cool down."

Ajax stripped off his shirt. "Well, let's not waste time, then."

Narissa found a ledge for them to store their outerwear, and she removed her shirt, revealing the not-two-piece bathing suit he'd told her to pack.

"Someone didn't follow my list."

She waggled her finger again. "Yes I did. I packed everything you told me, and then some."

His lips spread into a thin line. She would.

"And really, if this is why you told me to pack it, then there wasn't a reason to be so specific against me wearing my monokinis."

That's what they were called? He'd never cared enough about the two-piece design to find out, but they looked sexy on her.

Narissa, satisfied with his silence, removed her shorts and waded into the cold water, her shoulders going rigid as she dealt with the frigid water. Her reaction intrigued

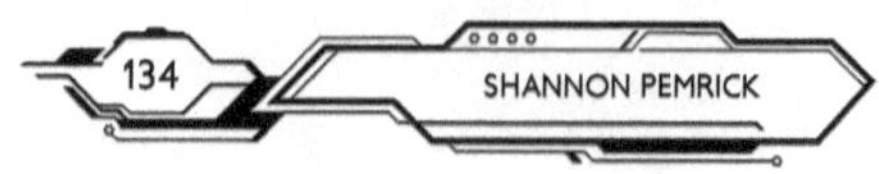

him. Yes, the water was cold, but he found it refreshing against the hot and humid air.

No matter. She'd get used to it. A wicked grin spread across his face and he snuck up behind her. A little faster than she may have liked.

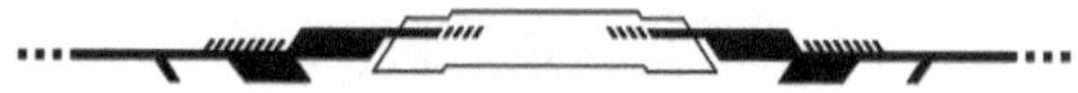

Narissa kicked off her wet shoes and swapped them out for dry ones. The hike had been nice, aside from the little fall mishap. That gorge was so beautiful. And even after Ajax was a jerk and tossed her into the water, she still enjoyed herself. *Nolan and I never did anything this fun together…*

She checked over her cut. It was doing okay, thanks to the water, so she decided first aid wasn't needed until later. Her leg had stopped hurting, too, thankfully. It hadn't been easy to keep Ajax in the dark about that. She just didn't need him fussing.

She leaned against the Jeep and looked over the photos they'd taken and saved one of them together as her wallpaper. The girls would tease her if they found out, but honestly, she didn't care right now. These past two days had been so amazing. Ajax really knew how to make a girl feel special. *It astounds me he's still single.*

He walked past her to the back of the Jeep, taking off his damp shirt as he went. Her eyes followed every movement, her tongue gliding across her lower lip. He was such a fine specimen of a man, it was sinful. And she was okay with that.

She looked around for the best place to change out of her bathing suit. When she'd changed into it earlier, he'd stepped away from the campsite for his own reasons, allowing her to duck behind the Jeep. And even that made her uncomfortable, as he could have returned at any minute. Or worse, some park ranger could have shown up.

She wasn't going to be so lucky this time, and she didn't enjoy the idea of running off into the woods to change. She needed to get creative. The tree next to the vehicle caught her eye, and got her wheels spinning. "Hey, Andrew, do we have any rope?"

He peered around the back of the Jeep, his brow raised. "Why?"

To tie you up and make you beg. She bit her tongue. *Stop it, brain.* "I need to do something. Blankets, too."

He looked back at the open back. "Yeah, I have both here."

She skipped over and took the rope when he offered it. She went about tying it to the Jeep and then wrapped it around the tree several times before tying the other end to the Jeep. Ajax watched her, intrigued.

She then took the blankets and laid them over the rope, creating a makeshift fort.

Ajax crossed his arms. "Clever girl."

She let out a raucous laugh and retrieved fresh clothes. "Have you been watching *Jurassic Park* again?"

He snickered. "*Crumbling Worlds* this time."

"You and those movies." She ducked into the fort and didn't waste time stripping out of her bathing suit.

"What, can you blame me? Dinosaurs are cool. The idea we could potentially bring them back is every young boy's fantasy."

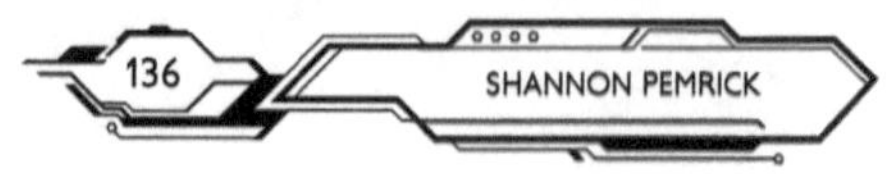

She slipped a t-shirt on and allowed herself to poke her head out of the little fort. "You mean wet dream."

Ajax held up his hands. "Whoa, hey now. Those were reserved for pretty pop stars whose music we couldn't admit we liked."

She chuckled and ducked back in. Ajax went back to rummaging in the back. "I see you don't trust me to not peek."

"I don't trust any man to say they're *that* much of a gentleman."

He chuckled. "Smart choice."

She shouldn't have been surprised, but she was. She was all too used to the guys she knew fumbling around with excuses and denial. *At least he's honest.* It made her unable to be mad, even if she wanted to be. There was a part of her that found excitement in the prospect of him finding her appealing enough to misbehave a little.

Narissa finished up, removed the blankets, and used the line to dry her wet clothes. Ajax wasn't in the back of the Jeep anymore, but his wet clothes were. She shook her head, glancing over to where he crouched by the fire he was attempting to start, and then picked up the clothes to hang them for drying. *I hope he doesn't make this a habit.*

Her stomach rumbled. She hadn't eaten since lunch, and that was just a small batch of chicken nuggets and water. She wasn't a particular fan of fast food. And then taking a hike, that'd just added to the chances of her getting hungry.

She pursed her lips as she looked into the back of the Jeep. He had various compartments and equipment back there for all sorts of things. Everything had a place, keeping it neat. She just didn't know the method to his packing. "Hey, Andrew, do we have anything to hold me over before dinner? I'm a little peckish."

"Peckish?" He laughed. "I thought my mom was the only one to use that word."

Her eyes narrowed at him. "Don't be a jerk, and just tell me if we have extra food."

He smirked and came over, rummaging around in a drawer. He pulled out an apple and then a bag of what looked like trail mix. Upon closer inspection it wasn't trail mix, but she didn't know what it was, except that it had chocolate and mini marshmallows in it. *Yum…*

"I can offer you an apple, or something less healthy, s'mores muddy buddies." He chewed on the peppermint gum in his mouth. "I also have more gum."

The chocolate snack looked really good. "What's in this… s'mores muddy buddies treat?"

"It's rice crisp cereal coated in chocolate, peanut butter, and powdered sugar, mixed with honey graham cereal, chocolate chips, and marshmallows."

Her mouth watered and she held out her hands. "Gimme."

Ajax laughed and handed the bag over. She scooped some into her hand and had to resist squealing when the delightful taste hit her tongue. "So good!"

"It's my favorite snack while out here. Trail mix is good, but this is better."

"I agree." She ate some more and then looked into the back. "What are we having for dinner?"

He smiled wide. "My gram's famous chili."

She pursed her lips. "Um, is it spicy?"

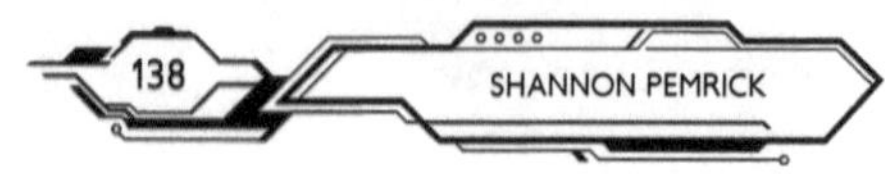

"Oh yeah." His brow twisted when she made an awkward face. "What's wrong?"

"I… don't do spicy."

"What? You eat jambalaya. How do you not do spice?"

"We just don't make it spicy."

Ajax exhaled. "Well…"

She frowned. "Sorry. You can still make it. I'll just eat something light. It's my fault for being picky."

He shook his head and waved her off. "No, that's not how this all goes." Ajax rummaged through his stuff. "Do you eat hotdogs?"

"Yes."

"And potatoes are okay on your list too, right?"

She laughed. "Yes. I just don't do spicy."

"Okay, then cheesy bacon garlic fries and pigs in a blanket it is."

She licked her lips. That sounded good.

"Also means the fire I've got going won't need to be made bigger."

Narissa pointed to a small grill. "Why not use that?"

"Because that only gets used if it's raining." He tilted his head up to peer up at the canopy. "And right now, it's nice, so might as well take advantage."

She nodded. "Makes sense. Do we have any other snacks, in case I get hungry after dinner?"

Ajax snickered. "Do you eat this much back home?"

"Yeah, pretty much."

"Well, good. Because I planned on doing s'more cones with fruit as a dessert."

Narissa licked her lips again. That also sounded delicious. "What type of fruit?"

"I packed strawberries, blackberries, and blueberries."

A wide smile spread across her face. "I hope you don't plan on eating those blackberries."

He pointed at her. "You're sharing those."

Interesting. Looked like they had some food choices in common. "Fine."

She then chowed down on her snack. Ajax went about gathering supplies and getting the fire going some more until it was perfect. Narissa sat in a comfortable chair, watching him. He had a process, even if she couldn't exactly see it, and he made for great entertainment. *And eye candy.* She could admit that to herself.

"Are you sure you don't want help?" She'd asked a few times, but he insisted on taking care of everything.

"Yep, I'm good." He placed a few tinfoil bundles on a wire rack he'd set over the fire. "Do you like your dogs crispy?"

She glanced at Crash and Helios, who lay nearby. "I like my *hot dogs* without burning."

He smirked and then nodded, going to the back of the Jeep and wrapping up some more food. He came back with two tinfoil bundles and two forked roasting rods. Four hot dogs wrapped in pastry were already skewered onto them. *Looks like he's going to eat like a horse some more.* She didn't know where he put it. Unless his intense workouts consumed it all, but she wasn't convinced it was solely that. Even she had to be careful with what she ate.

She may have joked about not working out with him this morning, but she did. She didn't do anything intensive, but it was enough to keep a good figure.

Ajax set up his roasting sticks and then pulled up a chair beside her. "I'll just have to remember to rotate them."

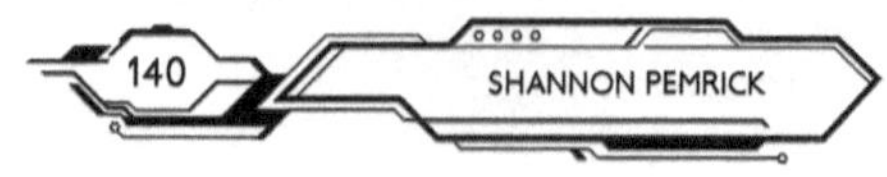

"Burnt meat, bleh."

"Open flame makes it crispy and adds an extra layer of flavor."

Narissa grimaced and then ate her snack. Her phone went off, surprising her. She didn't think she had service out here. Checking it, she found a text from Dylan.

How are you holding up?

She wasn't sure if she should smile at his thoughtfulness or curse because he reminded her. Her talk with Ajax this morning after her phone alert helped her calm down and focus on other things. But now it was at the front of her mind, and that same sensation of dread came back.

There was only so long she'd be safe from Nolan. She had to go back home at some point. And the fact the system failed her to where she didn't feel safe going home, it was wrong. It was wrong that Ajax felt the need to protect her like some damaged damsel—*You are a damaged damsel, Narissa.*

It's why he fussed so much when she fell. Why he took the time to drag her all the way out here. Without him stepping in, she'd be hiding in her home, too afraid to risk running into Nolan. Because everyone knew papers wouldn't stop him if he wanted to touch her.

She jumped when Ajax touched her hand. "Rissa?"

Narissa took a deep breath. "Sorry. I got lost in my head."

"Yeah, I know. What happened?"

She shook her head and replied back to Dylan, telling him she was doing fine and staying busy, in a good way. "Nothing. I just started thinking too much."

"It has to do with the text you got, doesn't it?"

Why did he have to keep pressing? It wasn't his job. "That's just a message from Dylan, checking up on me and all. Nothing major."

Ajax's eyes tightened at the mention of Dylan. He'd acted a little funny the last time Dylan texted her. She didn't understand why, though; Dylan was only looking out for her. It's why she wasn't mad when he reminded her of Nolan's release. His check-in came from the right place.

"Except it is major, Narissa," Ajax said. "I've been trying to keep you busy so you wouldn't think about that. Because I knew a reminder would bring you back into your mind."

She avoided eye contact. "I'm always going to think about it, Andrew. It doesn't matter what I do—at some point, I'm going to compare my past with the present, or something is going to make me think of Nolan. I'm always going to have to keep an eye over my shoulder for as long as he's roaming around, because legal papers don't protect people."

He slipped his hand into hers. "What can I do to ease that burden?"

She liked this contact. It felt safe. But deep down it also didn't feel right. Narissa pulled away. "You can't always fix things, Andrew. This isn't some princess story where the hero saves her from a tower and they live happily ever after."

She messaged Dylan when he texted back to be double sure about her answer. *Men.*

Ajax looped his pinky in with hers. "You're right, this isn't one of those stories. Because you got out of that tower on your own. I'm just the wandering adventurer you ran into after getting a little lost. You can either ask me for directions, or keep trying to go at this alone."

His explanation amused her. But there was one issue. "Who asks a guy for directions?"

Ajax chuckled. "We're fine at giving them. We just don't ask for them."

She found herself able to look at him again, the dread pushing down. "Then how do I know you're not lost either?"

He pressed his lips together. "That's fair." He brushed her hair out of her face. "Then, can we go on an adventure together instead of heading back to town?"

Narissa smiled. "I think I already said yes."

Ajax grinned at her. "Good. Only one rule—don't let Nolan get to you. Seriously. I get you're going to think about him. It's going to be hard not to. But I need you to not get lost in your mind because of him. If you think you will, tell me. I'll get you back on the path you wandered from."

"I'll try."

The dogs, now done investigating the bushes on the far side of the camp, trotted over to the pair. Helios made himself comfortable next to Ajax, while Crash came up to Narissa and pawed her leg with her cybernetic one. Her eyes looked to Narissa's treat.

"You little beggar." Narissa took Crash's artificial leg into her hand, but didn't give in to her. Not like yesterday with the ice cream.

Ajax watched her. "I'm surprised you haven't asked about that."

She shrugged. "Had she not slept in my bed at the

hotel, I would have. But I got a good look at the design and know you went to my cousin. She licenses my design and makes it animal-friendly."

Ajax sat back in his seat. "Of course Ava is your cousin. Is everyone in your family into this cybernetic stuff?"

She shook her head, a smile on her face. "No, but a lot of us are drawn to its possibilities."

"Like you?"

She nodded. "I grew up in my father's company. I saw all the advancements the technology went through, and how cybernetics changed lives. I wanted to be part of that."

He leaned on the arm of the chair closest to her. "Did you really start college at fifteen?"

She nodded and he exhaled. "Now I feel dumb. I didn't start until I was eighteen, and that was just because I had an early birthday compared to everyone else."

Narissa laughed and patted him on the arm. "Don't let it get to you. I was an exception to the rules. Even my parents weren't sure how to handle it, and were happy when Elijah had a 'normal' brain."

Ajax let out a raucous laugh. "I think I prefer you with a 'not normal' brain."

"My brother, too, since that's what saved his life."

Ajax gazed at her with interest. The focus made her feel a bit strange. "Can you tell me that story? Well, that journey? What I read before picking your company for my upgrade interested me a lot. But I've never gotten around to asking you more about it."

She leaned back in her chair. "It's not as exciting as you may think. Since I started college at fifteen, and because I already had experience in the field helping my dad where I could, I shot through courses, or tested out of them quickly. By the time I was eighteen, I was well into my Master's. That's when Elijah got sick."

Her lips curled down; the sting of the news still hurt to this day. "Something was wrong with his heart. The doctors said he was lucky he'd made it this long and he'd need a transplant. But as he waited, his health deteriorated, until he was on the verge of not being eligible for a transplant. That's when my father changed the focus on his projects and started working on a cybernetic replacement."

Narissa scratched behind Crash's ear. "Back then, the options for cybernetic organs were limited and not compatible with most people. And if you were lucky enough to get one that did work for you, you'd be on medication the rest of your life. My father was willing to accept that side effect, if he could just make a reliable artificial heart. But I wasn't okay with that solution."

She glanced at Ajax. He was already enthralled with her story.

"I worked with my professors and the college to allow me to rearrange how I did my courses to accommodate my RnD. My professors were eager to agree, as they wanted to see just how far I could push this. I'd shown promise in lab work and ideas I'd formed during my schooling, and many offered their assistance if I ever needed it."

Narissa shook her head. "It wasn't long into my research that I realized I would need to expand my skill set. That's how I ended up on a path to be surgeon. So not only was I balancing a double major, but I was trying to save my brother's life at any cost. And let me tell you, there was a point when my family thought they'd see both of us kids in the hospital. But the hard work paid off."

She smiled. "Two years after Elijah's diagnosis, I had a working prototype. My father was so impressed he stopped his work and helped me stress test the device. It wasn't flawless, but it worked better than the market design, and when we tested it against Elijah's white blood cells we'd gathered, it wasn't rejected."

Narissa sucked in a tight breath. "And then Elijah's condition worsened. It forced us to try it on him."

Ajax's brow twisted. "You didn't have to go through any channels?"

She shook her head. "No, because Elijah was a willing participant of the experiment, and he'd signed up before his health deteriorated, so there were no legal ramifications around presence of mind."

Ajax leaned closer. "Amazing. And that's when you saved him, right? You were twenty years old and made a brand new cybernetic."

She nodded. "Yeah. We did the transplant, and the brain surgery to implant the neuro-mod I'd designed, and it worked. It wasn't perfect, and I came back two years later with an even better design for him, but everything worked as I anticipated." She took a deep breath. "And then all the fame came. Everyone wanted cybernetics from us. Everyone wanted me to work for them, date me, or wanted interviews. Schools even wanted to recruit me to teach."

She half laughed. "It was overwhelming. But it was the boost I needed. Before I knew it, my father and I used

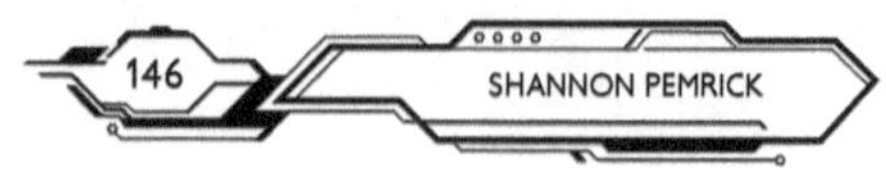

my knowledge to expand on organ cybernetics, and I'd updated the neuro-mod and cybernetic limb technology." Her excitement wavered for a moment. "Even with the hiccup with Nolan, I managed to do all this, plus get my degrees and surgical residency completed by the time I was twenty-eight."

When Ajax didn't respond to the end of her story, she looked at him. She found him gazing at her with his hand tucked under his chin, enthralled with her story.

"Amazing." He blinked. "Wait, I already said that."

She giggled. "It's fine. At least you liked the story. Most get bored. And I didn't even get into the technical aspect of it, which can happen sometimes when I get excited." Her nose scrunched when something awful wafted in. "Is something burning?"

"Shit, my dogs!" Narissa laughed as Ajax jumped to his feet and ran over to the fire, turning the skewered hot dogs. They were completely black on one side. "Just extra crispy. Nothing major."

Narissa grimaced. "Bleh."

He sat back down. "I can always slather it with cheese after, if it's too much."

She shook her head and the two fell into more conversation. When their food finished cooking, they ate, Narissa finding the meal delightful for something cooked over a fire. Even the dogs got to eat something other than kibble. Ajax explained that he usually had them on a raw diet, but that was hard to do while traveling without his mini fridge. Apparently, to accommodate for her stuff, he'd taken it out and opted for a cooler. She felt bad, but since they'd be arriving at the vacation home tomorrow, she didn't let it get to her.

She did start to feel chilled part of the way through dinner as the sun went down, so she retrieved the jacket she'd packed per his list instructions. Now she understood why. He didn't seem to need it, but she got cold easily.

When it came to dessert, she got to create her own cone. It was fun putting all the ingredients together in the sugar cone. Ajax offered chocolate, peanut butter cups, and peppermint candies as options to go with the marshmallows. And as promised, he also had berries.

She'd never done this before. When she wanted s'mores as a kid, they'd just roast a marshmallow over the stove burner. But stuffing a cone with the different treat mixes, along with some berries, wasn't something that ever came to mind as a possibility.

And when she finally got to eat it, after cooking it over the fire, she was in heaven. She knew she should limit herself to one, but she didn't. *I'm on vacation. I'm allowed to splurge and do something crazy every now and then.*

The two continued to chat long after the sun went down. It was nice connecting with him this way. Two friends, no distractions, and free reign of conversation.

When tiredness overcame them, they decided it was time to hit the hay. She changed into her nightgown again, but it was so cold out she threw some pants and her jacket on almost immediately. Ajax told her the sleeping bags were warm and they had extra blankets, so she wouldn't need them, but she kept them on. If she got too hot after, she could strip them off then.

Ajax had her slip into the Jeep and climb up into the tent first, finding it far roomier than she expected. Though that changed when he came in next. She always felt small next to this brickhouse of a man, but this tent put that into perspective better. Crash and Helios poked their heads up, but to her surprise didn't try to join them.

Curious, she peered down below, to find them curling up on some blankets Ajax had set up for them on the back seat. "They're going to be okay down there, right?"

"They'll be fine," he assured. "If they get cold, they'll burrow into the blankets."

"Okay." He knew his dogs better than she did.

Narissa curled up into her sleeping bag, finding it warm like Ajax promised, but not warm enough to ditch the warm layer she wore. They wished each other goodnight and Ajax turned off the lantern, plunging them into darkness.

Crickets and katydids played their nightly songs. An owl hooted in the distance. The sounds of nature were lovely. They'd have put her to sleep, if it weren't for the cold.

Narissa grabbed a blanket and pulled it into her sleeping bag, but still that didn't help. She shivered and huddled deeper into her sleeping bag, but the cold air continued to bite at her. She pulled into herself, controlling her breathing so she'd be able to focus on warming up.

Ajax shifted next to her. "Are you still cold?"

"Yeah, aren't you?"

"No. I ditched my shirt already."

"You're warm?" Narissa's brow furrowed and then she sat up. In the darkened space, she reached out to him and found his bare chest. He felt warmer than she did, at least.

Ajax rested his hand over hers. "You're freezing."

He then turned on the lamp on low, illuminating the tent.

Narissa migrated her touch up to his face and rested the back of her hand on his forehead. "Do you have a fever?"

He grinned. "If I said yes, would you be my doctor?"

She chuckled. "Only if you say *ahhh*."

Narissa pulled her hand away, the two laughing, and then she tucked herself into her sleeping bag. "I've always had trouble with the cold. I get it from my mother."

"You could always take off your clothes and curl up against me."

Narissa's eyes went wide and she stared at him. Ajax grinned at her. *Did he really just—* "What?"

His expression remained the same. "Basic survival 101."

Her cheeks warmed, an image of her stripping down and pressing against his hard muscular form entering her mind. Of him pulling her close, his hands running across her soft form—his hot breath against her skin. Against—

She ducked into her sleeping bag, trying desperately to not think of that. He was just trying to get a rise out of her—which was exactly what he did.

Ajax turned the light down. "Well, if you change your mind, offer still stands." He chuckled. "And I wasn't pulling a fast one over you. It is a survival technique."

Narissa held herself tight and thought about what he said. It wasn't like she'd never been naked next to a man before. Nolan wasn't her first, or her last. But this was Ajax. He was a friend. A sex-on-a-stick friend, but still a friend.

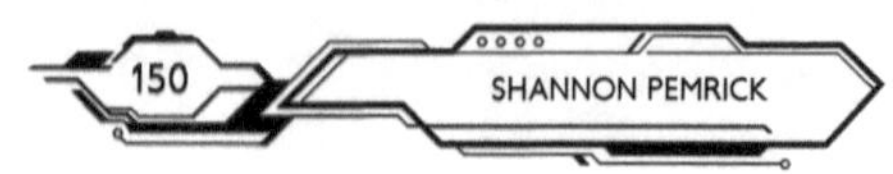

She shivered some more, her teeth chattering this time. *Splurge and do something crazy. Maybe…*

Narissa fussed with her jacket and then her pants.

"What are you doing in that sleeping bag?" Ajax asked. "Rolling around with a conjured person?"

Narissa laughed. "Disappointed it's not you?"

"I think I'll leave that question unanswered."

Her face heated. At this rate, he just had to get her mind going and she'd warm up.

Once she freed herself of her pants, she fussed with her sleeping bag zipper.

"Okay, that's it." He turned the lamp back on just as she started fussing with his. Ajax got a nice view of her in her nightgown. "Oh. You are taking me up on the offer."

Her eyes ticked up at him and then back to the bags as she zipped them together. "Not entirely. I'm combining our sleeping bags and then I'm going to sleep right up next to you, with some clothes on. I'll get the body contact heat needed to warm me, while not having to do anything embarrassing."

Ajax leaned on his elbow. "Smart. Though I have a correction. You'd have nothing to be embarrassed about when stripping down. Remember, I've seen you in a bathing suit."

Her face warmed some more as she finished the zipper part of her plan. "Bathing suits and nakedness are not the same."

Ajax shrugged. "If you say so."

Narissa took a deep breath and then curled into him, his musky, peppermint scent enveloping her. His warmth invited her, and she didn't resist. Ajax reached over and

pulled her close, tangling his fingers into her hair. She felt safe like this. Protected from everything bad in her life. None of it mattered here.

Ajax would protect her. He didn't have to, and yet still wanted to, without asking for anything from her. She knew it in the way he held her.

It was a strength she'd never felt with Nolan, or any other man who'd tried to take her heart. But Ajax, he made it difficult to keep it away from him.

Ajax turned the lamp off again and then pressed his lips against her forehead. "Good night, Rissa."

"Night, Andrew."

He made it very difficult.

Soft light and the neverending chirping of song-birds invaded Narissa's dreams. She clamped her eyes tighter, wanting to remain cocooned in the warmth surrounding her. A gentle hand brushed against her skin and slid into her hair.

Narissa's eyes fluttered open and she looked up to find Ajax smiling down at her. "Morning, beautiful."

It took her a moment to remember last night and why she was sleeping so close to him. She wet her lips. "Morning."

She looked around the car tent, soft light filtering in. "What time is it?"

He shrugged. "Didn't feel like checking, but sometime just past sun-up."

She rubbed her face and sat up. "Oh."

Ajax reached around her and pulled her on top of him. "You're welcome to stay a little longer. I don't mind if you go back to sleep."

Her face heated up and she pulled away, but remained seated on him. Her hands rested on his sculpted chest as she straddled him, his hands finding purchase on her upper thighs. Ajax gazed up at her, her wild curls threatening to curtain her face. She could feel his erection pushing against the fabric of their undergarments.

Warmth built in her core. The longer he stared at her with those breathtaking features, the more aware she was how easy it could be to lose herself if she wasn't careful.

Narissa pulled up one of her fallen straps and avoided his gaze. "We should really get up. We still have some driving to do before we make it to this getaway home."

"We don't have to." He sat up, one hand remaining on her thigh, though migrating up an inch or two. His other stopped her from fixing the other nightgown strap, his face so close to hers, their lips could brush each other if one of them moved. Narissa's heart hammered against her ribs, her mouth running dry.

"The house is only a couple hours away. And we could always stay here another day." He grinned. "There's no one around telling us we have to leave this spot."

Helios barked, making them both jump. Narissa's wits coming back to her, she pulled away and looked at the dog. He set both his paws on the opening down into the Jeep, his ears perked, and his tongue lolling out. She could see his back end swaying side to side as he wagged his stumpy tail.

Narissa giggled. "Except him. Mister Rising Sun is looking for his morning walk."

Ajax sighed and rubbed his face. "Fine, fine."

Narissa slipped off him. "While you walk them, how

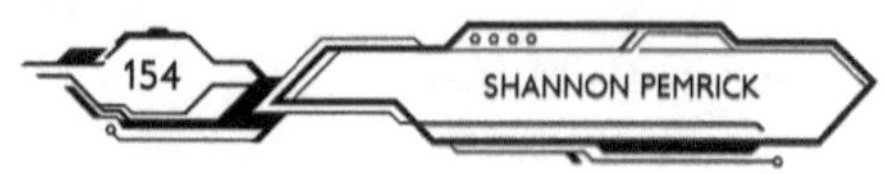

about I make us breakfast? I know how to make a mean breakfast burrito. And I think it's fair game to use your portable grill so we don't have to worry about a fire."

He pulled himself free of the sleeping bag. "Sounds good to me. We can eat on the way. I'll show you a good place to wash up, too."

Narissa sniffed herself. "Yeah, I could use a chance to freshen up."

Ajax touched her chin and then slipped down below, grabbing himself a pair of pants as he went. Narissa's fingers brushed against the spot he'd touched, her mind going back to a moment ago. That had not been subtle at all. No amount of logic could come up with ways to deny what could have just happened.

But why me? Sure, she could understand before he found everything out. Smart, successful, accepting, beautiful. She fit many criteria. But now? Now he knew she was just a broken mess with a crazy ex-husband and worked herself to death as self-medicating therapy.

That would make your average man high-tail it. *Then again, Ajax isn't your average man.*

Narissa shook these thoughts from her head and looked for some clothes to change into before going to make breakfast.

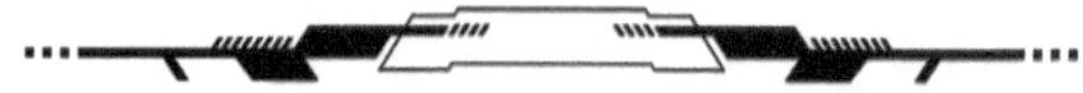

Frigid water splashed over Ajax's skin. If he wasn't awake after that run, he was now. He'd arrived back at the site to find Narissa gone, though he didn't go looking for her; he suspected she needed a moment alone. He figured it best then to wash up. As much as he liked the idea of bathing with her, after missing his chance this morning, nothing would happen now. *Dogs, they're like children. Always asking for something at the worst possible times.*

At least this cold water helped him keep his mind clear.

"Andrew?" Narissa called out. "Are you over here?"

There was something about her calling him by that name that he loved. Maybe it was because she only did it when it was just the two of them. She was the only one to call him by that name, and hadn't even told her two best friends about it. The frequency with which she used it had also increased this week. She had a tendency to swap back and forth, but that hadn't happened at all these last few days.

"Eugene Andrew Jackson, God so help you, you'd better not be playing some game on me!" she shouted. "I know you're around here somewhere."

The sound of her using his entire name both amused and frightened him. In the end, he just laughed. "I'm not hiding. You didn't give me a chance to respond."

Narissa bounded around the large boulder and tree obscuring him from sight. She came to a screeching halt, her face reddening instantly.

"Oh my God." She hid her face in her hands and turned around. "I had no idea you were bathing. I'm so sorry."

Ajax threw his head back as he laughed. She reacted just as he'd expected. "Narissa, turn around."

"Nope. Nope. A thousand times, nope."

"Wow. I didn't realize bathing in swim trunks was such a horrible sight."

Her back straightened and she stole a glance at him.

Ajax tugged on the swim shorts clinging low on his hips. She let out a deep sigh and relaxed.

He winked at her. "I can assure you that what lies underneath is good to look at, though. If you ever change your mind."

Narissa crossed her arms and looked elsewhere.

"Go change so you can wash up, too," he said.

"I thought when you offered to show me where we could bathe, it'd be a bath house. Like one just for park rangers if they get stuck out here or something."

He chuckled. "Just mother nature's bathhouse out here. It's why I told you to pack that specific bathing suit. Be too hard to wash if you wore too much in the water." He grinned. "Course, if you'd rather bathe with nothing on, I'm not going to complain."

Her face reddened more. "Not happening."

"Fine, be that way."

Narissa glanced down at the water. "Is it cold?"

"Just like yesterday." No point in lying to her.

She chewed her bottom lip. Normally, he'd allow himself the moment to indulge in the sight, but the way she held herself, something wasn't right. "Do me a favor?"

"Anything." He only ever wanted to make her happy.

"Don't… don't stare when I come back. Please?"

This piqued his interest. What did she mean by that? "I promise."

He'd seen her in a bathing suit before. And even though he'd never seen her wear a two-piece, another reason he specified it on the list, it really couldn't be that different than the sexy ones she wore. *She called them monokinis, right?* He couldn't remember. It was a bathing suit. He didn't see why it needed its own special name.

She left and after a couple minutes had passed, and when he wasn't sure how much more his body could take of the cold water, she returned, wrapped up in a towel. Ajax's hands rested on his hips, and she hesitated before removing the towel. When she finally found the courage to drop it, his whole body locked up.

Yes, she looked just as good as he imagined she would, but that wasn't what caught his attention. The discolored skin of the large scar on her lower abdomen did. *Is that where—* He tried to look elsewhere on her so he'd keep his promise to her.

Ajax now understood why she'd double-checked with him over text about the bathing suit. And as he thought about it, every monokini she wore covered this area.

Narissa dipped her toes into the water and squealed, yanking herself back. "Cold!"

She calmed, gave herself a small pep talk, and then counted down. It all amused Ajax.

Narissa jumped in when she reached one, and screeched again. "I hate this! So cold."

He drew up closer to her. "If it's that unbearable, you can wait until we get to the house. It's not that far from here."

She shook her head and splashed some water onto her arms. "I really need to try and do a rinse at least."

"Here, let me help." Ajax came closer and dripped water down her back. She reeled away and screeched. He chuckled and grabbed a hold of her, dripping more water on her. She wriggled in his grip, making the same high-pitched sounds, but they were muffled as his muscular form blocked it.

Narissa managed to slip out, but he was ready and

caught her. She gasped, but not because of his wet hand. His dry one had brushed against her scar. He pulled that hand away, and she remained still, one of her own hands touching the sensitive area.

"Can I ask—" he hesitated to finish that sentence. He wasn't sure if it was okay.

She gave a slow nod. "It is. After my fight with Nolan, I turned to leave, and that's when he pulled the gun." She took a deep breath. "The two bullets tore through me, fracturing my pelvis, tearing up my insides, and causing the damage to my abdomen you see here. The doctors did what they could, but there's only so much scarring they could minimize."

Ajax tentatively reached down to place his hand over hers, but she pushed him away. "Sorry. Had I known, I wouldn't have taken your inquiry so lightly. I—"

Narissa shook her head. "Don't be. This scar doesn't make me think of him. At least, not as much as it reminds me of the baby I lost. And…" Her body trembled. "How I'll never be able to try again."

The world around them disappeared. She couldn't have kids anymore? Then why would her mother make comments like she had recently?

"I know what you're thinking. My mom's comments." She took a deep breath. "She doesn't get it. Because the doctor only said I had a reduced chance of carrying a child to term, my mother thinks it's possible. But I did the math."

She took another breath, her shaking still present, as if the very thought of speaking this pained her. "The average healthy woman has a one-in-seven chance to get pregnant. That means within two years of trying, most women are able to conceive. But me… my math shows I have a one-in-three-hundred chance. And then my chances of bringing that to term without miscarriage…"

Narissa shook her head. "I couldn't bear to calculate that math."

Ajax wrapped his arms around her, holding her tight. He wished he hadn't asked. Not because he didn't want to know this about her, but because of the pain it brought. So many things made sense now.

She always had a strange look whenever she saw children. He'd never been able to place it, but now he realized it was longing.

And her reluctance to start a relationship. The likelihood of her finding someone who was okay with not having a family or going the adoption route, wasn't as high as some would hope, even in this day and age.

But he wasn't one of those people. He didn't care, as long as he had her.

Narissa's shaking ceased and she took several controlled breaths. "Thank you. I don't mean to dump all my problems on you."

Ajax lifted her chin. "I want you to. Whenever something bothers you, I want you to feel like you have someone you can come to and get it off your chest. No matter how silly you think your problem might be. I want you to lean on me."

Because I want you. He clamped his mouth shut. Now wasn't the time to go that far with confessions today.

"I need to at least repay you a little. Not even when we spoke about your past did it get this heavy." Her tantalizing lips curved into a deep smile that sent a rush through him. It made him acutely aware of how well

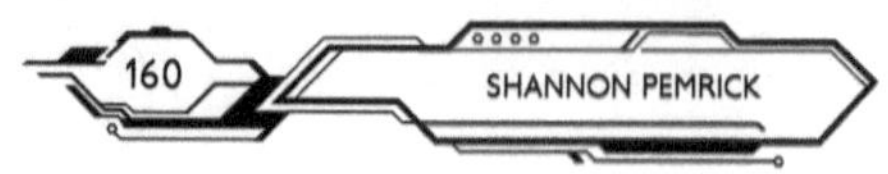

her body fit against his. How his hands fit perfectly into her curves. How tempting her soft skin was to touch.

Narissa pushed up onto her toes, her fingers fanning out across his chest, setting his skin ablaze. He sucked in a sharp breath when her lips met his. Her sweet scent invaded his nose, numbing his senses, and her taste seared into his mind.

All too soon for his liking, she pulled away. A playful smile sat on her lips as she turned and headed for the shore. He reached out for her, desperate to have her with him, but she was long out of his reach. She retrieved her towel and headed back to their campsite. It made him aware of how cold he was in this water.

He hurried out and followed her up, just catching her as she slipped behind the little fort setup she'd recreated from yesterday. It really was a clever idea, even if he wished she'd just be a little less reserved about changing clothes around him. *We'll have to work on that.*

He rummaged through his suitcase for clean clothes. When he dropped his swim trunks, he received a scoff from Narissa. "You couldn't wait for me to finish using this?"

"Why do I need it? I've got nothing to hide."

She muttered to herself, eliciting a chuckle from him. He was fussing with his shirt when she appeared around the Jeep.

"You're lucky I have pants on."

She tapped her lips with her finger, reminding him how much he'd like to devour them. "Hmm, it's as if I know something about male anatomy when it's cold." She grinned. "And how desperate men are to hide that knowledge, especially in the moment."

That may be true, but once the blood got pumping, that wasn't an issue. Especially for him. Ajax winked at her. "I could give you a hands-on experience if you're that eager to find out how right you are."

Her face flushed and she looked away. "No, I'm fine."

The change in her fascinated him. She switched between sexy vixen and shy innocence so quickly.

She held out her hand. "Hand me your shorts so I can dry them on my makeshift clothesline. Will be better than stuffing them wet into your suitcase."

"I was just going to toss them on the floor and deal with them later."

She scoffed and flexed her fingers. "Hand them over."

Ajax fussed with his pants and she gave him a stern look. "Behave, or you're not getting breakfast. And I'll use your first name for the remainder of the trip."

He exhaled and handed over his wet shorts. "Attacking a man's pride *and* stomach? You don't play fair."

She gave him a smug smile and disappeared behind the vehicle again. While she did that, he went about feeding the dogs—Crash making a mess like always, and then all too eager to clean it up herself. Narissa returned and pointed out what she'd worked up for breakfast.

She'd already created four average-size burritos, but she suspected that may not be enough for him, let alone her. There was quite a bit of egg and meat left, so he went to work making an "Ajax-sized" burrito, as she called it. He pushed the limit of the tortilla's capabilities.

As he finished, a couple chipmunks caught their attention. Narissa looked at the nuts she snacked on, and tossed a few to them. They scattered at first, but then returned to take their treat.

He wagged his finger at her. "Tsk, tsk. You shouldn't feed them. It encourages dependence."

She ducked her head. "Sorry. They're cute is all." Narissa then grinned, perplexing him. "But if feeding causes dependence, that means you can't be buying me food, else I'll become too dependent on you."

"That'd be true if you weren't such a stubborn and independent woman who needs no man."

This got her to laugh. He then smirked. "Besides, based on your logic, since you're cute, I'm still permitted to feed you."

She opened her mouth, and then closed it, unable to fight the corner she'd put herself in.

He bit into his burrito. "Not such a dumb jock now, am I?"

Her nose scrunched. "I'll get you back. Maybe by hiring a professional to teach you manners."

Ajax swallowed his food. "Mom already tried that."

She grumbled and then went about cleaning up. It wasn't long before they were packed, the dogs and Narissa were walked one more time, and they were back on the road.

About two hours later, they pulled into the long dirt road leading to the house. Narissa gazed out at the wooded scenery, enthralled just as she had been when they'd arrived at the gorge. She'd even made a few comments today on the way about how pretty the area was.

The car pulled up to the elegant open-concept home. Narissa's eyes widened and her lips made a silent "wow." The car pulled to a stop in the front and they climbed out. Narissa continued to gaze about as Ajax let the dogs loose. He pulled the suitcases and cooler out and

left everything else in the Jeep. He could take care of that later.

"C'mon, I'll show you inside."

She nodded absently. Narissa let out a gasp when she followed him inside.

"I guess I don't have to ask if you like it."

"It's amazing. I didn't expect such a cozy but modern and high-tech appearance to it."

He grinned. "What, don't tell you me you were thinking it was some sort of dilapidated shack."

Narissa chuckled. "No, but I did think it was a log cabin."

Ajax waved the thought off. "Too much maintenance."

He then motioned for her to come in further. "I'll show you to the guest room."

"What, not going to invite me to stay in yours?" She smirked.

Ajax chuckled. "Well, if you want to, be my guest."

Narissa shook her head.

"I did some food supply ordering a little bit ago, so we'll get that delivery soon. Mostly basic essentials. If we need extra we can always get more in."

She nodded. "Sounds good."

"I thought we'd just take it easy for today. Let you settle in and let us recoup from such a long trip."

"I think that's a perfect idea. Of course, we all know my idea of relaxation is working, just at a slower pace."

Ajax chuckled. "I'll be sure to keep work away. Now, let's get you settled in."

CHAPTER 10

arissa stirred, morning light filtering in through the window invading her dreams. She snuggled deeper into her pillow. She didn't want to wake up. She wanted to go back to her dream.

Eyes cracked, she touched her lips. She kissed Ajax again in her sleep. She didn't even know what came over her yesterday. She'd even approached it with more confidence than she actually had. And all because he listened to her problems. He didn't need to do all of this for her. *And yet he—*

A slobbery tongue smacked her face. She groaned and that enticed her "assailant" to nudge her with a cold, wet nose and more licks. "Okay, okay, I'll get up."

Reluctantly, she sat up, and Crash wagged her tail, her tongue lolling and flea-bitten ears twitching. She jumped off the bed and ran to the doorway, stopping and looking back. She then tore out of the room and into the house. She could hear Ajax chuckling downstairs, and then thumping she could only imagine was either Crash running into something or Helios and Crash playing.

Narissa glanced at the clock. It was only eight in the morning. *Dogs.* At least it wasn't as bad as children. She'd watched a few young cousins overnight before. She wasn't a fan of the four and five A.M. wakeup calls.

She went about getting ready for the morning. Her shower was a refreshing and welcome change from the cold river water from yesterday.

Ajax looked up from the bowl of cereal he ate as he leaned against the counter when she came into the room. From the looks of it, he'd also been reading something, based on the device on the counter.

Crash ran around like her maniac self. She'd seen firsthand these past two days just how hard it was to get all that energy out of her. And even if you did tucker her out, with five minutes of rest, it was back. Narissa wondered how possible it would be to harness energy like that.

"Morning." Ajax nodded to a coffee maker. "Coffee is in the pot."

Narissa nodded. "Great. What do we have for breakfast?"

Ajax took another bite of his. "Cereal. Granola. Fruit. Bacon and sausage. Eggs for various applications. Pancake and waffle mix. Lot of stuff to choose from."

She poured herself a cup of coffee while contemplating her options. She usually opted for fruit or eggs, but the concept of eating cereal appealed to her. She opened the cupboard and her brow furrowed. There were five boxes of cereal, but they were all Apple Jacks. "Um…"

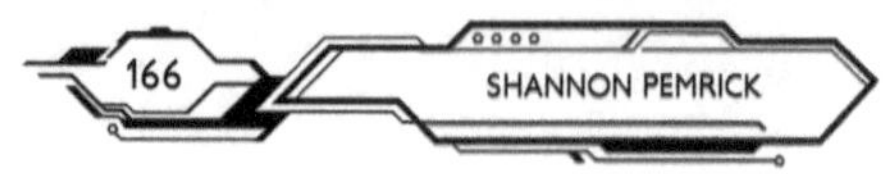

Ajax raised a brow, his spoon still partially in his mouth. "What?"

"What's with all the cereal being Apple Jacks?"

He frowned. "Do you not like them?"

"It's not that…" She'd honestly never had the sugary treat. She just didn't understand why he'd stocked so many boxes.

"Well, it's my favorite cereal," he said before eating more. "If it's a problem, I can order in something else for you."

His favorite, huh? That made sense if he had maybe two boxes. But five? That was more of an obsession. *Wait…*

The gears in her head turned. She placed her hand on the counter and stared at him. "This is how you got your name, isn't it?"

Ajax stopped chewing his food, his eyes going a little wide. "No."

She let out a half laugh and leaned against the counter. "It is. What the hell? Really?"

He'd never told her the origin of the name Ajax. Any time she'd asked, he'd always change the topic.

Ajax hung his head and sighed. "It's all Kiara. Because I ate so much of this stuff as a kid, she started calling me Apple Jack. It was so infuriating." He ate some more. "Then, I figured out how to own it. I thought if I could change it in a way that would sound cool, it could at least become bearable. Darius gave me a hand, too. Ajax came out of all the brainstorming, and Kiara liked it enough that she was convinced to call me that instead. Darius used the name as well, and it just stuck for everyone else."

He grinned at her. "Only a select few people are allowed to call me anything else, and even fewer can know the origins."

Narissa gave a closed-mouth chuckle and made a zipping motion to her lips. Such a cheesy origin, but she shouldn't have expected anything else from him. This man was all cheese. *Well, eighty percent, and twenty percent pure sexy eye candy.*

"Might as well give this cereal a try after that story."

A smile spread across Ajax's face and he helped her get a bowl ready. She took a bite and nodded as the various flavors coalesced on her tongue. "Not bad. Definitely a kids' food, though, with all the sugar."

Ajax held his head high. "Well, my inner child likes it."

Narissa snickered. "What do you mean, inner child? You're all child."

He pointed his spoon at her. "Watch it. Or I won't let you come into my fort."

She shrugged. "Fine. I'll just build an even better one. And I'll have dogs because they love me so much."

Crash barked, as if agreeing to her claim.

Ajax pouted. "Truce?"

Oh my God... She shouldn't put into words how cute that face was. An ordinary man, she wouldn't say that, but this was Ajax. So much so, how could she say no? "Can we actually build a fort? That sounds like a lot of fun."

He pumped his fist. "Hell yeah!"

She laughed as he ran off to retrieve various items for building. This allowed her to get her breakfast in her, as well as much needed coffee without disruption. By the time she was ready, so was he.

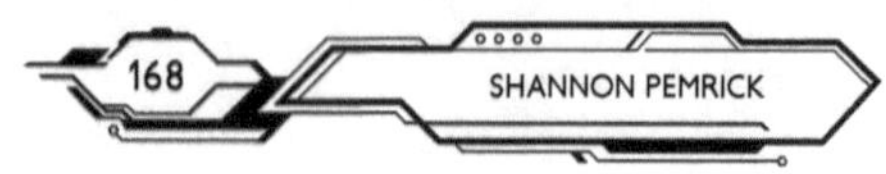

Using his strong physique, he singlehandedly moved the heavy furniture and chairs, while she did the blanket coverings and pillows. Ajax brushed his hands against each other, as if dusting them off, when they finished. "There, perfect."

Narissa giggled, looking at their adult-sized fort. "I can't believe we did this."

He shrugged. "Why not? It's fun to break the mold of adult and just do whatever. And forts are perfect for that." He headed for the kitchen. "And it'll be the perfect spot to do some work. I've been catching up on my reading for the cybernetics stuff you gave me. It's interesting, although I think you're going to have to clarify some things for me."

Narissa smiled. His excitement elated her. Sure, the fort had him acting a little giddy like a kid, but if he was reading her notes without prompting, that told her he was serious about all this. The partnership wasn't just a ploy to get her out here. He wouldn't have needed to go that far. *I'm glad he asked, though.* She really wanted to be part of this project. And to work alongside him.

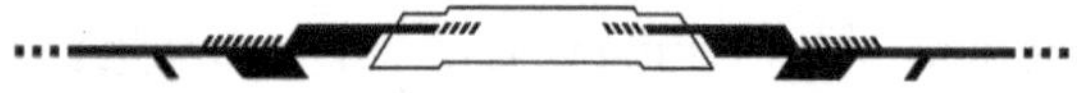

Ajax adjusted his glasses and pointed to a spot in the notes. "This is something I don't understand."

Narissa scooted closer, being careful not to disrupt the pillows she'd set up, and peered at his tablet. "Oh, that's explained back here."

She scrolled back to some notes earlier on. "See, this is the component that links the signals."

He gazed at her. "I'm not clear, can you explain in further detail?"

He did actually understand—there had been many times when he asked for clarification he didn't need, but he just wanted to hear her talk.

A lopsided smile appeared on her pretty face. "You sure?"

She was starting to catch on. He could see it. That intelligence of hers wasn't something he could pull fast ones over for long. *And it's sexy that I can't.* As much as it was infuriating, too. He was going to have to try something different soon. "Yeah. I think I'm almost there, but I believe if you explain it, everything will just click."

She sighed. "Very well."

Narissa jumped to the start of the reading section, rubbing her eye as if it were bothering her. This gave him an idea.

Ajax removed his glasses and handed them to her. "I know we have a difference in opinion on the effectiveness of blue-light-blocking glasses, but I think you should wear them. Protect your pretty eyes."

She gave him a long, suspicious look that amused him, and then took the eyewear. She slipped them onto her face, her eyes ticking up to him. "Better?"

Ajax's heart stopped. He'd seen her with her large sunglasses and they looked great on her, but this style of eye wear looked different on her. She looked even better than he'd imagined—sexier and smarter, if that was even possible.

A knowing grin spread across Narissa's face. *Busted.* "I'll take that as a yes."

She went to explaining further, referencing some

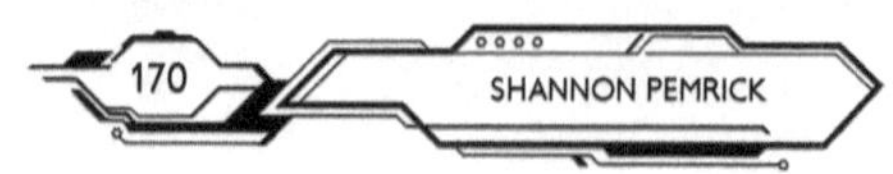

older material, as well as scrolling ahead to some notes he hadn't gotten to yet. *Saving grace for me.* He'd filled in the blanks, of course, but at least he could use that as an excuse. A poor one, but valid.

Her eyes squinted as she got into her lesson and her smile widened as she went. Ajax could listen to her all day.

He leaned on one hand, taking her all in under this fort they'd built together. So much passion in her. It was amazing. She was amazing. It came out even in random suggestions, like this fort. The effect this place had on her already was better than he could have hoped.

Narissa stopped abruptly and ticked an eyebrow at him. "Are you even paying attention?"

He grinned. "Have you ever listened to yourself talk? I mean, really listen? Even on a recording. It's amazing."

Her face tinted a shade and she looked down at the tablet. "I just know what I'm doing, that's all."

Ajax reached out and lifted her chin. "No, that's not it. Not solely. You have an incredible passion that's so amazing to see."

She struggled for words, making him grin. It was amusing to see her battle against genuine praise. It seemed to get worse when he gave it to her, though. Something about him causing her to fumble and need to collect herself drew him to her more.

"Why don't we take a break?" he suggested. He didn't want to mess with her too badly and cause an issue. Plus being this close to her in such an intimate space made her extra tempting to indulge in. But her actions with him told him to keep himself in check, for now.

"We haven't been going over all this very long," she said.

Ajax shrugged. "Breaks are good. And I'm getting the itch to play some Lusara Fates since we've been unable to for the last two days."

She sighed, but gave in. "Fine."

He knew it. She wanted to have a little bit of fun and change to her routine just as much as him. The two of them crawled out of their fort, the dogs taking their places, causing Narissa to laugh.

Ajax got some more food in him, as did Narissa, and then two of them headed for their stationary gaming chairs set up in each of their rooms.

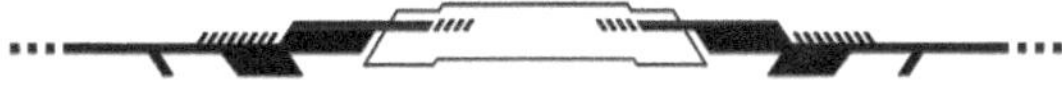

Ajax looked over his quests, Narissa waiting next to him. He was supposed to be going through the list to get an idea of the next expansion hype quests he'd already started, so they could do some together, but he found himself distracted.

Instead of healing on her priest, as she usually opted for, Narissa had chosen to swap over to her DPS specialization. And the gear she had for it, well, the tasteful side boob wasn't the only bit of skin showing.

Narissa's focus on him faded and she stared off into nothing. His brow ticked up. "What's up?"

"I have a phone call. I'll be right back." She logged off. He frowned. He was supposed to have her to himself this trip. But someone always seemed to take her attention away.

Ajax tried to busy himself in his quest log searching,

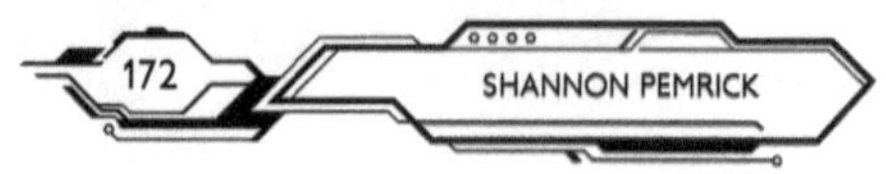

but after ten minutes passed, he couldn't stand waiting for her to come back. He opened his menu to log off when Narissa logged back in.

Her brow twisted. "Were you just about to leave?"

He nodded, dismissing the window. "You were taking so long I was concerned."

Narissa smiled. "Well, thank you. It's okay. I was just talking to Dylan. He wanted to make sure I was doing okay still."

Dylan. Of course she'd be talking to him. And of course, he'd remind her of her situation.

Narissa frowned. "What's wrong? What is with that face?"

Shit. He should have kept himself in check. "What face?"

"That displeased face you've given before when I mentioned Dylan."

Ajax shook his head. "I don't know what you're talking about, Rissa. Nothing is wrong."

She crossed her arms, her eyes narrowing. "Don't treat me like I'm stupid."

He scowled. "I'm not."

"Then what's the issue about me talking with Dylan?"

"Because he reminds you of this Nolan situation, instead of letting you forget about it." He didn't mean to word it that way, but his temper was rising, and that made him shoot off his mouth without thinking.

Narissa pressed her lips together and nodded. "So you think my friends aren't allowed to check up on me to make sure I'm doing okay?"

"That's not what I'm saying. I just don't see why he has to check in on you every day, as if a phone call is

going to make a difference." Wow, he was acting like a disgruntled teenager.

She shook her head. "And I don't see why you're acting like an ass all of a sudden. I don't have an issue with him checking on me. I quite like it, because it shows he cares. And unlike you, I do think that care being shown every day does make a difference."

Narissa opened her menu. "I'm going to go work. I'm not interested in playing with you if you're going to act like this."

Ajax's irritation flared up into anger as she disappeared from the game. He also logged out and sat in his gaming chair, stewing. He wasn't sure what he was more pissed about—his behavior, or Dylan. They were related, so it made sense.

Why did Dylan make him feel so threatened? He had no proof that he was after Narissa, too—and even if he was, Ajax had the upper hand by having Narissa here. Of course, if he was going to continue to make an ass of himself, he may as well hand it all over to Dylan on a silver platter.

"Ajax," Kirk said from the room. "I've got some research for you."

"I'm not in the mood to work right now," Ajax said.

"It's not work. Please take a look at your phone."

Ajax sighed and slipped out of his chair. He retrieved his phone and took a look. Kirk had pulled up two pages on his web browser. They were about Dylan. Dylan, who was married.

He sighed. Of course he'd let his mind get the better of him. He didn't have competition. Dylan was nothing more than a concerned friend, just as Narissa said.

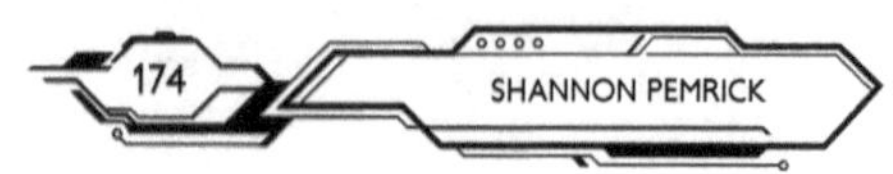

But that didn't make him feel better. He really had acted like an ass with Narissa. Friend or potential rival of his, his actions had been uncalled for. Dylan was allowed to check on her, and as often as Narissa deemed, not him.

Ajax knew why that part of the situation got to him, and he had no right to take that out on Narissa. He left the room. He needed to apologize. He didn't expect her to forgive him, but it was the right thing to do.

Ajax came to the guest room she stayed in and knocked on the partially closed door. "Rissa?"

"Yeah?" Her tone told him she wasn't thrilled he'd come by.

"Can I come in?"

"Sure."

He entered, finding her sitting on the bed, her phone in her hand. Ajax suspected she was ranting with Shira and Mercedes. Whenever something bad happened, those three went at it with each other. "Hey, I just wanted to tell you, I'm sorry about how I acted earlier."

Her brow rose. "Oh, really?"

Ajax nodded, licking his lips, as he found it hard to look at her. "I shouldn't have taken my frustration with myself out on you and your friendship with Dylan."

Narissa's shoulders relaxed. "What do you mean?"

"It's true that Dylan's check-ins irritate me because it reminds you of Nolan, and we had discussed how much I'd rather you not think about that half-a-meatball as much as possible."

Narissa couldn't stop herself from giggling at the stupid term he'd picked.

"But, his check-ins reminds me how much I might

be failing you. I haven't once asked you how you were feeling. I just assumed because you weren't talking to me about your feelings, or obviously shutting me out, that you were fine." Ajax ran his fingers through his hair. "And that wasn't fair of me to do to you. So, I'm sorry for doing that."

Narissa took a moment to respond, and that made him twitchy. "Thank you for the apology." She looked down at her phone and then back up at him. "And just so you know, I'm happy with the way you've handled this. It's nice having at least one person not fuss every day, when I've been doing fine as long as I haven't had constant reminders."

Well, at least he did one thing right. He turned. "I'll leave you be now. If you need me, I'll be in my work room."

"Andrew," she said as he left. He turned back and she smiled so wide her eyes squinted. "Thank you. For caring enough to bring me here."

The expression brought a smile to his face, too. "Always."

CHAPTER 11

Ajax transferred new reading material to Narissa's tablet. After their little fight, she'd talked with Shira and Mercedes, who were convinced Ajax was jealous for some reason. She couldn't see that happening with someone like him, but they were adamant about the possibility. When he came in to make up, his words eased the tension out of her and shut out what the girls tried to claim. She'd gone back to studying after all that.

Narissa had gotten through the introduction bit he'd provided the other day, and now had another chunk to go through. Ajax offered to go over it with her, but since it was late, she figured she'd read a little before going to bed.

"I'm going to be up late working," he said. "I have a few things going through my head that won't let me sleep for a while."

"Okay, if you need me for anything, give me a shout,"

she said. "If this is as engrossing as the last packet, I'll be up for a while."

He nodded and let her leave his work room. Crash padded after her. She'd become Narissa's faithful companion these days, and Narissa didn't mind one bit. She enjoyed the scrappy dog's company. And she wasn't a bed hog.

Narissa changed into her nightwear and curled up in her bed. She started her research, keeping one hand on Crash as she fell asleep next to her. The sounds of the forest drifted into her open window. Narissa read page after page, but got to a point where some of what Ajax wrote wasn't clicking. She reread, and even pulled up the introductory information to make sure she wasn't missing something. But it still didn't click.

She sighed and slipped out of bed. Looked like she'd be bothering Ajax after all. She didn't want to interrupt him; he should be allowed to work on his project without her getting in the way. Sure, they were going to be partners in all this, but she didn't want to step on his toes and hinder any progress.

Narissa descended the stairs and made her way to Ajax's work room, tablet in hand. As she drew closer to the room, she heard odd sounds coming from it. *Sounds like… grunting.* She rolled her eyes. He really couldn't stop himself from working out. Yes, it helped him develop the nice physique she loved as much as he did, but it was an addiction he needed to be careful with. *He could hurt—*

She stopped dead in her mental tracks when she opened the door and didn't find him working out. He sat in a chair by one of his desks, phone in one hand, hard manhood in the other.

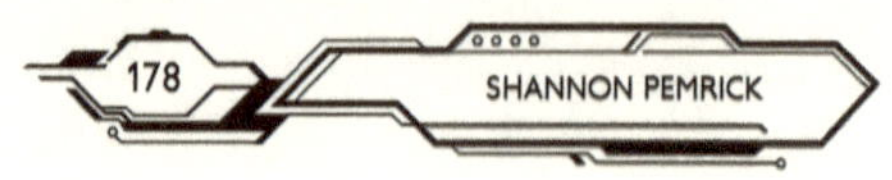

The two stared at each other—Ajax surprised, Narissa embarrassed. Her whole body felt like it was on fire.

"Hey, Rissa," he said, the greeting so casual, like nothing was weird about this.

Maybe it's not. She really had two options here. She could turn around, and walk away as if none of this happened and hope things were fine between them in the morning. Or she could own this situation.

Scared and damaged twenty-two-year-old Narissa said to run. That nothing could come of any confidence here, and Nolan was right about her. That she wasn't worth anything, and that the only reason anyone wanted her was because she had fame and money, and had a decent body to use. But thirty-year-old Narissa disagreed.

She said she was worth it, Nolan was wrong, and that she needed to own this situation and this fine man. That there was nothing wrong in indulging in life's pleasures. To splurge and do something crazy—do something crazy with a sinfully hot friend who wouldn't judge her in any way, and would be more than willing to get a little liberal with the friends line without losing that friendship.

Thirty-year-old Narissa was older and more experienced, and that made her wiser. Or in the very least more willing to take risks for the sake of adventure.

Narissa tapped her tablet against her hand. "Well, I came down to ask for some help, but it seems you might need some instead."

Ajax leaned back in his chair, letting himself go, but not facing her as his eyebrow spiked. "You want to give me a hand?"

She shrugged. "Only if you want me to." She grinned,

trying to be confident even though she didn't feel it. "I did say if you needed *anything*, after all."

Ajax faced her then, erect manhood on full display. *Lord have mercy… He really is a fine specimen.* There were no steroids used on this man. Not with his impressive size.

His eyes pinned on her, his mouth curved into that devil half-smile of his, and he beckoned her with a single cybernetic finger.

With everything she had in her, she took long, confident steps toward him, breaking eye contact to drop the tablet on his desk. Instead of focusing on him immediately, she stood there and took in what she had to work with on the desk. Tissues, lube. It was all there. And then there was his phone. She swiped the screen, curious about what he'd been using for material.

Long dark curls, and curvy form, a sensual and still tasteful image of a dark-skinned porn actress displayed on full view. *Bella Stazra again.* This particular actress focused on particular angles and poses mainstream media still couldn't understand worked for both men *and* women.

Narissa's eyes ticked to him. "You have good taste."

Ajax pulled her closer by the hips, his hardness pressing against her protected femininity. This rewarded him with a small gasp from her. He was tempting. "Actors are just that. The person they pretend to be isn't real. I'd prefer to focus on what's real in front of me."

A smile curved up Narissa's lips. He knew how to entice a woman with words, that was for sure. She rocked her hips against his hot swollen flesh as best she could in her current position. She received a small groan from him, curling her smile more.

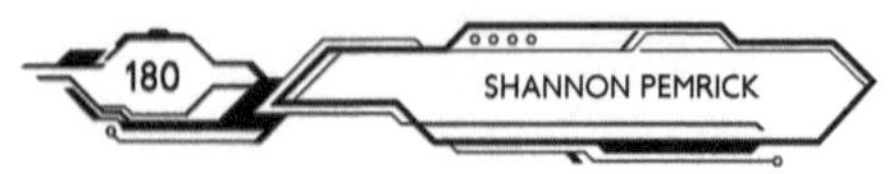

She applied some lube to her hand and then leaned in, her lips hovering over his. "I'll show you just how real I am."

Narissa captured his lips with hers as her hand dipped between them and grazed his aroused shaft. Ajax's grip on her hips tightened and accepted and deepened the kiss. His musky peppermint scent enveloped her again. She loved it, wanted it around her always, like the most addictive drug. But this wasn't about her. The agreement was for him. And that's what she'd give him.

One hand firm against his sculpted chest, she wrapped her hand around him and stroked, gentle and rhythmic. The kiss broke for a moment as his breathing hitched in tune with her touch. Then came the need.

Ajax's hand tangled in her hair and pulled her in for a demanding kiss. A small whimper came from her throat, a quick wave of excitement bursting through her. It surprised her. Such an action with Nolan wouldn't have cause the same reaction. Then again, Nolan wouldn't have come anywhere close to this route of fun.

Ajax's other hands squeezed her ass and then migrated. His massive hand roamed her body—feeling every curve, teasing every nerve. The sensation was better than she'd imagined.

She pulled away and gasped when cool air hit her chest. Taking a controlled breath, she looked down at her exposed full breasts, dark nipples taut from all the excitement. She didn't expect this. This was just him, after all.

Ajax cast an appreciative glance over them before locking gazes with her. Narissa's breath caught. So much lust and want filled those eyes. Nolan never looked at

her this way. Never made her feel—*Fuck Nolan!* He didn't matter right now.

Ajax took both his thumbs and rolled them over her sensitive peaks. Narissa gasped and then bit her bottom lips as she moaned, her eyes hooding. Heat and need built in her core. Her strokes increased, and for a moment she thought of pushing this farther than planned, but kept her wits about her.

Ajax's touch stopped and he suddenly pulled her closer, resting his forehead on her. "Keep going."

She complied, and added a little extra. Dipping her head closer, she nipped his lower lip. He twitched in her hand and she repeated the action, this time sinking her teeth into his flesh and holding on for a moment. Ajax placed both his hands on her face and kissed her hard, until she saw white. He pulled away and threw his head back as his breathing labored.

Her strokes continued, long and hard, like him. His breathing became quick gasps, and his shaft swelled in her grip until he grunted and spent himself in her hand. She slowed her rhythm until she stilled as he had. The only sound in the room now was his ragged breathing.

Ajax wet his lips and lifted his hand, but then dropped it, no words able to come from his mouth as euphoric sensation still coursed through him. Smirking, Narissa pulled away, cleaning herself up, and then him. It was only polite.

She fixed her nightgown and then retrieved her tablet. "Good night, Andrew."

Narissa didn't make it more than two steps before his strong hands grabbed her by the hips and pulled her back. She gasped when her back hit his chest and she found herself sitting in his lap, facing away from him.

He bent close to her ear. "Where do you think you're going?"

His hot breath sent a shiver down her spine. "Bed? I did what I offered, so we're done."

His teeth grazed her ear, causing her to gasp again. "That's not how it works. This isn't a one-sided arrangement."

There was more to this? It'd be one-sided with Nolan more often than not. If he got off before her, then that was it, they were done. It was honestly a miracle she got pregnant, with that kind of lackluster treatment.

Ajax's cybernetic hand slid over her thigh and between her legs, grazing her wet center. "You don't leave here until you're satisfied, understand?"

Momma said no touching the devil's doorbell, but I'm all too happy to let him ring that. Narissa swallowed hard, her breath hitching. "Then why are you stalling?"

"Stalling?" His teeth grazed her neck and he took her tablet away. "No. Waiting for your invitation."

Ajax nudged her panties aside and slipped his finger into her slick heat. Narissa gasped and moaned as he found rhythm in his strokes. Heat built up in her core, spreading through her body.

Ajax's other hand found the front of her nightgown and tugged it down again. She sucked in a tight breath as cool air once again bit at her sensitive buds. He rolled a dark peak between his thumb and index finger. Her back arched, need building in her.

She never felt this with Nolan. Something so basic, it became a means to an end by itself. But with Ajax—she moaned when he tweaked her nipple. Her fingers curled against his arms, his rhythm between her legs increasing.

"Please, Andrew," she whispered. She should have specified what she wanted, but the words wouldn't form.

Ajax slipped a finger inside her, then another, pushing in deep, increasing her pleasure just as she asked. Words weren't needed for such a request. A man like him, he just knew.

Narissa moaned, deep and heavy. She reached back and grabbed a fistful of his hair, pulling him closer. He nipped at her skin again, sending quick, amplified bursts of desire across her body.

Desire built deep within her. She didn't know which sensation to focus on. She bit her lower lip.

"Don't hold back like you did earlier," he murmured in her ear, his voice husky and deep with need. "I want to hear how pleased you are."

The flush stinging her cheeks amplified. Nolan had preferred her quiet. And so as to not disturb her neighbors during her own alone time, she'd kept up the habit.

Ajax rubbed his thumb against her pleasure button while still keeping rhythm with his other fingers. All of it was too much and still not enough for her.

Her grip tightened and her breath labored. Her hips bucked. Narissa whispered out his name and then screamed with pleasure as ecstasy flooded over her. Ajax didn't let up until she rode out her high to the end.

He kissed the tip of her ear as she relaxed into him. "Such a beautiful sound you make."

She gave a lazy smile. "Thank you."

It was weird to thank someone for such a compliment. But it seemed right. Or maybe she was thanking him

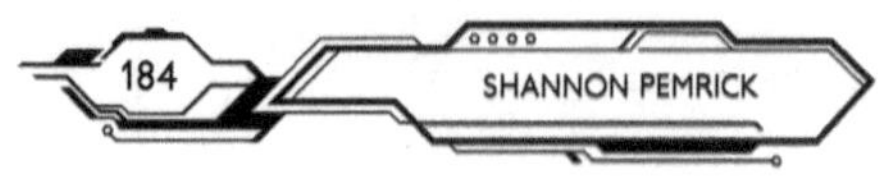

for this sensation she still felt. Not even she'd gotten herself off this well.

Narissa gasped when he slid his real fingers between her thighs. "Andrew?"

He kissed her neck. "I want to hear it again."

Another? "But I've never—"

The confession lodged in her throat. She was lucky to get one with Nolan, and she'd never tried for more on her own.

Ajax chuckled in her ear. "Well then, we'll find out if you can now. I really want to feel that this time."

He found rhythm in his strokes. Narissa bit her lip as overwhelming sensations rushed through her. She'd almost forgotten he didn't have the upgraded cybernetic with nerve stimulation. With him constantly destroying his, he wasn't a possible candidate for selection.

God, this feels amazing. She moaned and ground her hips into his hand, her blood simmering. He continued his touch, pushing his fingers inside her at the same time. Narissa gasped. Apparently she'd done well at mirroring his cybernetic against his natural limb. She couldn't tell the difference between the two as she teetered on the edge.

Ajax cupped her breast with his artificial hand, squeezing and playing with her. Her eyes hooded and her lips parted as another orgasm burst through her. She swore her cries could be heard miles into the forest, and she didn't care.

She sighed as her high dissipated, leaving her a pile of mush in his arms. Ajax dragged a finger across her skin, tiny little residual sensations pricking through her.

"I guess I can," she said, her voice lazy.

He pulled her close, smiling into her neck. "You're welcome."

Narissa allowed herself to remain like this in his arms a moment longer before pulling away and fixing her clothes. She swore she caught a disappointed sigh from him.

"You came here with a question," he said as she retrieved her tablet.

She glanced over her shoulder, grinning at him. "I got my answer. Thank you."

It wasn't a lie. This change in routine had cleared her mind, and now the answers she needed formed in her mind all on their own.

"Good night, Andrew."

She sashayed out of the room. She'd either continue reading into the night, or sleep. Maybe even dream of Ajax. She wouldn't mind that.

CHAPTER 12

Ajax pointed to the diagram. "No, no. This piece here is what allows the conversion."

Narissa's brow furrowed and then she pointed to her notes. "But this here says that is only a stabilizer."

He opened his mouth and then shut it, taking the tablet to read. He then looked at the diagram. Which was wrong, his memory or his notes? They'd come across a few of these discrepancies today. He was pretty sure the notes were wrong. He wasn't the only one who wrote them. And that wasn't an excuse not to move. Her sitting next to him, with her legs over his acting as a table for the various paper diagrams, in those cute shorts that accentuated her curves—that wasn't an excuse, either. *Yes it is.*

He couldn't get last night out of his mind. It followed him through sleep and even now. Her soft form against him—her irresistible figure on display. He wanted to

ditch the work and pin her down on this couch—hear her scream his name again. It was addicting.

But Ajax knew he needed to be careful. Last night could have been a fluke; it most likely was. His little vixen priestess had chosen to own the situation she walked in on, but had he not been caught in such a position, last night would have gone far closer to the status quo.

She tilted her head, smiling. "You know, we could go to your lab and take a look at each of these issues I've found. Hands-on experience can help clear up any confusion."

He'd show her some hands-on experience, long into the day as she rode him. Ajax pinched his nose. He needed to clear his head. "Yeah, you're probably right. Some fresh air could do us some good, too."

Narissa's phone rang. She picked it up, but didn't answer, intriguing him. "Picard, why isn't a name coming up?"

"Sorry, Doctor," her assistant said from the phone. "I'm struggling to obtain identification."

The called ended, but then soon after rang again. She swallowed and they both guessed it was the same person.

"Could it possibly be a client?" he asked.

She shook her head. "Clients always have to go through the main company line."

The phone rang a third time. Ajax held out his hand. "Let me answer."

Narissa nodded and handed the phone over. He swiped the screen and placed it up to his ear. "Andrew's Painting Service."

Narissa pressed her lips together, trying not to laugh. This was his typical prank line, but in a situation like this, it came in handy.

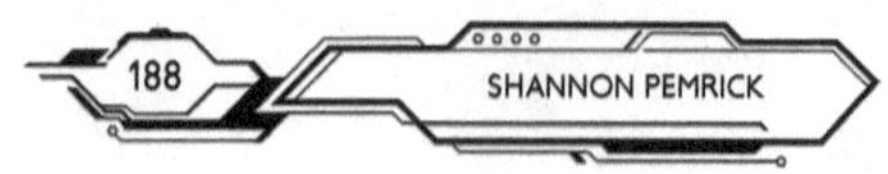

"Who is this?" a male voice questioned on the other end. He didn't sound pleased.

This sent a red flag immediately. Narissa froze up, the volume of the phone high enough for her to hear.

"My name is Andrew, sir," Ajax said. "I own this painting service. How can I help you?"

"Where is Narissa?"

"I'm sorry, who?"

"Put Narissa on the line."

Ajax glanced over at Narissa. Her eyes were wide with terror and her hands trembled. She shook her head.

He knew what to do. "I'm sorry, sir, but I don't know that name."

"I know she's there." The man sounded more irritated. "She hasn't been at work. Gone away. Vacation perhaps. With a friend, I know. With you? You're the replacement. That means she's sitting right next to you. Isn't she?"

"Who is this?" Ajax asked. "If this is some sort of prank call, I'm going to call the authorities for harassment."

"I will talk to her." The line went dead.

Ajax looked at the phone, brow furrowed, and then to Narissa. She looked ready to go into a panic. "Rissa."

"T–that was him. That was Nolan."

He was afraid of that. "Rissa, I need you to stay calm for me, please."

"I changed… I changed my number and made it so no one could find it in a public space." She snatched the phone from him and dialed. "Dylan?"

As irritated as a part of him was to hear that name, he shoved it away. This was the best person for her to call.

"Dylan, he called me." Her voice cracked. It hurt to hear. "He just called."

She stood up and paced, making it impossible for him to hear Dylan's responses.

"No, he didn't give a name. No, my friend picked up the phone and tried to get information from him without giving away any of mine. No, he didn't cooperate, but no matter what my friend said, he was insistent he had the right number and would speak with me."

"Officer Dylan," Picard said, the AI's voice coming through its usual speaker, though Ajax knew it'd go through the phone as any normal voice would, too, for the other person on the line. "I have the data and recording packaged for transmittal, if you'll take it as evidence. The line used was either public or encrypted; I couldn't trace much during the call."

Ajax waited as silence permeated the air. Narissa fidgeted as she listened. Then she spoke. "Thank you for looking into this. I'll do as you suggest."

She hung up the phone and Ajax opened his mouth, but she held up a finger and dialed another number. "Lilian. It's me, Narissa. Something's happened."

Ajax was forced to endure this half-sided conversation again, as she told this Lilian person what happened and recounted her conversation with Dylan. From what he picked up, he guessed Lilian might be a lawyer. *That's good. Maybe she'll have some advice.*

"Thank you, Lilian, I will." She sounded dejected. The call ended and Narissa stood there, her hands shaking.

"Rissa, come over here," Ajax said, patting the couch. He didn't want to approach her in this state. He was

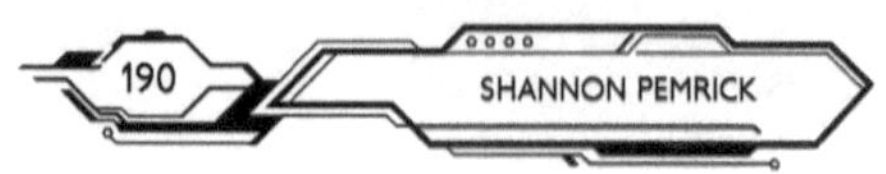

afraid to trigger something, and that was the last thing he wanted to do.

Narissa complied but didn't look at him. He reached out and lifted her chin with a single finger. Her dark, fear-stricken eyes welled up with tears. "Dylan can only look into it, and what he can do is limited. Lilian's hands are tied. They can't help me."

There went that idea. Ajax pulled her close and she cried into his chest. He stroked her back, rage boiling inside him. *How dare he do this to her!* "You're safe here, Rissa. He can't get you here. I won't let him."

She snuggled into to him more, her sobbing continuing.

He nuzzled her. "Don't let him get to you. Don't let that corndog win."

Narissa hiccupped as her crying ceased immediately. She pulled away and gave him a questioning stare. "Did… did you just call him a corndog?"

He smirked. "Yep. I almost called him a dildo, but corndogs don't bring as much excitement in someone's life."

Narissa giggled and sniffled. He wiped a stray tear off her cheek. "There we go. Don't let him steal your laughter."

He kissed her firm on the forehead. "And I promise, as long as I'm around, he's not getting near you. I'll go to jail before that happens."

A small smile spread over her lips. "I'll make sure there's bail money in the bank."

He grinned. "I'll be sure to keep the prison tatts to a minimum while you do."

Narissa laughed, making him happy. He didn't want

this dickwad to loom over her like some sinister cloud of doom.

"Let's go into town and do something?" he suggested. "It'll get us out of the house and get something fun done."

She looked down at the research notes. "But, what about me learn—"

He pressed his thumb against her lips. "We can get to it later. There's no rush getting you up to speed. I'm okay with making this project wait a little longer." He smirked. "Won't kill me."

She laughed. "Okay, fine. Where do we want to go?"

"Well, since you really want to see a bear, and we haven't yet, I thought we'd pay a visit to the zoo."

A big smile spread across her face. "Yes."

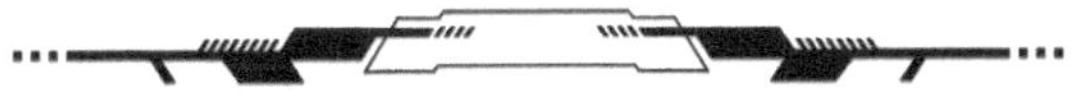

Narissa giggled as several Loriini birds sat on her arms, wanting a taste of the sweet nectar treat she offered in her hands. So far their trip to this zoo had been fantastic. Seeing all the animals roaming around in large enclosures designed just for them was such a wondrous sight. She even got to see some of the baby animals born this year—a little Asian elephant named Citra, and some wolf cubs.

She laughed some more, and birds in the aviary flocked to Ajax. Some even landed on his head. He didn't mind, on the contrary, he seemed to enjoy the birds' attention. This side of him made it hard for her to resist him. He was all kinds of perfect. *But Nolan...*

As much as this trip was supposed to help forget about

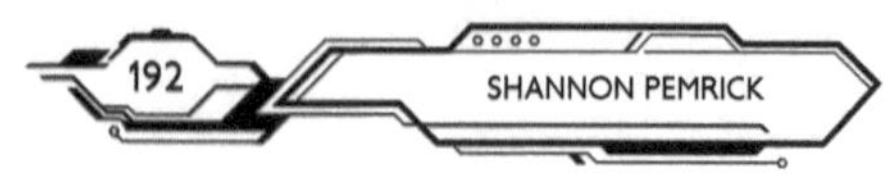

him, she couldn't. His calling her added to her fears. She knew he wasn't going to leave her alone. He'd never forgive her for getting him thrown in jail, even though it was his own fault. But a part of her had really hoped he'd just go on his way and leave her alone finally.

And now Ajax… He was going to get caught up in it all. His promises to keep her safe made her feel better. She could feel it in the way he held her, they weren't just words to him. But at the same time, it was wrong to get him mixed up in this mess of hers. He deserved better.

Ajax lifted her chin. Her heart jumped. Every time he did this particular action, her body reacted. Something about it made her feel different. *Something about the way he looks at me—*

"Narissa, stop," he said. "I know that look. You promised you wouldn't think about him."

She looked away. "I'm sorry. I'm trying."

He frowned. "Are you not having fun?"

Her eyes widened. "Of course I am! This trip is so amazing." She giggled when one of the birds tickled her ear. "And this interactive enclosure is one of the best things we've done today."

Narissa frowned. "I'm just having a hard time shaking earlier. It's going to take me a bit."

He stroked her cheek, sending another jolt through her. "What else can I do to help?"

She shook her head. "Just keep doing what you've been doing. I promise it's helping. Without all this treatment, I'd be far worse off."

She wasn't lying. As much as involving him in her problems wasn't right, she knew she'd be worse off

without him there, by her side. *It makes it so hard not wanting more.*

"Are you okay with all this treatment?"

The question surprised her. Upon looking up at him, she found, for the first time since ever knowing him, uncertainty crossing his face. *Good going, Narissa.* Now she was making someone as confident at Ajax question his own actions, when he shouldn't.

She looked away out of guilt. "I'm just… not used to it. Each time you do something nice for me, it reminds me how poorly Nolan treated me. And you and me? We're just friends. It's painful knowing how naïve I'd been to accept what he offered. Looking back and seeing how little was there, and yet I'd been so completely fooled."

Ajax reached out with his cybernetic hand, the only side the birds couldn't congregate on, and wiped away a tear rolling down her cheek. *Shit.* Narissa rubbed the eye, trying not to disturb the birds too much, and turned away. "I'm sorry. You don't need to deal with this."

She took a few steps to walk away, but came to a halt when Ajax hooked his finger into her belt loop. He tugged. "Come back here."

She stepped backward until she pressed against his strong form. Ajax rested his face against the back of her head. "Please do not run away from me. Or how you're feeling. You're not a burden."

In that moment, nothing around them mattered. She didn't care how other visitors saw them. "That's not true."

"I wouldn't say it if it weren't. I don't have a filter. It's gotten me into more trouble than I can count. You know this."

He had a point. *But still…*

"We all make mistakes. I'm no exception. Hell, I make a lot of them. Regularly. But my decision to help you isn't one. I want you to be happy, Rissa, and I will do whatever it takes for that to happen."

Her bottom lip quivered. "Why?"

"Because I care about you. And that's the only reason I need."

She swallowed. How was she supposed to interpret that? Her friends would scream "more than a friend." And a desperate, lonely part of her wanted that so much. But the jaded and damaged side shook its head, saying, *only a friend would stand by you in this.* She didn't know what side to follow, and that scared her almost as much as Nolan.

Ajax pulled away and convinced one of the parrots to perch on her head. "Now, let's finish up here so we can go look at the bears."

The pain melted as she smiled at him. Her picking didn't matter right now. The level of care he had for her didn't matter. It was enough; he prioritized her happiness, and she needed to stop taking that for granted right now. "I want to see a bear."

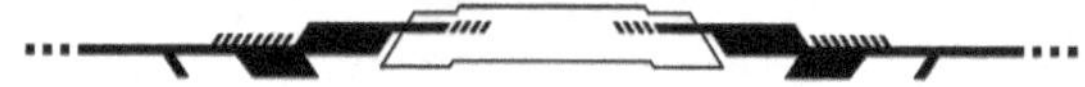

Laughter echoed into the house as Crash charged inside, Helios not far behind. After the zoo visit, Ajax had treated Narissa to another meal, and then they'd come home to walk the dogs. It felt more like a mini-hike to her, due to the wooded nature of the area, though she'd enjoyed it regardless. But boy, was Crash a wild child. She wasn't sure how Ajax handled it. And Helios could get wound up just as bad, too.

Narissa kicked off her shoes at the door, and Ajax flicked on a couple lights. She bade him goodnight and went upstairs. It was well past bedtime, and she could use it after such an emotionally exhausting day. But she didn't find herself alone.

As she dressed for bed, Crash and Helios pushed their way into her room and picked their spots on the bed—Helios at the foot, and Crash right on the side edge, where she always chose. They were such good dogs. The moment Ajax and she arrived home, they'd chosen to stick close—well, closer than normal while roaming around.

Dogs were man's best friend. And it was said they knew a human's emotional state, sometimes even better than that person. She believed both. She was a wreck. A fearful wreck, and they made her feel safe.

Narissa climbed into bed, and both dogs adjusted themselves so they were both touching her, even a little. She really needed to get a dog of her own. They were a lot of work, sure. But the right one would keep her safe once she was home. Because she knew this arrangement couldn't last forever. She'd have to go home eventually, and Ajax couldn't protect her when he wasn't around.

A figure appeared outside her partially closed door. Then Ajax's voice whispered into the room. "Are you awake?"

She sat up and flicked on the nightstand light. "Come on in."

He did and then looked at both dogs. "Oh, that's where they went."

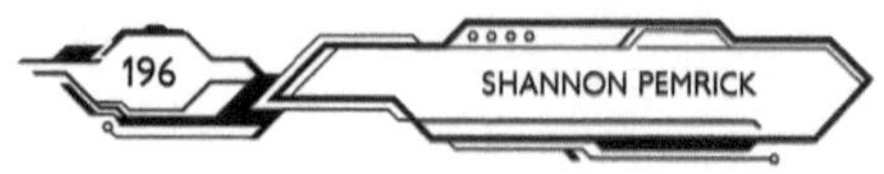

Narissa giggled. "Sorry. When I said I'd take them for my fort yesterday, I meant it as a joke."

He shook his head. "Nah, it's okay. As long as you're okay with it. If they're bothering you, I can call them out."

"No!" She ducked her head when he jumped back. "Sorry. I like them here." She hesitated a moment. "It makes me feel a little safer."

Ajax frowned. "Do you not feel safe here?"

"It's not that it at all!" She took a moment to sort her thoughts to make sense. "I feel protected here. But these two are adding to that feeling. So I'm okay with sharing my bed."

Ajax nodded and turned to leave. "Well, goodnight then."

He patted the doorframe, but then halted his exit. Narissa tilted her head. "Everything okay?"

He didn't respond, only stood there, his brow furrowed and his lips pressed into a thin line.

"Andrew?"

Ajax turned around and came back into her room, walked around her bed and then jumped on, curling right up to her and pulling her close. Narissa's heart skipped, and for a moment, she thought she might experience a similar situation as the night before, but nothing happened. He simply laid there, holding her like no one else had held her before.

Calm wasn't the right word for how she felt at the moment. It was more than that. *Safe.* He amplified the protected sensation she experienced.

"Do you feel safer now?" he murmured in her ear.

Narissa reached out and turned the light off. She rested her hand over his. "Yes. Stay here a while?"

"As long as you want."

CHAPTER 13

Ajax scratched his head. He thought this cybernetics stuff was going to be easy. But the part Narissa had him working on now wasn't making any sense, and she wasn't helping him. *That's what I get for pretending I don't know anything.*

It wasn't as though she wouldn't help him eventually, but since he'd pretended too many times, she chose to focus on an analysis around the gaming pod. *It's the better action to take anyway.* Whereas him knowing about cybernetics wasn't necessary for their partnership to work, her getting to the bottom of the machine versus cybernetic issue was.

"Okay." Narissa leaned back in her chair, shifting her gaze to him. The concentration in her gaze sent a jolt through him. "Picard is doing a test, but it'll take a while. Now I can help you."

Ajax ran his hand through his hair. "I don't know if you can help me. This has gone several levels over my head. Your brilliance is a little overwhelming, in a good way."

Narissa's cheeks tinted. Man, did he enjoy seeing that. "Yeah, well, don't cut yourself short. There's a reason I have Picard helping me on this analysis."

Ajax set his tablet down. "Let's take a break."

She gave him a long, hard look. "We've only been at this for two hours."

He leaned back. "Yeah, but breaks are good."

"Laziness isn't."

"Oh, c'mon, Narissa. I can't force this information into my brain. Trying too hard causes more problems. If I take a small break, then I can come back with a fresh mind."

She gave him a look that screamed *I don't believe you.* "And how long will this break be? Because these past few days have been quite telling as to what you see as a break."

Ajax grinned. "A break is as long as it needs to be."

Narissa scoffed. "It's a wonder you get anything done."

"Some may say my procrastination is so unhealthy, it may kill me."

"I believe it," she muttered.

"I've been getting game announcements all morning. I'd really like to take a look at some of them. They could be fun."

Narissa sighed and then relented. "Fine."

"Yes!" Ajax pulled up the game notifications on his tablet. "Looks like there's a massive treasure hunt going on."

"No doubt Mercedes and Takashi are already all over that."

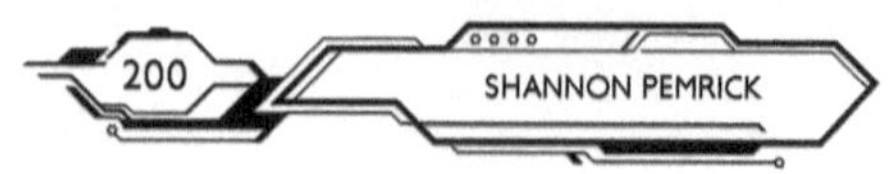

Ajax snickered. "We could bet on how long it'd take them to switch targets to each other."

Narissa threw her head back and laughed. "You're ridiculous. Everyone knows they'd save that until after, as a type of reward for each other."

He had a hard time disagreeing with that. Those two could get quite focused on their task for something so slow-paced. Ajax took a look at the other notifications. "There's a reminder about the brawl event, but I'm not much for PvP."

Narissa shook her head. "I'll pass on that one, too. We'll leave that to Shira and the boys."

"There's one last one. The tower event." Ajax looked over the rules. "Though *tower* is misleading. Teams of two fight a single boss battle; what they'll face is randomized. And the boss' abilities and weaknesses are as well, making it impossible for players to predict what would be needed to fight."

Narissa pressed her lips together. "Isn't that the popular one that's live-streamed?"

Ajax nodded, and then realized her question had more meaning. He noticed the tightness in her eyes. "What's wrong? You don't like the idea?"

"It's not that..." She struggled to meet his gaze. "It's the live stream part. It doesn't sound... safe for me."

Oh. He should have realized that'd be her concern. They'd discussed the possibly of Nolan trying to track her. He'd run an IT company back in the day, and they both knew what Jason did to Emi, Takashi, and Mercedes with his IT skills. Because of it, they'd chosen to turn off their locations on their phones, with the added padding that no one knew where they were.

In theory, that should have made it harder for him to track them down, even if he had their phone numbers. Since they'd done that, Ajax didn't see an issue on that end. "I don't think it'll be a problem. Besides us using avatars, the stream displays our character names. You don't have character names Nolan would know, right?"

She thought for a moment. "I don't think so. But are there any other protective measures, just in case?"

Ajax scrolled through the information. Narissa wheeled herself over and peered over his shoulder. The closeness reminded him of last night. He'd planned to only stay until she fell asleep, but before he knew it, he was waking the next morning, still in the same position as before. Well, she'd rolled over and curled into him at some point, tempting him to remain with her. But Helios wanted his walk, and he wasn't sure if her vague permission last night was enough for him to justify staying the entire night. He'd chosen to cut his losses and slip out before she knew.

"Here it is," he said, finding it. "They do have a security option to keep your name hidden. And you can enter a name, so that if a partner or you speak during the match, it'll be censored."

She placed a hand on his shoulder. The tender touch made him ache. "That sounds like the perfect solution. What else can you tell me about this event?"

"Not much else to it. You can only attempt the tower three times a day. And only a handful of people have successfully completed the challenge. Sounds difficult, but fun. And from what I know, prizes are worth it." He glanced at her. "You want to try?"

"I'd like to watch a few of the saved streams, to see what we're up against."

Ajax agreed. It could help.

An hour later, after watching streams of both well-coordinated teams and ones that didn't last more than a few minutes, the two of them were sure they could at least do better than the worst attempts. Hopping into the game, they met up in the guild hall and then ventured into Balgara, the home city of their guild.

Buildings of wood and stone with shingle roofs lined the roads—some businesses with signs, others NPC houses. Unlike most other cities, this one didn't have a designated business district. It made the place unique, and a reason Darius picked the town for the guild hall. He thought it helped embody what he wanted from the guild.

Ajax and Narissa stopped in at a few shops, both NPC-controlled and player. Narissa also slipped into the cathedral, gaining a few items specific to her class that she may need. While she did that, Ajax ran off to a large stone-and-wood building with a large mahogany double-door entrance. An ornate sign hung over the entrance, reading *Baten's Auctions*.

This was where players could trade directly, without the need of a storefront or meeting face-to-face. Rare and useful items were usually posted here. Ajax had a few in mind that he wanted, but it all depended on the cost.

Upon entering, he was bombarded will all sorts of sounds you'd find in an active auction place. Most were sound clips to make it seem more realistic, but the actions were all driven by game prompts. Ajax strode up to an NPC auctioneer and activated the auction panel. He did a few searches, but the first couple came up empty, or well over a price he was willing to make. He expected this endeavor to be a long shot. With all the events going on, prices shot up, and limited stock became scarce.

He tried one last item—star lily elixir. One hit. The price wasn't ideal, but it could be worse, and it was a useful clutch item for Narissa. Ajax decided to buy it. She'd complain and try to pay him back, but he wouldn't let her. He enjoyed spoiling her.

Satisfied with his purchase, he left, to find Narissa making her way to the building. "Get anything?"

"Just one item."

He opened a trade with her and offered the elixir. Narissa narrowed her eyes. "How much did it cost you?"

Ajax smiled. "Doesn't matter."

She sighed and tried to offer some money, but he refused to accept the trade. "No, this is a gift."

"No gifts!"

He didn't budge. She canceled the trade. "Fine, then keep it."

She turned and Ajax grabbed her hands, forcing the bottle in and opening a trade again. "Please take it, Rissa. It may come in handy."

Narissa gave him her best pleading eyes. He swallowed as guilt fell over him. She was good at this.

"You can pay me back some other way, but no gold." If he was going to give in, he'd make it a compromise.

She pursed her lips. "Sounds like you're expecting sexual favors."

His brain stopped. That hadn't crossed his mind, but

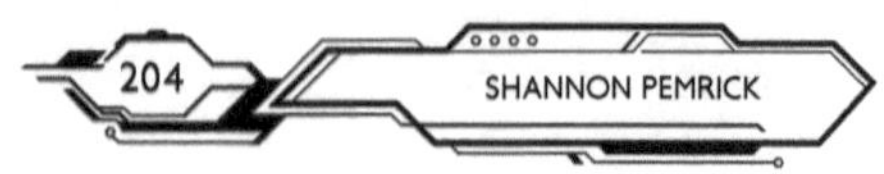

now—Ajax pulled her close against him. "Well, I'm not going to say no if you offer."

That pretty face of hers reddened again. He really didn't mind a possible repeat of the other night. He'd just want more than only her hands on him this time around.

Narissa accepted the trade and then pulled away, walking off without another word. This confused him. Did his bold action put her off? The corner of his mouth twisted up when she glanced back at him, her cheeks still red. Or maybe the idea interested her.

Ajax was learning that as long as Nolan's effect on her wasn't strong, he had a better chance of getting through to her. It was the only reason the other night had happened. And as long as he kept Nolan out of her mind, he'd be able to keep stepping on the friend's barrier until he crossed it with her. He had no intention of making this some sort of friends-with-benefits arrangement, and he suspected this may be running through Narissa's head. But at the same time—he sighed—it may be all he'd get with Nolan causing issues. He had to figure this all out, and soon, or he might really screw this up.

"Hey, we going to do this or what?" Narissa called out to him.

Ajax snapped out of his thoughts and realized she'd wandered off quite a ways. He ran to catch up with her and they hit up the flight master to travel quickly to the tower.

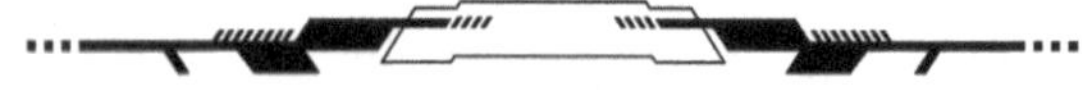

Narissa paced while Ajax watched. He'd tried to get

her to stop three times now as they waited their turn, but she continued. He wasn't sure what he could do to calm her down. Not even his attempt to fluster her had worked.

The only reason there was a turn-based system was due to the live stream. Otherwise, this would go faster and she wouldn't have time to let her nerves get to her.

"Narissa, it's going to be okay," he said. "We've got a good dynamic that makes us a great team."

"Yeah, but we both know a priest and berserker don't put out the same numbers as some of the groups that get farther along in this. Even with me going as a DPS-healing hybrid, we're putting ourselves at a greater disadvantage."

Ajax reached out and cupped her cheek. "And? We know these two classes. We know each other. We've worked hard to get to the level of skill we both have. All of that is why we do so well in our raids." He chuckled. "Why I'm the only one allowed to call you my priestess."

She stared up at him, with those eyes… those eyes she'd done well picking that looked so much like hers. She then closed them and leaned into his touch, placing both her hands on his. This acceptance both excited and surprised him. She'd never done this before. He was tempted to see how far he could push it, when a bell went off.

Narissa pulled away. "I guess the other team finished, in some way."

Ajax took a deep breath. That meant they were up. The rounds were back-to-back, winners transported to a separate instance of the tower to claim their prizes, and losers sent outside to wait for their next chance or leave to go about other tasks.

The door of the corridor they stood in creaked and whined, the light beyond spilling in as it opened. Ajax squeezed her hand and she took a few breaths to calm and steel herself. No matter how nervous either of them were, they needed to put on a brave face for those watching. And they needed to remember, this was for fun. The outcome didn't matter as long as they had that.

The two of them entered the boss room to find it was a giant colosseum. Ajax snorted. "What do they think I am, a gladiator?"

This got Narissa to laugh. *That should help her.*

The two of them looked around, expecting a boss of some sort. But they were the only ones in the pit. *Did it glitch?* It was possible. No game was perfect.

He froze when the ground shook. Ajax swiveled his head looking for the source. The shaking grew worse, and Narissa drew up closer to him, her mace at the ready. Her class' DPS side was ranged damage, but if it helped her stay calm, he wasn't going to say anything.

The wall on the far side of the colosseum cracked and then burst as a hulking monstrosity tore in. The creature had a sloping forehead and enormous, sharp tusks that protruded from its massive underbite. A long, dark tongue hung out of the poorly formed mouth. Its four arms, rippling with muscles, swung wildly at nothing. Vines and moss clung to its hardened, stone-line skin. Dark, shadowy tendrils protruded from its back, lashing out in its rage. The creature stood ten stories, looming over them, its coal-like eyes swirling with a chilling emptiness, sending a pit of dread through them.

Balls. They were facing a jungle troll afflicted by dark celestial magic. This was one creature he had hoped they wouldn't face. Trolls had high defense, making battles against them DPS races. This one had extra arms, so Ajax knew it could also pack some damage of its own. And the added magic made them unpredictable, as that was a random effect. Although if he had to guess, those tentacles needed to be avoided at all costs.

"Spread out, so we're not caught up in the same attacks," he said as he pulled away from Narissa.

"Just try not to get too far out of my range," she said, going in the opposite direction.

The troll roared and swung his arms wildly. Ajax chuckled. "No promises, with that thing throwing a temper tantrum."

Ajax activated a taunt, driving the creature's attention away from her. The troll roared and lunged at him, already starting its rotation of attacks. Ajax dodged the first two attacks, but misstepped, and the troll's massive arms slammed into him twice. He winced, though noticed they hadn't hurt as much as he expected. He did, however, have a debuff. Dancing around the boss, he had a moment to take a look at its effect.

It was a stacking damage debuff. *Tradeoff, I guess.* Each hit would be less than one large one, but the damage stacked. What would happen if he let it hit him more than twice, he didn't want to find out.

With its back now turned away from Narissa, she struck it with a blinding light from the sky. She followed up with the same attack, and then a heal to Ajax when he wasn't able to evade an arm just before his debuff ran out. This attack hit harder because of the debuff;

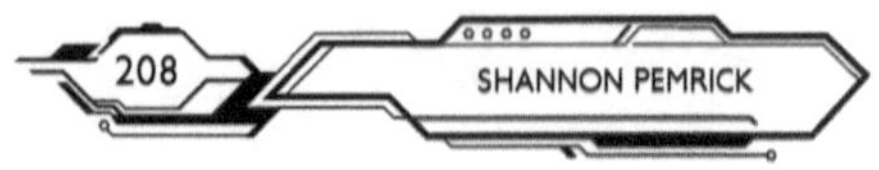

it also managed a critical hit, doubling the damage on top of the debuff amplification. *I need to be careful of that.*

The troll grunted in pain with each attack, but the damage to it wasn't enough for Ajax's taunt to fail. It still had twenty seconds. They also needed to put out more damage if they were going to stand a chance.

Ajax slashed at the boss, learning how it moved and what type of timer its four-armed attack was on. This helped him evade damage from four more swings, and his debuff ended. Narissa attacked again, the same way as before. Priests didn't have a variety of attack spells when they went the hybrid route. It was the risk they chose to take by going with a hybrid setup to keep essential healing spells available and not cost any extra mana, wasting their limited pool.

The troll's tentacles lashed out at them both, too far away from Narissa for it to touch her, and too slow to snag Ajax this time around. While Ajax wasn't sure what these tentacles did, there were two common effects in this game—stun and grapple. Grapple was the most common, and he didn't want to find himself in that predicament.

Ajax activated his taunt again and rolled out of the way of one of the four-armed attacks. The debuff stacked three times, each new hit taking out a heavier chunk of his health. No attack crit, or *critical damage*, so he wasn't exactly sure what percentage chance the boss had for that with those swings.

Several flashes of light hit him, as Narissa gave him some supplemental healing before attacking again. She wouldn't bring his health higher than seventy-five percent, as that would waste too much mana, so he needed to be careful with the abilities he chose. He had one that could boost his damage for a short time, but with this tank build, it syphoned a heavy chunk of his health. Narissa couldn't out-heal that while also attacking and rationing her resource pool. *It's too risky.* He'd have to rely on other attacks to get him through, no matter how useful that spell might be.

Ajax slashed his large axe into the leg of the boss, but misjudged the troll's next attack and found himself pummeled by all four arms. Two crits came out of that, hitting his health pool hard. Narissa slapped some healing on him. *Fuck.*

The second attack and the last attack had been the crits. The first crit had an effect on the power of the third strike, which made for a devastating blow with the second crit. Ajax surmised the debuff increased the crit chance of the hits, and had a sneaking suspicion the last hit was an auto crit because of the success of the prior attacks.

This theory was proven correct when he repeated his last mistake and found himself suffering from four hits. The first three didn't crit, but the last did, and it consumed the debuff in the process. Luckily, this time he'd managed to activate a damage reduction ability with his class' built-up rage resource, keeping Narissa from killing him herself. He did catch some swearing in her grumbling as she healed him.

Narissa then slammed the troll with holy light, three of the four attacks critting. *Yes!* The troll roared and broke free of Ajax's taunt, but he was ready. He taunted again and attacked its legs, using a trip attack to knock it off balance. It worked.

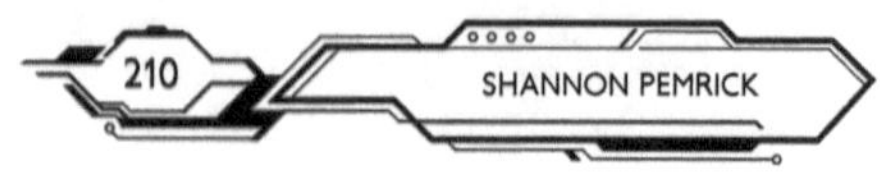

The troll fell to one knee, stunned. This allowed the two to unleash a variety of attacks, taking out a decent chunk of the creature's health.

"Look out!" Narissa yelled.

The stun wore off, and the tentacles on the creature's back lashed out. Ajax wasn't expecting this and found himself grappled. But that wasn't all. He couldn't move at all as the troll got back to its feet, and his health drained out, absorbing into the boss. He looked to the debuff obtained from the grapple. *A whole minute? Shit.* These were worse than he could have imagined. It was no wonder these fights were difficult.

Narissa split her spells, attacking the tentacles and healing him. But without Ajax there to act as her defense, the troll could now attack her, putting her on the run.

"Don't worry, I'll have you out in a moment!" she yelled out. "Just hang in there."

He'd have made a retort back about having no choice, but the stun kept him quiet. She screamed when the troll swung his massive arms at her. She managed to evade three of the attacks, but as a cloth armor wearer, she couldn't take these hits as well as he could. *Dammit!*

He hadn't thought about that in his damage assessment. It was a common mistake of his. Ajax looked at his timer, still thirty seconds remaining. *Balls.* And there was nothing he could do unless she broke him free before the timer ran out.

Bright light slammed into the troll, forcing Ajax to squint. He'd never seen such a bright attack from her. The ones she used on the tentacles were much dimmer. This attack, though, seemed to have done a substantial amount of damage to the boss. Taking a peek at her mana bar, Ajax noticed whatever it was she used, it took out a lot of her resource. *Tradeoff, I suppose.*

More light rained down on him and the boss, the attack interchanging between the tentacles, the troll, and him for healing. Then a tentacle broke, and Ajax fell to the ground. The boss was not oblivious to this and lashed out with an arm. Ajax rolled away from it, but found himself rolling right into the back swing of his other hand.

A holy ring formed around his torso, and his health slowly regenerated. But as he glanced to Narissa to see how she was holding up, he noticed one around her as well. That's when he saw her health changing.

She's rebalancing our health. He'd never seen her use this ability before, but had heard of it. It was risky, especially in a situation like this, but that troll had done a number on his health, so Ajax assumed her hand was forced in order for her to ensure he didn't go down too much while she prepared other spells.

Ajax went to taunt the boss, but it failed. Narissa hit the boss with another powerful attack, not realizing her mistake. *Shit.* The troll roared and brought its arms up to swing at her. She screamed, and a bright flash sparked in front of the troll's eyes. The creature roared and thrashed about wildly, its eyes squeezed shut.

"Ack, not my brightest move combo," Narissa said as she ran past Ajax.

Ajax rolled away from a wayward troll arm swing. "No, but it provides good entertainment value."

She narrowed her eyes at him, and attacked the boss. The troll roared and frenzied. It stomped and flailed, making it difficult for Ajax to get in close. *Not one of*

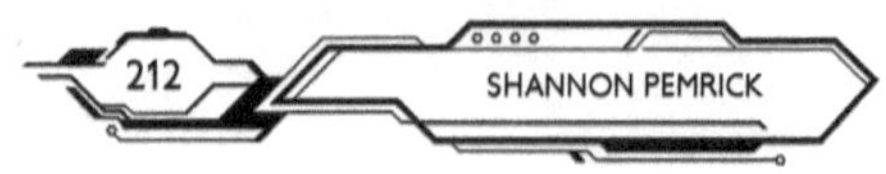

our brightest moments. But he'd rather this than see her squashed by those clubs-for-arms.

The two of them circled the creature, and once he found an opening, Ajax ducked in and swiped at its legs twice before having to roll away from some arms. He repeated this attempt, this time getting three swings in before having to dodge, getting clipped by one meaty hand in the process.

"How are you holding up?" he called out.

"Um, depends. I just used a mana potion," Narissa said as she threw out a heal on him. "Look out!"

Too late. The troll regained its sight and grabbed him, slamming him into the ground, twice, and then threw him across the colosseum. Pain raked through him as he crashed into a wall. "Ow…"

The troll roared and went for Narissa. She high-tailed it toward Ajax, throwing on a magical shield and calling down radiant light from the sky. This attack took a nice chunk of health from the boss, as well as her mana pool. *That must be the attack she used earlier.*

Ajax rose to his feet and charged in. Narissa tossed a shield over him as they crossed paths, and he took a swing at the boss, also activating his taunt. This pulled the troll's attention away from her, and it lashed out, its attack pattern not what he expected.

It came in for eight consecutive hits. Four of them hit him, three of those crits. He also wasn't able to get a defensive ability off until the last one, but it came in handy as the tentacles attacked then and grappled him. This forced Narissa to use stronger healing and attacks to free him. She managed to do so, and also used the health equalizing ability, but it all came at a great cost to her resource. *We're dragging this out too long.* The boss' abilities would become more erratic and strengthen as this dragged out.

Not only that, but Narissa wasn't going to be able to last much longer at this rate. The boss's health had been reduced down to about thirty-five percent. That was great for how this had gone, but if they didn't think of something fast, they wouldn't come out on top.

Ajax could use his clutch ability. It would increase his attack power significantly, but it didn't use rage. Instead, it siphoned his health. In a raid, this was fine to use, as Narissa had all her healing spells and single focus at her disposal. But this situation would be too risky.

He dodged another four-armed attack. His health would sink too low for Narissa to handle, and that could cost them this match.

The troll hit him again, lowering Narissa's mana more as she healed him. "Hon, this isn't looking good."

Hon? He could get used to her calling him that. After this was over, of course. She looked exhausted. Mana reduction had that effect on players. It was one reason he didn't play classes like that. They needed to think of something clutch, and fast.

"The elixir," he mumbled.

"What?"

He looked to her. "Rissa, the elixir I bought you!"

Her eyes widened, realizing she had it. Of all the potions he could have bought her, this one would be the most perfect in this situation. For casters only, the star lily elixir would give her clear casting for ten seconds that wasn't used up when a single spell was activated. That meant she'd be able to get off any

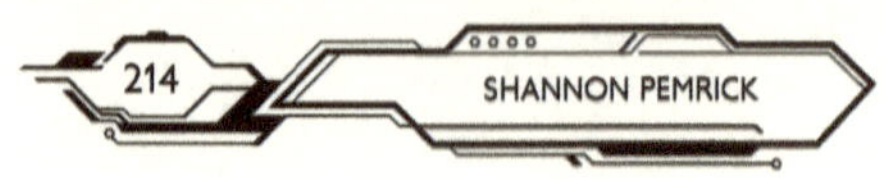

spell of her choosing as many times as she wanted, for no mana.

What she'd use it for, he wasn't sure. But he knew Narissa would use it well for this situation.

She healed herself, and then glanced to him to signal she knew what spells she wanted to use during the clear cast. He put all his faith in his priestess and taunted the boss, facing it away from her. Narissa consumed the potion. Her hands and eyes glowed, and three blasts of energy rapid-fired from her hands.

Ajax knew this spell, though had only ever seen her use it a few times. It was a five-second channeled attacking spell that converted a portion of the damage into health, healing a random party member, including the caster. *She knows what ability I want to use.* It only made sense playing such a risky spell.

This choice was a huge gamble, considering it wasn't guaranteed to heal him, and there was only a certain percentage of a chance based on how she geared to give her the much-needed critical hits that would be the true saving grace in this maneuver, as that translated into the healing. Narissa would understand this gamble as well as he did, maybe even better. But it was the only thing they could do in this moment. They'd lose if they didn't try, and if it didn't work out for them, they'd still lose.

Ajax's health went up when the two lights made their mark on the troll, and then Narissa's health, with the last light. No criticals. *Shit.* He slammed the boss and caught Narissa powering up the channel again. *She's trying again?* Now that was a risky move. She could have tried to get off her bigger damaging attacks, instead of channeling this spell. It'd give them a better chance of getting the boss' health down in larger chunks, increasing their chances of success.

Ajax kept the troll busy. He had to trust her.

A volley of light slammed into the troll. The first light healed her, and then the second. *Shit. This didn't work*— The third force of light bashed the boss, critically striking him. And then Ajax's health shot up to seventy-five percent.

Before Ajax could process this amazing turn of events, Narissa yelled out to him. "Andrew, now!"

She did know what I wanted to do. This whole setup was on the same wavelength. *I'd kiss her if I could.* After this, even if they didn't make it through victorious, he just might.

Ajax activated his damage mitigation ability, and then the attack-boosting skill that siphoned fifty percent of his health. Power welled up inside him and he unleashed a flurry of blows. Narissa used the last of her mana to get his health up with that equalizing heal, and then shot off one last attack. By the time Ajax's ability ended, the boss was at five percent health. *We can do this.*

Narissa stumbled, the draining effect for her resource taking its toll on her, but she refused to give up. As Ajax slashed the boss, dodging and reducing damage where he could, she came up and slammed her mace into its heel. The troll roared in pain, and then it fell to the ground. It didn't move, and neither did they.

CHAPTER 14

Silence permeated the air. The troll remained motionless on the ground. Narissa wasn't sure if this was real. They beat it? That risky move she pulled off worked? They actually won?

Excitement burst through her, coming out in a shout of glee. "We did it!"

A wide grin of joy and relief spread up his avatar's half-orc face. Ajax rushed over to her and lifted her up, spinning them both around. Narissa wrapped her arms around his muscular neck, laughing all the while.

Their celebration died down when the game prompted them to look at a box that appeared in the air and they both smiled. Narissa couldn't stop herself from hugging Ajax tight as the system took their picture for the charts. She also couldn't stop herself from pecking him on the cheek right after, and climbing down.

Ajax rubbed the spot she'd kissed. "Do you think my tusks looked okay?"

Narissa laughed. "You looked fine." She tossed her thumb to the boss. "You don't need to over-compensate like him."

Ajax laughed as well.

Then, they were phased into another instance of the colosseum, the boss' body disappearing, and a large chest and shiny and sharp objects appearing on the far wall.

Ajax rubbed his hands together. "Let's see what we have for rewards."

She held up her hand, her blinking chat prompts catching her eye. "Hold on. The guild is going nuts."

They both connected to the voice chat. Shira noticed them first. "You two were amazing!"

"Yeah, wicked awesome show, guys!" Zach said. "Way to show the world what our guild is made of."

"And to give us officers something to deal with," a heavily accented voice said.

Narissa's neck twisted. "Eli, is that you?"

"*Si, signora*," he said in Italian. "No family business keeping me away today."

Narissa chuckled. "Well, it's good to hear from you. Hope the guild requests aren't too bad after that craziness we pulled off."

"We're at a hundred and climbing," a female voice said.

"Sorry, Alana!" Ajax said.

"Yeah, no you're not. Wait until Darius finds out."

"Oh, I'm here," Darius said. "I watched the whole spectacle from my work station. And now my coworkers are all up on me with questions about the guild. I don't think I'm going to get this model finished at this rate."

"You will," Narissa said. "You'll just pull an all-nighter and get Kiara all worked up and mad."

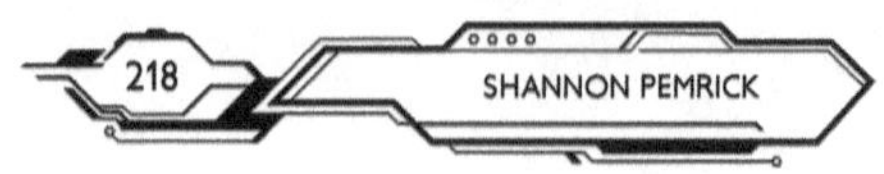

Those in chat laughed while he sighed. "Just go collect your rewards. And think about either doing it again or another event. The guild gets special items, ranking, and the like when these events are over. That goes for everyone else."

"I think Mercedes and Takashi are working on those big treasure hunts right now," Zach said.

"Everyone knows that's not the treasure they're pillaging right now," Shira snarked.

Ajax nearly fell on Narissa as he laughed. "She's not wrong!"

"I heard that," Mercedes said. "And you both are wrong. We're top score right now with this *legitimate* treasure hunt."

"The other hunt comes after," Takashi quipped.

This time the guild joined in on the laughter. There was a reason they listed this guild *for adults only*.

"So, Narissa, Ajax, how do you feel?" Shira asked.

"Like a million bucks." Ajax said. The guild snickered.

Narissa placed her hand on her chest. "My heart rate has returned to normal. Is that an appropriate answer?"

Her friend chuckled. "Yes. That was heart-pounding to watch. I can only imagine what it was like participating."

"You can always try yourself," Darius said.

"Nah, I'll pass. But the brawl looks fun."

Ajax laughed. "I think her idea of fun is a little messed up."

"I'll join yah," Jasper said.

"Same," Zach said.

Narissa grinned. "Correction, all three of them."

People laughed, and banter continued for a bit longer before Narissa and Ajax disconnected from the chat to go over their reward. Her excitement built up again. There were a few items she hoped they'd get. One was a particular mount. A mount was guaranteed as loot, but there were six that could be randomly awarded.

They both received a great deal of gold, and some real world currency, as well as rare potions and scrolls for them to either use or auction off.

Ajax opened his personal loot and received a new axe, three times the size it should have been for a one-handed axe. *Oh fantasy games.* The head of the blade had an eye much like the troll's, the darkness swirling the same way, and a dark essence oozed from the blade.

He also received a new shoulder piece. Berserkers didn't exactly wear much for armor, but for some reason shoulder pieces were part of the armor design. He equipped it. A large jaw-like bone now curved over his shoulder, large jagged tusks protruding out. Shadowy whips, like the tentacles from the boss, lashed out at times.

"Badass," Ajax said, admiring the two rewards. "What did you get?"

She opened her loot prompt to find out. She also received armor and a weapon. A new staff for her, made of bone and wrapping vines, with a gorgeous purple crystal. *I can pretend it's tanzanite.* This staff had a similar aesthetic to Ajax's axe, with the odd-looking eye right up in the crystal, but instead of the staff oozing darkness, shadowy tentacles lashed out from it.

Ajax gave a nod of approval.

Narissa equipped the armor, finding it didn't cover much of her, as it showed off more than just a bit of cleavage, her stomach, and a great deal of leg. She

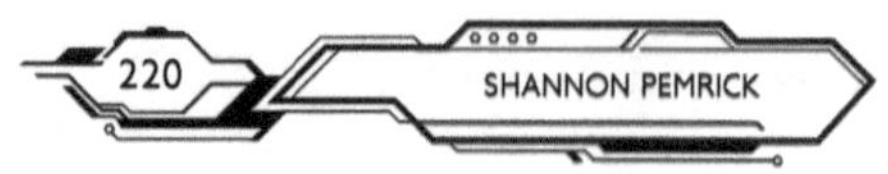

bounced, as did her breasts, the game's coding keeping her covered even when it logically shouldn't. *Female fantasy armor at its finest.*

Narissa didn't mind. She liked the sexier armor. And at least in this situation, it made some sense due to the theme of the armor, with the shadows and bits of bone and vines. And Lion Rage did a good job balancing the gear options as a whole, between practical and sexy fantasy. They'd also allowed a transmogrification magic to be applied to the gear to alter its appearance artificially to suit the tastes of the player.

Ajax's eyes bugged out of his head. "Well… uh… that looks great on you."

Flustered? That was interesting. She didn't see that side from him often. He was always so confident. Narissa placed her hands on her hips and leaned forward, pouting her lips for effect. "Only great?"

Ajax struggled for words and then turned to focus on the loot chest. "I think we missed the item for the mount."

She smirked. That was satisfying. She liked seeing Mr. Confident acting all out of sorts. He came across as more real—more attainable. *No, definitely not that.* Not for someone like her. Line blurring on the temporary was all she could get. And really, she should be happy with that. It was way better than anything she'd ever gotten in the past.

"Found something," Ajax said. He pulled out a rusty key they'd ignored earlier. "I think this has a quest attached."

Her brow ticked up. A quest? That old rusted thing? She shouldn't be surprised. The devs liked to mess with the players. So, what could it possibly lead to? Without a mount item inside, logically that'd be the reward. But was the key's appearance an indicator to the mount type?

There was a sludge-like creature as a reward, so it was possible. *Means I don't get my pretty pony.* Even though she wasn't sure this wasn't the mount, she couldn't help but be a little disappointed.

Narissa accepted the quest the key offered, and followed Ajax to a different wall where a locked door had appeared at some point—possibly during the phasing. The two of them heard loud breathing, and Narissa's heart skipped when she heard soft nickering and the stomping of hooves. *My pony!* With an overwhelming burst of excitement, she shoved the key into the locked door and turned it.

The door creaked and then opened inward. A huge smile curled up her face as two enormous black horses walked out. The moment the light hit them, their fur shimmered and swirled with light colors. Their snow-like eyes swirled with bits of darkness, and their white manes wisped about like ethereal flame. White and black horns shimmered on their foreheads.

Celestially-touched pegasi. Quick ground mounts, they also sprouted ethereal wings for flying. And, as an added bonus, their colors inverted at night.

So overcome by excitement, she squealed as she completed the quest, obtaining the reins of the beasts, and jumped onto Ajax, kissing him smack on the lips.

Realizing her forwardness, she pushed away and took a few steps back. "Sorry. I—"

Her back hit the wall, and Ajax's lips crashed into hers. It stole her breath and sent a wave of arousal through

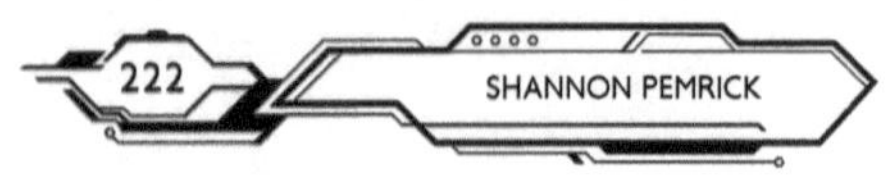

her. Ajax pinned her hands next to her head and pulled away, though not far.

"You tease me with that first outfit. Then you bring that sexy brain of yours into the mix during the match. Then you tease me again with a quick kiss, and then this new outfit." He took a controlled breath that made her heart pound in her chest. "You don't get to kiss me again after all that and then say *sorry* like you didn't mean for it to happen."

It was an accident… right? Maybe it wasn't. He had a point. Sure, the first kiss was innocent, yes. But she didn't have to pick the gear she had during the fight. She didn't care what random people thought of how she looked during the match. She had cared, though, about his opinion, and she knew he appreciated that armor set on her.

She also didn't need to tease him with the new gear. But yet she had.

Narissa swallowed hard as she stared up at his smoldering eyes. He had one goal in his mind, and the only thing in the way was her saying yes. Need called from inside her. She wanted to feel his touch again. She wanted to explore and not draw lines. She wanted to say yes.

He called her brain sexy. It was time to put it to good use and tell it to sync with her body's want. She unlocked the "safety" mode that kept interactions with her PG-13, and the area around them shimmered. "I think there was some loot missing from that chest."

Ajax grinned against her lips. "I think I found it."

She sucked in a tight breath when he reclaimed her lips. Her eyes hooded as she wrapped her arms around his neck, pulling herself closer. She needed this contact.

Ajax's hands roamed her body, his own body pinning her to the wall. Even with this avatar of his, it felt like him. There was no mistaking this touch, identical to what she'd experienced the prior night.

His hands found her breasts several times before remaining there, squeezing and teasing the exposed skin. Then he pulled the cloth material to the side, her suppleness spilling out. Their kiss also broke as he dropped to his knees and kissed between them, down to her navel, and then back up, his hands taking the fullness of her breasts and kneading them. His thumbs circled and rolled over her aching peaks. This pulled out a quiet moan from her.

Ajax grinned against her skin. "There we go. No holding back, remember?"

She remembered. How could she not, when he brought on such strong, euphoric sensations after she gave in?

His tongue slid over her taut buds. Narissa's mouth parted for a gasp. Ajax then slipped one nipple into his mouth, sucking hard and flicking his tongue over her captured bud. Narissa threaded her fingers into his hair, moaning as need and desire filled her. Ajax split his attention between both breasts, sucking and nibbling one, kneading and teasing the other with his hand.

"Andrew," she moaned. She needed more than just this.

Ajax's hand dragged down her body, finding her thigh and slipping between. She squirmed, and her breath hitched as his fingers touched her slick heat. She didn't know how the game code made this feel so real, and right now she didn't care.

Her back arched, and her hips thrust into his touch. She needed more.

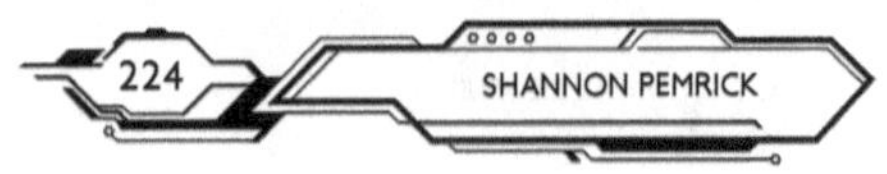

Ajax kissed between her breasts, his fingers finding rhythm and making her writhe. He held her hips down with his other hand. "Be good—or I'll tie you down."

Narissa bit her lip, her eyes hooding, his words kicking up her excitement. She'd never been one for adventure in bed. But he brought out a different woman in her. "Is that supposed to be a threat, or a reward?"

"You always know what to say." He kissed lower, trailing down to her navel. Narissa's breath hitched. She knew his intent, but she'd never—Nolan had expectations that he never reciprocated.

Ajax pulled her robe to the side, spreading her legs apart as he did. He could rip everything off, so nothing was in the way, but his choice—his need to touch her without doing so—simmered her blood.

His tongue darted between her legs, finding her velvet heat. She gasped and then moaned, the sensation foreign and pleasant. Her knees threatening to buckle under her.

Ajax continued, causing her breathing to labor. Need built in her core—her whole body set ablaze. This was amazing, yet not enough at the same time.

He looked up at her as he continued to please her. Her mouth dried with the intensity. Licking her lips, her hands found her breasts, where she played with them. Her fingers rolled over her nipples, exaggerating their play for him. Ajax rewarded her for the display, slipping two fingers inside her, his tongue never letting up.

Narissa's panting changed to constant moaning. So many sensations—so much pleasure. Her pulse hammered in her ears.

Her head flew back and she lost control of her legs

as an orgasm ripped through her. Ajax held her up with one arm, not ceasing his other motions until she rode out her high to the end.

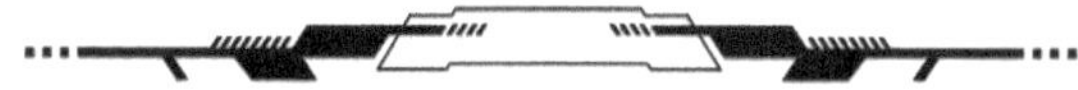

Ajax eased Narissa down onto his lap, listening to her heavy breathing. He kissed her neck and collarbone several times. His erection pressed against her, what little clothes they had in the way of him slipping inside her this very moment.

Narissa kissed him on the neck. "Your turn?"

His body warmed at the thought of her wrapping her lips around him, stroking him until he reached his peak. But he also wanted more than that. "No."

"You sure?" She pecked him on the lips, grinding her hips into him. He groaned. "Or is there something else you had in mind? I'm willing to discuss anything that can make this better for us."

His pulse quickened. "The only thing that'd make this better is if we logged out of game and I came over to your room to take you in a manly fashion."

She grinned against his lips. "Cause I'm pretty?"

"Because you get prettier and sexier for every geek reference you understand."

"It's a good thing you're unwed."

Oh, that was it. Hunger gnawed at him. He couldn't stop himself from indulging with this kind of geeky wit thrown at him. He flipped her over, getting a satisfying inhale of anticipation from her. The sound made him throb. The sight of her in this position, wearing this tempting robe, and the prospect of showing her just

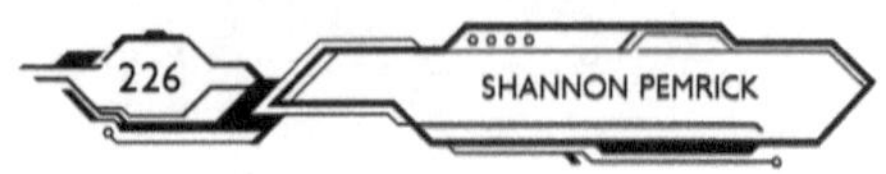

how manly he could be with her while she was still in it, sent his mind into overdrive.

He bent closer to her, running his hands along her thighs, occasionally slipping one between her legs for a moment to tease her. "I've been told there's no down-time here. I hope it's true. I want you to scream for me more than twice this time."

Narissa gasped as he continued to stroke her. "If you manage that, I'm going to have to punch your frequent sinner card."

Ajax slipped two fingers inside her, receiving another satisfying gasp from her. "I think that would fill my card, granting me a free punishment from my priestess."

Narissa moaned. "You sound excited by the prospect."

He bent over and nipped her shoulder blade. "Not at all. That would mean I'd enjoy it. And we can't have that, can we, Priestess?"

Her hands curled and her back arched. Labored breath and tiny gasps, moans, and sighs replaced her words as he continued to pleasure her. Seeing this reaction made him unable to resist any longer. He needed her. Now.

Ajax activated his menu and removed what little armor his class wore. Using some special prompts, he allowed the armor to clatter to the ground so she knew what was coming. Narissa glanced back at him, her face flushed and her eyes dark with need.

He angled his swollen shaft behind her. She swallowed and begged. "Please."

How could he say no to that? Ajax eased himself into her with the last bit of control he still had. Narissa's fingers dug into the ground, and her back arched as she let out a deep gasp. Ajax himself found his own breath halting as she accepted him. He gave them both a moment to process this new sensation before thrusting.

Narissa moaned loud and deep. Hearing that sound drove him on, finding rhythm and digging his fingers into her hips. His pulse hammered in his ears, need building within him the more she verbalized her pleasure.

And when she begged for more, he obliged, thrusting harder. Ajax also reached down and grabbed a fistful of her hair, pulling her head back. Hooded eyes stared at him, her mouth parted as she panted and moaned. Her breasts bounced with each rapid thrust. He wanted to see that sight next. *But first…*

Ajax reached around her with his other hand, slipping his fingers between her legs and touching her pool of velvet moisture. Narissa's moans increased in volume, her eyes shuts as she focused on the sensations he fed her, stroking his own flame of desire coming to a cusp. She rocked her hips in rhythm with him. This sent them both over the edge.

She screamed his name and euphoria ripped through her. Her screams drowned out his own grunts as he abandoned himself in her.

Ajax's movements slowed until he stilled, taking deep breaths. He released his hold on Narissa's hair and she breathed, face down, strong and heavy, trying to recover from her second high of the night. He appreciated she still had her perfect ass in the air for him to gaze at, even with her robe covering the important bits.

"That was amazing," she murmured.

Amazing, was it? He looked down and found his avatar just as ready as before. He grinned. "Good. There's more where that came from."

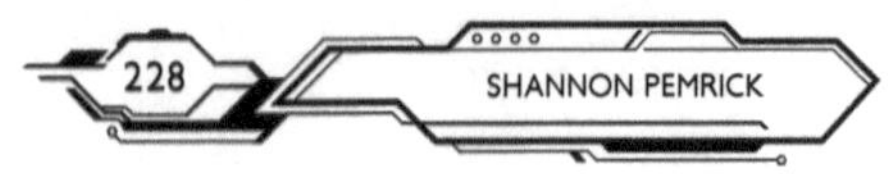

Narissa moved then, disappointing him. She flipped herself over and sat with her arms behind her and her legs casually spread apart. A grin sat on her lips. "Still going for more than two?"

Ajax leaned closer. "Of course. I need to hear more of that from you."

Without breaking eye contact, she reached out and grazed his hard shaft with her fingers. He swallowed, his pulse picking back up and his member throbbing with need again. "Are you sure it's not because of what you get out of it?"

Ajax pulled her hand away and leaned further over her, forcing her to lie back and allowing him to pin her arm above her head. "There's more than one answer to this question."

She tried to reach out with her other hand, but he pinned that one above her head, too. "No, no. You have to behave."

Narissa gave him a tempting look. "Do I? I quite enjoy punching this sinner card."

Ajax's lips brushed hers. "Are you saying you need to be punished?"

Narissa licked his lower lip, taking him by surprise. "No. But I'm enjoying the pleasure you offer."

Well, if that's the case… Ajax pulled away without letting her go, and searched his inventory. He found a low-level belt from a quest he'd completed the other day. *That'll do nicely.*

Ajax grabbed his new axe and slammed it into the ground above her head. He tied the belt around the handle. He then slipped it around her pinned wrists, restraining her.

"There," he said, pulling away to gaze at her. His blood simmered at the view of her ravaged and ready for more. She squirmed under him, her eyes pleading. Not for escape, though. That was good. He liked seeing her like this, all trussed up and on display for him. The sight made him harder—hungrier for her.

Ajax slid his hands up her thighs. "Now, where were we, Priestess?"

CHAPTER 15

Bacon popped and sizzled in the pan as Narissa focused on scrambling the eggs in another. The nutty aroma of coffee brewing in the pot filled the kitchen. Toast shot up from the toaster and she scrambled over to retrieve and butter the slices before going back to the eggs. She hummed to herself, getting lost in her cooking and her mind.

Narissa couldn't get yesterday out of her head. It'd been so amazing, for a digital experience. The way he touched her, made her feel physically and emotionally, she could barely tell a difference between reality and virtual. Even when she'd gotten out of the game, her physical body thought she'd really had that high. *Those highs, Narissa.*

That man knew how to please a woman. It could get addicting. With the virtual experience feeling so real, she wondered just how different reality would be with him.

But that left her to wonder, what were they? If it was

a lack of control around emotions that'd flared up these past few days, and they were friends who had a sexual history together, she could accept that. If it could be something more than that, though, she wasn't all that opposed anymore. Ajax was proving to not care about her broken nature, or that Nolan was going to be a problem for some time.

Her phone buzzed and she took a look. It was a group message from Mercedes, including Shira.

> *Okay, you. Spill what happened yes-terday. We saw you and Ajax both go into DND for hours before just up and logging off.*

That was code for "Do not disturb then, means kiss and tell now." Her friends' nosey nature made her chuckle.

> *I'll tell you later.*

Shira responded next.

> *Oh no. Details. Details!*

Narissa shook her head and typed back.

> *No, later when I return from my vacation.*

Shira came back with an angry emoji, but Mercedes had her back, sort of.

*Shira, leave her be for now. She's spend-
ing more time with her "work" partner.*

She shook her head and put her phone down. Her mind wandered back to Ajax.

Strong arms wrapped around her from behind, pulling her into a familiar, strong form and out of her thoughts. Ajax's low, husky voice murmured next to her ear. "Something smells good. And breakfast does, too."

While she smiled from the absurd comment, her body involuntarily tensed at his touch.

Ajax's grip on her loosened. "It's just me, Rissa. You're safe. I promise."

"I know." She took a deep breath and eased the tension out. "I guess I'm just not used to anyone doing that anymore."

The doorbell rang. The dogs barked like crazy and the tension returned, this time all over her.

"It's okay," Ajax whispered before going to answer the door.

She busied herself with breakfast. She did find herself listening as Ajax questioned the person about what sounded like a delivery. Knowing that, she relaxed more. Deliveries were nothing to be worried about.

Narissa finished just as Ajax closed the door. "What did you get?"

She didn't receive an answer. Brow furrowed, she looked at him. He stood by the couch, staring at the long white box in his hands. "Andrew?"

His lips spread into a thin line as he looked up at her. "It's not for me. It's addressed to you."

Her hands began to shake; the dread returned. "I

didn't tell anyone. Not even Mercedes and Shira. Or my mother." She licked her drying lips. "I only posted a few photos on social media, and nothing in them would help anyone recognize where we are."

Her heart raced and her jaw clamped shut. Ajax put the box down on the couch and rushed over to her, pulling her into his arms. "Easy. Easy. It's okay."

He continued to soothe her until she finally calmed. She took two more shaky breaths before pulling away. "Thank you. I think I'm okay now."

He nodded and glanced to the box. "Do you want to find out what's inside?"

Narissa took a moment and then nodded. Ajax stepped aside and she set the box on the back of the couch. After another calming breath, she removed the ribbon wrapped around it and lifted the lid. Her eyes widened. Inside laid a large, beautiful bouquet of flowers.

She lifted them up, amazed at the lovely assortment. Inhaling deeply, the wonderful aroma of floral scents didn't disappoint. "These are so lovely."

Ajax reached into the box and pulled out an envelope. "There's a note."

Narissa set the flowers down and she opened and read the letter.

My dearest Narissa,

I hope these flowers find you well. I saw them and immediately thought of you. I wanted to wait until you returned, as I know traveling with such a gift would be quite difficult, but I couldn't help myself.

Her blood ran cold. She knew this handwriting. And yet, she couldn't stop reading.

> *I also wanted to congratulate you on your special win in Lusara Fates. You performed so spectacularly. As I always know you do. I must say, the hobby surprises me, but you look so happy, so I can't complain.*
>
> *I can't wait until we're able to speak face to face. You can go into detail about this new hobby of yours. But please be sure to leave that mongrel you're so attached to at home. I'd prefer a nice meeting between the two of us. And you wouldn't want anything to happen, now would you?*
>
> *Until then, doll.*

The paper slipped from her shaking hands.

"Rissa, what is it?" Ajax asked, taking a step closer.

"It's from… it's from him. He didn't sign it. But I know… I know…" Her chest tightened. She couldn't handle this anymore. She just couldn't take it.

She broke down. Her knees gave out, forcing Ajax to catch her. She didn't understand. Why did this have to be happening? All she wanted was to be happy. She dedicated her life to helping others. She just wanted a small slice just for her. Was that really too hard to ask for? Was that really such a bad thing to want?

Ajax hushed her softly and murmured calming words. The dogs even came over and nudged her. When none of that worked, Ajax had her hold onto Helios while he collected the note and the flowers and put them outside.

He crouched down next to her again when he returned,

his phone in his hand. "Kirk, please find the number for Ornate Orchids. It's a name I found on a tag."

"Of course, Ajax," Kirk said from the building's infrastructure.

Narissa found herself able to calm then. Ajax's ability to stay strong and levelheaded in this situation gave her something to ground herself to.

"Ajax, I've found the number and am dialing it now," Kirk announced.

Ajax placed the phone to his ear and rubbed Narissa's back. He smiled at her, giving her something more to grasp.

"Hello, yes, my name is Ajax Jackson. I need to speak to someone about an unexpected shipment we received from your company, addressed to my girlfriend that has us creeped out and upset."

His girlfriend? Well it made sense to use the word in this situation. Why else would a "friend" call on her behalf? The people on the other line would also be more likely to listen to him if he had a deeper connection to her.

"Yes, that's the order I'm talking about," Ajax said. In her musing, she'd stopped paying attention for a moment. "I need to know who sent it." A pause. "I don't care about your confidentiality bullshit. Whoever sent this sent a creepy letter with it." Another pause as the person spoke. "Yes, it was creepy. It's completely stalkerish and has my girl all freaked out!"

Ajax listened and then sighed. "Alright, thank you. You'll be hearing from the police, then."

He hung up before the person could defend themselves against that threat. Narissa swallowed. "What did you find out?"

"Barely anything. They've got a few locations throughout California, Oregon, and Washington. They have some stupid confidentiality clauses that protect their clients."

Her chest tightened. "No name, though?"

Ajax shook his head. "No. Though, if this person paid cash, I doubt they even gave a legitimate name. It'd be foolish."

Narissa rubbed her arms. "I need to call Dylan and tell him about this."

"Picard, please call Officer Dylan," Ajax said.

"Of course."

Narissa's phone dialed on speakerphone and after three rings, a man picked up. "Officer Dylan."

"Dylan, it's me, Narissa," she said.

"Narissa," he sounded surprised. "Are you okay? You sound like you're on speaker."

"It is. And no, I'm not okay. I received a package today at a location I'm staying at. No one but the person I'm with, and my AI assistant, knows where I am."

The sound of a chair creaked on his end. "Is your friend with you right now?"

"I'm right next to her, Officer," Ajax said. "My name is Ajax Jackson."

"Ah, the good friend of hers I hear about a lot. Pleasure," Dylan said. "Can you both tell me what has happened?"

Narissa swallowed her fear as it clawed its way back up. "I received a package from Nolan."

"It has his name on it?"

"No, but there's a handwritten note."

"Did you talk to the company that delivered it?" he asked.

"I did," Ajax said. "The company is Ornate Orchids. They refused to give me information because of confidentiality."

"I was afraid of that. No doubt, whoever this is used cash." Something made a tapping sound on Dylan's end, and then he sighed. "I can't promise anything, like before, Narissa, but I can see what I can do. Even if it's not him, this is grounds for investigation."

Narissa's heart sank. She knew it'd be hard, but hearing it from him just made that reality more real. "Thank you, Dylan."

"Officer, I'll send you a copy of the note received. And if you need it delivered, I can mail it out if we haven't returned to L.A. before then."

"Thank you, Ajax. I would appreciate the photograph; that will be good evidence. I know it will be difficult for her, but please keep the note until I know further if we'll need the hard copy. I suspect we will."

"I'll store it away where she won't have to look at it."

"Thank you. And, Narissa?"

She swallowed hard. "Yes?"

"Because Nolan is on parole, if he moves anywhere he's not supposed to, we'll know. Please don't let this get to you too much."

"I'll try."

"Good. I'll be in touch."

The line went dead. Narissa remained sitting, her mind going a mile a minute. Dylan couldn't help her right off, and now Nolan definitely knew where she was. Would he show up next? Dylan sounded sure that'd be a no, but that didn't mean anything. Nolan was crafty. It was

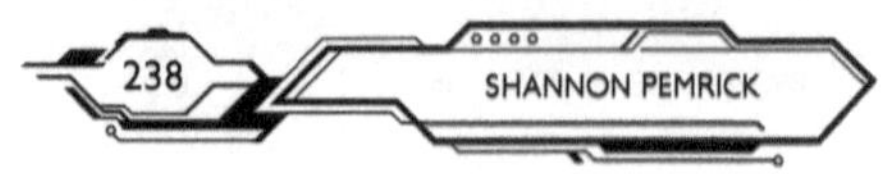

a quality that drew her to him back then. And now, that trait was coming back to bite her.

Ajax pressed his lips against her forehead. "Come out of your head, please, Rissa."

She shook herself. "Sorry."

He stood and held out his hand. "Let's go for a hike. Fresh air will be good, and it'll get you away from here."

She nodded. That sounded like the perfect idea.

Sticks and dead leaves crunched underfoot as Ajax led the way through the hiking trail he and his family had forged over the years. Animals had a habit of using it too, so he hoped one would cross their path to cheer Narissa up.

The hike was supposed to save her from her own mind, but it wasn't working this time. Even the dogs noticed, sticking by her side instead of wandering off to explore. At least she found comfort in their presence, but it didn't make him feel better.

He needed to pull out the kid in him. "You know, I'm surprised a city girl like you can handle these walks."

Narissa's brow furrowed. "What's that supposed to mean?"

He looked to the sky. "Oh, you know. By this point you'd be gasping for breath, begging to go back."

She placed a hand on her chest. "I'm so sorry to disappoint. How's this?"

To his surprise, she threw herself dramatically against a tree. "Andrew, wait! I cannot go on any longer. We've been walking for days! Please let me rest to catch my breath, even a little."

He threw his head back as he laughed. "That was so not you."

She sucked in a tight breath. "Fine, how about this one?"

She sashayed over to a large rock, giving him a nice view of those swaying, sexy hips of hers. What he wouldn't give to grab onto that again—this time, the real ones. Could he make love to her until she completely forgot about Nolan permanently? He wished. That'd only happen if the prick would stop waving his small dick around in their faces and just leave Narissa alone.

Ajax had read the note. The guy was a complete nut job. And now that Nolan had also pinned Ajax as a threat, he wasn't going to leave her side.

Narissa lay across the rock she'd found, resting her arm over her forehead. "This is it! This is the end. This is my life. I have climbed this hill and now I shall die upon it!"

Ajax held his sides as he laughed. "Now that's more like it!"

Satisfied, she slipped off the rock. His breath caught when she stumbled and fell. He rushed over to her. "Narissa, are you okay?"

She grumbled and picked herself up. "Yeah. That sucked. I'm fine, though."

He fussed and looked her over. "Are you sure? You're not hurt at all?"

She laughed. "Well, my hands and knees sting, and my ankle is complaining, but nothing major."

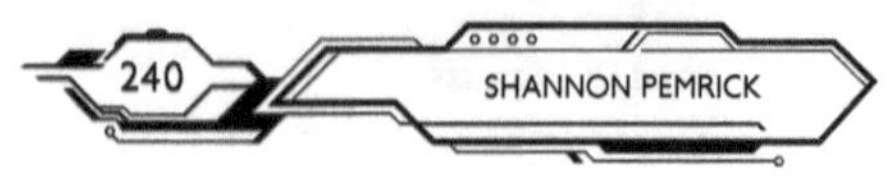

He'd make a dirty joke if he weren't so worried. *I'm acting like a mother hen.*

Narissa dusted herself off, wincing a little, and then smiled at him. "Let's continue, shall we?"

They did. Ajax kept a close eye on Narissa, finding her mood improving as they went, though her pace slowed. He worried she may have hurt herself more than she wanted to admit. Or he could be overanalyzing, and she was just taking in the forest.

Narissa gasped and stopped, gazing up into the trees. Ajax tilted his head and looked up as well. A great horned owl sat high in a tree, peering down at them.

"He's so beautiful!"

Ajax smiled. At least she got to see one creature out here.

The two of them jumped when water splashed their skin. The clouds had been gathering for a while, but Ajax had hoped the weather would hold out until they made it back to the house.

Thunder rumbled in the distance. He tossed his thumb back down the path. "We should head back before we're caught up in this."

Narissa nodded and then smirked. "Race you."

She took off before he could react. "Hey!"

The two of them sprinted down the path, the two dogs peeling off ahead. More water fell from the sky, pushing them faster. Ajax pulled ahead of her, laughing a bit when she made a complaining sound.

Then, Narissa screamed. He turned back to catch a brief glimpse of a chipmunk dashing across the path, right in front of her. Everything around him slowed. In her attempt to not step on the creature, she'd stumbled over a jutting tree root and crashed to the ground.

"Narissa!" He rushed back to her.

She complained and moaned, lifting herself into a half-sitting position. Ajax crouched next to her. "Are you okay?"

"This is just not my day." Narissa touched her ankle and winced. "I think I twisted it."

He hoped it was just that. A sprain or a break would not be fun for her. But even a twist would need some ice. Ajax lifted her up into his arms, noting how well she fit, even for a position such as this. "I'll carry you the rest of the way."

She wrapped her arms around him, helping with her weight distribution. "Are you sure? You're strong and all, but we're still a ways away from the house."

He locked his cybernetic arm into place and smiled at her. "I got you, don't worry."

Ajax rushed up the stairs as the rain pelted them. Narissa tried to shield them both with her arms, but it wasn't working all. The dogs, on the other hand, enjoyed tromping through the mud and weren't too pleased to be called by a whistle from Ajax once he got the back door open.

He continued to cradle her as he waited for the dogs to enter, and then carried her into the living room, setting her down on the arm of the couch. Crash shook herself off in the kitchen, but Helios wandered farther into the house before doing the same. Ajax grumbled about having to clean up after the two "slobs."

Narissa tugged on her drenched shirt; her shorts weren't much better. Staying in wet clothes wasn't good—she was going to need to change. But this ankle of hers was going to make getting up and down those stairs difficult. *I could just ask Ajax to grab some clothes for me and change down here.* She'd have to ask Ajax to not look. Or would she?

Her in-game model wasn't too different from her. Her hair was the only big difference, and she changed her character's hair style all the time. Narissa wasn't big on the whole "its fantasy so be someone you're not" thing. Games were an escape for her, so why not be her in a different world?

That meant Ajax had a decent idea of what she looked like without clothes, beyond what he'd already seen the other night. *Minus the ugly scars, and less-than-perfect figure.* And he seemed to enjoy what he saw.

It wasn't like she'd strip all the way down. Just to her under garments, which, as he put it before, wasn't much different from a bathing suit.

She needed to mull over this. While she did, her shoes at least could come off. Narissa fussed with her good foot first, but with her bad one propped out to the side, the angle made it a bit more difficult than she'd hoped.

"Here, let me help," Ajax offered.

He worked on the shoelaces and pulled the shoe off.

Narissa smiled and couldn't help but crack a joke. "It's like a reverse Cinderella."

His brow cocked as he glanced at her before focusing on her bad foot. "Reverse? More like better. What Prince Charming gives a woman an uncomfortable death trap made of glass when he can make her feet feel like heaven with a foot massage and fuzzy slippers?"

Narissa winced when the shoe refused to budge. "Are you offering to be Prince Charming?"

A sinfully tempting grin spread up half his face. "For you I could be."

She could get used to that—to this. Undressing in front of him wouldn't be a big deal. Especially if she got her foot massage. It'd been a while since she'd gotten one. Elijah was the only one to ever offer. *Not even Nolan…* Screw Nolan. Not really. Not even with a ten-foot lance. Although, impaling him with a lance was a tempting image. So was picturing Ajax's reaction when she took off her shirt. *Yep, so doing it.*

Ajax finally managed to remove her shoe and touched her tender skin. "We need to get some ice on this. You should"—his eyes widened as she pulled her shirt over her head—"Uh, not that I'm complaining, but what are you doing?"

Once extracted from the shirt, she looked for a place to hang it, being sure to keep an eye on Ajax to gauge his physical response before speaking. She wasn't disappointed. As expected, he looked shocked, but pleased and enticed by this new turn of events. "I don't enjoy sitting in wet clothes. So they're coming off."

His brow tick up. "All of them?"

Narissa chuckled. "Just the shirt and shorts. Everything else is fine. Where can I hang this?"

"Oh, I can go hang it up, and get you a towel so you can dry off." He took the garment from her. "I'll also fetch you some clean clothes."

She shimmied out of her shorts, careful of her bum foot. "Towel would be great. Clothes aren't needed. I'd prefer a heating pad for this ankle."

He hesitated. "Heat… right."

He wandered away, leaving her chuckling to herself and looking for a temporary place to hang her shorts. Ajax got a bit more flustered than she expected. After everything they'd done, she didn't expect something like disrobing to faze him.

Narissa lowered herself onto the couch to make it easier for her stretch out. She grabbed a couch pillow and tucked it under her ankle and leaned back, thinking of ways to distract herself from the pain.

She could ask Ajax to grab some work files. Narissa watched him chase Crash, who had a small towel in her mouth. She giggled. "Hey, after you're done playing, and get me that heating pad, can I have my tablet so I can work?"

"Uh, one sec."

She shook her head. *He didn't hear a word I said.*

Ajax shouted in triumph, but Crash wasn't going to be counted a loser yet. She bounced up and down, following him back into the kitchen. Narissa watched him disappear into the adjacent downstairs bathroom for a moment and then return, a heating pad in his hand. One of his hands was also balled up. He procured a glass of water before coming back into the living room.

Ajax offered her the glass of water and some pills. "Pain killers. It's the good stuff."

That could only mean one thing. The best over-the-counter you could get, which were amazing. It'd bring down the swelling and numb her pain for a while.

While she took the medicine, Ajax rested the heating pad on her ankle and wrapped the towel around it, adding pressure. When he turned the device on, she let out a sigh, the heat spreading all over the tender spot. Ajax's gaze lingered on her for a moment before he dashed off. *I might be a little too tempting for him.* She considered

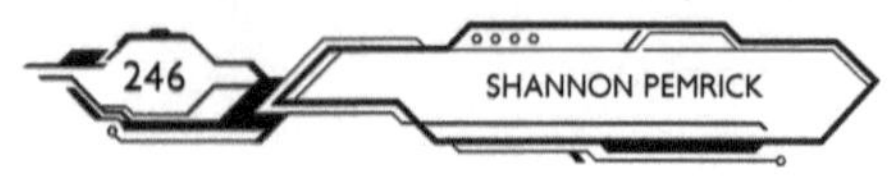

retracting her stance of not covering herself with more clothes. She didn't want to be a problem.

Ajax returned, shirtless and with a new pair of pants, chasing Crash with a towel. Narissa's eyes pinned on his rippling muscles, resisting the urge to lick her lips. She laughed when Crash managed to rip the towel free from his grasp and take off with it. Ajax waved her off and retrieved two more. He dropped one on her head, getting a brief murmur of complaint from her, and then went about drying Helios off. Narissa ran the towel through her hair, watching as Helios enjoyed his pampering, especially getting his butt rubbed. She related to that.

When Narissa finished with her hair, she draped the towel around her neck and relaxed, watching Ajax scurry about, taking care of a few little things when he finished with Helios.

He carried in blankets and pillows, setting them up in front of the couch. Narissa's brow ticked up. "Are you going to make another fort?"

"Nope."

Once he finished setting up what looked to be a really comfortably bed, he went upstairs. When he returned, he carried a gray object with cords. He set it down on the coffee table. She recognized it as a PlayStation One.

She pursed her lips. "You brought that with you on this trip?"

Ajax chuckled. "No. I bought a second one at some point, to have one here and one at home."

She shook her head. "Most billionaires spend their money on multiple houses, yachts, and fast cars. You buy expensive old game consoles."

He held up his hands. "Gamer, what do you expect?"

She grinned. "That you'd have enough for every room of every place you live."

He held up a finger and went to speak, but clamped his mouth shut. She could see the wheels in his mind turning now.

"I was joking. You don't need that many."

"No, I think I do."

Narissa smacked her forehead. What had she done?

"But that can wait." Ajax handed her a controller.

Her brow rose. "What's this for?"

"We're going to play games, and not work." He chuckled. "Yes, I did hear you. My selective hearing wasn't active."

She threw her head back as she laughed.

"Now, let's get you moved down to this setup I've made." Before she could protest, he moved her heating pad and lifted her in his arms. Careful not to jostle her ankle too much, he set her down in the cradle of comfort, wrapping the heating pad back around her elevated ankle, and then turned on the game system before settling down behind her.

Ajax encouraged her to lean back against him, and she didn't resist. She enjoyed the warmth radiating off of his sculpted body, and embraced how comfortable it was to lay here like this with him. She could definitely get used to this.

"So, what game have you thrown in?" she asked.

"Crash Bandicoot."

Narissa laughed. "Of course. But isn't that a single-player game?"

"Like most PS1 games. I thought we'd see who could beat levels with more fruit and gem points."

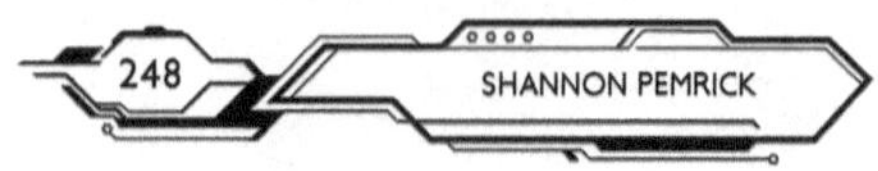

"Well, since I've never played, I'm going to predict you're going to do better."

Ajax rocked his head. "Maybe. This is the third game, Warped. I haven't played it as much."

She wasn't convinced, but would try regardless.

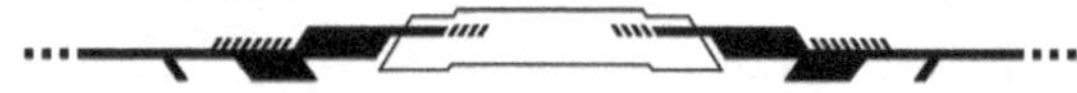

Twenty minutes in, and she wasn't doing too badly. Ajax did better than her, but she wasn't too far behind in points. The assistants were even making comments, going as far as to heckle the other person. It was quite comical, especially when they interacted. Narissa enjoyed these advanced AI upgrades that came out earlier in the year. It improved their use on so many levels.

Narissa cheered when she received the crystal at the end of the level. Ajax hung his head. He'd tried this one before her and had trouble with it.

"Those points put you in the lead, Doctor," Picard said.

She smiled at Ajax. "Your turn."

He sucked in a tight breath and snaked his arms around her, taking the controller in his hands. "I'm trying that level again."

It wouldn't gain him any points, as they were only allowed to attempt a level once unless they both failed. But he seemed determine to beat it, so she let him.

Ajax restarted the level, but didn't make it any farther than his first try. He tried yet again, and did better, but not great.

He groaned. "Why can't I beat this stupid level?"

Narissa peeked down at her chest, where his hands

rested underneath, pushing them up a bit. This had become his standard placement during the game. She didn't mind. She'd put herself on display for him. And it's not like she told him to stop. "I may be mistaken, but it's possibly due to your controller and hand placement."

Ajax pulled his hands in, pushing her breast up more. "No, it's helping."

She glanced up at him, half her lips curving up. "I'm sorry to disappoint you, but my breasts don't act as controllers."

He regarded her for a moment and then grabbed one of her breasts. The action sent a jolt through her. "You sure?"

Narissa had two choices: keep going with this play, or stop it before it went any farther. It wasn't a choice. Each action she'd made leading to this one steered her toward one already—the one she wanted from the start.

She reached up and grabbed his hand, moving her breast around. "See, characters don't move."

He sighed and placed his hand back on the controller. "Fine."

This surprised her. She didn't expect him to go back to the game after that. Did she do something wrong? *Maybe I looked too far into this…* Wouldn't be the first time.

Narissa pulled her knee up, and rested her arms on her stomach. Might as well get comfortable.

Ajax failed another time, and then tried again. He rested his head against her, and she didn't know what to make of it. She was getting one too many conflicting messages here.

When he failed again he hung his head. "Why can't I figure this out?"

Narissa turned and kissed him on the temple. Not wanting to push this boundary any more, she figured it was best to leave it be, but just to encourage him a little. "For luck."

Ajax smiled and tried the level again. This time he got much farther before getting too careless with a jump, and ended up in a bottomless pit. Narissa couldn't stop the laughter. Those were becoming the bane of his existence.

Ajax pouted. "Not fair."

"Do you need some more luck?" She was pushing hers, but she couldn't help it.

He locked eyes with her. The intensity built warmth in her core. "I think I'm going to need something a little stronger."

This was it. They'd either keep playing hot or cold, or—Narissa wasn't sure anymore what they were playing. But she could do this one last thing to see what would happen. If nothing, then yesterday and the night before were just flukes based on the situations and heightened emotions. And she could live with that.

She reached out, touching his face with a single finger, before pulling him in for a kiss. Ajax inhaled deeply and Narissa's heart skipped with the sensations flooding over her.

She pulled away and settled back against him. "That should be enough mojo, yeah?"

Ajax took a moment to respond. When he did, he tossed the controller aside and grasped her face. "Alright, enough of this flirty tease game."

Flirty… tease? That's what he thought this was? That explained the mixed messages.

His lips crashed into hers, cutting any more thoughts. She reached up and threaded her fingers into his hair, locking him in close. Ajax's hands roamed her body, one sliding over bra and then under it. Narissa whimpered as his fingers touched her sensitive flesh.

His other hand went to her back, following her band. But when his hand came to where the clasp would be on a standard bra, everything stopped. He pulled away and looked behind. "Dammit, this is a front clasp, isn't it?"

Narissa smiled at him and he groaned. "Damn man-hating contraptions."

She sputtered on a laugh. "Man-hating?"

"Yes, they lock into place on the front—"

"Because we need to be sure our breasts don't escape."

He held up a finger. "No, it's because you want to give us men a harder time. It's annoying enough dealing with back clasps, especially the bras with multiple. Why can't you ladies just go without? Would be so much easier."

She let out a closed mouth chuckle. She enjoyed his silly rants.

"Besides, you could go braless no problem, so it's not like you need it." He tried to undo the front clasp, but struggled.

Narissa removed his hands and placed them on her thighs. "I'll take that into consideration. But first, let me give you a hand."

She hooked her fingers around the locking clasp and undid it with ease, her supple breasts spilling out, though his roaming hands did add a minor difficulty.

Ajax's hands stopped moving as he stared, his voice coming out husky and throatier than before. "Witch craft."

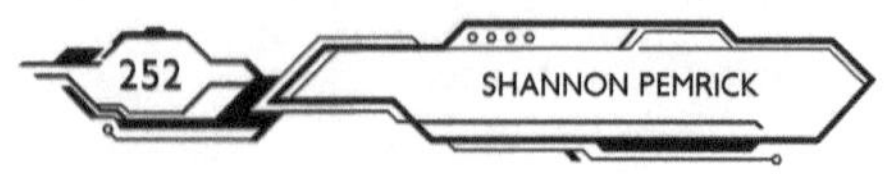

Narissa's head flew back as she laughed. "Is it now?"

"Yes."

Narissa turned to face him, pushing up on her knees, thankful those painkillers had kicked in some time ago. "Now, am I a witch, or a priestess?"

Ajax's hands found purchase on her hips. He looked her over with an appreciative gaze. "A dark priestess? I never asked the deity you followed."

She leaned in closer. "I'm pretty sure some of the deities out there aren't evil, but fit this domain perfectly."

He pulled her tight against him, pulling a quiet gasp from her. "Aphrodite has nothing on you."

Narissa grinned. "Careful, she'll curse you if she hears that."

That wickedly sinful grin spread up half his face. "Curse me? Why would she do that when she sent you to me?"

Ajax's hands ran down her thighs and his thumbs slipped between them, finding her slick and ready heat. Narissa gasped. "And now it's time to appreciate the gift."

He stroked her, the sensation of both fingers breathtaking. Ajax kissed her collar, her neck, under her chin. Need swelled inside her, her swollen breast aching with desire to be touched. Narissa arched her back, pulling him closer to them. He reciprocated, circling his tongue around her taut peaks, before dragging it across and then capturing them between his lips. She drew in a sharp breath and moaned as he sucked and teased.

Her mind shut off, passion and want taking over. She ground her hips into his touch, wanting more. Ajax thrust a few fingers inside her. She arched her back, her eyes hooding, moaning loud; the sensation of his various assaults set her core ablaze. She needed more. She needed him.

Narissa reached for the button of his jeans, but he stopped her. She whimpered as all pleasure halted. "What's wrong?"

Ajax kissed her jaw, using a finger to stroke her again. "I don't have anything on me. And I don't want to stop this to get some."

Her teeth caught her lower lip. She didn't understand. It wasn't like she could get pregnant. She figured he wasn't on anything. Plenty of men chose not to take any of the market birth control, due to a lack of effectiveness compared to female birth control. Those who did opt to use it, usually were in committed relationships. "Are you clean?"

Female birth control reliability made condoms really only needed for STI prevention, and an added layer of peace of mind.

He kissed down her neck and over her collar bone. "Yes, but that's not the point."

Then what was his point?

"No more talking or thinking." He licked her taut nipple, getting a sharp inhale from her. "Just feel."

Ajax captured her dark bud again, sucking, teasing, driving her mind wild as he continued to stroke her between her thighs. Her core pulsed with desire again. He slipped his other hand between her thighs again; amplifying her pleasure back to before she'd stopped it in her impatience.

"Andrew…" she moaned. She cusped on the edge of release. "More…"

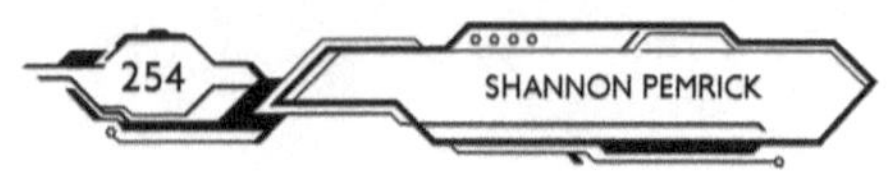

Ajax's touch never faltered, pushing her closer and closer. And when she thought she couldn't handle much more, ecstasy burst through her. Narissa screamed, her hips bucking and her back arching, her whole body consumed with pleasure. Ajax pulled her close, still refusing to let up until she shuddered out the last of her orgasm.

Narissa rested her forehead on his shoulder, her breath ragged. Euphoria pulsed through her as Ajax held her firm against him. When the sensation ebbed, she attempted to pull away, but he held fast. "Not yet."

She stopped resisting and leaned into him, waiting for an explanation.

"I just want to keep pretending a little longer."

Her brow arched as she turned her head to peer up at him. "Pretending what?"

"That you're mine."

Her pulse skipped. *Does he mean that?* The way he held her made it hard to believe otherwise. And did it mean he only wanted to keep pretending, or—

Narissa pushed herself away from Ajax, despite his attempt to keep her close. She eventually won.

She didn't go far, though—only an arm's length away, as she rested her forearms on his muscular chest. She looked at him, noticing the concern lines creasing his face. It wasn't hard to guess he was assuming he'd said something wrong—that she didn't want him saying such things. But it was the complete opposite.

At this point, what Narissa wanted outweighed her past fears. Words tumbled out of her mouth. "Does it have to be pretend?"

Ajax's face relaxed, a smile slipping up his face. He

reached out and brushed her cheek with the back of his hand. "Not if we both don't want it to be."

Narissa leaned in and kissed him, her heart swelling. She wanted this—wanted him. She wanted to get it right this time. To pick someone who respected and cared for her for real. She wanted Mr. Right to be Ajax. Her dumb nerd of a jock who'd do anything to make her happy—do anything to keep her safe.

Both of his hands cupped her ass. "I think it's time to check you for ticks."

Narissa giggled. "Only if I get to return the favor." She ran her fingers through his hair. "And fleas."

He grinned. "Well, Nolan did call me a mongrel."

She placed a finger on his lips. "I'd rather not talk about him."

Ajax pushed her hand aside and his dark pools stared into her. "Tell me what you do want."

"I want to forget. I want to get so lost in this, in us, that he doesn't matter. That what he did can't touch me anymore."

"I can do that." He pinned her arms behind her back. "And while I'm at it, I'll do so many unholy things to you, not even a bath in holy water will cleanse you."

She swallowed, desire building inside her. She'd never been the adventurous type, but he tempted her to try. Being restrained yesterday had been far from unpleasant. And even now it was exciting. *I wonder how he'd enjoy it with the roles reversed.*

He'd also introduced her to a few positions she'd never tried but had fantasized about. All without prompting. It had been... quite the amazing experience.

Ajax threaded his fingers into her hair and kissed her

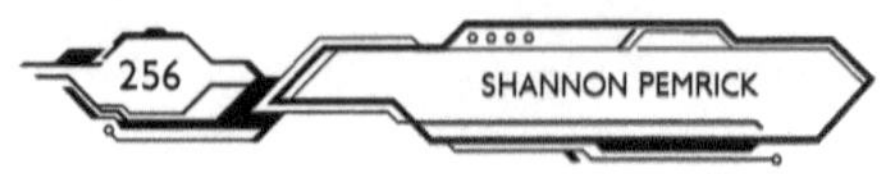

hard. She whimpered into his mouth, want and need driving her. It didn't matter he'd given her a release only a moment ago. She was becoming accustomed already to this multi-euphoric experience with him.

Narissa ground her hips into him. With her hands pinned, she could only give limited body cues, and her grinding was the best one. She needed him. Now.

Their lips parted and Ajax grinned. "If you're really that impatient…"

He released her arms and grabbed her thighs. With what seemed like inhumanly smooth motions, he got to his feet, still carrying her.

Narissa kissed his neck as he carried her to the stairs. "Impressive."

He squeezed her. "And there's more where that came from."

Her teeth grazed his skin. "Good."

Before Narissa knew it, her back hit soft sheets. Her arms spread across the silk material as she took a quick peek around. He kept the room relatively clean, the walls mostly bare, save for an old promotion poster or two, and a single shelf with some collectable figures. Most of the game-related items were tucked in the corner around his gaming station. "Nice place you got."

He smirked. "It's even better now that you're here." He turned for his closet. "Stay there."

Narissa pursed her lips, curious what he was doing, and sat up. She never said she was any good at listening. Ajax rummaged through the closet and pulled out a tie—from the looks of it, 8-bit-themed. She shook her head. She should have known.

Ajax turned back around, his eyes narrowing. He

wrapped the tie around his hand as he came back. It appeared to be his way of staying focused, nothing more, based on her careful observation. "You're not listening."

A smirk curved up her face. "If I was good at that, I wouldn't have saved my brother's life and made that nice cybernetic you sport."

He chuckled and knotted the tie around the headboard. "Your smart mouth is going to get you in trouble here."

Narissa reached out and fussed with his jeans. "Me? You're the one who filled out all the punches on his frequent sinner card."

Ajax managed to finish his task as she pulled down the zipper of his pants. "Someone is eager."

She worked him free of the material confines. His impressive aroused flesh sprang free and stood at attention, as eager as she was. Narissa's eyes ticked up to his, a grin on her face. "Who's eager now?"

The intensity of his eyes made her heart skip a beat. "Rissa."

Without breaking eye contact, her tongue darted out and teased him, receiving a satisfying inhale, before she took him into her mouth. Ajax groaned and his hands found her hair, balling up into her curly locks.

"Rissa…" he groaned.

Narissa sucked and slid his shaft in and out of her mouth with rhythmic strokes. She kept eye contact with him, the intensity of their locked gazes further building her hunger.

Ajax's grip tightened and his hips rocked, his member swelling more. "Rissa…"

Her rhythm picked up, her desire building with each moan of pleasure he let out.

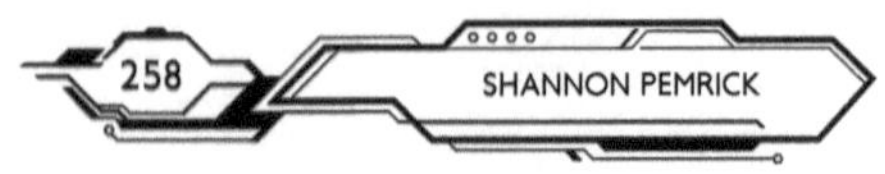

Then suddenly, he jerked away from her and pushed her back on the bed. Without a word, he bent over her and ravaged her, trailing kisses all over her body. She gasped as powerful, needy sensations built in her.

Ajax's hands roamed her body—her sides—her breasts—her hips—nowhere was safe. It only fanned the heat of her desire. Her heart pounded in her chest and she pressed herself against him, craving the feel of his flesh against hers.

His hands found her panties and slipped them off before reaching out for her inner thighs. No stalling, no hesitating, allowing the pleasure to build up. He used his other hand to pin both of hers above her head. She moaned, embracing this feeling—this experience with him.

Then suddenly and all too soon, it stopped and he pulled away. She let out a hiss of frustration, sitting up and watching him go through his nightstand. He was going to pay for that; it didn't matter what he pulled out.

Lube and a condom. Still didn't matter.

Her eyes ticked to the tie hanging from the headboard and then back to him.

Ajax tore open the packaging, his eyes darting back to her. "Don't look at me like that. I promise it'll be worth it."

Narissa kept eye contact as she scooted back on the bed, a fake scowl on her face. It wasn't going to be that easy for him. Not with the idea brewing in her head. "You didn't need those."

Ajax rolled the condom on. "I want to be safe, even if your statics say otherwise. And we'll be going at this long enough that I don't want you getting uncomfortable."

His logic made it hard to keep pretending to be mad—or not aroused. His respect and care for her was more endearing than she felt like she deserved. And the view she had of his perfectly sculpted form—*Don't let it sway you, Narissa. Not right now. Stick to the plan.*

Ajax sighed when she managed to keep up her poker face, and climbed onto the bed. "Come here."

She scooted back more, luring him farther until she had him in the right spot. His brow ticked up when she smirked. Narissa pushed herself forward, onto her knees, and wrapped her arms around his neck, capturing his lips with hers. Ajax wrapped his arms around her waist, leaning back as she applied pressure with her body.

When he lay on his back, Narissa's hands slid over his torso, memorizing every peak and valley of his muscles. She rocked her hips. Ajax responded in turn, his kisses and touches becoming more demanding, just as she'd hoped.

Her hands continued to glide up, over to his shoulders and along his arms as she encouraged him to let her go and rest them over his head. Their hands entwined, Ajax was oblivious and consumed with the promise of pleasure. His erection pressed against her unprotected femininity. It tempted her, but she needed to stay focused a little longer.

Her thumb touched the tie hanging from the headboard. Their kiss ended, leaving Ajax staring at her. "Rissa."

Narissa grinned and slipped from his grip. She latched onto the tie and went about tying him up, though he didn't make it easy. He "fought" back, making no attempt to hide he was just trying to make this harder on her

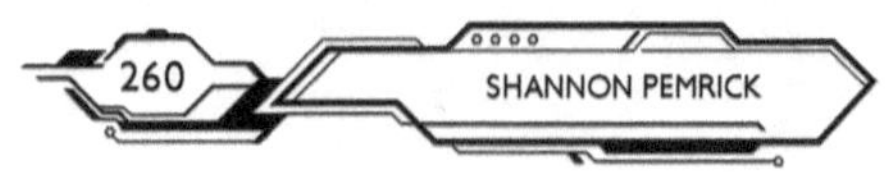

and not stop her. *If he wanted that, he'd just be able to throw me under him.* She wouldn't mind that, either.

She let out a triumphant chuckle once she got the knot tight, and sat up, her hands gliding over his skin. Ajax sucked in a breath as he watched her, his mouth curving up, and then looked up at his hands. "We really need to work on your knotting skills."

With no effort at all, he slipped his cybernetic hand free. Narissa huffed. "You're no fun."

Ajax rested his artificial limb on her thigh. "Don't be like that. I'll submit, even though this wasn't my intent for setting that up." He waved his captured arm. "This one is in there good though."

She let out a breath. "I suppose a consolation prize is good enough."

He bucked his hips, forcing her to brace her hand on his chest. She narrowed her eyes. "No. You behave, or I'll leave you here and finish myself off."

Ajax's eyes glowed. "I would like to see that."

She wore a smug smile. "I'll go in the other room."

His mouth spread into a thin line. "Fine. But I'd recommend getting some stimulation going, or I'm going to lose this hard-on."

She faked innocence, though she did rock her hips some. "What, you mean you can't keep that going? Am I not pretty enough?"

Ajax squeezed her thigh. "There's a reason the Viagra commercials say to see a doctor if an erection lasts longer than four hours."

A smirk curved up her face. "So up to that point is okay?"

He chuckled. "What are you getting at here?"

Narissa shrugged and leaned over to kiss him quick. "Just being weird."

His false hand threaded through her hair and he managed to kiss her before she could pull away. "I like it when you're weird."

Narissa sat up and rocked her hips. Ajax swallowed and gripped her thigh again. Ajax's eyes pinned to her, following her every movement. "Are you going to punish me now, Priestess?"

She would, if she knew how. She honestly wasn't sure what she was supposed to do in this position. She'd really only done it to mess with him, and thought he'd pin her to the bed instead of allowing this. *I wouldn't mind that at all.*

A thought came to her. Something he said earlier surfaced from the back of her mind. She grinned. "No. You assumed filling that card would grant you punishment. It doesn't. It's a reward."

His eyes glowed again, his voice deepening. "I like rewards."

Narissa slipped her hand between them and grasped his aroused member. She stroked him, careful with the condom he'd rolled on. She only needed to ensure he was ready for her, and she for him. She wasn't entirely sure his impressive size would fit in her. Textbook theory said yes, but practical wasn't always the same. *Here goes nothing.*

She lifted herself up and hovered over him, waiting until she could see the anticipation in his eyes killing him. When she'd seen enough, she lowered herself over his shaft. Her mouth parted, and her breathing came to a halt as she accepted him.

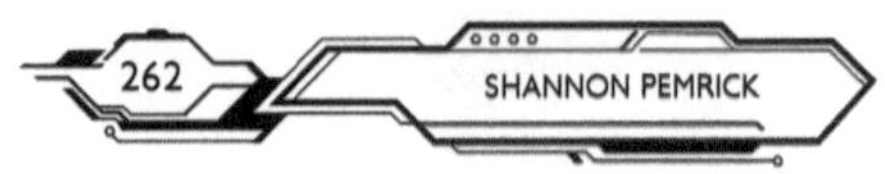

"Oh, God," tumbled out of her mouth. Game-model him was amazing. Real him was godly. She may just go over the edge from this one act.

Ajax's grip on her leg tightened for every inch he buried inside of her. From the look on his face, he was experiencing this much the same as her.

Once he filled her completely, the two of them remained still, processing this new sensation. Ajax was the first to move, thrusting deeper inside her. She gasped, louder than she'd ever expected, as intense pleasure hit her.

Ajax tensed. "Did that hurt?"

His concern made her heart swell. "No. On the contrary." She rocked her hips. "I want you to do that again."

A heart stopping grin spread across his handsome face and he thrust again. "As you wish."

Her breathing hitched again, this time finding that expecting the pleasure made her reaction less crazy. She placed a hand on his abs and met his thrusts with her own grinding. The two found rhythm quickly, the sensation overwhelming. She didn't even try to stop the quiet moaning that came from her throat.

But it wasn't enough. She reached between her legs and dipped her fingers into her own slick heat. Narissa threw her head back and moaned; Ajax groaned as well. She glanced down at him, finding his eyes intent on her while also fighting against his restraint.

"You're not allowed out yet," she said.

"You said this wasn't punishment." His cybernetic hand slipped up her side. "Me not being able to touch you—feel you—is torture."

She grinned. "I lied."

Narissa grasped his false hand and made him touch her bouncing breasts—roll his fingers over her aching nipples—pinch and tweak them. It sent so many pleasurable sensations through her, on top of what she was already experiencing below.

Ajax watched with hungry eyes; the lack of feeling from the cybernetic tortured him, but the sight of her pleasure excited him. He tried to move his hand behind her head to pull her close, but she fought him. He wasn't in control here.

"Rissa, please," he begged.

She licked her lower lip. "Please, what?"

He swallowed, his breathing strained. "I need… I need you closer."

She liked this side of him. The vulnerable side of Mr. Confident.

Narissa complied, but just a little. Still upright, the new angle increased the intensity of his thrusting and the touches from her fingers. Ajax wasn't satisfied. He tried to coax her closer, but she wasn't listening. He made his frustration clear, and for a moment she thought he'd beg some more.

He seemed to have other plans. Ajax cupped her face and pressed his artificial thumb on her lower lip. Interested in what he was trying to accomplish, she let her jaw go slack, opening her mouth as he pressed. He grinned and inserted his thumb into her mouth. *Oh*.

She didn't mind this, and gave him what he was looking for. She sucked the artificial appendage, not easing up on anything else she did, her eyes hooding.

A pleased grin appeared on his face. "I think my doctor may have a cybernetic fetish?"

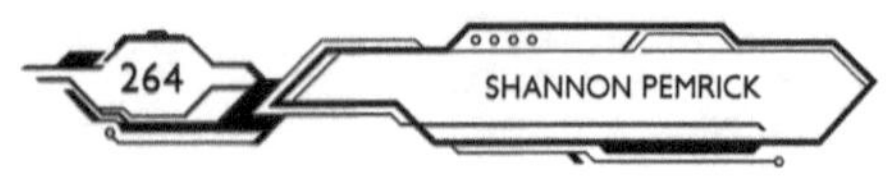

Did she? She never thought about it. Cybernetics were cybernetics to her. She didn't see the augmentations any differently than a natural limb or body part. But even if it wasn't one, she could play along. She pulled away with a *pop* and smiled. "And if I do? Is that a problem?"

Desire deepened the rich hue of his eyes. "Not at all. In fact—"

Ajax dragged his hand down her skin to her center, and took over the job of pleasuring her. Narissa gasped, and the freedom allowed her to brace herself with both hands on his chest.

Need and desire renewed and coursed through her. "I guess you have a fetish for pretty, broken things, then."

Ajax stared at her with intense, sincere eyes. "You're not broken."

Thank you. She picked up her pace, bouncing against his thrusts, each plunge sending bursts of pleasure through her. Ajax's body tensed, his breathing labored. Narissa grinned. His final punishment was upon him.

She immediately slid off of his hardness. Ajax let out a frustrated hiss. "Rissa."

She chuckled as she straddled him. That had worked quite well. Took a little longer, but the journey had been more fun. "Consider it payback for earlier. And the final piece to your punishment."

He stared at her with intense eyes. She couldn't read them, though. "That's it."

Ajax yanked at the tie with his cybernetic hand and broke himself free. With how quickly he'd undone the restraint, she thought for a moment he might have just Hulk-ripped his way out. That was really the only thought to go through her mind before she was flipped onto her back, her arms pinned next to her head.

The intensity of his gaze as he hovered over her made her mouth dry out and her heart pound hard against her ribcage and in her ears. "Is… it my turn to be punished?"

She wasn't sure why she said it, but given the circumstances, it may have been a possibility.

"No." He reached out, grasping a fistful of hair, and crashed his lips into hers, devouring her. Narissa let out a small whimper, her insides melting.

Ajax gave her no time. With his other hand, he lifted her hips and plunged deep into her. She moaned and pressed into him, wrapping her arms around his neck and meeting his thrusts. Their tongues wrestled, hungry and demanding, drinking in each other's taste.

He reached up and fondled her breast, his other hand still locked in her hair. Their kiss broke and his teeth grazed her jaw, her neck—so much of her neck. Her nails dug into his skin, heat searing her core. Her breath labored as she teetered on the edge.

Ajax reached between her thighs; the sensation pushed her over the line. She arched her back, her mouth hanging open as a scream erupted with the burst of ecstasy coursing through her. Ajax's grip on her hair tightened, losing control. He grunted into her neck as he spent himself.

Their movements slowed until they both stilled, breathing heavy and deep. Ajax nipped her shoulder, pulling out a quiet gasp from her, before rolling off and disposing of the condom. Narissa remained there, coming back down to earth. She understood now why people were so crazy for sex. It wasn't just a means to

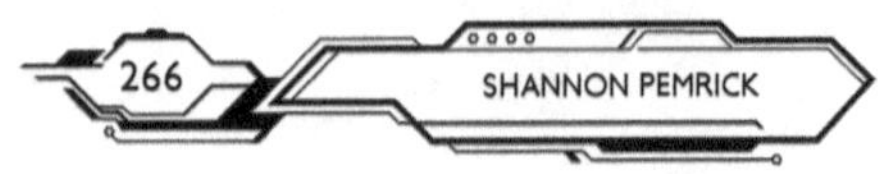

an end. It was fun, exciting, thrilling even. She could definitely get used to this.

Ajax returned and curled her into his strong form, her back facing him. His comfortable musky and peppermint scent enveloping her. *Yes, I could get used to this.*

Crash's nose poked over the bed, sniffing away. Ajax chuckled. "Well, at least she waited to bother us."

"I'm half surprised she didn't jump on the bed." Narissa was no stranger to that type of behavior with dogs. Bruno, and some dogs they'd watched or fostered for a time, were always curious beasties during times of intimacy. Even if it was just something as tame as cuddling.

"I'm sure it'll happen sometime." Ajax squeezed her. "How is your foot doing?"

"Between the painkillers and endorphins, it's not screaming at me."

He kissed the back of her head. "Good. Now, I owe you a foot massage."

She glanced back at him. She'd assumed that wasn't happening since they'd jumped right into playing the game. "You don't have to."

Ajax's brow furrowed. "What woman says no to a foot massage?"

She shrugged. "Me? Elijah was the only one to ever give me one."

"Have you never been pampered?"

Narissa didn't want to answer that question. It was a sad response.

He pulled away. "That's it. Full-body it is. Roll on your front."

Full body? "You don't have to, Andrew."

"And with that response, it's definitely happening." His strong hands forced her to roll over. "Now relax and enjoy."

She let out a contented sigh as his hands worked her back. "You don't have to give up Bella."

His work stalled for a moment. "What?"

"I don't care if you have porn," she clarified.

"Oh." He continued working. "Well, I won't need her now that I have you."

She glanced back at him. "What do you mean?"

He smirked. "I chose her because she looks like you."

Narissa' brow ticked up. "You mean I look like her."

Ajax bent over and kissed between her shoulders. "No."

Narissa sucked in a tight breath. "Okay, whatever you say. But, should I expect this massage to lead somewhere? And if so, how often should I expect it to have the same results when you offer?"

He chuckled against her skin. "About ninety percent of the time."

She stifled a moan as his hands worked her in ways that weren't intended to feel like a typical massage. "What happens with the other ten percent?"

"You say no and I listen." He nipped her shoulder. "I won't ever do anything you don't want me to. I promise."

"I'll hold you to that." She grinned. "Now, focus on this wonderful massage, then seducing me after."

Ajax chuckled. "Looking forward to that second part."

CHAPTER 17

Warmth surrounded Ajax as he stirred from his sleep. Birds chirped a morning song, welcoming him to the realm of consciousness. He stretched, finding his arms didn't run into another body. This woke him even more as he blindly patted the bed to find Narissa gone.

Ajax bolted up. The sun shone in through the windows, his clock reading *9:09 AM*. His dogs weren't in the room and neither was Narissa. Panic flooded over him and he bolted out of bed, finding some pants lying around to throw on.

He dashed out the room, his hands landing on the mezzanine as he peered down into the living room. Helios lifted his head from where he lay behind the couch, his butt wiggling as he wagged his stumpy tail. *There's one.*

Clanking echoed from the kitchen, and then Narissa's giggling. "No, you can't have this."

There's the other two. He relaxed and descended the stairs. Helios met him at the foot and happily accepted some loving pats. Ajax entered the kitchen, finding Narissa leaning against the counter, a bowl in her hand. She scooped up something green with dark flecks and ate it. Crash stared up at her with big puppy-dog eyes.

"Morning, sleepyhead," she said, eating more of her food. "I took the dogs out for you. Figured you'd like to sleep in for once."

Ajax's eyes gazed over every curve of her sweet form, sending an ache through him, before he ran his hand through his hair. "Thanks. Are you eating ice cream?"

She smiled and nodded. He glanced back to the TV, but no sappy chick flick played.

Narissa laughed. "I'm not eating it from a pint, so it's not a mood thing."

Ajax let out an exhale of relief. "Well, at least I didn't cause you any sort of trauma or anything like that last night."

"Nope. I just wanted ice cream for breakfast." She pointed her spoon at the fridge. "With how health conscious you can be, I'm surprised you have ice cream here."

Ajax shrugged and came further into the kitchen. "Normally we only have boxed cake mix, but I know how much you love ice cream, so I had some delivered for you."

Her nose scrunched. "Boxed cake mix. That's not real cake. You need to make that stuff from scratch."

Ajax drew up close. "Well, if you're offering, I won't say no. You'll just have to wear a cute little apron." He chuckled and bent to her ear. "And only an apron."

Her eyes shifted up to him, a tempting smirk on her lips. "You'd have to bake with me."

Ajax poked his chest with his thumb. "I've got a 'kiss the cook' apron my sister gave as a birthday gift. It's got a lot of frills and color. I'm sure that will suffice."

Narissa laughed and placed both her hands on his chest. She looked up at him through her lashes, sending a jolt of need through him. "Well, if that's the case, we'd need to cross out 'kiss' and write in 'blow,' because a man who cooks is too sexy for words, and if he's going to be comfortable wearing that train wreck of an apron, he deserves a nice reward."

That offer was so tempting. Though her words kept him slightly more preoccupied—for now. "I didn't think I'd ever hear you say anything remotely vulgar like that." He twisted some of her gorgeous hair into his finger. "I didn't even get anything remotely close while I was making you beg."

Her gaze fell elsewhere as she pulled away. "Yeah, I fight my upbringing all the time. Sometimes I feel real stupid staying things because of its nagging voice, so I don't."

Ajax tucked his finger under her chin so she'd look at him. "Don't. You can say whatever you want with me."

She smiled and then went back to eating her melting ice cream. He'd have to work with her on that. It did bring something to the front of his mind, though. For a moment, he thought it best not to ask, but then realized it was okay if he approached it the right way. "Can I ask you something personal?"

She glanced up at him, finishing the treat on her spoon. "I don't see why not."

He scratched the back of his head. "I'd like to understand your religious and spiritual stance a bit more. It's not something I'd normally ask, as I've been raised not to since that's so personal, but you and your mother are complete opposites."

Narissa placed her empty bowl on the counter and shrugged. "It's not all that complicated, or invasive. While it's true my parents are Baptist, and raised Elijah and me as such, I struggled to embrace the idea of religion as I got older. It stemmed from us devoting our lives to helping people. I couldn't understand how innocent people could be allowed to suffer."

She leaned on the counter. "Then, Elijah got sick and I saved him, but people praised God instead. It bothered me, when he had nothing to do with it in my eyes." She took a deep breath. "And then came my situation with Nolan. That was the final nail in the coffin. I'd lived my life a good person. Sure, my faith and acceptance of the concept of God wasn't strong, but that didn't make me a bad person."

She looked up at him. "So why did that all happen to me? What did I do to deserve that?" Narissa looked away. "And on top of that, Nolan's church sided with him. Tried to make me out to be the bad one, like I framed him or forced him to do all these horrible things."

She shook her head, her curls bouncing about. "I have no ill will toward my parents and others like them for their beliefs. I know not all people were like that one church. My parents and their church tried to defend me, so I know they're good people. It just stopped being something I could possibly believe in."

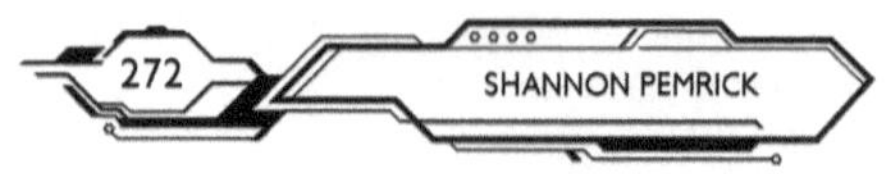

Ajax tucked some of her hair behind her ears. "Thank you for sharing."

She smiled at him. "What about you?"

He shrugged. "Agnostic. Most of the family is. Couple atheist and Buddhists in the extended family. We're all just an accepting lot overall."

"Thank you."

He kissed her forehead and pulled away when the dogs barked, and someone knocked twice on the front door before the lock clicked open.

"It's your sister," Kirk said from the house infrastructure before anyone could panic.

His brow creased. What was his sister doing here? Ajax went for the living room to meet her halfway.

A woman with tan skin and long, raven hair entered the house.

"Baby brother, I have something important to tell you," Allyson said as she entered the house.

"What are you doing here?" he asked her.

Her brow knitted, bright blue eyes flickering with annoyance. "Did I not just say I have something important to talk to you about?"

Duh, Ajax. "Yeah, I heard that. But could it really not have waited until I got back?"

Allyson glanced behind him. Narissa approached. "Am I interrupting something?"

He went to say yes, but Narissa spoke instead. "No. He's just being weird."

Well, there went that.

Narissa looked at him. "I don't know why you have to ask so many questions. She came all the way out here, so it must be important."

Allyson held out her hands to her. "Thank you."

It was like they were both conspiring against him. Ajax sighed. "Okay, okay. What do you have to tell me?"

"I figured out the issue with the gaming pods!" his sister beamed.

His mouth fell open. She figured it out? "Really?"

"Yep!"

His pulse quickened and the need to jump around like a little kid threaten to take over. "This is fantastic!"

His joy died when he noticed the perplexed look on Narissa's face. "Aren't you excited?"

"No, and I'm trying to figure out why you are."

That answer surprised him, and he could see it didn't please his sister one bit. Allyson crossed her arms, her eyes looking Narissa up and down. "Who the hell do you think you are?"

Shit. The women were about to get catty on him.

Narissa mirrored the pose. "Doctor Narissa Okafor. The pioneer of cybernetics."

Allyson's hardened expression faltered a moment but quickly returned.

Narissa continued. "I've worked for several days analyzing much of the information needed to understand this design in full, and I've found numerous errors that not just any person could find."

Allyson licked her lips. "Well, sounds like your analysis is off, because I found them and fixed them. This change will work."

"It will? What background do you have in cybernetics that makes you this confident?"

His sister shrugged. "I looked up what I needed to know on the internet. It wasn't that hard."

Narissa's eyes burned. "Not that hard? Are you kidding me?"

He needed to diffuse this. "Ladies, please—"

Narissa fixed him with a hard stare. "Do you really believe she knows more than me with what she just said? That her quick internet search trumps my eight-years-plus of school and hands-on field research? Do you really think I'm going to take such a blatant insult from the two of you?"

He didn't know how to answer that. His sister was brilliant. She wouldn't come here unless she knew for sure—

She shook her head. "Didn't you bring me on in the first place because no one else could help you like I can?"

He did, but—

Narissa's lips pressed into a thin line and she nodded as if piecing something together in her head. "I see. A ruse, then. I should have known."

What?

She headed for the stairs. "Picard, call a car."

"Doctor, I—"

"Call a car, or I will."

"Yes, ma'am."

Ajax's brow furrowed. "Call a car for what?"

Narissa placed her foot on the first step. "So I can get to the airport. There's no point in me being here." She gestured to his sister. "It'd be one thing if she was in my field or had some sort of extensive knowledge from self-studies. But that's not the case, and you're siding with her over what I know."

She shook her head. "I went through this with Nolan

once. I will never be foolish enough to repeat that mistake."

His shock twisted to anger. She was comparing him to that manipulative asshole?

"Since you no longer need me, once I arrive in L.A., I'll send over the termination clause of our business partnership. You'll also receive the client service termination contact with Cybro Industries, as your continued patronage relied on you changing your behavior. You'd better hope your sister is right, Ajax, because you will not get a replacement arm from us again." Her eyes softened for a moment, before going back to stern. "And let's hope, for your sake, that's the only thing that breaks."

Numbness fell over Ajax. He wanted to feel something else. Confusion, for knowing that as upset as she was, she wasn't screaming at the two of them. Pain, knowing she was so done she went back to calling him Ajax like everyone else. Or even fury, because she was so proud of herself she couldn't see someone else might be able to come up with safe alternatives without the same type knowledge as her. But it all compounded into emptiness.

And the absurd termination of both contracts… *It's just her anger talking. They're just empty threats to make me change my mind.*

Narissa marched upstairs to collect her things.

One emotion finally cracked through—irritation. *Fine, let her act like a child.* He faced his sister. "Give me what you have." When his sister looked at him, confused, but didn't speak, he snapped his fingers at her in his irritation. "Hello? Allyson, do you have the information or not?"

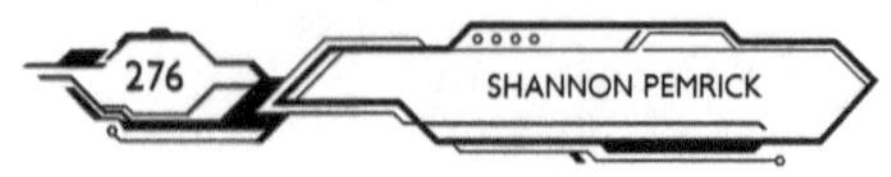

Her eyes fluttered and she shook her head. "Oh, right, yeah."

She whipped out her phone, and he retrieved his from the coffee table where he'd left it last night. It *pinged* when he received the file. Ajax opened it up to take a look at it. Without looking too far into the notes, he did see a great deal of improvements. Something deep inside nagged him to have Narissa look at it, either to prove she might be wrong, or to make sure he wasn't making a huge mistake.

Would she listen to him at this point? Did he have a right to backpedal and ask after siding with his sister so quickly?

"Brother," Allyson said after a moment. "It wasn't my intent to cause problems between you and your girlfriend."

"I'm not his girlfriend," Narissa said as she passed them, her packed suitcase in hand. She didn't look at either of them as she did.

The numbness and confusion returned. *What?* She was just supposed to be mad. The termination threats were just that. She'd leave and then in a few hours, few days at most, they'd work it out. He'd spent all this time trying to convince her to give him a chance. What they said in the living room last night—

He let it go. Everything he'd done for her these past few days, didn't matter to her.

Narissa said her goodbyes to the dogs, both acting a little off, as if they knew something was wrong. And then she left without saying anything to him. Crash paced back and forth in front of the window, whining. Helios stood in front of the door, his head cocked and one ear up, listening, as if Narissa would come right back through that door. But she didn't.

Ajax watched her walk down the long driveway, so desperate to get away she wasn't even willing to wait outside until her ride arrived. *Whatever.*

He'd prove her wrong. Ajax faced his sister. "Let's get to work."

Keys clicked and data flew across Narissa's computer screen. All day she'd worked on improvements for her cybernetic design. She was so close, she just had to keep doing a little more. And that wasn't an excuse to not think about anything else. *Yes it is.*

For the past five days, after returning home alone, she'd jumped right into working. Long hours—the weekend, too—sometimes not even going home. It was an all-work-no-play she was used to, and now embraced.

Her fingers brushed her lips as she contemplated how to word her next note. An unbidden image of her last passionate night with Ajax flashed through her mind. She shook it off.

She hadn't talked to him since the day she left. The one email exchange they had over the contracts was formal and brief. Then nothing. No contact to work things out. No phone call to gloat she'd been wrong, as unlikely as that was. And no phone call about any more accidents, begging her to take care of him at least one more time, against the contract he signed.

Her friends quickly noticed something was up, beyond the fact that she'd returned home early. According to Mercedes, Ajax had also canceled on raid night like she had, to focus on work. Her guildmates were worried, but she wouldn't drag them into her problems.

Narissa typed away. She knew what they'd say. She'd overreacted. She was being stubborn. She should really talk it out with him.

Her fingers faltered. *They'd be right.* She did overreact. Ajax's defense of his sister, even if only non-verbalized by his lack of defense against Narissa's accusing words, had been the biggest slight she'd felt in such a long time. Of all the people she knew, she thought Ajax would be the first to defend her position in her field.

Memories surfaced—of Nolan making snide comments about her knowledge, brushing off an accomplishment, trying to convince her she was wrong when she wasn't.

I thought Ajax would be better than him. Her lip quivered. He didn't even have to pick a side. All he had to do was suggest they all work together instead of assuming his sister had all the answers right out of the gate. But no. He picked his sister over her. *I don't know what I expected. He's never listened to me before. Why would he start now?*

She shouldn't have even tried with him. She knew better. Doing anything for herself was always met with walls and pain. *I don't know why I expected this time around would be different.* At least this time she knew the signs so she wouldn't repeat the past. *As much as it hurt to walk away…*

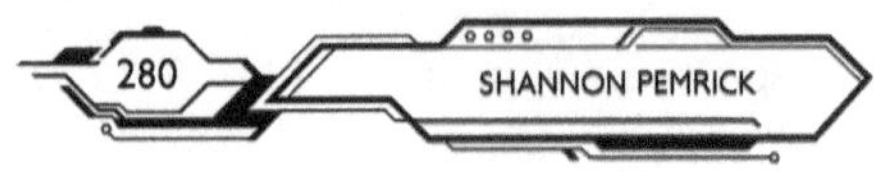

The door to her office opened. She glanced up to see her mother entering. Narissa looked back down at her screen. "On your way out for the night, Mother?"

"Yes. Try not to stay late tonight, darlin'," she said. "I don't want to find out from security that you's slept at your desk again."

She smiled at her mother. "Don't worry. I'll leave soon."

Her mother forced a smile, not believing her at all, but by now knew not to argue. Narissa had slept in her office two out of the four nights she'd been home. It just made sense. Security was better, so Nolan was less likely to get her. They had a shower and gym. Ideal location for eating out. And no commuter traffic.

"Well"—her mother turned away—"you have a good night, babydoll. And remember, there's always a hot plate and warm bed at home, if you's eva wanna stay there."

"Thank you, Momma."

She watched her mother leave before going back to work. It'd be a while before she decided if she'd stay all night or not.

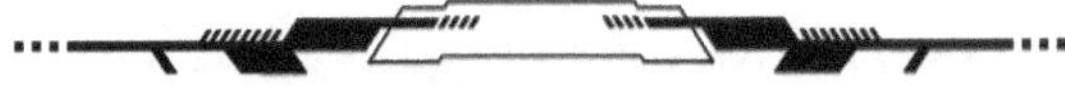

Ajax tightened a screw on the pod and then wiped away a bead of sweat forming on his brow. The AC in the building had crapped out hours ago, and he wished it'd get fixed already. *It may be September now, but that doesn't mean the heat goes away here.* Even this far into the evening.

He looked up when someone knocked on the work-room door. A tan woman with long, wavy hair in tight pants and far too low-cut shirt for dress code compliance stood in the doorway. In her hand she carried a large cup of what looked like iced coffee.

"Lilah, I thought you'd gone home already." For a human assistant that he didn't ask for but his mother had hired recently regardless, she was not good at staying after hours. "How can I help you?"

Her painted red lips curved into a deep smile and she entered. "You've been working so hard today, I thought I'd run out to get you an iced coffee before I left."

He didn't like iced coffee. And if she'd paid attention on her first day working here, she'd know that. He gestured to the table near her. "Thanks. Just put it over there. I'll drink it once I finish this."

Her gaze lingered on him before doing as he'd asked. "Is there anything else you need assistance with, sir?"

"No, thank you."

She drew a little closer, her eyes assessing him for a moment. "You sure? I'm pretty handy with tools."

He exhaled. "I'm not interested, Lilah. So why don't you go home for the night? And while you're there, re-familiarize yourself with the company dress code. We may allow casual, but there are limits set in place."

She hesitated, her confidence now gone, quickly switching to irritation. "All right. Have a good night, Ajax."

He didn't watch her leave. He didn't have time. This machine needed to be done. Allyson wanted to test it by tomorrow, but at this rate, it'd take him two more days at least.

"That wasn't very nice of you, Eugene."

Ajax looked up to see his mother standing in the room. He refocused on another bolt in need of tightening.

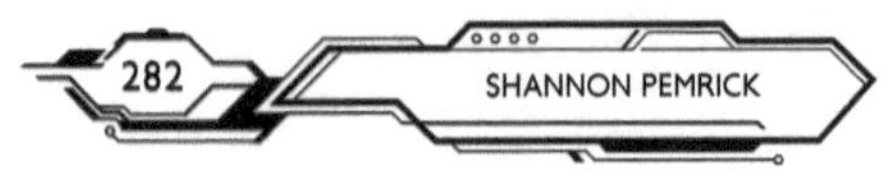

"I said what needed to be said. She's breaking dress code, and I didn't want her to keep up her antics. I'm not interested."

"Yes, but you could have been kinder. At the very least, more professional." She sighed. "Honestly, you've been in this mood since you came back. I'd hoped you'd cool off by now."

"I'm not in a mood." His mother didn't respond, but he knew what she would say. That he was poor liar. And she was right. He was still angry Narissa would leave like that. That she'd compare him to Nolan just because he sided with his sister.

"Kirk, analysis results?"

"Negative, again," Kirk said.

He stopped his building. "Say that again?"

"This test came up negative, like the other five."

That couldn't be right. It had to come up positive.

"Sir, you may want to consider that you made a mistake in believing your sister. I cannot find any reduced risk in her schematics."

No. He had to be right. He had to have picked the right side on this.

"I've tried to tell you this before," his mother said, turning away. "Your faith in your sister makes you blind, Eugene. And your stubbornness will lead you down the same path as your father if you're not careful."

She left and he stood in a room alone. He didn't have his mother's support on this. That hurt just as much as Narissa walking out on him. That lack of goodbye hit him later that day. And the lack of communication with her since…

Ajax reached for his phone and went through his

messages. Nothing new. Nothing from Narissa, and nothing from their friends. Not since they found out. Well, they didn't know the whole story, just that he and Narissa weren't working together anymore, and that they hadn't spoken for a few days.

Shira had a few choice words for him, as he expected. She'd been dubbed "the attack dog" for her friends. Her bite was just as bad as her bark. Luckily the others got her to calm down, and while they weren't able to help, let him know they were there for them both if they needed it. That's how he found out Narissa was burying herself in her work again.

Guilt gnawed at him, knowing he'd caused her to do that. He could see her now, sitting at her desk until she fell asleep. Pushing herself further than she should. All because she needed a distraction—an escape.

Ajax tapped the screwdriver in his hand. He knew that place. All he did was work or take care of his dogs. He didn't even work out anymore. Normally, that'd drive him crazy. Now, he found no passion for it. Saw it as just another distraction.

"Kirk, run the analysis again."

"I won't."

His brow furrowed. "What?"

"There isn't a point. If there was any chance your sister was right, Ajax, then I would have found it in one of these six checks. You need to face the fact, she was wrong."

No. He wouldn't accept that. She had to be right.

His grip tightened on the tool.

If she wasn't, then he'd lost Narissa for nothing. And that wasn't a reality he could accept.

CHAPTER 19

Two more days had passed, and Ajax still hadn't had any contact with Narissa. He stared at his phone, his thumb hovering over her name in his contact list. He should call her. Apologize for being so hasty and make things right between them again. He should have her come look at the machine he and Allyson had finished this morning. The one Kirk still insisted wasn't ready.

He wanted to believe his sister. He wanted this to go right this time. But now, the voice inside him spoke louder than it had before. *"Dumbass, you screwed up and need to fix it before it's too late."*

Even if he did get this right, was it worth it? Was it worth watching Crash lose her spunk and keep an eye on the door at all times, as if Narissa was going to waltz in any minute? Was it worth the awkwardness with their mutual friends? *Was this stupid machine really worth losing her?*

"Baby brother." His sister's voice cut through his wallowing. "Baby brother? Earth to Ajax, you in there?"

He looked up from his phone, her hand now waving in his face. "Yeah, sorry. What?"

She sighed and placed her hands on her hips. "Are you ready to test this machine yet?"

Was he? Doubt clawed him. His phone went off, a clip from a cooking show the tone. He'd set that for Kiara.

Hey, just wanted to tell you I got a bad feeling today. Please don't to do anything stupid.

His doubt latched onto those words. Her intuition wasn't often off. The day he lost his arm, she'd given him the same exact warning.

"Everything okay, brother?" Allyson asked.

Ajax stashed his phone. "Yeah, let's get to testing."

He'd already screwed up the best thing to ever happen to him, so he might as well not back out now. Ajax lifted the lid and hopped in. His heart pounded in his chest. He wasn't sure if he should be excited or terrified.

Ajax gave his sister a nod and she closed him in. The machine sounded off as she started it up. The first of three power conduits roared up. *So far, so good.* By this point he'd have already screwed something up.

Allyson activated the second. Ajax's body tingled but he attributed it to nerves. "Keep going, Ally."

"Okay."

Did he catch a waver in her voice? Concern flashed through him. Was she not as confident about this as she'd let on?

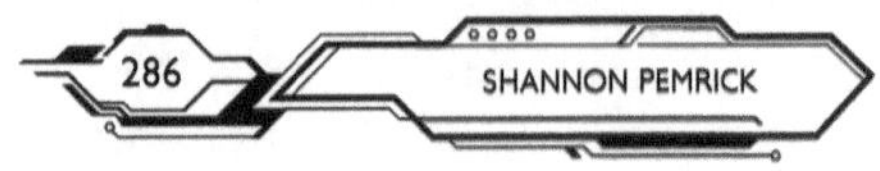

The last conduit activated, the tingling sensation he felt earlier progressing to pulsing pain, and sparks ignited around his cybernetic. *Shit!* He'd ignored the signs when he shouldn't have. "Allyson, shut it down! Shut it down!"

It was too late. Ajax shielded his face as sparks flew and pain raked his body. He let out a guttural, horrifying scream.

"Ajax!"

"Are you sure you're okay?" Dylan asked, his voice bouncing off the office walls.

A weak smile crossed Narissa's face. She typed more on her computer. "Yeah. I haven't had any more incidents. I'm not letting my guard down, but I'll gladly take the quiet for now."

Even with him on the phone, his next breath told her he didn't like her wording. What else was she supposed to say? She didn't feel safe. She never would as long as Nolan walked free. And with Ajax now out of her life, that made things worse.

"What about that friend of yours?" Dylan asked. "How's he handling all this stress?"

She typed away on her notes some more. "I don't know. We haven't talked in almost a week."

"What happened?" His concern was endearing, but not needed.

"It doesn't matter."

He sighed. "Yes it does, Narissa. This is the guy you'd been eyeing for a while, right?"

"Yeah." She frowned, the guilt she'd been trying to

ignore all this time rising up. "But it didn't work out. Nothing else to say."

Dylan sighed again. "Alright, I'll stop prying. But if you need someone to talk to, I'm here." He chuckled. "James says he is, too, and you should stop by for dinner sometime."

This got her to smile. "Dinner with you two would be nice. I'll have to see what I have for empty spots in my schedule."

"Good. And stop working yourself to death. I want you to be able to meet our precious little girl."

He'd sent a photo of the toddler he and James were adopting. She was so adorable. And she was happy for them. After a number of failed adoptions, this one was finally going through. She'd be home with them in the next few weeks.

Narissa rested her hand on her lower abdomen. Thinking of the little girl sent a great deal of longing through her. She'd gotten ahead of herself with Ajax. The way he'd treated her around the subject… How he treated her like there was a chance, even with the slim likelihood… *Let it go, Narissa. You screwed that up.* "I'll do my best, Dylan. I should get back to these notes. I'll talk to you later."

They said their goodbyes, and the call ended. A text came in soon after. It was another group message with Shira and Mercedes. The text was from Mercedes.

How are you holding up?

She typed back.

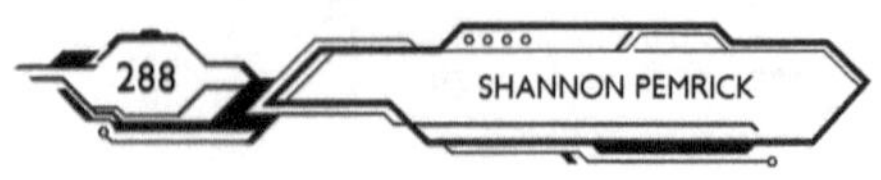

I'm doing all right.

She knew better than to lie, but at the same time she didn't really want to talk about it. The two of them had pestered her all week to find out what happened, but she wasn't ready to loop them in.

Shira sent the next message.

Are you finally going to tell us what happened?

Straight to the point. One of the qualities Narissa loved to hate about her.

Not yet. I need more time.

The moment that text was received, her phone rang. A video call. *Great.* She answered, moving the video to her tablet for a better view of the two. They sat in the same room—from the looks of it, Mercedes' condo. *The text was just an ice breaker for their real plan.* "You expect my answer to change on the phone?"

"Yes," they said in unison.

She sighed, her shoulders sagging. "No. I just want to get over it on my own time and move on."

Shira's brow spiked. "So you think killing yourself in your work is a healthy way of getting over this?"

Narissa pointed to her computer. "I've made a bunch of breakthroughs with this work. You don't have to like my methods, but this is how I keep this company afloat, and how I ensure cybernetic improvements soar. I do it for people like you two. So you can have happier lives."

"But what about your happiness?" Mercedes asked.

The question made her falter. "My happiness comes from others. It's why I dedicate my life to it."

The two looked at each other and then at her. They weren't buying it; she didn't exactly sell it well. Not even enough to convince herself. Narissa sighed. "Fine, I'll tell you."

"It'd better be everything," Mercedes said.

Shira winked. "And she means everything."

That wasn't going to happen. But she did retell the events between her and Ajax, starting from when she found out about Nolan getting out of jail, which she at that point realized she never told them about either, adding even more to her story. She went through the subsequent days of her spending time with Ajax and how she fell a little too hard, skipping the exact details of their more intimate escapades, much to Shira's vexation.

When she finished her explanation about the fight, she was resting her chin on her folded arms on the desk. Her two friends stared at her, trying to process.

"So," Shira stared. "Where do I find steel-toed boots to kick him in the balls?"

"Shira!" Mercedes scolded.

She shrugged. "What? He deserves it."

"No, don't do that," Narissa said. "I don't want this getting out of hand." *It was my fault anyway. It's always my fault...*

Shira crossed her arms. "Then what do you want? To talk some sense into him?"

Mercedes nodded. "We could help. People make mistakes. Maybe he's sorry it got out of hand and doesn't know how to talk to you about it?"

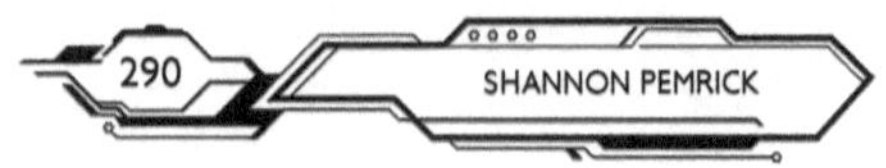

Not likely. Narissa shook her head as she sat up. "No, I just want to let this go and move on with my life. It didn't work out. It happens…"

Her two friends frowned, unable to help. This talk didn't make her feel any better, as she suspected.

Narissa turned her gaze when her office door opened. A well-dressed older gentleman with a complexion matching Narissa's entered. A wide smile spread across her face. "I have to go. My dad just got back from his trip."

"Hello, Doctor Okafor!" the two greeted.

Narissa's father chuckled. "Hello, ladies. I'm not interrupting anything, am I?"

"No, we're just pestering our friend," Mercedes said. "We'll let you two catch up."

Narissa said her goodbyes to her friends and hung up. She stood and embraced her father in a loving hug. "It's so good to see you again, Daddy. I hope your trip went well."

"It was a bit rocky at first, but worked out."

The two pulled apart and he pulled up a chair.

Narissa gazed at him expectantly. "So, tell me about the new recipient. How'd they take to the surgery? How well are they taking to the cybernetic?"

Her father smiled. "Your dedication to this company and the people we help brings a smile to my face every time." He frowned. "I just wish you didn't use that passion to cover up your emotions, sweetie."

Narissa's gaze fell away. "What did mother tell you?"

"Just that you've gone back to working so much you sleep in your office again. And that it may have something to do with a man around your age." He tilted his head as she tried to not look at him. "One I suspect you were discussing with your friends just now."

Narissa rubbed her arm. Her father was a sharp man. He knew exactly which person this topic was about. "I really don't want to talk about this, Daddy. I already rehashed it with the girls, and it didn't make me feel any better about the situation."

"Please? I want to help you, sweetie. Was it something he did? You did?"

Her lip quivered. "We're both to blame. We both did and said things that can't be fixed."

Her father reached out and lifted her chin. "That's not always true. We're human. We all make mistakes. Some are worse than others, but the ones that aren't, should be forgiven."

Narissa turned away. "I learned from the past. I won't let it repeat."

Her father tilted his head. "Are you learning, or running?"

She looked at him, confused.

"The pain of the past can teach us, yes, but it also has way of deceiving us. It throws a mask over the truth, dressing it as a lie."

Her brow knitted as she mulled this over. Was he right? Did she project onto Ajax and ruin things between them because of it?

Narissa's phone rang, and Picard came over the room infrastructure. "Doctor Narissa, this is an emergency phone call from the community hospital."

Dread spread through her. *Please don't be about him.* She wanted to be wrong. She wanted Allyson to be right so he wouldn't get hurt. She wanted…

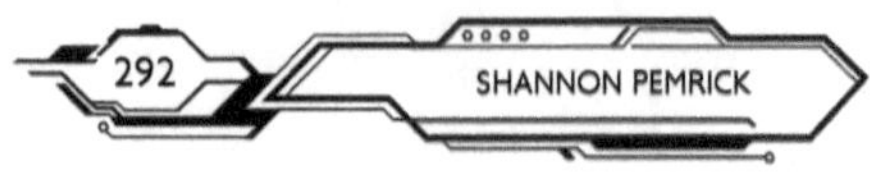

She answered the call. "Doctor Narissa Okafor."

"Doctor Narissa? Thank goodness you answered," a female voice said. "We have an emergency situation we're not entirely equipped to handle. An individual with cybernetic enhancements has been rushed here after an accident involving them."

Her hands shook. *No.* She wanted to be wrong. She wanted him to have listened to her for once. "Please don't tell me this patient's name is Eugene Jackson."

There was a pause. "Yes, ma'am, though his sister insisted we call him Ajax."

"Fuck!" she shouted. She ran her hands through her hair. "I told him not to do it."

Her father glanced at her and then took over. "Ma'am, I'm Doctor Benjamin Okafor. Can you please tell us his condition so we know how many to send down to assist?"

"From the limited assessment we've done, his cybernetic limb is eighty-five percent destroyed. He's sustained severe lacerations, and possibly internal injuries as well. We're trying to get him stable now. Preliminary scans have us concerned about his brain and the implant that comes with cybernetics of your design, which is one reason we called you."

Her father took Narissa's hand. "Rissa, you need to stay calm and keep your head clear. It's the only way we're going to help him."

Narissa took a deep breath. He was right. She nodded. "Picard, I need Sam notified to meet us down in the lobby."

"I've already done so," he relayed. "And I've called a car to the front and notified police. You will have an escort to get you through traffic."

"Thank you, Picard." She and her father rushed out of the room. "I need whatever data you can give me, and status updates so I can assist until we reach the hospital."

"Of course," the woman on the other end said. "I'll bring you to the room so you can converse with the doctor working with him now."

CHAPTER 20

Narissa ran through the barely opened doors of the emergency room, her father, and one of their surgeons, Sam, close behind. A nurse standing at the reception desk glanced up at their approach.

"Doctor Narissa, you made it!" Narissa recognized her as the nurse she'd spoken with earlier. She motioned for them to follow. "Please come with me."

"Narissa?" A familiar female voice said.

She looked around to find three people she knew sitting in the waiting room a few feet down the hall: Darius, a tall, well-built man of dark-tan complexion; Kiara, a short, curvy and buxom woman with red hair, several piercings, and tattoos scrawled over her light skin; and the one to have called out to her, and still sitting and staring at her lap, Allyson. Allyson's blue eyes appeared bloodshot, as if she'd only recently stopped crying.

On her way to Ajax, her path crossed the trio, allowing Kiara to grab her hand. "Please, save him."

Narissa nodded to her father and Sam. "Go scrub up. I'll be right behind you."

The two ran off with the nurse. Narissa gave the best sympathetic smile she could to Kiara, considering the circumstances, and she patted her hand. "I'm going to do everything I can."

Kiara smiled and nodded, letting her go as to not impede her any further. Darius placed his hands on Kiara's shoulders, staring at Narissa with a silent plea.

As Narissa passed Allyson, who hadn't moved, she placed her hand on the woman's head. Allyson reached up and grabbed her. "Please… please don't let my baby brother die because he listened to me. You were right. He should have listened to you. I'm sorry… I'm so, so sorry…"

Narissa could gloat, tell Allyson exactly how wrong she was. But Narissa knew better in this situation. And the guilt of what Allyson had done would follow her longer than any words Narissa could spin. "I'm going to save him, I promise. He's not going to die as long as I have a say."

She pulled away. "I'll come back to tell you all how things went once we're done."

"Thank you, Narissa," Darius said.

Narissa dashed down the hall. *You'd better not make me a liar, Andrew.*

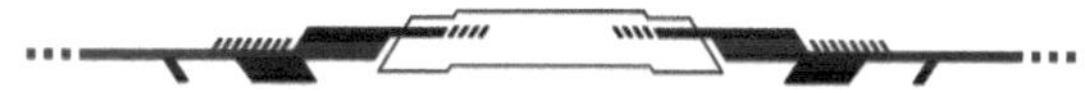

A buzzing sensation assaulted Ajax's mind. He didn't like it. He wanted it to go away, but his mind felt… heavy? Foggy? He wasn't sure. *Wait…*

Last he remembered, he had jumped into a machine. *What machine, though? Oh, right…* He'd tried to test his new pod. His failure machine. The pain he experienced surfaced in his memory.

But wait. He wasn't dead; he didn't think so, at least. So, what happened to him after that? He needed to push through this head fog.

It wasn't easy, and the resistance he experienced caused a great deal of pain. But he pushed through.

Odd beeping and hissing sounds hit his ears. Soft, dim light hit his eyes as they fluttered open. The beeping sounds surrounded him and the hissing coincided with his breathing. Pain crawled all across his body.

He looked around. He was in a bed in a small white room, the shades to the large windows pulled to keep it peaceful inside. Machines of a medical nature stood on both sides of him, all of them hooked up to him— including the not-so-pleasant oxygen port in his nose. *A hospital room?*

His sister lay asleep on a couch on the far end of his room. She must have rushed him here after… what happened? *Machine malfunction, I think. Yeah.* Why was his memory off? He should know what happened. Did he sustain brain damage? Narissa said it could happen if he wasn't careful. He'd always thought there were fail-safes with the neuro-mods, but maybe he'd overloaded even those.

Ajax's gaze wandered around the room some more until they landed on Narissa. She sat in a chair just to his right… *Knitting?* He didn't know she knit. From the looks of it, she was maybe making a blanket. A tiny one, but still a blanket. That's when he noticed more next to her. They were definitely blankets. And maybe even a tiny hat. *Are those for preemies?*

It made sense. She was certain she couldn't have a baby, so why wouldn't she help other parents with their own babies' fight for survival?

She always thought of others… even him. She'd only warned him of the risks and gotten mad when he ignored them because it was dangerous, not be because of her pride. She'd even pushed him away because of Nolan, not wanting to get him involved. Narissa had only ever looked out for him, and he could barely do that once for her when she really needed him to. *And it was my own selfishness that drove that one time.*

"Rissa," he croaked.

Her head snapped up and her eyes went wide. "Andrew…"

Ajax's chest swelled. She'd used his name again.

She threw down her work and rushed over to him. He smiled at her, but it didn't last long. All of his excitement sunk. What he'd hoped would be a caring, intimate touch or embrace turned out to be nothing more than a clinical assessment.

Narissa checked various vitals and even flashed a light in his eyes. He didn't like it, but he knew better than to complain.

She pulled away. "Everything looks good so far. No signs of extensive trauma. You've been out for four days."

He didn't care about that. Well, he did, but he wanted her to stop looking at him like just another patient. Ajax tried to reach out to her with his false limb, only for nothing to happen. He looked where he was missing a limb, expecting it to move. *Right, shithead.*

"Most of your lacerations were caused by that prosthetic getting blown off. I couldn't salvage any part of the cybernetic, so the whole thing was removed," Narissa said. "You lucked out, though. The safety protocols on the neuro-mod worked and kept that from short-circuiting your brain. And the damage you sustained physically didn't require you to need any extra cybernetics."

Her gaze faltered for a moment. "Of course, I wasn't sure if your brain sustained any other damage while you were unconscious. You seem to be doing okay right now, though."

His lip ticked up to a smirk. "Well, I *am* Ajax. I'm stronger than Greece."

Her brow twisted.

"Ajax soap? Stronger than grease?" He shrugged. "Stupid, I know. Darius came up with the joke when I took the nickname."

To his surprise, she laughed quietly. At least he'd managed to break the ice with her. "You two are idiots."

Ajax held up his hand and shrugged again. "Berserkers have low intelligence."

Her gaze fell away. "Yes, you certainly do."

He frowned. He was losing her again. "Rissa…"

Ajax cringed when she suddenly threw herself on him. Her whole body shook. "You stupid, stupid man. Why did you do that to me? Why couldn't you have just waited a few more days? Why couldn't you have allowed all three of us to work on this project, instead of just up and taking your sister's word?"

Her face in his chest, her words came out muffled, but he was fluent in muffled speech. Ajax rested his hand on her back, gripping her tight as she sobbed. "I'm sorry. I'm sorry I didn't listen to you. You're right, I should have asked you to go over my sister's notes before jumping in. I should have listened to my gut right before testing, when it told me to not do exactly that. I should have called you and apologized. I'm sorry."

Narissa continued to cry. The longer this continued, the more the guilt consumed him. If his pride hadn't been the size of Texas, she wouldn't be like this. There may have been fault on both sides, but he needed to own his end of it.

Her sobbing slowed and then she pulled away. Disappointment pulsed in him as she wiped her tears and stood up. "I should go get your doctor. He needs to know you're awake."

"Have the assistants do it." Ajax reached for her, ignoring his body's pain. She was already too far out of reach. "Please, Rissa. Stay and work this out with me."

Narissa collected her things and headed for the door. She paused when she opened it, glancing back at him. "Allyson and I talked. I've made an amendment to the contract. Once you're healed up, Cybro Industries will give you one last replacement, but only under the agreed condition that you'll be fitted with our newest prototype nerve-simulated model. For the sake of the company's reputation, this was the only route I could take in the agreement, to ensure you won't do this again."

Her lips pressed together for a moment. "Acting as your next of kin, due to the absence of your mother, who is stuck in another country, your sister signed paperwork for us to install the new neuro-mod while you were in surgery, in the deactivated state, of course. When you are released from the hospital and ready to be fitted with the new model, you can make an appointment."

He didn't have sufficient words. Watching her waver between professional and concerned… friend, made it hard for him to understand what was going on with her. Did she not believe his apology? Did she feel she needed to be professional in this situation and found it hard to do so? *Does she still care like I do for her?*

Before Ajax could come up with a way to get those answers, Narissa left. Emptiness filled him. He didn't want her to go; he wanted to work this out. Not later, not when he was discharged. Now.

His gaze ticked over to his sister, who now sat upright on the couch. "How long have you been awake?"

Her gaze didn't meet his. "I was never asleep."

She had a habit of doing that when guilt got the better of her. "Don't blame yourself."

Her eyes snapped to him. "I'm the one that convinced you to try my 'fix.'" She gestured to the door. "And I'm the one who screwed that all up."

Ajax shook his head, finding it not such a great experience. The longer he was awake, the more he realized how poorly his body handled the situation. "I chose to go along with your words. You didn't put some gun to my head. And I'm the one who didn't listen to Narissa when all logic said I should have. You're not solely to blame for this."

Allyson came over to his bedside. "How are you feeling?"

He let out a long breath. "Like a blue turtle shell ran me over, and then backed over me for a good second measure."

His sister chuckled and did her own check of his face. "You interested in seeing how ugly you look now, baby brother?"

Ajax snorted. "Ugly? You mean badass and rugged."

Allyson shook her head. "No. It looks like you got mauled by a bear."

He grimaced. That wasn't good. He may need some surgery to fix some of that. "I think I'll stay in a state of ignorance for a while longer.

His sister nodded, her lips pressing into a thin line. "I hope what little I was able to do will help you patch things up with Narissa."

Her eyes cut to the door, where a masculine and a feminine voice came through. The two sounded as if they were approaching. "You did well connecting with her again before she left. She even almost accepted your apology outright. I'm sure if she wasn't still a little mad at you, it would have worked."

Allyson's lip quivered. "And since I convinced her to give you one last appointment, maybe you can use that time to drive the point home? I don't know. I tried to help."

Ajax reached out and brushed away a lone tear streaking down his sister's face. "Thank you. I'm not ready to throw in the towel. I'm going to fix this and get her back."

"And keep her safe from guy name Nolan?"

His eyes darkened. "What do you know about that?"

Allyson shrugged. "Not much. She talked to someone on the phone a few times when she thought I was asleep. They talked about some creep by the name of Nolan. Something about her not having any more incidents with him?"

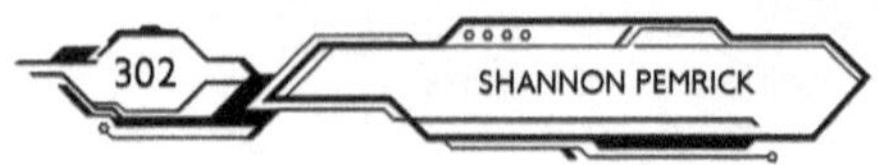

His mouth spread into a thin line. That was both reassuring and alarming news. Something wasn't right about that. He needed to get out of this stupid bed and fast.

The two of them looked to the door when someone knocked. An older gentleman of pale complexion wearing a doctor's coat entered. A young man in scrubs following him. "Good to see Doctor Narissa's words are true, and you're awake, Mister Jackson."

"Good morning… afternoon…" Ajax's brow furrowed. "I don't know what time it is. Hello, doctor."

Chuckling filled the room. The doctor then spoke. "Let's go over what happened, and we'll do some tests to ensure a swift recovery."

Ajax was willing to do whatever he needed to get out of this hospital bed. He'd rather be in his, with Narissa in his arms.

CHAPTER 21

jax's fingers drummed on his knee as he waited in the lobby. He never had to wait before to see Narissa. But then again, he hadn't had to set up an appointment with her since they became friends years ago. *It's been what, six years? Or is it seven now?* He lost track of time. He knew his friendship with Mercedes and Shira happened around five, almost six years ago, but when he started calling Narissa a friend wasn't as set in stone for him. *Maybe it's because of how it began.*

Their first meeting, while professional, had been the most friendly he'd ever had with any doctor. She genuinely wanted to get to know him as a person rather than a client. It's how he found out she'd been dabbling in Lusara Fates and he invited her to the guild Darius had created.

At first, he'd never seen the possibility of them becoming romantically involved, even though he'd been stunned by her beauty the moment they'd met—*Pictures and TV*

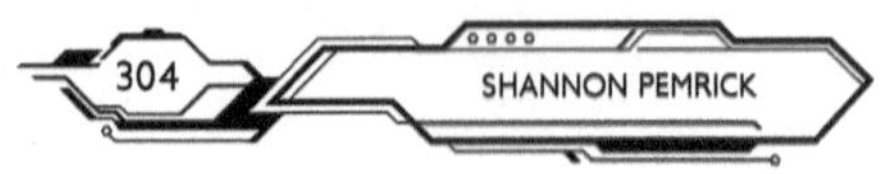

have never done her justice—because of the doctor-client relationship, so to speak, that they'd had. He figured it'd be off limits, and she didn't seem all that interested. But as time went on…

Ajax looked up when someone approached, their jingling jewelry alerting him to their presence. Mix in the clicking of heels on the floor, and he had the impression the person was a woman.

His heart came to a screeching halt at the sight of Narissa approaching, her tight pants clinging to her seductive hips as they swayed. Want thrummed inside him. The moment he sorted things out with her, he was going to bend her over that bloody desk of hers.

They hadn't spoken much in the past few days during his recovery. Without any formal reconciliation, he didn't think it was right to talk to her so informally. And when she contacted him, it was either a standard inquiry about his condition status, or an update on this specialized arm.

"Mister Jackson, thank you for waiting." Her formality confused him. And since she was smiling, he couldn't place the reason. Until a brief moment from his past surfaced in his mind.

Ajax smiled and stood. "Doctor Okafor, it's a pleasure. I'd shake your hand"—he gestured to his missing limb—"but that'd be a bit impossible at the moment."

A grin spread across her face. "I'll just make sure it happens on the way out after your fitting."

The two gazed at each other for a moment before sputtering out laughter. When they'd first met, they'd had this exact conversation.

His prior prosthetic had been so poorly made it

required monthly repairs. By the time he'd decided to switch to Narissa's product, he'd chosen to go without the limb until a better replacement could be found.

Narissa smiled at him after she'd gotten herself under control. "I'm glad you made it, Andrew."

His pulse skipped almost down into his stomach. If she was calling him Andrew, he had a good chance.

She waved him to follow her down the hall. "Sorry I made you wait so long. I had to be sure everything was in order, and I had to make a few last-minute cosmetic alterations."

He cocked his head. "Cosmetic?"

"I had an intern work on building the shell. But they didn't do the mirror process correctly, so there were several areas that would make an arm… not look right."

Ajax shrugged. "That wouldn't have bothered me. I'd accept it as added punishment for my poor choices these past few weeks."

Narissa's lips spread into a line and she didn't respond. *Nice going, Ajax.* He wanted to kick himself.

The two entered her office and she gestured him toward the examination chair. "Go have a seat."

He nodded and sat down, placing his phone on a table next to him and watching her retrieve her tablet. She then walked over to a cybernetic arm displayed on a stand. Narissa worked on her tablet and the fingers moved. She then made another command and the wrist rotated. *Ah, one last-minute test.*

Narissa pressed down on various sections of the arm and hand, nodding when she finished, and faced him. "Everything is good to go. Are you ready?"

Ajax nodded. "What do I need to do?"

"Installation is the same as any other, except for calibration. Your neuro-mod won't activate until I turn it on." She lifted the arm off the stand and transferred it to one sitting on a table nearby. "This is where you'll find a difference. Not only is the process too quick for us to put patients under anesthesia, we found it hindered the brain's ability to accept the new sensations."

Narissa attached a claw-like machine to the false limb. "The neuro-mod will turn on in quick waves. This will cause you to feel a pins-and-needles-like sensation. Once it's gone, the false nerves should register in full, and then we can do some testing for you to acclimate, and perform a calibration, so you're at a normal human strength and not the Terminator."

He snickered. As much as he'd probably enjoy being the Terminator for a bit, especially if he got the chance to cross paths with Nolan, he knew it wouldn't be good in the long run. The rest sounded simple enough to him.

She placed a soft hand on his chest, gazing at him with those incredible eyes of hers. "Do you have any questions before we begin?"

Just one. Ajax grasped her hand with his. "When do we get to talk?"

Her gaze remained warm as she smiled and slid her hand away. "After I get this arm installed. I need full concentration for that. Talking after that will help keep your mind engaged, and not focused on the pins and needles while the mod activates."

Disappointment prickled inside him. He wanted to talk now and deal with the arm after. But if he pushed this wrong, she may refuse to work things out. *Why do women have to be so complicated?*

Narissa used the crane arm to move the cybernetic limb into position. She then checked over the small skin-covered stump that was left of his arm. A nod of approval sent her working. The precision and accuracy mixed with utmost care she worked at fascinated him. He didn't catch a single fumble or struggle. *Is there anything she can't do?* If there was, it'd be a tiny list.

When she finished, Narissa sat back and wiped her brow as if she'd worked up a sweat. "There. That was the easiest install I've done lately."

Ajax smirked. "You're welcome."

Narissa laughed and then reached for an object that looked like a metal card deck box. "Okay, ready for that neuro-mod to start up?"

He took a deep breath. He'd lain awake for hours wondering how this would go. So many years had passed, he wasn't sure if he could remember what it was like to feel on that side. And if the residual memory was there, would this live up to the talk? Shira and Mercedes had gushed about it to him several times.

Even his friend Kane had gotten in on the program, thanks to him… and Kiara. Of course, that little brat got a discount on her tattoo coloring. *And, without fail, Darius helped her out with that deal, too.* Darius was a little too obsessed with seeing their friend covered in tattoos, in Ajax's opinion. He didn't hate tattoos, he just believed there needed to be a limit. And Ajax wasn't even sure how much free body space that small woman had at this rate.

"Okay, I'm ready."

"Close your eyes," she instructed. "This will help with the transition."

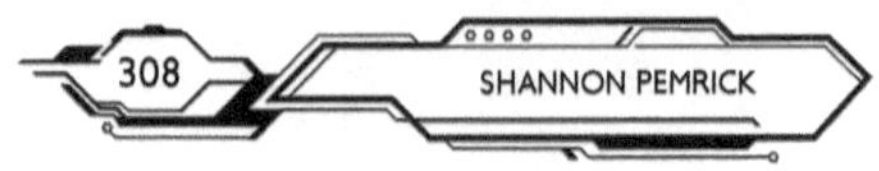

His brow cocked. "Will it now?"

Narissa chuckled. "Yes. I'm not pulling anything over you. Now do as I say."

Ajax fake grumbled and closed his eyes. She pressed the square object to his head and it beeped. He felt nothing, but when a mod turned on, if done correctly, there should never be any extra sensation.

A few moments passed before the tingling sensation hit him. His breath hitched, taken off-guard by the sudden rush of joy. He'd never been so happy to feel pins and needles in his life.

"Andrew, are you okay?" Concern lined her words.

He swallowed. He didn't need to get emotional in front of her. "Y–yeah." *Real convincing, Ajax.* "It's a lot to take in. That's all."

"Talk to me about it."

"I'm sure you've heard it from the girls. When you get so used to not feeling anything, even when you touch an object but your limb still does what it needs to without any issues, a new feeling of discomfort on that side suddenly becomes the best thing in the world."

Narissa placed her hand on his chest again. "Are you happy?"

Ajax rested his head against the chair, his eyes still closed. "So much."

He wiggled his fingers, the sensation intensifying just as it would his real hand.

"Hey, none of that," Narissa chided.

A tight breath entered his lungs. "Okay, then I need a distraction, because that's too tempting."

Narissa's fingers grazed his cheek. "You're healing well."

"Can I open my eyes yet?"

"No." Her fingers traced his jaw and his neck, sending an intense wave of desire down to his groin.

"Well, if you're going to explore my body"—he cracked one eye to look at her—"Then I'd rather be allowed to watch."

A deep flush fell over her face. She tried to retract her touch, but he caught it. *Too late, Rissa.* She was going to own up to her actions. And he wasn't letting her get away this time.

"I'm sorry."

Her apology took him aback. He wasn't mad at her. "Sorry for… what exactly?"

Narissa shook her head. "Dense half-orc. I'm apologizing for my behavior back in Oregon."

"I'm the one who needs to apologize," he said. "Again. In a way that doesn't sound like a desperate plea for you to stay, and does sound sincere as hell."

A small smile spread across those kissable lips of hers. "Maybe, but I do as well. When you mentioned you were sorry for not thinking about asking Allyson to join the project, you're not the only one who should have offered that as an option. I could have easily done that as well."

Her gaze fell. "But I had my head up my own ass too far to not see it as a personal slight to me. And that was wrong to do."

Ajax shook his head. "No. It was me. Had I not hesitated to answer your upfront questions, you would have been far more willing to listen to options. I've never doubted your abilities. Not even in that moment. But my respect for my sister clouded my judgment, and my

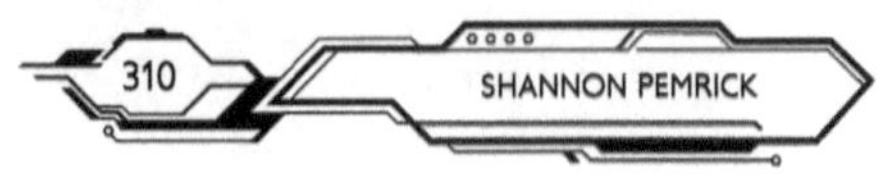

subsequent actions. I let spite drive me to continue, even when I knew it wasn't going to work like Allyson said, and it'd prove you right all along."

Her lips pressed together but she didn't look at him. He reached out with his real hand and lifted her chin. "I'm sorry, Rissa. I truly am. I can't take back what I've done, and I can't promise I'm not going to be an idiot and make a similar mistake, but I'm going to try my damnedest. If you'll let me."

Her lower lip quivered and for a moment he thought he'd lost this battle. Then, without warning her lips crashed into his. Overwhelming joy flooded through him, overpowering the tingling from his cybernetic.

Narissa cradled his face with both her hands. Ajax reached up and tangled his fingers into her hair. His pulse beat hard in his ears, and thoughts of anything but her stalled. He wanted to pull her onto his lap and watch her writhe under his touch. Make her beg and scream. The glass walls of the room had the capability to tint and shut out the rest of the building. It'd give them the privacy needed to keep her out of too much trouble for enjoying a mid-day romp.

But he knew she wouldn't go for that. Not while this artificial arm needed calibration. *I'll just bend her over the desk after.*

Their kiss broke and Narissa murmured, "I don't want to lose what we have."

He stared into her eyes. "Me either."

"Oh, how sweet," a smooth masculine voice said.

The two looked to the door where a tall man in a black suit stood. He had slicked-back black hair and a pale, angular face. Glasses partially obscured his ice-blue eyes.

"I'm so glad I made it in time though." His voice reverberated deep in his chest, but was also silky-smooth. Ajax could tell, this man could charm a woman just by speaking—and make a man want to punch him.

Ajax didn't need a name to know who this was. He only had to look at Narissa's wide eyes, clenched jaw, and tight shoulders.

"N–Nolan," Narissa said. "What… what are you—"

"Doing here?" He grinned. "Paying you a visit of course, doll. I tried the other day"—Nolan's eyes cut to Ajax—"but your mongrel's *accident* caused quite the ruckus, pulling you away."

Ajax's eyes narrowed. This guy knew way too much. His family and legal team had made sure his hospitalization didn't make the news.

Narissa's eyes flashed to Ajax for a moment. "How did you know about that? And how did you get in here?"

Nolan shook his head, making scolding sounds. "Have you forgotten, Narissa? Have you forgotten about the IT company you stole from me by sending me to jail? Of course I have ways to get around your pathetic security. I even know the schedule of that sexy piece of ass you have sitting in the lobby. No one knows I'm here. And no one will, because I've disabled alerts to emergency responders."

Nolan's eyes darted to Ajax. "I'll only tell you once, mongrel, remove yourself from my wife. Now."

Ajax couldn't stand this condescending attitude of his. How often had he used it on Narissa before things went south? He guessed a lot, which explained her spotty self-esteem.

That issue wasn't there now, though. As terrified as

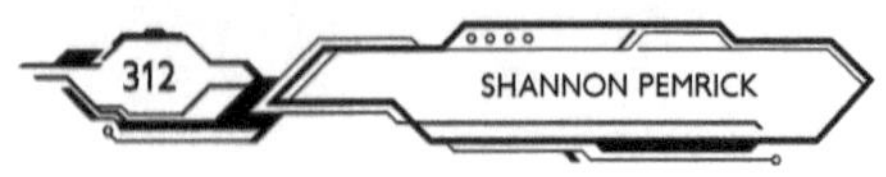

she was, Narissa wasn't standing down. "You can't just waltz in here and make—"

Nolan lifted his hand, a gun grasped tight. How had they both missed that detail? He aimed it at Ajax. "I admire your spirit, doll. The years have been good to you, beyond your body. But for his sake, I hope you learn to reel it in."

Asshole. This just escalated to a whole new level of bad.

"Now, step away from him, doll. You don't want to be the reason he dies, do you?"

Narissa swallowed and took several steps away. Ajax noticed her fingers shaking as she tried to keep her fear controlled. He'd sworn to protect her from this bastard, but he was at a loss as to what to do. Ajax would take a bullet for Narissa, but he wouldn't cause her any more pain by playing hero for nothing.

"Keep going," Nolan instructed. "Until you're standing by your desk."

Narissa continued to move as he asked.

"Good girl."

Ajax wanted to spit at the asshole. Treating her like some dog. But he kept himself controlled and instead ran as many possibilities through his head as he could, trying to find one way to get that gun out of his hand. A blinking light on his phone caught his attention. He knew that light. Kirk was making a silent phone call. But who—*Dylan.*

Knowing Nolan's brilliant yet unstable nature, he probably locked down Picard from reaching anyone. He'd know Narissa would have good contacts to circumvent his emergency contact block, like a direct line to a cop. But maybe he wouldn't have the same information on

Ajax. And while he'd never spoken to Dylan himself, Kirk had done that search.

The two of them just needed to keep Nolan distracted long enough. *God, I hope this works.*

"Why are you here?" Ajax asked him. Better to play dumb and stroke his ego.

Nolan chuckled. "Why? Why wouldn't I? I'm finally able to see my wife after seven years of being unfairly locked away."

Unfair, right.

"We're not married anymore, Nolan," Narissa said. Her response caused him to narrow his eyes at her. "You know this. Your sentencing came with—"

"Shut up!" He extended his arms further toward Ajax. "We're still married. Just because you decided to act out and lie doesn't mean you can walk away."

Act out and lie? How many loose screws did this guy have?

Narissa frowned. "Nolan, I didn't lie. All those things you were sentenced for doing, you did. I don't know what happened to the man I married, but you're not—"

Nolan aimed the gun as Narissa. "Don't you dare say it. This, all of this, is because of you. Because you wouldn't be a good, obedient wife. And I had to remind you of that the moment I got out. I had to go through so many hoops to remind you I own you."

Narissa's hands went to her stomach as she shrank back, like they always did when something scared her. To a normal person, it would appear to be a defensive posture, but with the way Nolan's eyes narrowed, he was reading into it.

"What are you hiding, Narissa?" Nolan asked.

She shook her head, swallowing hard. "N–nothing."

He took a step closer to her. "Why do you hold yourself so protectively like that?"

She shrunk back more. "It's a reflex."

"No…" Nolan's lip curled and he grabbed her by the hair, aiming the gun at Ajax. "He knocked you up, didn't he? Didn't he!"

Fuck. Nolan's instability was worsening as this continued. At this rate, they'd both be dead. Ajax needed to think of something.

Tears welled up in Narissa's eyes, Nolan's grip on her tightening. "No. No, he didn't, Nolan. Please…"

Nolan aimed the gun back at her, this time aiming to her midriff, his eyes darkening. "Don't—"

"Don't hurt them!" Ajax called out. Nolan snapped his head in Ajax's direction. He wasn't sure what he was doing, but he knew this guy's instability couldn't be reasoned with. If he believed it, no words could sway him. "Please, don't hurt them."

Narissa's eyes screamed, *What are you doing?*

Nolan's dark gaze swiveled back to Narissa. "At least one of you can tell the truth." His grip on her head tightened and he pulled her closer. "Now I'm going to have to punish you, Narissa. Had you just told me the truth, I wouldn't have to."

He shoved her toward the desk. "Bend over."

Fuck you! Ajax bit his tongue. If he made that outburst, that gun would go off. He needed to act fast and get out of this chair and remove that gun from this maniac's hand somehow. There was no way he'd let Nolan do that to her.

Ajax's eyes shifted to outside the room. His lips

pressed into a line when he caught a glimpse of someone crouched behind a half wall. From the looks of it, they may be in uniform. *Thank you, Kirk.* Of course, a hostage situation wasn't a good one, and would force them to act slower in fear any force would send this unstable man into making a drastic action.

Narissa's voice shook. "Nolan, please… please don't."

Nolan grasped the back of her head and forced her down, bending himself closer to her face. *There.* With Nolan unable to see him, this was his best chance. Ajax prayed he'd be quiet enough.

"You're going to listen to me, doll," Nolan growled out. "I'm going to remind you that you're mine. I'm going to remind you, had you listened and been a good wife, this wouldn't be happening."

He pulled her head back as he leaned against her, simmering Ajax's anger. "Then we're going to leave here, and you're going to get rid of that *thing* inside you. We'll start our marriage over, and this time you'll be a good, obedient wife."

He yanked her, making Narissa gasp. "Do I make myself clear?"

Narissa's hands curled on the desk. Even though Ajax couldn't see her face, he could only imagine the terror in her eyes. *Hold on, Narissa, I'm almost there.*

Nolan aimed the gun to where he thought Ajax still sat. "You will confirm your submission to me, or your toy—"

His words caught when he realized Ajax wasn't there. But it was already too late for him. Ajax grabbed Nolan's arm with his cybernetic hand—the sensation of touch unable to get far through the adrenaline pumping

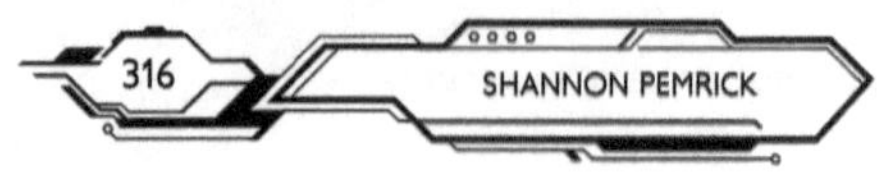

through him—and the back of the lunatic's head with his real hand. Ajax slammed Nolan's face down into the desk, twisting his arm at the same time so he'd drop the weapon.

The gun fired, and a woman in another office screamed. The sensation of bones breaking and tendons ripping registered through the adrenaline. It startled him. With everything going on, he'd forgotten about the calibration. If he didn't have such a strong stomach, he'd have wretched up his lunch.

Nolan screamed and fell to the ground, holding his mangled arm. His dark eyes seethed at Ajax through broken glasses. Ajax had enough of his wits about him to kick the dropped gun away and stand between Nolan and Narissa. She pressed against Ajax, her body shaking.

Just then, the police rushed in and apprehended Nolan. Ajax didn't have any words for the crazy as they dragged him away. Instead, he wrapped a protective arm around Narissa. His claim to her wouldn't be taken, and if that was the last thing Nolan saw before going back behind bars, then he would gladly rub salt in that wound.

"Are you okay?" Narissa whispered.

Ajax let out an exhausted laugh. "You were just manhandled by your unstable ex, and you're asking me if I'm okay?" He leaned in and kissed the top of her head. "You're something else."

"I know." She pressed her face into his chest. "Thank you."

"I told you I was going to protect you," he murmured into her head. "I'm just sorry it took so long."

She shook her head. "Don't be. With that gun in his

hand, I didn't think there'd be any help. I should have known you'd be stupid enough to pull something."

"Protective." Ajax pulled her in tighter. "I prefer the term protective."

Two officers approached them; one a short woman of fair complexion and the other a tall man of darker complexion. Narissa's eyes lit up and she pulled away from Ajax. "Dylan!"

Dylan wrapped her in a tight hug. "I'm so glad you're safe, Narissa."

Ajax fought his instinct to punch him. He knew Dylan wasn't an issue. And had it not been for him, Nolan would have gotten away with a whole lot more.

The other officer with Nolan approached Ajax. She introduced herself as Officer Elise Smith and asked him several questions. Ajax relayed what he could remember through the adrenaline fog, and explained how he was able to destroy Nolan's arm.

Narissa, hearing this, gasped and ran over to fuss. "You have the new prototype active. Did you—"

Ajax nodded. "I did feel it. But the situation numbed me to the worst of the sensation. I think."

Various emotions played across Narissa's face. "This was not how I wanted you to experience this new arm."

Dylan laughed while Ajax rubbed his face. "That's what's going through your head right now? You really are unbelievable."

She gazed up at him with innocent eyes that drove a wild need through him. Why did there have to be people here? "Well, yeah. Y—"

"Narissa!" Her mother's voice screech. "Narissa, babydoll, are you all right?"

Everyone turned to see Ayana forcing her way into the room, followed closely by Benjamin. No police officer could stop this mother. She rushed to Narissa and pulled her into a tight embrace. "Oh, my baby. Oh, my darlin'."

Ayana continued to repeat herself, her worry and relief for her daughter overwhelming her. Narissa managed to pat her mother's back. "I'm okay, Momma. Ajax made sure of that."

Ayana pulled away from her daughter and framed Ajax's face with her hands. She pulled him closer and kissed his forehead. "Bless you. Bless you."

She repeated her words as she continued to kiss his forehead and cheeks, until Benjamin pulled her away. "Dear, let the man breathe."

Ajax, while happy for Ayana's response to the situation, was grateful for Benjamin's help. His wife's love was a bit much right now.

Narissa grasped her mother's hand. "Mom, why don't you and Dad go into his office and spend some time calming down?"

Ayana placed her hand on her chest. "Narissa! Lawd have mercy, suggestin' such a—"

Narissa laughed. "What are you talking about? I was thinking of tea." She snickered. "Whatever you two do after that is your own business."

Ajax pressed his lips together so he wouldn't laugh. Her father, on the other hand, did, loudly, as he ushered his wife away. "Come, dear. Our daughter is right. The police will want to speak with them more, and your fussing won't help."

"Benjamin, you better not be ins'nuatin' I'm—"

"Not at all, dear. I just…"

The two walked out of earshot, though Ajax wouldn't have minded hearing more of their amusing banter.

The officer he'd spoken to before returned, having slipped away during the interruption. A rotund middle-aged man in uniform accompanied her.

"Doctor Okafor?" the man said. "I'm Officer Gawain. I've been informed the injuries the suspect received were due to an uncalibrated cybernetic?"

Narissa nodded. "Yes, sir. Nolan showed up before I had the chance to do the calibration. I'd like to get that taken care of, if I may."

The officer nodded. "That is what I came over to request. Seeing as one of the AI assistants linked us to the security cameras, we have no reason to request either of you come down to the station with us. But I can't allow this man to walk around as he is now."

The two of them understood. With police taking a look at the examination chair that had been the unfortunate victim of Nolan's gun, Narissa had him sit in her desk chair, and she went to work testing his new simulated nerves and calibration.

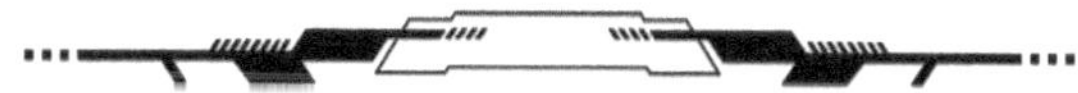

Narissa made another adjustment to Ajax's arm and had him grasp a glass cup this time. This was always her last test to make sure everything was in order. He complied and passed with flying colors.

She brushed her hand up his false arm, sending the artificial nerves into a frenzy for him. His eyes went wide and his breath sucked in tight as he registered it all. She

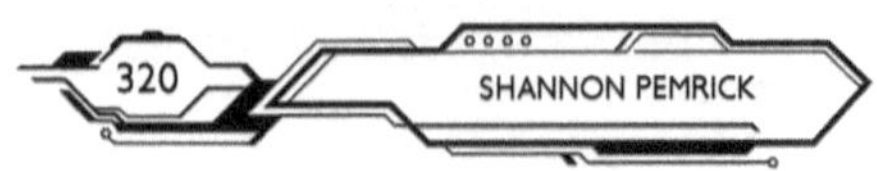

giggled and then tried to slip off his lap, only for him to stop her. The moment she'd begun the calibration process, he'd pulled her onto him and wouldn't let her say no—not that she wanted him to.

"Can't you just be nice to me?" he asked, taking a deep breath as the artificial nerves settled down. "I did help get rid of Nolan."

She wore the most innocent look she could. "You'll need to get used to those sensations somehow."

He pulled her closer and murmured in her ear. "I had something else in mind for that."

Heat rose to her face. She knew exactly what he meant, and while she didn't hate the idea at all, right now wasn't the time. Narissa slipped away, earning a grunt of contempt from him. "Behave."

She then went over to Officer Gawain to report the finished calibration. He thanked her, asked a few more questions about the situation, and then gave her and Ajax the okay to leave. It appeared her father would continue to work with the police so she could go and rest. One glance at his happy face, and her mother's attempt to hide her disheveled appearance, and she didn't need to guess why he'd offered to take over. *At least he convinced her to take my advice.* It was a good way to distract and refocus. She knew from experience.

"Narissa," Dylan said. "Are you going to be okay?"

She smiled. "Yes. What he did was scary, but I'm okay. I've had time to calm down, and with Nolan in custody, I'm able to breathe. How did you all know what happened to get here?"

Dylan gesture to Ajax, who was making his way over. "His assistant called me."

She couldn't stop the surprise from showing in her face as she looked at him. Ajax shrugged. "Kirk did it on his own."

"Because I'm an intelligent AI," Kirk said from Ajax's phone, still over by the examination chair. "With Picard shut down, he was the most logical contact I had in my memory bank."

Narissa gasped. "Picard was shut down? I need to check on him before—"

"Doctor Narissa," Picard's voice said through the room. "I am okay. Once I sensed Nolan's attempt to infiltrate the emergency systems, I transmitted the one contact to Kirk and shut down all confidential and important channels to protect them. This included myself in the process, though."

"Ah, so the truth comes out," Ajax said. "Kirk was trying to steal all the glory. Again."

Narissa laughed. Sounded like his AI's quirky behavior did that a lot. They all had at least one of them.

Dylan chuckled and then held his hand out to Ajax. "Thank you for keeping her safe. That was a risky move, but I'm glad you took it. We were struggling with the best way to approach the situation, with his unstable nature."

Ajax grasped Dylan's hand. "I'll always keep her safe."

Dylan smiled and looked to Narissa. "Bring him with you when you finally join James and me for dinner."

Narissa glanced to Ajax. "How does Saturday night sound?"

His smile widened. "I'll let James know. Don't back out on us."

"I wouldn't dream of it."

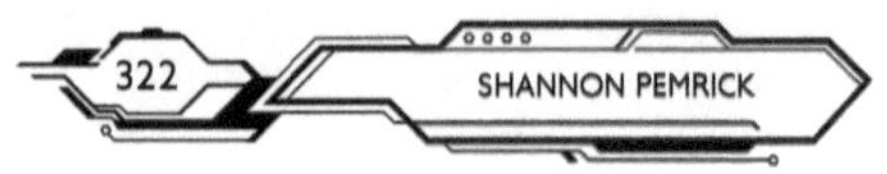

"Good." He kissed her on the forehead. "Now go home and rest. You both need it."

Rest was the farthest from her mind as Ajax subtly rubbed his finger against her wrist. They still needed to test his arm in various ways. And they needed to finish cementing their relationship.

The two of them collected their things, said good-bye to her parents, and walked down the hall, hands entwined.

"Doctor Narissa," Picard said from her phone. "Your friends have blown up your phone with concern. It appears the incident caught the news."

Narissa pinched her nose. "Great."

"I can relay a message on your behalf if you'd like."

"Please do. Let them know everything is okay. And tell Cede and Shira I won't be alone tonight, so not to worry about that."

"I will inform them the Klingon will be sharing your bed tonight, per your instructions."

Her face grew hot. "Picard!"

Her assistant chuckled. "Kidding. Mostly."

Ajax chuckled next to her. "I don't mind being a Klingon."

"That's not the point," Narissa muttered.

He squeezed her hand and pulled her into the elevator. They had the box to themselves, which gave Ajax the impression it was okay to get handsy.

She pushed his hands away from her butt. "Behave."

He let out a long sigh. "You can't tease me and expect me to behave when we're alone."

She pressed against him and pushed up onto her toes, kissing his strong jaw. "Yes, I can."

Her back hit the wall, her hands pinned next to her head. Ajax's breath came out strained. "Christ, Rissa, you know how to push a man's patience and control. I haven't had release in two weeks. You tease me right before Nolan shows up uninvited. I have to watch while he assaults you. And then you proceed to tease me more. I'm all sorts of pent up right now. You're playing with fire."

She knew. He didn't have to tell her to know how cruel it was for her to do this to him. But she was getting so much satisfaction from it.

Narissa noticed the floor level they passed and kissed his chin. "We're almost to our level. And we haven't discussed where we're going."

Ajax sighed and pulled away. "I figured my place would be good."

Narissa leaned in closer to him, tempting fate some more. "We could always go back to mine. We can watch Lord of the Rings." A wide grin spread across her face. "Extended edition."

Ajax's hand ran up her side, his eyes intent on her. "Only if I can dive into your volcano."

The two of them stared at each other, and then sputtered out laughing. Narissa doubled over, holding her sides. "Really?"

Ajax's hand rested on half his face, the other holding him up against the wall. "I thought it'd be funny."

Well, he wasn't wrong.

The elevator came to a stop, forcing them to compose themselves. When the doors opened, they walked through the underground parking, reaching Ajax's corvette. Ajax opened the passenger door for her. She hopped in and it wasn't long before they were cruising down the road. The two's hands entwined over the console.

"How are you feeling?" Ajax asked. "No sugar coating."

Narissa glanced down at their hands, his finger caressing hers. "Are you trying to distract yourself?"

He let out a breath. "Yes. And because I want to be sure you're okay. You went through a lot today."

She nodded, looking out the window. "I won't lie. I was scared out of my mind. But with you there, I was able to get through it far better than if I had been alone."

He reached out and turned her chin. "That's better."

She gave a sheepish smile. "It's going to take me a bit to get over what happened, but I will. One day at a time."

Ajax leaned over and kissed her on the forehead. "I'll be there with you. I promise."

She kissed him back and then trailed a light touch up his artificial arm. He sucked in a tight breath. "Please don't. Not unless you aren't going to stop me again."

"You're going to wait until we reach the house." She pushed him back to relax in his seat. "But your reaction is strange."

She applied pressure with her entire hand, all in one spot. "What does that do?"

He inhaled. "The same thing."

She slid her hand up and he nodded. "It's the same. All of this is just one giant turn on for me, and it's frustrating. Even holding your hand isn't easy."

Narissa's brow furrowed. "That isn't right. No one has reported that happening. Did I get something wrong?"

She ran several scenarios through her head. She could

have crossed a wire by mistake. *You know better than to cross beams, Narissa.*

Ajax lifted her chin. "It's nothing you did wrong, Rissa. It's just you touching me. Between me feeling something for the first time on that side, and you being the source, it's got me overwhelmed."

Well, that was better than her wild imagination. She sat back in her seat. She could allow them to indulge in the car. But she wasn't really in the mood for being cited for lewd activities in public. Or not wearing a seat belt. Or… well, car sex just sounded uncomfortable. Mercedes said it was fun, but Narissa wasn't sold on the idea.

She'd just make it worth it later for him.

As the minutes passed, Ajax's grip on her hand became increasingly hard to ignore, clearly indicating his desire for her. It made her pulse skip. It was strange, feeling so wanted, but she did like it.

The car pulled up to a large apartment building under a shaded area. Just based on the cars around them, she could already tell a room here would cost a fortune—and Ajax lived in a penthouse suite, meaning he paid out the rear for it. *I'll have to show him the benefits of modest living.*

The two climbed out of the car and he slipped up behind her, resting his hand on her hip and guiding her into the building. The large lobby amazed her, decked out in all manner of luxury furniture and fine art. Ajax led her to the elevator. It only took a few moments for it to arrive. Hopping in, he selected the top floor. A few other people joined them and selected their own floor levels.

They rode the elevator up, the other residents' presence

keeping Ajax's behavior in line… for the most part. Since he'd chosen the back corner, her ass wasn't safe from the occasional squeeze.

At this rate, they weren't going to make it far into his apartment.

Reaching the top floor, the elevator opened to a short hallway with a single door at the end. Ajax pulled her by the hip to follow. She went along with him, gazing about the sparsely decorated corridor.

When they came to the door, she noticed the Star Trek-themed welcome mat. She couldn't stop a quiet laugh from escaping her mouth.

Ajax swiped his key, and even before he could let them both in, the dogs barked. She could tell this was an excited bark, and not a protective one to ward off intruders.

The moment the door swung open, Crash and Helios bolted out and jumped around them. Crash whined and pawed at Narissa, while Helios did a whole lot of spinning.

Ajax laughed. "They missed you."

Narissa tried to pet them both. "I can see that."

"This is the first day in two weeks Crash has had this amount of energy," he admitted. "She really took to you."

The idea made her heart swell. She missed having a dog. And it seemed she had one again.

"C'mon, I'll show you around."

He ushered her into his home, both taking their shoes off at the door. "Welcome to my home."

Narissa gazed around, her eyes wide. Open concept with high ceilings, wood floors, and glass windows.

Simple furnishings, but stylish. The place had a large kitchen with marble counters, and as she wandered in, she found two rooms beyond the living area, as well as a full bath. A set of stairs led to a second-floor loft. She guessed that to be the bedrooms and at least one more bath, if not more.

The balcony outside had a nice patio and pool, and some minor landscaping, emulating a small backyard.

"What do you think?" Ajax asked.

She continued to peer around. "It's amazing. Cleaner than I thought it'd be, but for all I know, you hire someone to clean it for you."

"I plead the fifth."

She snickered and went to check out the view. The hot California air slammed her when she stepped out onto the balcony. A lovely view of the city sprawled out before her. Nothing as amazing as the view in Oregon, but this was nice nonetheless.

Ajax came up behind her and wrapped her up in a strong embrace. He kissed the side of her head and then rested his chin in the crook of her neck. "So? Impress you enough to stay?"

She shifted her gaze to look at him. "What, you mean move in with you?"

His eyes moved up to her. "Yeah."

"You don't think it's a little too soon?"

Ajax shook his head. "No. Someone else, sure. But not you. Not us."

She turned to face him. "I dunno. Might be a little ritzy for me and my modest-living self."

Ajax dipped his head, his lips brushing hers. "An empress such as yourself deserves the finest."

"Empress?" Her tongue flicked out to tease him. "I thought I was a priestess."

"Oh, don't worry, you are." Ajax grinned. "You're just my priestess. And only mine."

He crashed his lips into hers, searing heat stealing her breath, and cutting off any more conversation. She slid her hands over his broad shoulders, up his thick neck, and tangled her fingers in his hair. Ajax's hands roamed her body, the sensations of touch flaring up his artificial nerves, based on his staggered breathing.

His hands found purchase on her rear and lifted her up. She wrapped her legs around him. Their desperate kiss broke when he sat them down on nearby outdoor furniture, instead of bringing her inside.

"Out here?" The concept frightened and excited her.

Ajax nipped her chin, his hands digging into her ass. "I'm the only top floor resident. And, if you're worried about it, no one from other buildings can see us here. Tallest building in the vicinity."

Narissa released one hand's grip and glided it over his artificial arm. Ajax sucked in a tight breath, the richness of his eyes deepening. "Good. Only you get this show."

She slipped off his lap, though he didn't make it easy. "Come back."

Narissa grinned and began unbuttoning her shirt. "You sure?"

He leaned back, resting his arms across the back of the couch, watching each button release as the shirt slid open inch by inch. "My request is on hold for the moment."

Pleased, Narissa continued her slow undress. Her shirt hit the ground and her bra was next, her supple breasts spilling out on display. Ajax's hands curled. Narissa shimmied out of her pants, looping her fingers into her panties and dragging them along with her pants.

Bare and on display, Ajax's eyes took in every inch of her. The desire—the appreciation—she'd never tire of his gaze.

He reached out, but she pushed his hands away. "Your turn."

He let out a strained breath and then whipped his shirt over his head, tossing it somewhere. Ajax didn't waste time with his pants, kicking them off and letting his erect member stand proud and eager. Ajax beckoned her with a finger.

Narissa complied, stepping out of her clothes pile and slipping onto his lap, her hands running over his sculpted chest, and his hardness pressing against her.

Before anything else could happen, though, Crash jumped up on the couch and whined, cocking her head to the side. The two of them laughed. Ajax gave her a quick pat on the head and then shooed her away.

His neck exposed, Narissa leaned in and nipped his skin. He groaned. A grin slipped up her face. "Like that?"

He inhaled when she repeated the action, his hands clamping down on her ass. "You have no idea."

She continued to bite him, testing different areas—his jaw—collar—anywhere she should without become a contortionist—testing what he responded to. The right places rewarded her with a light tap on her ass. She assumed it was a reward, with the unexpected excitement her body received from the action.

Exploring with him was going to be fun.

Done with the teasing bites, and desiring more from

all this, she kissed him deep, both of them sucking in deep breaths.

Ajax's touched roamed her body, engulfing her in a blaze of needy desire. Narissa rocked her hips, pressing him into her more. His artificial hand found her swollen breast and teased her, each touch exciting him through the false nerves as much as it excited her.

His hand trailed down her belly to the wetness between her thighs. He groaned against her whimper, desire intensifying inside her. Narissa rocked her hips, desperate for more.

He pulled away and groaned. "Fuck."

Her brow ticked up, her rocking ceasing. "That's the idea."

"That's not"—he chuckled, realizing what she'd said—"cheeky. But that's not the issue. I forgot the—"

She placed a finger over his lips. "It's not needed. I told you, one in three hundred."

Ajax grasped her hand and kissed it. "There are more than three hundred days in a year."

"I don't think you understood the statistic. That's one in three hundred per month."

"Well then, challenge accepted."

Her core pulsed. That was a lot of sex he was promising. But knowing him, it wasn't an empty one. And she was not complaining.

"And if something did happen by chance, we'd talk about it." She swallowed when he kissed her wrist, her pulse kicking up again. Such a simple, intimate gesture. "But if it'd make you more comfortable, we can—"

His eyes shifted to her, the intensity lodging the words in her throat. "We have two extra bedrooms.

And I might be willing to trade this all in for a white picket fence."

Her heart slammed against her ribcage. A family with Ajax? She could get behind that—wanted that.

Narissa leaned in, her lips hovering over his. "Don't worry, I won't make you trade in the Corvette for a minivan."

Ajax nipped at her bottom lip, his hands gliding over her skin. "No one said we can't have a few cars. We'd make Mini's hot."

She giggled and kissed him deep. "I love you, Andrew."

He kissed her back, his hands pulling her closer by the hips, digging into her soft flesh. "I love you more, Rissa."

Ajax nipped her neck. "Now, about that baby."

She gasped and her back arched when he thrust into her. The two found their desired rhythm quickly, driving closer and closer to ecstasy. Over and over again. No inch of skin was safe from each other. No surface in the suite was safe.

Everything was right in her world now. Nolan couldn't reach her here. Never again. Not as long as Ajax was around. And she wasn't letting him go this time.

EPILOGUE

Narissa popped a blackberry in her mouth. The sweet treat made her smile, as she didn't feel the nauseating sensation she normally felt when eating. She was glad she could at least eat these.

She listened to the game developer on stage. Gamer-Nine reveals this year were big, but none were as big as the work she and Ajax had done with the new pods. It'd been a lot of work, but they'd gotten several safe prototypes created. The investors were happy, and today was the day the world would find out about them, and even test drive.

Mercedes and Takashi stood with her, and Ajax's mother and sister stood some ways off, talking with crew and employees. Narissa's fingers curled as she tried to keep her nerves contained. She'd done these types of things before, but without fail, she had to fight off the fear of being in front of so many people.

Kiara, Darius, Shira, Jasper, and Zach were supposed

to join them, but she was pretty sure the first two were setting up for the big Lion Rage reveal right after GameTech's presentation, and latter two were still in their semi-final match. While Kiara and Darius probably wouldn't make it to this presentation, Narissa hoped the other three would.

The PvP finals for Lusara Fates would be using the new designs, to put them through their paces and show what they were made of. But she was also just happy Shira made it to the convention. That milestone was big, though those men of hers had to take most of the credit.

Strong hands wrapped around her from behind and she squealed when they spun her around. "Careful, I'm eating."

The spinning immediately stopped and Ajax moved in front of her, concerned. "Are you feeling sick?"

She shook her head. "These berries have the green light right now."

Ajax stole one from her, and she protested. "At least our little girl has good taste in food from the get-go."

He placed his hands on her slightly less-than-flat belly and then frowned after a moment. "She still won't kick."

She shook her head. "I'm only seven weeks along, hon."

"So?"

Mercedes and Takashi snickered. Not only did he insist they were having a girl, he honestly believed if he focused enough, he could get her to kick. Narissa never thought she'd ever see someone as happy to be a father than him. It excited her, knowing they were on this journey together. She honestly still couldn't believe that week after Nolan showed up resulted in this. The math didn't add up, but here they were.

She was high-risk, and had to do a lot of extra things to ensure nothing would go wrong, but she'd do whatever it took to keep this baby. And she knew he would, too. And with Nolan back in prison for life now, without the possibility of parole, she had one less thing in her life to cause her stress.

The crowd cheered as the current presenter finished. Ajax checked his microphone and then clapped his hands together. "Okay. Our turn. You ready?"

Narissa took a quick calming breath. "No, but I doubt I ever will be."

She didn't understand how he enjoyed these presentations. She could put on a good show and hide her nerves, but this man of hers was on a different level. And that meant he was driving this show. She'd help where he requested in advance, but that was about it.

A host thanked everyone and then spoke about GameTech. Ajax rubbed his hands together, excitement radiating off of him.

"Wait, Rissa!" a young girl called out.

They all turned to see a girl of light tan completion, and around the age of seven, running down the hall toward them, her brown hair bouncing behind her.

Narissa waved to her. "Hey, Serenity."

"Rissa, wait!" she called out again, not realizing Narissa hadn't gone anywhere. Hearing her nickname from the young girl made her smile. Much like with Shira, Serenity had difficulty with Narissa's name, so she allowed the cutie to use her nickname.

Behind her, Jasper, Zach, and Shira followed. Snake,

Shira's service dog, trotted along with her. Jasper was a tall man of muscular build, and tan skin covered in tattoos, dark hair and green eyes. Zach had a slightly slimmer, more athletic build, blond hair pulled back into a short ponytail and ice-blue eyes. And Shira, she was a walking poster model, like always. The two men were good looking, but there was a reason Shira had modeled a long time ago. *And why I wish she'd accept my proposal.*

Serenity ran up to Narissa and latched onto her leg, staring up with her bright green eyes. "I have something to tell yah before you go out there."

Narissa looked to Ajax and nodded. She'd come on stage after. He was fine with it and ran out onto the stage to get the crowd all hyped up. Narissa focused on Serenity. "Now, what did you want to tell me?"

Serenity beckoned her closer. Narissa crouched down and the little girl kissed her on the nose. "Good luck."

A unison of "awws" sounded around them. Even Narissa's heart swelled. She kissed Serenity back. "Thank you, birthday girl. You're going to like what we reveal. And the gift I have for you."

Her eyes lit up. "You remembered!"

Narissa laughed. "Of course I did."

How could she forget? Jasper and Zach had asked her to watch Serenity for a bit during the convention while they dealt with something with Shira. She and Serenity did some quality bonding, and was sure to remember the number of times Serenity kept telling her when her birthday was, and what she *really* wanted for a present: for Shira to become her mom.

While Narissa couldn't help with that, even though from the looks of the trio and their hand holding, that

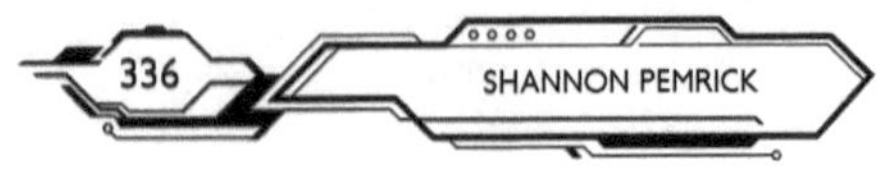

might have happened, Narissa could offer the little girl a unique gift. She'd already talked it over with Jasper.

Narissa stood up. "I can't give it to you right now, though. I have this presentation to get through."

Serenity nodded several times. "I'll wait!"

Shira came up to them and whispered in her ear. "We'll be sure she's ready."

Narissa nodded. As she turned away, she noticed a folder in Shira's hand. It piqued her interest, but she didn't have the time to ask. There was only so long Ajax could stall. She went to the offstage entrance, waiting for Ajax to call her out. He was eager to do so, and she received a loud reception walking out. *He really knows how to get a crowd going, that's for sure.*

"Look at this beautiful woman, huh?" Ajax said.

And here he goes. She put on her most confident act. "Just a reminder, we're not talking about you here."

The crowd laughed, and Ajax placed his hand on his chest. "Well thank you for the compliment, but I'm not talking about myself."

She crossed her arms. "For once."

Ajax shook his finger at her. "Careful, now. Or I won't let you do the slides."

Narissa held up the remote and smirked. "I don't need permission."

Ajax searched his person, finding she'd nabbed it from him before he headed out. The audience loved it.

Ajax shook his head. "Sneaky little thief. And here I thought you were a good little priestess."

"That's not what you said last night!" Shira yelled from offstage.

The room roared. Even Narissa and Ajax were amused.

"She's talking about the guild raid last night," Ajax said, trying to ensure it was disguised as a "family friendly" event.

"No, I'm not!" she yelled out.

Ajax pinched his nose and Narissa tried in vain to control her giggling. "Careful, Shira, our intellectually-challenged berserker is going to go into a rage at this rate 'cause his head hurts."

Shira and the audience laughed, Ajax pointed at her. "Watch it. Or I'll make you do this presentation on your own."

Narissa shrugged and turned. "Or I could go play with the new toy instead."

She clicked the remote, the screen behind them displaying the first slide of the presentation. Cheers and shouts of excitement echoed through the room.

Ajax shook his head and started up the reveal. As he did the intro, Narissa motioned for some of the GameTech employees to roll the covered pod out onto the stage. They'd left the lid up for the reveal, and to throw off people's guesses. The timing was all perfect, as planned, and the crowd loved it.

When it was time to uncover it, she and Ajax took an end each.

"GameTech would like to announce its newest virtual reality gaming model." The two pulled off the cover.

They received "oohs" and "ahhs" and a lot of excited clamoring. Ajax made a few "Vanna White poses" to add to it all. They let the audience go for a few moments before Ajax calmed them down. He got down into the nitty-gritty of explaining the changes from the chair-to-pod setup, and why Narissa had partnered with them for this.

He did receive a wayward shout about him just trying to impress her to become his girlfriend, which he didn't exactly deny. To most who paid attention to social news, their relationship was no secret at this point. Media flocked over the finding, as top singles hooking up was a "big deal." *Nosey bastards need a life, if you ask me.*

Narissa went through the different slides as needed, until it came to her turn. "So, as Ajax told you, there were logical health reasons behind this complete redesign. There's also better inclusion. For those who can't sit for long periods of time, now you don't have to. For those who couldn't afford the major modifications to the chairs to accommodate you, either based on height, or some other physical disadvantage, this pod reduces that burden."

Happy murmurs responded to that information.

"And by partnering with Cybro Industries, we've been able to help push a limitation that's been a thorn in everyone's side for many years." She clicked to the next slide and the audience gasped. "Age limitations are mostly a thing of the past now."

Narissa let them take in the news before continuing. "Children, who all love games, can now get a taste of this world as young as five. And those who are as old as Master Roshi are able to continue to enjoy the gaming experience instead of giving it up."

"I'm not old!" a cosplayer yelled out.

Narissa laughed. "Now, to show you—"

"Hold up, Narissa," Allyson said as she came out on

stage, oozing with confidence. "We all know I can't let my baby brother have all the fun today."

Narissa smiled and Ajax threw his hands up. "Why are you two so mean to me?"

His sister winked, and held up a newly designed portable gaming helmet. "The stationary designs aren't the only ones to get an upgrade."

Loud cheers erupted.

Allyson smirked. "I couldn't let you traveling gamers be left out in all this. The new designs will feature upgraded hardware, greater stability, and also the same approved age range, thanks to Narissa's involvement."

She then nodded to Narissa as the crowd clapped. She'd only planned the quick reveal. Allyson didn't see a need to drag it out when the pod design was a bigger deal. She'd really only crashed in to get on Ajax's nerves.

"All right, now back to what I was about to say," Narissa said, the crowd quieting down. "To show off this new age range, I've got a very special birthday girl here waiting offstage."

Narissa heard Serenity gasp. "She-ra, does she mean me?"

She looked over to see Shira and Serenity standing just off stage. Shira held her hand out for the little girl. "Yes, she does. Let's go out there."

Serenity took the offered hand and the two came out on stage. Snake followed on Shira's other side. Shira's presence was unexpected. Jasper had said he'd come out with his daughter. *What have they done with this woman?* Shira walked with all the confidence of a model. She was made for the stage.

Serenity tried to emulate Shira's bravado as the crowd

gushed over how cute she was. Narissa could see how the attention scared her. Even Snake sensed it. He swapped sides and padded next to her, and the young girl placed a hand on his vest for added support. When they made it to the three of them, she asked Shira to hold her. Shira picked her up, and Serenity curled into Shira's neck.

Shira already had a headset. "Honey, can you tell everyone your name?"

She took a moment. "Serenity."

Several people melted. Shira smiled and turned a bit so that Serenity could see the crowd. What astounded Narissa was that it also exposed all of her cybernetics, including ones she usually hid with a false skin on the market. *Really, what did those two men do to her?*

"And can you tell everyone how old you are?" Shira said.

Serenity played with her fingers. "Seven. Today's my birthday."

She received a huge happy birthday, making her hide her face, but she managed to muffle out a "thank you."

"And is that younger or older than the virtual reality minimum age?" Shira asked her.

"Daddy says I can't play his game until I'm ten yeahs old."

Ajax placed his hands on Narissa's shoulders. "And what if we told you, someone your age can now play?"

A big goofy grin spread across her face. "I want to kick his butt like She-ra can."

Laughter boomed through the room, everyone unable to contain themselves.

Narissa smiled. "Well, a friend at Lion Rage helped

us out and set up a demo just for you to try and show off to everyone. Do you want to do that?"

"Can She-ra play with me?"

Shira kissed her on the forehead. "Of course. That's why I'm here with you."

Ajax patted the gaming pod. "You can either use this, Serenity, or you can use the portable device my sister holds."

Serenity hesitated, scared about making the wrong choice. "The pod looks scary."

Ajax hung his head while she received some sympathy from the attendees around her. Narissa was mostly amused by his reaction. He knew it would be a possibility, especially with her onstage, but he'd been hopeful.

"I'll be more than happy to use it, Ajax," Shira said. "As a cybernetics user, I'd like to give it a safety test."

Ajax grinned. This would be the big moment in front of everyone. Narissa prayed it went well, like all the other tests this month.

People scrambled around to set up the devices. Serenity sat in Narissa's lap while Shira climbed into the virtual pod. Serenity giggled as Allyson strapped the portable helmet to her head and made the correct safety size adjustments. Then, she was given a countdown and sucked into the game.

The audience looked up at the large screen where they'd set up a view of the demo action, along with technical monitor overlays Narissa had added for the demonstration. *So far so good, for them both.*

Serenity squealed in-game and ran around, taking to the game faster than most adults. Shira chased after her, trying to get her to focus. It didn't work. The audience

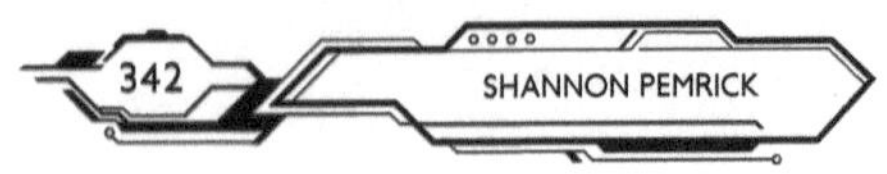

didn't care. Their favorite part was when she experienced the texture and smell of another creature. It actually looked like she might cry petting the wolf Darius had put into the demo for them.

Narissa took the moment to explain a few key things to the audience. Particularly, what type of safety measures were in place for younger children, stressing how important it would be for parents to set the systems up correctly for their child's age. She and Ajax bounced off each other until Serenity's time was up. She complained that she wanted to have more fun, but Shira reminded her she was only doing a demo, and could play later.

When they came out of the game, and the portable device was removed from Serenity's head, she wrapped her arms around Narissa's neck. "Thank you, Rissa! Best birthday, evah!"

Narissa hugged her back. "You're welcome, sweetie. I'm glad you liked the surprise."

The little girl hopped off her lap and ran over to Shira. "Momma, I want to go tell Daddy and Dad about the fun I had."

Shira smiled down at her. "We'll do that after I say one thing."

A grin spread across Ajax's face. "What do you have to say about the new machine, Shira?"

"Yeah. Goodbye gamer neck."

The three of them laughed, as did the crowd, as Shira walked off with Serenity, Snake close behind.

When things quieted down, Narissa had the screen display the Q&A title screen. "Okay. I think we're ready for some questions. Don't you think, Ajax?"

He grinned at her, but didn't say anything. She found

that peculiar but went to the next slide. "Alright, so to submit your questions, all you have to—"

She stopped, realizing the audience was whispering and confused. Brow furrowed, she turned to see the slide not displaying the instructions she was trying to relay. Instead, it read:

Hold on.

"What on earth?" She went to the next slide.

One more thing before questions happen.

Narissa pursed her lips and glanced at Ajax, who looked a little too innocent. She'd been the one to get all these slides worked up, and had even done a double-check this morning to make sure it was right. Someone had touched her file.

She hit the next slide and her name popped up. Only her name. She swallowed. Something was up here. Narissa pressed the button for the next slide.

I have an important question for you.

Her heart stopped. *He isn't—* The crowd gasped and murmured with excitement. Narissa turned to face Ajax. He wasn't standing anymore. Instead, he was down one knee, a small box in hand. Her breath caught. Glimmering inside it was a white gold tanzanite ring.

The display remote clattered to the ground and her hands flew up to her face.

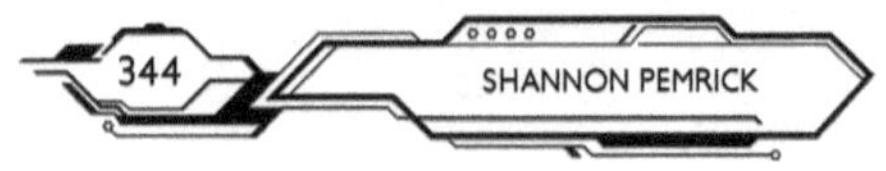

"Narissa, will you make me the happiest man alive, and stay my player number two, until game over?"

Her heart swelled. It was so cheesy, so him, and she loved it. But the words lodged as her emotions flared in all directions. She was pretty sure the waterworks would start popping up too, though she could blame out-of-control hormones on that one.

Narissa nodded—the only thing she could find herself able to do to was say yes. The biggest smile since she announced her pregnancy spread across his face and his eyes shone. Within seconds he was on his feet, lifting her in the air, and spinning them around. The crowd went wild.

She dipped her head and kissed him, her heart feeling as if it was going to burst. Ajax had shown her a love she'd missed. One she thought once would never come to her after her experience with Nolan. She didn't want to be with anyone else. She didn't want to love anyone else.

The cheering died down as she was set back down on her feet. Ajax planted a kiss on her forehead and slipped the ring on her finger just as someone offstage shouted. "Hallelujah, about time! Now give me lots'o grandbabies!"

The two laughed, along with the crowd. Narissa gestured to the hidden person. "My mother, everyone."

More amusement filled the room. Ajax kissed her again before retrieving the remote she dropped and flipped to the next slide, which had the Q&A information on it.

He grinned at her. "Glad I know you so well, or that would have been a real extra-life killer."

Narissa shook her head and addressed the audience

with how to submit their questions. They gave them ten minutes, and then had the AI assistants filter out the duplicates and order the rest based on popularity.

Twenty minutes later, they'd covered most of the questions, and had to cut the rest. Ajax let them know test plays would happen soon, and the championships for Lusara Fates would be using the approved prototypes.

The pair exited the stage, and Narissa was assaulted by her friends' excitement. She had to show off her ring several times before things calmed down. Ajax had to run off to be around for the public demos, and Zach and Jasper had to get ready for their last match—they were in the finals. Narissa wished them luck, and then looked to Shira when she didn't leave with them. She usually waited on the side, cheering them on with Serenity.

Shira held out the folder she had brought, as if hearing the unspoken question. "I'd like to talk to you about something before I join them, Doctor."

Everything clicked, and Narissa grinned. "Step into my office, Ms. Schneider. I'd love to go over the documents you've brought me."

Shannon Pemrick is a full-time USA Today best-selling author of slow-burn romantic fantasy, fuller-time geek, and dragon obsessed. She also has too many novelty mugs, not enough chocolate, and a forbidden love-affair with all things shiny. When she's not burning her fingers across a keyboard handing out adventures and HEAs, she's rolling dice and getting lost in RPGs or searching for brides for her dragon overlords.

You can learn more about Shannon by visiting her website at:
Shannonpemrick.com